Finding a sovereign

Eric Jones

Finding a Sovereign

Published by The Conrad Press in the United Kingdom 2020

Tel: +44(0)1227 472 874
www.theconradpress.com
info@theconradpress.com

ISBN 978-1-913567-51-4

Typesetting and Cover Design by: Charlotte Mouncey, www.bookstyle.co.uk

The Conrad Press logo was designed by Maria Priestley.

Printed and bound in Great Britain by Clays Ltd, Elcograf S.p.A.

Remembering our dear friend,
Sally Mills

1

Not much to live on, plenty to live for

September 1878

Poverty in itself, so we are told, is relative. One can be as poor as a mouse in a church when the harvest is over, and yet be content, even happy, with one's lot. A child with loving parents, some food to eat, the warmth of a cuddle and a scattering of laughter-filled moments, is rich indeed, though money be hard to come by.

A child deprived of the close comforts of a mother who cares, with food on the table and clothes to wear, a handsome bed in which to sleep, but nobody to stroke your hair when one is falling asleep, or read a story from the myriad of books on the nursery shelf, might as well be as poor as the barefoot waif. Crying oneself to sleep, without much to look forward to on the morrow, is poverty of a kind. Smiling back into the face of a loving parent, who sits by your side until sleep takes you into a happy dream, is wealth untold.

But of course absolute poverty is hardly relative; it is absolute.

And so it was with Adam Warkin, a boy of seven with spindly legs and arms, the sallow look of someone who could have derived some benefit from a warm pie-crust, or a chunk of well-buttered bread, but with the smile of an angel when sat beside his mother or father in their tiny grey cottage. Adam was unencumbered with brothers or sisters, of whom there had been two born before him, neither of whom had survived more than a few weeks.

Adam loved to skip along the single village road, happy in his own skin, eager to earn a penny or two, carrying shopping or walking a dog, but happy too simply saying, 'Hello, can I help?' to any villager, whether there was a penny in it or not. His smile was known and enjoyed by all whom he met, his teeth were strong, his fingers nimble but his shoes well-worn.

The Warkins knew real poverty, living in virtually one room behind a flimsy wooden front door, with a small bedroom above, with access to a well nearby, a few homely utensils and pieces of furniture but frankly, not much else. The uncurtained window, in the downstairs room, let in light, but also allowed the cold air and unwelcome wind to permeate their living-space. There was not often a fire to cook by, or to warm the tiny family in their home.

Adam's mother, Louise, would make bread or occasionally cook a small piece of pork. She would also boil vegetables and serve whatever came into the mix on three wooden plates, the only ones the family of three possessed.

She was thirty-one, friendly and smiling, with brown hair tied back revealing her smooth skin. Her eyes lit up when she laughed or tried to make things comfortable for the three of them, wearing a twice-turned dress, and a short blue woollen coat, when the dress did not provide much warmth or comfort.

Father, Henry Warkin, would have liked to work regularly but was not a strong man and could only bring in the occasional sixpence, doing odd jobs for the vicar at the nearby church, or a neighbour with some pennies to spare needing wood chopped, a patch of garden dug over or a fence painted. He was not feckless or lazy, but lacked the energy, or good health, which would have encouraged him to seek anything more permanent.

Two years older than Louise, he too had dark brown hair, with emerging streaks of grey, covered almost permanently with a wide-brimmed brown felt hat given to him eleven years earlier, in lieu of cash payment, for moving furniture, when a young couple arrived new in the village. They had been Mr and Mrs Redman, although Mr Redman had died after just four years in 1871, the year of Adam Warkin's birth.

Henry Warkin's brown trousers, the leather belt, the long dark grey coat and a couple of shirts were all he owned. His boots were, fortunately, strong, but would not last for ever. He was kind but could not offer his wife, and child, much beyond what they now possessed. He was not greedy for more, and so his son, too, grew up to be content, and occasionally joyful, when a small bonus of extra food, clothing or comfort came their way.

The Warkins lived in the village of Melton Ford, in Dorset. With just one hundred and eighty residents it was hardly likely to offer much in the way of employment to Henry Warkin, but today he had found a day's work at the blacksmith's, just beyond the village on the Weymouth Road, where a shilling could be earned in ten hours, holding the horses still while they were shod, collecting wood for the fire or keeping Tom, the blacksmith's furnace alive and hot. A shilling was enough for a day, but it could not often be repeated, certainly not tomorrow!

Young Adam could not resist his daily skip along the single

village road, after he had helped his mother with some wash-ing, hanging out the shirts and vests she had washed, or her apron, or their thin sheets once everything had been thoroughly scrubbed and rinsed. He ran, skipped and jumped his way past the houses of others, all of whom he knew, holding on to his oversized flat cap, when he jumped across the stream. He waved and smiled at his father, carrying a bundle of wood, and they earnestly discussed how much more could be carried or collected in a single day.

He offered to pick some apples from a tree, belonging to the elderly lady, in the cottage alongside her orchard, and was offered a bag of apples in payment for his welcome assistance, as well as three home-baked scones and tuppence. He raced another local boy, young Will, and the boy's sister, Helena, from the blacksmith's yard around the back of the village houses, along the leafy lane back to the main road, finishing back at the blacksmith's. He was out of breath, but he came in first, even carrying a bag of apples, and they all laughed, quenching their thirsts with handfuls of water from the nearby stream. All of this welcome occupation took up his morning, a morning well spent.

He smiled, returning to the cottage and to his mother who was folding three sheets, and a couple of shirts, before lunching on some bread and cheese which she shared with Adam. Father returned when sundown approached and the evening was spent exchanging stories of the day, smiling, and even laughing, as they retold what they had seen, the antics of the birds and cats they'd come across, the people they had met. They felt rich with the pennies they had earned, each one of which went into the tin, on the mantle, above where there was no fire.

2

Plenty to live on, not much to live for

Two hundred miles away from Melton Ford – and exactly fifty years earlier, in 1828 – a nine-year-old girl sat on an ornate chair, with a book on her lap. She was wearing a silk dress with pure cotton underwear, trimmed with lace.

Her lustrous hair was well cared for, clean and brushed, and two biscuits lay, uneaten, on a plate nearby. Her tutor sat alongside her, monitoring her reading skills, for she was never alone but always lonely. Poor Princess Alexandrina of Kent was indeed as lonely as ever.

'Can we not go outside?' said the young girl to her tutor, the formidable Louise Lehzen, a haughty German lady, sitting bolt upright in the adjacent chair. 'We could listen to birds singing out there and look at the trees.'

'You know that is forbidden, unless your mother or Sir John grant permission,' said Madame Lehzen.

Indeed venturing outside, on a whim, to see trees or flowers, or anything else in Kensington Palace garden, was unthinkable.

'But I never see anybody of my own age,' said the girl. 'Just you and the servants, and sometimes my mother when she comes down to check on me.'

'And that is the way your mother requires it to be.' Louise Lehzen knew that enjoying the company of other children, of the same age, was completely out of the question, so that, for Alexandrina, a weary shroud of loneliness covered her days, seeing few adults other than strict and humourless servants and a stiff mother-figure, actually her mother, the widowed Duchess of Kent just once or twice, for an update on her reading or writing skills, or to glance perfunctorily at a drawing or painting just completed.

The Duchess had been widowed in 1820, when Alexandrina was less than a year old. She was, by royal standards, a poor relative of her brother-in-law, King George IV, whom she, and her young daughter, seldom saw.

And the girl was poorer still, lonely, pampered but bullied by strict adults, developing a temper which burst into tantrums when she was compelled to practice playing the piano, or return to her studies. By the age of seven her tutor had been given a formidable list of books that the young princess should read, including twenty religious texts, twenty-seven French books, classical Latin and grammar volumes, Ovid, Virgil and Horace as well as the poetry of Pope, Cowper, Shakespeare and others. The list would have daunted the most eager student at Eton itself.

It was a never-ending cycle of lessons, in French, English (for German was the first language of the family, although Alexandrina herself preferred to speak English), history, geography, some dance, some reluctant piano practice and a great deal of silence.

'We shall take a short walk,' said Madame Lehzen, 'keeping strictly to the gravel paths in the gardens. And you will hold my hand, as we descend the staircase, for fear of your falling and being injured.'

Alexandrina was not even allowed to walk up or down a staircase alone. That was all part of The Kensington System, imposed by her mother and encouraged by Sir John Conroy, her Mother's Comptroller of the Household.

With some simple mathematics and a lot of drawing – which Alexandrina did enjoy – she passed her days, without any understanding or even hope, of how it might ever change. She cried herself to sleep some nights, knowing full well what the next day would bring. But this Alexandrina, although lonely, sad and frustrated in many ways was of great value to the nation. She was the one most likely to be the next heir to the throne after her Uncle George died, and then later her Uncle William.

Apart from this knowledge, which she barely understood, as her mother tried to keep any comprehension of her potential inheritance away from the girl herself, Alexandrina had one rich chink of light in her otherwise dreary and tedious life. She loved her dolls.

'You are my friends,' she would confide to them. 'We shall go to bed in Mother's room tonight, and nobody shall hear how we cry ourselves to sleep. We shall imagine how the birds make friends and sing to each other; we shall pretend that we are running headlong into the breeze with our hair loose and our eyes stinging. We shall imagine, you and I, what it must be like to go for a long walk, with just each other for company, along a path, or by a river, that leads to somewhere unknown or exciting. We shall meet new people, like ourselves, who are not approved by mother or Sir John.'

Substitutes the dolls may have been for the real thing, for real friends and cherished playmates, but substitutes they were, and loved, cared for and treasured. She was, in truth, a very deprived girl indeed, sleeping every night on a smaller version of her mother's bed, but always in her mother's room. She longed for whatever it was she felt was missing, but which she could never speak out loud, nor even picture easily, in her lively mind, or her girlish understanding.

And why was this girl the likely monarch after the next? That accident of birth was generated by her grandfather's disconnected and dysfunctional family.

Her late grandfather, King George III, who had died in 1820, when Alexandrina was just one, had reigned since 1760 and had no less than nine sons and six daughters, leaving little doubt that the next generation would be well supplied with sons and heirs to the crown and more. It was never to be. Leaving aside the brothers, the daughters of George III had either died in infancy or married and produced no living descendants. Even this should have presented no problem for their father, hoping for male heirs through his male offspring.

But the brothers fared little or no better, so that by the time that the King's own life looked to be coming to an end, in the early years of the nineteenth century, several sons were in the line of succession, but almost nothing beyond them to another generation. Plenty of illegitimate offspring were scattered around London and the surrounding counties, but virtually none in legitimate line through George's sons. The one exception was George, Prince of Wales,

'You are my one hope, for the monarchy and for the next generation, don't you know?' King George III might have said to his eldest son George, if he had not been struck down since the year 1810 in a miasma of madness, which rendered him incapable of saying virtually anything at all. That eldest son had been appointed Regent in that year ruling in his father's stead.

The Regent's daughter, and only legitimate child from his estranged wife Caroline of Brunswick, Charlotte, was the hope of the Royal family's future and of the nation. Several suitors had been considered for her hand in marriage, an eligible hand indeed, as the heir to the British throne.

'I have summoned Prince Leopold of Saxe-Coburg Saalfield to Brighton,' said The Prince Regent to his daughter, who had declined several other offers of prospective husbands suggested by her overbearing father. This was in late February 1816, and so the Prince came to dinner with the Regent and his daughter.

At the end of a successful evening the Prince Regent told his daughter, 'Your Prince Leopold has every qualification to make a woman happy.' And Charlotte herself wrote her diary that evening in a state of great happiness.

'I find him charming, and go to bed happier than I have ever done yet in my life… I am certainly a very fortunate creature, and have to bless God. A Princess never, I believe, set out for marriage with such prospects of happiness, real domestic ones like other people.'

She had been married in 1816 to her Prince Leo and raised everybody's hopes for the dynasty by becoming almost immediately pregnant. But then very little needs to be left to the imagination, of how the nation, and the family mourned when, not only her baby boy was stillborn, but Charlotte, the one legitimate descendent of the monarch, also died within hours of the birth.

The nation was plunged into grief. It was as if every family in Britain had lost a child. The stock market plunged, shops closed for a fortnight, black drapes were hung from the windows of homes throughout Britain and the family despaired over who could succeed George IV, and subsequently William, his brother, with no living heirs.

So, as of 1817, the race was on for the remaining brothers, sons of George III to provide a legitimate child. The King's fourth son, Edward, Duke of Kent did his duty, marrying in 1818 the widowed Victoria of Saxe-Coburg Saalfield, sister of the recently widowed Leopold, and producing a daughter, Alexandrina, in 1819.

This was the poor girl, the only child of the almost penniless Duke and Duchess of Kent, fatherless by 1820, surrounded by sycophants and an adoring but cold mother, reading the book on her lap, hardly daring to move, let alone dream of escaping from 'The Kensington System of bringing up a child', rich by most people's standards, poor by the royal norms of the day and lifeless in a state of familial penury, in dire need of love, company and affection.

Hers was a form of poverty indeed. It would not last forever, but Princess Alexandrina had no vision of any change in her foreseeable future, as she sat, aged nine, on the gilded chair under the watchful eye of her tutor, reluctantly reading a book.

3

Melton Ford

Young Adam Warkin wished that he could read a book. Now he too was aged nine, having run and laughed his way through two more years. He had befriended the lady with the orchard, Birgitta, the widowed Mrs Jonathan Redman, who made such delicious scones and allowed him to keep some of the apples he picked. He often helped her with jobs around the house, carrying shopping, cleaning out the small barn and coming home with a few pence to top up the family fortune. This was the Mr and Mrs Redman whom his father had helped move into their cottage, in the year of Adam's birth. She was thirty-seven, but old in the eyes of Adam.

'And why can't you read, young man?' said the good lady. 'A bright young thing like you could help himself to better things in life if you could tackle a book or a newspaper'. She smiled at him, lovingly, as she almost reprimanded him for not being able to read. Her well-pressed dress was a beautiful green, with some embroidery on the neckline. She surrounded her slight shoulders with a shawl of soft knitted wool, and her white bonnet, always worn, kept her prematurely greying hair tidy.

Adam was not much short of her height which made him feel quite grown up, but behind her smile and friendship he knew that she was wise and clever, wiser and cleverer than he, perhaps, with a wonderful history of her life to tell. He had no idea that perhaps he was clever too. He was just Adam.

'Nobody every taught me,' he responded, as he sat in a chair in her sitting room and enjoyed a glass of weak cider. 'My dad can sign his name, my mother never needs to, but would use a cross if she did. But I would like to know what some of the things in your books say, I really would.'

'Then I shall teach you, and you will unlock the secrets of my books, one by one, and learn about the world beyond Melton Ford.' said Mrs Redman. 'We'll start tomorrow.'

Adam had never even opened a book, let alone tried to read one, so when he arrived at Mrs Redman's on the following morning he was tingling. He'd always been satisfied with his lot in life, without ever actually verbalising his contentment, but this was promising to be something different and very special indeed.

He'd met his friend, Will, as he came along the road, and they had raced as far as Mrs Redman's pretty little cottage, but then Adam peeled off to go through her gate and waved a cheery goodbye. Maybe he was waving goodbye to his past, to his ignorance, even maybe to his innocence.

The 1870 Education Act had been formulated to provide elementary education for all children up to the age of ten, but had not as yet permeated the land, through to all towns and villages, or to all children. Certainly it had not reached Adam Warkin in Melton Ford in Dorsetshire. Indeed it had been only forty short years since sending indentured boy sweeps up chimneys had been outlawed.

The Act did not specifically make education compulsory, it excluded some children, on the grounds of being more than three miles from the nearest school, be it church or local authority, even assuming the authority had yet set up a school, let alone built one. The idea that all children needed to be educated, at all, had hardly filtered through to those in villages or small towns, where parents could not read or write, and children were part of the family's working day, making their valuable contribution to survival.

In town halls, across the nation, and even in parliament, all the old excuses had been wheeled out against educating 'the masses' which so many elite citizens – and factory owners – thought entirely unnecessary.

'Not everybody needs to read and write,' said many, 'especially when there are large numbers of servants in the home.'

'Educating everybody will lead to too much 'thinking,' and self-awareness.'

'Nobody will be willing to go into service.'

'What's the point of educating children above their station?' And so it went on. There emerged the very old chestnut, which scared the life out of the manufacturing *nouveau riche*; 'Putting all children in schools would deprive factory owners of the 'right' to employ child labour.'

There had been so many attempts to educate the poor, throughout the century, including Ragged Schools and Dame schools, but, even with gradual changes in the law, it would be sometime before compulsory education for all became the norm. Adam Warkin, along with about a fifth of the population of young boys in the mid-eighteen hundreds, seems to have missed the boat.

And there was always the fear that when everybody was educated it would lead to discontent and revolution. The

European revolutions of 1848 and 1870 had put the fear of God into many a wealthy citizen.

Adam was, however, completely unaware of any such considerations. He was still tingling as he rang Mrs Redman's little brass bell, hanging on the doorframe. He wasn't sure how to say good morning, or even enter the house. The dynamic had changed, although he would never have said any such thing. He even felt compelled to remove his cloth cap, as he entered, and followed her with small hesitant steps, clutching the cap in front of him, into her sitting room where he stood until she spoke.

'Come along now, sit yourself down. Cat got your tongue?'

'Don't think I'll be clever enough to read, Miss.' he said, as if this had suddenly become an ordeal outside his comfort zone, and thinking perhaps it was not such a good idea. 'I'm probably better just collecting firewood or apples.'

'Nonsense.' she responded. 'You have a biscuit and a glass of water, and I will go and get some paper and a pencil.' She was out of the room in one swift move and Adam found the biscuit and the drink near to where she had guided him to sit. He couldn't touch them.

'Why do I feel scared?' he thought to himself although the actual words were hardly there even in his head. Just the thought, 'Why'. It was as if, unbeknown to him, the idea of being educated, knowing more, gathering knowledge, was scary, or maybe even dangerous. The more one knows, the more responsibility you have, the more decisions need to be made on one side or another of any argument, the less secure you are in your innocent existence, not having to make choices or decisions.

But, of course none of these ideas were actually forming in Adam's head, just a feeling of uncertainty and still the nagging, 'Why'.

Mrs Redman breezed in holding some sheets of yellow paper and a couple of worn-down pencils. 'Here we are,' she said, suddenly realising, as she proffered the pencil that Adam had never even held such a thing. She told him it was a pencil.

'What about books?' said Adam. 'Do I need one of these 'pencils' to read a book?'

'It's about letters.' she assured him. 'You learn some letters and then you will see how the words, and the books, are written.'

The morning sped by, as Adam gained some confidence in learning how to hold the pencil, how to make the shapes of an A or a B, a T and so on and learning quickly what each sound meant.

And he really enjoyed putting one A, two Ps an L and an E on the paper in his own hand to make the word which resulted in him being given a juicy red fruit, from the orchard, to eat on the way home.

Reading was fun. Writing was exciting. Making words was a revelation.

Day after day, Adam turned up at Mrs Redman's cottage, sometimes with a pencil, having been given his own on day two, and sometimes with bits of paper covered in words, which he had spelled out at home before darkness came in the mid evening. Even his mother and father had joined in, enjoying what Adam could now do, making a game of spelling out everything they owned in their small home; T-A-B-L without the final E, the word F-L-O-R missing one O, more and more, until they laughed or hugged, being somehow empowered to communicate with each other in a new way.

And every word was corrected by his new teacher the next day with no hint of criticism, just kindly words to encourage accuracy and understanding.

The day came, sooner than one might have thought, for him to look at one of Mrs Redman's books. He had the small volume on the table in front of him, moved the glass of water out of the way, and peered inside. It was, of course, full of words, but now he could distinguish the letters, the separate words. He so enjoyed the gradual understanding that, put together, each block of letters turned into a fact, a piece of information, a description or view of the world from somebody's else's point of view. He decided it was indeed, marvellous.

It had been barely a month, since he first rang that little brass bell at the front door, but Adam was a quick learner. He read from one book, a special black volume opened and spread before him, '*In the beg-in-ning* – that was a hard word – *God cre-at-ed the Heav-ens and the earth*'.

'I've heard that before,' said Adam, 'in church from the reverend. He told us that God created everything, and here it is, in your house, in your book!'

'Try this one,' said Mrs Redman as she put another book in front of him. He opened it and his eyes fell forward in amazement, not knowing where to look first. It was an open page full of the most beautiful pictures of birds and other country creatures, each one with words written underneath.

Closer inspection revealed the words for size and colour and names for the birds, *Chaff-inch. Spar-row, blue, bro-wn,* and even *'plum-age.*

'No, not *plum-age*,' she said, 'it's pronounced *ploom-ij*.'

'Oh, yes,' announced Adam. 'Of course, I know that word, and now I know what it looks like and how to write it,'

He knew how to write so many other words, even phrases and sentences, by the time the winter months set in that year. He had even taken some books home, one at a time, to read aloud to his parents.

Stories of heroes and princes, of Robin Hood and Sir Gawain, courageous men and women and girls who'd battled injustice or climbed mountains, including Mary Jones, the fifteen year-old Welsh girl, who, in 1784, had walked twenty-six miles barefoot across the countryside to buy a copy of the Welsh Bible. What a story that was.

By the time Adam was twelve, he too had walked a thousand miles, or so it seemed to him, back and forth between his modest home and Birgitta Redman's cottage, with every step bringing him closer to the dream of reading fluently and even writing imaginatively. He had progressed beyond all the expectations of either he himself, or the good lady who was mentoring him.

They sat and talked one day, long into the afternoon after they had finished reading together. Theirs was an unlikely friendship, but friendship it was, as they supped some tea, something else Adam had grown to like, and enjoyed a cherry scone, which Mrs Redman was so expert at creating, with a thick layer of butter.

'When did you come to the village?' asked Adam, holding his cup of tea between the palms of both his hands, partly for warmth but mostly to secure it from spilling. 'Have you lived here since before I was born?'

'Oh, certainly,' she responded, 'ever since I was married sixteen years ago. I was twenty-six years old, just a little more than twice your age. My husband was Jonathan, a clever man, who knew his way around gardens and orchards.'

'Were you happy?' Adam rather hesitantly asked. 'My mother and father are very happy, although father is not always very well, and mother does not cook scones quite like this!' he said.

'Ah,' she said, 'you have learned to read, your mother and father are good at many things, I am sure, and I too have been blessed with some skills, as was my husband. It is what you do with your talents that make you the person you grow up to be.

'You will grow up to be a bright and, I hope, an honest young man with, perhaps, a brighter future than your mum and dad, but always remember it was they who brought you into this world, who love you and made you who you are. It is perhaps, always our task to help the children have a brighter future than we adults experienced. Except that...' she broke off.

'Except that... did you have any children, Mrs Redman?'

'Sadly not. We were married just four years and he was taken from me before we had a living child. I was heartbroken, of course, but I also have many memories, even some objects that I treasure, for which I am always thankful, although... having a child was never to be.'

'Does that mean you have treasure here in this house?' said Adam, intrigued.

'Good lord, certainly not,' she replied. 'But I do have a few things which I treasure.'

'Such as?' Adam sat forward on his chair.

'Well, all I will show you is this.' she said, and got up to go to the little bookcase near the window behind where Adam was sitting. 'This was given to us when we were married by the lady I worked for.' She picked up a small silver box and handed it to Adam.

'Is it real silver?' he said, looking very closely.

'Oh, yes,' said Mrs Redman. 'That's the real thing. And I do love silver. '

This was probably the first time that Birgitta Redman had opened up her heart, in words, to anyone in recent years. She wept inwardly, grateful for the moment, as she retrieved the box and replaced it in its place, on the bookcase.

'Tell me some of your memories,' said Adam, putting down his empty cup and sitting forward again on his chair, as if he were about to be regaled with a new adventure story. He hadn't quite grasped the enormity of her remembering that she had never given birth to a living child.

'Goodness me, no,' she replied. 'You don't want to know about an old lady's memories.'

'But I think I would,' said Adam. 'Just one... for today?'

'You would be bored stiff, my boy,' she responded, but, with a twinkle and a blink of her eye continued, 'But supposing I were to tell you that, once upon a time, I saw the queen?'

'You saw the queen! Queen Victoria? Our queen, you actually saw her once? But surely nobody has ever seen her who lives in these parts. Don't you have to be in London, or Windsor? That's what it says in one of the books you showed me... or Scotland... at Bal...'

'Balmoral,' said the old lady. 'Yes, the queen lives in all these place, at some times during the year, and on the Isle of Wight,

23

sometimes, where she has another home.'

'Fancy having four houses to live in. But when did you see her?'

'She came to Weymouth once, arriving in the Royal Yacht, docked in Weymouth and took her carriage from there all the way to Windsor. I saw her there, at Weymouth.'

'You saw the Queen of England,' exclaimed Adam, again, 'Tell me some more, please. I would like to see her one day.'

'And maybe you shall, one day, but no more stories from me today. I am tired, and your mother will need your help at home.'

'Oh, please, when was it you saw her?' Adam just had to ask one more thing.

'It was 1865, before you were born. My husband and I saw the queen in 1865 and that is all I am going to tell you today.'

'In 1865?' the boy thought it out for a moment and then said, 'But that's before you were married. Did you live in Weymouth before you were married? Did you know Mr Redman a long time before you and he were married?'

'Maybe I am confused.' she responded. 'I'll tell you more another day… or maybe I won't, because it is not really very interesting'.

'Not interesting?' said Adam. 'You see the Queen of England and you don't remember when it was, and you don't think it is interesting! If I saw the queen, I think I would remember and tell everyone, every day.'

'Yes, I think you probably would. But for now, off you go and look after your good mother who is probably cooking you a meal.'

Adam was still buzzing as he went out through the front

door, ran down the road, clutching a pencil and a book, and into his own front door. 'You'll never guess,' he began, 'Who Mrs Redman once saw.'

'No, I probably won't, so I won't try, just now. You go and wash your hands.'

4

Kensington

Fifty years earlier, in Kensington Palace. 1833, the washing of hands and the daily bath, were, as ever, closely supervised. The world of Princess Alexandrina (Drina to the family) was slowly being unlocked, in some small ways by her mother who meticulously took the advice of her Comptroller of the Household, Sir John Conroy.

Alexandrina hated him, and believed he was controlling her mother in an unhealthy way. Her uncle, the twenty-stone, indulgent King George IV had come and gone as monarch. He died in 1830 and Alexandrina, the one and only legitimate granddaughter of George III was now heir presumptive to the crown of Great Britain.

Much to the annoyance of her Uncle, King William IV, she had been taken on arduous touring visits to various parts of the kingdom in her early teenage years. One such, in 1833, had been to The Isle of Wight, the island with which the 14-year-old Alexandrina fell in love.

Falling in love with the Isle of Wight or not, Alexandrina was nevertheless a capricious child, who also hated these nationwide tours and, despite the close supervision of her every move, exhibited the most dreadful temper tantrums when it suited her to do so.

She wrote, years later, '*I led a very unhappy life as a child — I had no scope for my very violent feelings of affection — had no brothers and sisters to live with — never had a father — and from my unfortunate circumstances was not on comfortable or at all intimate or confidential footing with my mother - and did not know what a happy domestic life was.*'

Now, two years on another royal progress was arranged, and the young princess went with her mother and, predictably, Sir John. Alexandrina was not keen, and believed that travelling with one-night stopovers at various noble houses would make her tired and ill. She was right. The king was never keen, either, on these yearly travels by his niece and her motherly entourage, accompanied by municipal addresses, and with so much pomp and ceremony,

He regarded them all as something approaching a rivalry to his own position as Monarch. But then there never had been any love lost between King William IV and Alexandrina's mother, the Duchess of Kent.

On 21 September 1835, they passed through Stamford, Lincolnshire, having spent the previous night at Belvoir Castle, and were due to spend this night at Burghley House, home to the Marquess of Exeter. There was never any shortage of titled families with large country estates falling over themselves to welcome the young Princess Alexandrina, and, to a lesser extent, her mother, and the Comptroller of her household. The day did not begin well, having been pouring with rain since early morning.

'Mother, dear,' said Alexandrina, as their carriage approached Stamford in Lincolnshire, 'I feel completely wretched and ill. The weather is foul and now we have yet another Mayor and

Corporation, turning out in their robes and regalia, for us to listen to another, so called, Loyal Address!'

'Sir John thinks that it is better for us to stay here,' said her mother, 'and greet these people from inside the carriage.'

'But look,' the girl replied, 'everybody is soaked, the sodden band is playing the National Anthem and…'

'And we must bow our heads and show our thanks,' said her mother, as they passed by the windows of the Town Hall and the houses beyond, acknowledging the ladies of the town, who had stayed indoors rather than risk the downpour. Alexandrina was not comforted.

At Burghley House, the teenage princess found herself, as always, sleeping in her mother's bedroom, on a camp bed alongside the magnificent state bed occupying the best bedroom in the duchess' allocated suite of rooms.

Being heir to the throne never got in the way of The Kensington System, and the motherly smothering of this girl. The magnificent banquet at Burghley House was an ordeal, even though it comprised thirty six dishes on gold plate.

'Drina, you will open the evening's dancing with a quadrille, as you have been invited by Marquess of Exeter,' said the Duchess of Kent to her grumpy daughter.

'I feel tired and ill,' said the sixteen year-old princess. 'I know hardly anybody here. Lord Exeter's children are plain and boring, and I have a splitting headache.' The marquess extended his hand to her and, dutifully, she got up, and performed the quadrille to perfection.

'You have a fine large and handsome house here, Lord Exeter,' said the princess, as she danced with him. And I must thank you for the very elaborate welcome you extended to us, with the Royal salute and the military band playing the National Anthem, as we came through your gates.'

'Thank you, Your Royal Highness,' said the marquess. 'I hope the dinner was to your satisfaction.'

'It was a magnificent dinner,' said the princess. 'Thank you so much. And now, if you will excuse me...'

She excused herself from the dance, much to her mother's annoyance, stayed another half an hour, exhibiting a very sullen look in her chair at the head of the ballroom, and then left. She went to bed grumpy and feeling very unwell.

The broadening of her horizons, and introduction to the people of Britain, was not something the Princess Alexandrina took easily in her stride, although she had some fond memories of the kindnesses shown to her during these few years of travelling. Her mother, the duchess, always used very much the same words when replying to loyal addresses. That was, of course, if Sir John Conroy let her get a word in, before he, presumptuously answered for her, which he did quite often.

She - or he - would say that it was *the object of her life to assist her daughter to be deserving of the affectionate solicitude she so universally inspires, and to make her worthy of the attachment and respect of a free and loyal people.*

She went about this 'object of her life' in an unforgiving and aggressive way. Indeed she began to spread the rumour that her daughter, the princess, was so immature that she would require the duchess to rule for her, until at least the age of twenty-one.

Things almost came to a head when the princess contracted typhoid, when visiting Ramsgate in 1835. Now that Alexandrina was sixteen years old, Sir John, and the duchess, conceived a plan to retain power, even in the event of the child becoming Queen.

'Drina, my darling you must sign this document,' insisted her mother standing alongside Sir John, and looming over the girl whilst she was weeping with a fever. 'You will need guidance and support when you are well, and it is necessary that Sir John should become your Private Secretary when you are Queen.'

The duchess was sure, too, that she should be Regent, in the event of the girl assuming the crown, whether she be under or even beyond eighteen. The girl was almost delirious, but urged herself not to sign a thing. For once, her wilfulness and stubborn hate of Sir John, served her well.

'I will not sign,' she repeated again and again, despite Sir John's insistence and even his threats to have her locked up. 'Neither you, nor Sir John Conroy will control my decisions or my money... ever! In spite of your harshness, I will not sign!'

King William, too, was resolute. He was determined to stay alive. He hated the duchess and the very last thing he wanted was for her to become Regent. Every day he willed himself to stay alive.

During her seventeenth year, in August 1836 she and her Mother were invited to the king's birthday party at Windsor. In a speech, following dinner, His Majesty pointedly made an announcement.

'It is my sincere hope that I would live another few months, at least, beyond the eighteenth birthday of the Princess Alexandrina here, which would allow her to become queen, and spare the nation the Regency which Parliament has designed for a 'certain lady' sitting near to me.'

The gauntlet was down. The princess knew that her uncle wanted her to inherit, entirely alone. The duchess knew that the great familial chasm between her and her brother-in-law was as wide as ever, and unbreachable.

'This lady,' the king continued, 'has far exceeded her authority, and occupied more rooms in Kensington Palace than she had been allocated. She is, even now, surrounded by evil counsellors'.

The duchess was incensed and left the room. The break between her and the king was complete and never healed.

The following May in 1837, on the morning of the 24th the Princess Alexandrina of Kent wrote in her diary, '*Today is my eighteenth birthday.*'

It was a giant gala day for the country. Kensington was festooned with banners and there was an official reception at the palace, and a ball. For the duchess, however, it was a day of despair. Alexandrina was 18 – and the king was still alive

Barely a month later, during the early hours of the 20th June, King William IV expired.

It was then the duty of The Archbishop of Canterbury and Lord Conyngham, The Lord Chamberlain, to journey through the night and inform the Princess Alexandrina that she was now the Queen.

The Lord Chamberlain and the Archbishop had found it difficult to enter the Palace, the porter refusing to rouse the Princess or her mother. Eventually the young Alexandrina's tutor and mentor, who was by now Baroness Lehzen, was sent for and she, somewhat reluctantly, agreed to wake the Princess. She asked them to wait in her sitting room.

Alexandrina arrived, in a flowing white dressing robe, with her long dark hair loose and a shawl around her shoulders. She was less than a month beyond her 18th birthday; the kingdom had been spared the Regency of The Duchess of Kent. They kissed hands at just after 5.00am.

Lord Coyningham dropped to one knee, addressed the girl as 'Your Majesty' and kissed her hand. The Archbishop did likewise, as Princess Alexandrina of Kent was informed, and became aware, that the king had died peacefully that night.

'And my aunt,' said the new Queen with a note of anxiety. 'Is my aunt Adelaide quite well?' The young girl, now queen, immediately moved out of her mother's bedroom and into a suite of rooms of her own. She declined to be known as Queen Alexandrina, discarding that given name for ever and using her middle name, assuming the title Queen Victoria, Victoria Regina.

Not only King William IV, but also The Kensington System died that day.

5

Weymouth

Adam's parents died within a hundred days of each other when he was just fifteen. Now a strapping young man, clever beyond his years, but maybe not yet as wise, Adam had developed strong limbs and weathered skin. Handsome, with a great crop of brown hair sometimes hiding his sparkling eyes, he would have turned the head of any young girl looking for someone to walk out with, but, up to now, had met few girls of his own age.

Helena, still living nearby, was a friend, and they sometimes sat by the river at the end of the village, with her brother, Will, and half a loaf of bread. This might be, when time allowed, a break for them to enjoy exchanging news, if there was any news, although more often than not just to sit quietly together.

Twice, within a period of three months, he had been left stunned and puzzled by the death of a parent, experiencing a mighty jolt in what he had always thought might be a unchanging and continuous way of life. The upheaval was bad enough when Henry died, and Adam and his mother had managed what came next. When she weakened and died, perhaps of a broken heart two months later, Adam was bereft.

For the second time Mrs Redman held his hand, as a simple coffin was carried a few yards on a farm cart, through to the land, beside the church, which was the village graveyard. His father and mother were together now, in a space furthest from the church, and furthest from the road. The body was followed by the reverend, by Adam and Mrs Redman plus Adam's friends, Tom, the blacksmith and a handful of village neighbours. It was lowered to lie within the same plot as Mr Warkin, who had not had long to wait for his beloved Louise to join him, silent and unknowing.

'What to do next?' mumbled Adam as they walked away after the committal prayer. The other 'guests' followed. There was no wake, as such, although Mrs Redman provided tea and some scones, as she had two months earlier.

On that occasion she had entered the home of the Warkins for the first time and been welcomed by Adam's mother. This time she welcomed everyone to her home, and, for an hour, they comforted Adam, spoke of the departed and slowly departed themselves, returning to village life which, of itself, never changed. Adam's life, however, was at a turning point.

'You know what you must do,' said Mrs Redman. 'You have been the breadwinner now for quite a while and you can carry on until you decide whether you want to stay in this village.'

Adam had, by then, indeed become the bread winner, earning an almost regular wage of two shillings a week at the blacksmith's as well as working for Mrs Redman, performing so many domestic tasks as she became a little older.

He also worked in the grounds of the church which owned the little Warkin cottage where he and his mother had been allowed to stay, after Henry died, and where Adam was now allowed to live, when Louise had followed her husband into a church grave.

'The reverend is charging me a truly peppercorn rent of just sixpence a week,' Adam told his mentor, 'and has allowed me to stay on there. I can afford to stay if I keep working and...'

'And yet you are wondering what might happen in the months and years to come?'

He never stopped reading, or learning from the books that he read. He was no shirker and worked hard at one thing, or another, in a well organised, busy day, every day, between sunrise and sundown. His friendship with Mrs Redman never diminished, indeed probably grew in its intensity. She encouraged him to read more and more, introduced him to new ideas, even arithmetic, and to new books.

One morning, some months before Adam's father had weakened and died, Mrs Redman had suddenly announced, 'If your parents agree, we shall go to Weymouth, you and I.'

'To Weymouth! But I have never been outside this village or the next. What is it like? How do we get there? How long will it take?'

Mrs Redman had assured him, 'You leave all that to me. We shall join the train, which stops at the Halt nearby, on its way from Dorchester to Weymouth. It will take us less than an hour, and we can look at some books, have some tea, and even take a look at the sea.'

Adam was agog. He'd seen pictures of Weymouth, and Dorchester, and even London, in some of her books. He had heard the train, when it passed a mile or so away from where they lived. He'd seen pictures of how the sea meets the land with a sandy beach in some places, and crashes into the land on rocks and cliffs in others.

He had seen pictures of trains, now gradually weaving their

way with glistening parallel rails across the whole of Great Britain, but never imagined travelling in one.

The day came. Mrs Redman pulled out four pence from her purse to give to the conductor, who travelled with the passengers and Adam sat, mesmerised, by the window facing forwards, his eyes glued to the window and his consciousness overflowing, almost hypnotised, with sights and sounds he'd only ever dreamed of… or read about.

Too soon the train pulled into Weymouth and the pair of travellers ventured out. Mrs Redman knew her way around the town and she soon found one of her favourite bookshops where they scanned the shelves and found a new volume or two, which Adam hinted at, and Mrs Redman bought. They enjoyed a tasty hour at the tea rooms, yet another first for Adam, and together they looked at the sea, a sight which Adam relished.

Mrs Redman somehow, seemed to know an awful lot about everything. He was impressed without ever saying so, but sat in awe of her wisdom and knowledge, without ever finding out much about that special day, the day that she had seen the queen.

Back in Melton Ford and in the days and months following his mother's funeral, the boy now lived, of course, alone. Never a day passed without he visited Mrs Redman. Hardly a day went by without his earning a few extra pence, or a shilling, on which to survive. He even managed to save a little here and there, and within a year emptied the tin, which sat on the mantelpiece, finding in it ten shillings and seven pence. It was not a fortune but more than he had ever seen in one place at one time.

'What would you like to do by the time you are eighteen,

or twenty one, or thirty?' asked Mrs Redman one day. 'You are a bright young man, healthy and handsome, with skills, especially of reading and arithmetic.' something which Adam and she had also practised, at great length, over these past few years.

'I've no idea,' he said, 'but maybe be a blacksmith, or work in the gardens of a big house. Do you think I should leave Melton Ford? I've been to Weymouth, with you and seen some great houses from the train.

'I've seen pictures, and read of even greater house and other towns, and people, where they make cotton fabric or grow vegetables by the thousand, where boys can be trained to be silversmiths or stonemasons. Perhaps I should learn a trade, but that would mean moving away from here. I would hate to leave you.'

'But one day you must. One day you will. I will not be here for ever and you don't know yet how your life will turn out in years to come. Perhaps you should turn a corner, go on a journey on your own.'

Her words rattled around in his head. He worked every day, but Birgitta Redman knew now that he seemed to be looking ahead, not chained to this village, but apprehensive about leaving it, without ever actually voicing his fears. She knew how he both feared, and yet felt the urge, to move on.

'You could join the army. Her words came out of the blue one morning, when he had been cutting back hedgerows at the rear of Mrs Redman's cottage. 'You could join the army, perhaps learn a skill with the Royal Engineers, or become a musician. Guard the queen!'

'The queen's army,' he mused. 'Maybe I could. I have seen some soldiers in Weymouth and they look very smart. I never thought that I could be like that. I have hardly worn anything different to my dad's old trousers and shirts ever since he died.'

'It's not just about what you wear,' she said. ' It's about who you are.'

'And who am I?' Maybe it was time to decide.

6

The young Queen

At the end of a continental visit in 1843 the young Queen Victoria, married now for two years, and the mother of a bouncing baby girl aged nearly three, and an infant boy, returned to England with her husband, Prince Albert, landing near Weymouth at Portland Harbour. The Queen had been violently sea-sick, which may, or may not, have influenced the newly formed Commission for Harbours of Refuge, to build a new breakwater at Portland. But all of that came too late to help the Queen on that day.

Her Majesty alighted the yacht and entered one of three horse-drawn carriages, waiting for her, ready to begin the journey to London. The obligatory loyal address was read by the Mayor, itching with the delight of being in a position to address Her Majesty during his year of office. He stood proud, with a bulging belly under his red coat, black hat slightly tilted, gloves gleaming white.

He spoke words, the like of which the young Queen had got used to hearing, in various forms, during these first six years of her reign.

'We hereby tender to Your Majesty our humble offering of gratitude and dutiful obedience. And we shall ever pray that it will please Almighty God to shower his choicest blessings upon Your

Majesty, upon the illustrious Prince, your honoured and much-loved Consort and upon the youthful members of Your Majesty's family; and that it may please Him in His great mercy to grant that Your Majesty may long reign, in uninterrupted happiness, over a loyal and affectionate people.'

She was cheered by crowds, lining the streets through Weymouth, with children and grown-ups alike, waving flags and hands, delighted to have caught sight of the young Queen and her handsome husband.

As the queen and Albert waved, and smiled, from the carriage her Majesty spoke to him through tight lips.

'Remember, Albert, that even though we two will seldom be able to remember, individually, any of these thousands of eager folk we meet during our travels, nevertheless each individual met and greeted will never forget, as long as they live, the day they saw the queen.'

But it was not on that excursion to Weymouth that the young Mrs Redman had been amongst the crowd or seen Queen Victoria. Birgitta Gustasson, as she was then, was but two years old, and did not even live in England.

Her Majesty had moved on indeed, self assured, confident and regal, from the eighteen-year old who greeted the Archbishop, attired in just a dressing gown and shawl and with her hair loose. Now married, and the mother of two healthy children, more travel plans were made to enable Her Majesty to meet her people.

7

Leaving home

It was towards the end of the beautiful, if rather wet, summer of 1887 and Adam was making plans for travels of his own.

He was clutching fifteen shillings and eight pence, carefully saved in the tin box, and Mrs Redman had given him another ten shillings, a new shirt, two pencils and a book about England. The one bag he owned, he had packed with all the other clothing he possessed, a small knife and his late father's strong shoes as well as his large, felt hat. He had given up the Warkin cottage and he stood now at Mrs Redman's cottage door.

Tucked into his jacket was the letter from the head gardener, at The Manor House in East Hambley in Hampshire, offering to meet him and perhaps take him on as a junior gardener. Adam was approaching his sixteenth birthday.

'You're a grown man,' said Mrs Redman, 'and you look as though you could take on the world.'

'I feel like a lost boy not knowing where I am going and what I shall do,' he responded. 'But actually I am excited. You have taken me to parts of the world outside of our village, taught me how to buy a train ticket, how to speak with strangers, and... a whole host of things I never would have known.

'You have taught me so much about some of the big houses

in England, how the staff work for the great families who live there. I will never be able to repay you, and I certainly cannot see how I will ever repay this ten shillings!'

'If Mr Granger takes you on at The Manor House,' said Mrs Redman, 'you will earn enough money to allow you to save a little. They will give you somewhere to sleep, and you will eat with the other servants. You may be given some shoes and, possibly, even a suit to go to church in. You don't have to repay me, but if you come home to Melton Ford for a visit you can bring me a little gift or a trinket you can buy in the village, or in Southampton.'

'I will bring you something silver,' said Adam, 'and I will. I will come back as often as I can to see you.'

'No, you won't,' she replied, 'but you can write to me. It would be such a joy for me to receive a letter from you, and you very well know how to do that.'

'Perhaps I should go.' he reluctantly decided. 'I have to walk to the Halt and pick up the train to Dorchester. From there I get a train going towards Southampton, but I must get off at the little station serving East Hambley. I am sure I shall do something wrong and get lost!'

'No, you won't,' she repeated, 'but, yes, you must get started. Never allow the bag out of your sight, keep your money safe, deep inside your pocket and take off your hat when you meet, and speak, to somebody at the Manor House.'

So it was coins, totalling twenty-five shillings, and eight pence that left the village that afternoon hidden deep in the pockets of Adam Warkin, aged sixteen, almost. He glanced back only once, as he strode away from the cottage. He was leaving behind the boy who was his former self.

'I will write, and I will visit you,' he called back, 'And one day you will tell me about the day you saw the queen.' Adam had never forgotten the telling of that moment in Mrs Redman's life, which she had mentioned those few years ago, and his surprise at hearing it, but she had never elaborated on the experience. He had always been curious, but settled for that snatch of conversation which had so enthralled him, but about which she had never revealed anything new.

'One day I might,' she said, as he walked away. 'Perhaps you will see the queen yourself one day.'

'You will be the first to know if ever that happens,' he said as he walked away, without actually believing that it ever would.

'If I ever see the queen, I will write to you immediately,' he shouted back. And he was gone. Once out of sight of her cottage, he looked ahead and heard the approaching train.

There had been a motherly kiss on the cheek and an embrace. Birgitta Redman stood at the gate until he was out of sight, and wiped her eye, wondering who was going to pick the apples for her in the autumn. She stayed at the gate until she heard the train departing from the Halt.

8

Golden Jubilee

In that same year, after breakfast on the lawn, the now sixty-eight- year-old Queen Victoria had taken a short train ride from Frogmore near Windsor, where her beloved Prince Albert had lain since his death, twenty-six years earlier, to Paddington. It was then that the nation began the celebration of the Golden Jubilee of Her Majesty Queen Victoria. It had been fifty years since she ascended the throne as Queen of Great Britain and Ireland and now, by the Grace of God, but more by the machinations of Benjamin Disraeli, she was also Empress of India.

A magnificent banquet had been arranged at Buckingham Palace for that evening, attended by fifty kings and princes, with consorts, along with Heads of State of neighbouring nations, and British colonies and territories overseas. The room was awash with uniforms and diamonds, beautiful gowns and the sashes and badges of rank.

Her Majesty had presided over her people now for half a century. The next day dawned and with it came the journey to Westminster Abbey in an open landau, escorted by Colonial Indian Cavalry, and thousands of troops, who marched in time to several bands, and lined the streets of the procession itself. Nothing of the kind had ever been seen in London, certainly not within living memory.

Heading up the guest-list were Prince Frederick William, the Prussian Crown Prince and later Emperor of Germany, with his wife, Victoria, the Queen's own eldest child, representing the German Emperor. There was also the Prince of Wales, Her Majesty's eldest son and heir, with his wife the Princess Alexandra of Denmark, Princess of Wales.

There were appearances on the balcony of the palace after the procession on that 21st June summer's day, and a grand ball in the evening, for which the queen wore a lilac gown lavishly embroidered with silver roses, thistles and shamrocks. Afterwards she received a procession of diplomats and princes before she was wheeled in her chair to sit and watch fireworks in the palace garden.

9

East Hambley

There was little or no such welcome for Adam Warkin at The Manor House in East Hambley a month or so later in that year of 1887. His journey had been uneventful and he quietly congratulated himself for having successfully negotiated the two trains, and the stations, which brought him to Hampshire. He had asked the way to the house from the little station and enjoyed the evening sun, as he approached the gates of the house. He had bought himself a sandwich, and a bottle of weak beer, when he changed trains, and eaten the piece of cake which Mrs Redman had slipped into his bag.

However he searched in vain for a way into the grounds of The Manor House. There were big gates indeed, but no way through them and nobody to be seen on the inside to let him in.

At length, but not long before the sun was due to dip below the horizon a maid came by, stopping momentarily to observe the boy shuffling around, and looking lost, near the big gates.

'You'll not get in there,' she said. 'Nobody gets in there without an invitation or a carriage,'

'But I am due here. I'm Adam Warkin and I need to see Mr Granger, but I cannot get in. Do you know how I can get through?'

'I've told you, you'll not get in there,' she told him again, 'But, if you follow me, I'll show you the lower gate to the garden and the stairway entrance.'

'That would be very kind,' said Adam, noticing that the girl was about his age, shorter with dark blond hair, and not much of a smile. She was wearing a long grey woollen dress, covered with a white apron, which came almost to the hem of the dress, and a white bonnet not unlike that which Mrs Redman always wore. He picked up his bag, which he had been standing astride and followed her.

Within a quarter of a mile, she took him through a small, cracked, painted wooden door into a large kitchen garden, through lines of vegetables, growing successfully under the evening sun, and into a side door to the great house which had come into view as they rounded the end of the garden. Inside was what he recognised as a kitchen, although bigger than almost any room he had ever been in, except possibly the Tea Rooms at Weymouth.

'You should have been here several hours ago. I thought the train brought you to East Hambley by half past five, so the walk from there should not have taken you this long.' It was Mr Granger, and Adam had been led to him by the girl, whom he quite quickly learned was Daisy.

'I couldn't get through the gates...' began Adam.

'The silly boy, he was waiting by the double gates leading in from the main road, sir,' enjoined Daisy with half a smile on her face.

'And you thought you were important enough to come in that way, did you, boy? Well that may be the last time you come in here at all.'

'I'm sorry, I did not know there was more than one way in, sir.' said Adam, but Mr Granger had turned away and was walking away, shouting instructions to other boys who scuttled around to do his bidding.

Adam stood still, transfixed both by the movements of everybody nearby, by the imposing nature of the enormous kitchen, where he stood, and with what was going on all around him. It was as if he was nailed to the floor, being unable to make a move, which would contribute in any way to the activity of the kitchen, and being unable to leave as he contemplated which way he would leave even if he thought he should.

'Are you still here?' It was Mr Granger taking a momentary breath between barking orders and supervising the coming and going of so many underlings.

'I thought I'd made it clear that you would not be staying here.'

'I was very much mistaken, sir, thinking that the big gates to the house were where I might be allowed to come in. I just didn't know.' He intuitively remembered quite suddenly what he had read in one of Mrs Redman's books about the hierarchy of such a house, and knew that he had possibly one chance to redeem himself, or find himself on the early train next morning, having, by then, possibly slept under a hedgerow, after being thrown out.

Daisy had come back to stand by his side. He was still clutching his bag.

'Mistaken indeed!' exclaimed Mr Granger, 'and how many more mistakes might you think you'd be allowed to make before you are rendered useless to me in this house?'

'Possibly not more than one more, sir,' said Adam. Daisy smirked.

'Are you the boy with the letter I sent to Melton Ford?'

'Yes, sir.'

'And you,' he barked at Daisy, 'go and fetch more vegetables for Mrs Browne, and stop that smirking,' he added, as she sidled off.

'Are you,' he started again slowly, 'the boy with the letter I sent to Melton Ford?'

'Yes, sir.'

'Well, why aren't you showing it to me?'

Adam suddenly sprang into action, knowing full well where the letter was but appearing to have to search for it from one pocket to the next. Suddenly it appeared and thrust itself between his fingers and thumb towards Mr Granger's face. 'The letter, sir.'

He read it very slowly.

'You know how to grow things? And look after a garden?'

'Indeed, sir,' said Adam. 'I've learned a lot in the village where I grew up.'

'And what about Mrs Redman? Did you learn a lot from her?'

'Yes, sir. Do you know her, sir? Is that why she chose you for me to write to?'

'That doesn't matter now.' said Mr Granger, who turned out to be the Head Gardener. Now he just stood there, then stood back a little and just stared at Adam.

He was not a slight man. He had enormous arms and apparently muscles to match. He stood nearly a foot above Adam, wearing rough woollen trousers and a rather grubby pale green shirt, with sleeves rolled up above the elbows. His tough brown leather apron almost covered him from top to toe and side to side and he stared down at the new boy with only a hint of acceptance. The large mouth on his rosy face and beneath his balding head moved about as if he was chewing something.

'Right! Let's get you sorted out. Freddie!' he shouted at another boy, passing by carrying boxes. The boy, just a few years older than Adam, but looking slighter and weaker, stopped in his tracks. He had dirty blond hair and was wearing a cut-down version of Mr Granger's attire. His hands were filthy, but his hair and neck were clean. His eyes were brown and he blinked a lot. He put the boxes down.

'Get this boy up to your room. You'll be sharing from now on. Get him stuff to wear and show him the vegetable plots, fruit trees and… well, show him around. You've all been hoping for another pair of hands. Well here they are. His name is ..' Mr Granger took a quick look at the letter and said, 'Adam.' There was moment's hesitation and a pause in the proceedings.

'Well, are you both still here?'

'Thank you, sir,' Adam tried to say as Freddie pulled him away. He barely had time to turn around and pick up his bag, but he managed it and followed Freddie.

'And get those boxes outside first,' shouted Mr Granger, at which point Freddie did an about turn, followed by Adam, manhandling both his bag and a couple of the boxes.

Together they removed the boxes and themselves from the kitchen floor, piled the boxes up outside on to another collection of empty wooden crates before returning to the kitchen, to weave their way through everybody else towards a set of double doors.

'You still here?' It was Mr Granger, emphasising the word 'still' as his way of telling them both to get a move on. 'Don't dawdle, the pair of you!'

'I'm sorr…' began Adam, before Freddie pulled him again.

'Don't bother answering. Just do as he says.' Freddie advised by which time they were through the doors and into a long corridor.

The pair of them climbed several flights of stairs until they were in another corridor, which looked as though it ran the length of the house, beneath the roof, with doors leading off, all painted green.

Freddie took Adam in through the seventh door, the furthest from the staircase where he found himself in a tiny room, with sloping ceiling, two flimsy looking 'camp' beds, one chair and not much else. He looked out of the window and, apart from seeing a sloping roof beneath the room, he enjoyed the view.

Perhaps it was the highest he had ever climbed inside a building of any kind. He just looked - at the hills, the green fields, winding paths and cattle. He thought he saw a river. He thought of Melton Ford, but was glad that he had moved on and found a position.

It didn't take long for Adam to settle in to what was a completely strange environment. It was all new to him, but somehow he seemed to take it in his stride, learning skills and ideas as he went along, soaking up the routine and being occasionally thanked and congratulated for a job well done. Adam had never been, nor ever would be, a shirker.

This was a large house to navigate, although he occupied so little of it. It was a large kitchen garden, with Mr Granger handing out orders to everyone, but everyone actually knowing what to do. There was row upon row of vegetables to tend, to hoe, to trim, and sometimes to pick. Fruit trees having already blossomed were now ready for a harvest, so the wooden crates came into their own when Adam and Freddie managed to fill them as everything ripened. There were large lawns, too, and a glorious avenue of rhododendrons the like of which Adam had never seen.

He ate well, with the others servants, about thirty in all, headed by Mr Johnson, the Butler who was clearly in charge of everything and everybody. Adam soon learned the pecking order for seating and standing up if Mr Granger or Mr Johnson entered the room where they were eating or resting. Even Mr Granger stood up if Mr Johnson came in.

To his surprise and joy he was given the extraordinary sum of five shillings, every Friday, when the staff lined up at the butler's pantry door, entered when told and signed a book to say they had received their wages.

The money was then handed back to the butler who put it in a black metal box. Everyone's wages were being saved for them, and although Adam would have quite liked the idea of having the money in his hand he knew it was his, could calculate what he had 'saved' by his labours and enjoyed the thought of owning thirteen pounds at the end of a year.

Almost all of the money he had saved to travel away from home with was still in his trouser pocket. He wrote to Mrs Redman, bought a stamp at the nearby Post Office when he had been sent to a local village on an errand, and enjoyed putting it into the post box. He thought of her reading it.

The Manor House,
    East Hambley.

Sunday 20 November 1887.

Dear Mrs Redman, my dear friend,

I have thought of you often since leaving Melton Ford, and appear to have settled in well at The Manor house, here. There is so much to do and I am kept very busy by Mr Granger.

I nearly didn't get in to the house at the start but I was shown the correct way to the garden entrance by Daisy, who is a maid, and now I know my way around very well, although I have yet to see much of the house and have never seen the family. I am so glad that you suggested that I write to Mr Granger. How do you know him? He will not tell me, but then, I suppose that is not important. That is what he says.

Often I think about our times together when you were so patient with me, learning to read and write. I shall ever be grateful for that and wonder, sometimes, how you put up with this boy who made so many mistakes. And, of course, I think of mother and father, too, who brought me into this amazing world, but knew so little of it themselves.

I have read in the newspaper, which appears every day in the kitchen from the house upstairs, about terrible scenes in London last Sunday. It seems that above twenty thousand men and youths were in Trafalgar Square in a riotous assemblage which was severely met by the police and even soldiers. I am so pleased that nobody lost their life but have yet to understand fully why such scenes should occur. Mr Granger says that the men were protesting about not being employed. Some people here say that they may be among the unemployed one day. I am so grateful, of course, that I have employment although sometimes the work is hard.

I have a good friend, Freddie, who showed me what to do and where to go when I arrived, and we share a room at the top of the house. Daisy is a very cheeky girl, but she and I get on well. Perhaps I can come to see you at Easter next year. I would like that, but for now, I remain,

Your dear friend,
With much affection,
Adam.

Then it was back to growing more produce, learning from Mr Granger, but also from Freddie, what worked well in the process and how to get the most out of the earth. Adam was growing every day in every way.

10

Kingston Lacey

At the end of a long day for the sixty-eight year old Queen Victoria, a few months earlier on 21 June 1887, her Golden Jubilee Day, she had sat down, as was her custom, to write her journal.

She had been delighted with the reception which the crowds had given her, and noted that a beautiful beam of sunlight, from the Westminster Abbey window, had lighted on her while her eyes were closed, during one of the prayers. The future Queen Liliuokalani of Hawaii had observed this, and noted it as a mark of divine favour. Queen Victoria, never one to refuse a mark of divine favour, had thanked her, and God, and now wrote it in her diary.

She sat quietly and recalled earlier days, when she had been with Albert, whom her generous, and usually co-operative, God had taken from her far too soon, twenty six years earlier.

She remembered 1843 and visiting the Isle of Wight, deciding to buy a home there which Albert re-designed and re-built into the beautiful Italianate Osborne House. Everybody knew now that this was her favourite home.

And she recalled 1865, having by then been a widow for some four years, again setting foot in Weymouth. Accompanied by her son Bertie, The Prince of Wales and his young wife, the beautiful Alexandra, the Queen had sailed from the Isle of Wight to Weymouth, and been taken on, by carriage, from there to visit Kingston Lacey in Dorset, a house owned by The Rt. Hon George Bankes MP, and his wife Georgina.

The Queen had been determined to visit Kingston Lacey, and this was the opportunity, along with the Prince and Princess of Wales, and their entourages. She had heard previously of the bravery of George Bankes' son, Cornet William Bankes who had died during operations in India in 1858, some seven years earlier, aged just 21.

Young Cornet Bankes was the fifth child of Rt. Hon. Mr and Mrs Bankes who, after a good education and a period of paid work as a librarian at The House of Commons, had enlisted as a cornet in the 7th (The Queen's Own) Regiment of (Light) Dragoons (Hussars). William, initially, had no great enthusiasm for the military but was very keen to spend time with friends who were serving in the regiment. The story of his untimely death after just a few months in India, following the Indian Mutiny was sad indeed and came to the notice of the queen. She remembered it now.

Bankes had lain desperately wounded in hospital in Lucknow.

Queen Victoria heard of his courage and was so deeply moved by his plight, that she wrote to her daughter, Vicky, the Princess Royal, who was preparing for her own wedding.

'There is a poor young man, of the name Bankes, who has been cut almost to pieces. He fell and was surrounded by a set of fanatics who cut at him, so his thigh was nearly severed from his body and so was his arm! Besides six other desperate wounds! He has had his right leg and his right arm amputated and yet they hope he will live. This is, they say, the pattern of patience and fortitude.'

Despite all the efforts to save him, Bankes died in hospital in Lucknow, on April 6, 1858, after contracting blood poisoning. He was unmarried, aged just twenty-one.

Her Majesty had created, and introduced, the Victoria Cross during the Crimean War of the early 1850s and was now inclined to award this honour to the deceased William Bankes, although there was no precedent for awarding the VC posthumously. Indeed current practice was for those who died valiantly in the service of their queen to be mentioned in the press as 'deserving of the Victoria Cross, had they lived.'

In this case, however Her Majesty had been determined to award the honour to William's father and made the journey specifically to Kingston Lacey to do just that. It was honour indeed. No other posthumous VCs were awarded for many, many years. Visiting Kingston Lacey that day, to be there when the queen arrived, was Dr William Russell who travelled with his wife, Mary, from their home at The Manor House, East Hambley.

The staff had prepared carefully for the visit and had the honour of working alongside the personal servants of The Prince and Princess of Wales. The queen's own staff were housed separately and worked independently of the remainder of the household. The house at Kingston Lacey was a hub of activity, from the back stairs entrance up and through to the main rooms and front hall. It was very exciting.

Dr Russell and his wife had been invited specially. He had been in India when the young William Bankes had arrived and, so soon, been wounded in the attack. He had tried to save the life of the young cornet who, despite being in such pain, stayed remarkably cheerful having lost both an arm and a leg.

'They tell me, doctor,' he'd said to Russell, 'that if I get over this I can go yachting.'

Alas, it was never to be. Dr Russell, also acting as a war reporter for *The Times* in London, sent the story of the brave young man to his newspaper and so it came to the attention of Her Majesty, the Queen. Now they were all gathered in the pink drawing room at Kingston Lacey, Dr and Ms Russell, the boy's parents Mr and Mrs Bankes, The Prince and Princess of Wales and Queen Victoria, for a simple handing over of the Victoria Cross to George Bankes, who handed it immediately to his wife.

The jubilee day had been a long day indeed for Victoria, as she sat now, looking at her journal, remembering that day at Kingston Lacey and many others. What brought to her mind the story of Bankes eluded her, but she was always prone to sitting and remembering days, and years, gone by, as she wrote her notes and made ready for the end of a day. And little did she know, nor ever would, what a momentous occasion it had been for others when she visited Kingston Lacey on that summer's day back in 1865.

11

The family

Young Adam Warkin had never yet met the family for whom he worked. He knew the master was a doctor, Dr William Russell. That much he had been told. And he had seen some of them come and go from the front of the house, usually in carriages, but sometimes on horseback.

Adam had spent his days during those first four months harvesting fruit from the orchards, picking vegetables which might be ready for storage, or for the table, learning new skills and being very tired at the end of each long day. His days began at 7.00am and were punctuated by drink, or meals, at 8.00am, at midday, once during the afternoon and a final meal at 8.00pm, usually after the family had eaten.

The food was always good, his wages were being saved up slowly. He hardly spent a penny on himself, and he now had two good shirts, one necktie, a suit to wear on Sundays and a spare pair of shoes, all this as well as the clothes he was given to work in.

He and Daisy, along with Freddie and, on occasions, one or two other young servants, went to the village. Sometimes it was on errands, but more often than not it was to sit and dream, or talk and waste their break-time hours until it was time to resume their duties.

When December came all the servants were called to the main hall at the front of the house on Christmas Eve, to receive a gift from Dr Russell. Adam was apprehensive, but Freddie and Daisy guided him, behind so many other staff members, led by the butler, Mr Johnson.

Adam made a point of standing between Daisy and Freddie, so that, whichever way the gifts might be handed out, coming from the left or the right, he would see how they had responded and be able to imitate one or other of them.

The hallway was bright with lights and had a large fir tree standing at the bottom of the main staircase so that anyone coming down the stairs would pass by the top of it, which Adam would be hardly likely ever to do. With the staff lined up and looking their spruced up best, Dr. and Mrs Russell came through from the sitting room, with three other adults. Adam guessed which were the master and his wife, although he had never spoken to them, and he had no idea who the others were.

The doctor and his wife came down the line, with Dr Russell shaking the hands of each servant. He was tall, upright and looked severe. He had grey hair and bony fingers which Adam noticed. Mr Johnson made sure that the doctor knew each person's name, although in fact the doctor knew most of them. He was less sure as he headed towards the younger end of the line-up.

Behind him came Mrs Russell, looking very frail. She was shorter, looked very delicate with grey hair also and a silver gown, attended by one of the male servants from the house, who carried a tray on which there were gifts. Each gift was handed over by Mrs Russell with a nod of the head from the men, or a brief curtsey from the female staff. Adam could make out that sometimes a few words were being exchanged. As they approached Adam's end of the line, he was even less sure that he knew what to do and he hoped that they would perhaps not speak to him.

The moment arrived, and by now Mr Granger had taken over the introductions. It was the turn of the garden and ground staff to receive the Christmas gifts. They arrived in front of Freddie, who bowed his head very slightly and said, 'Thank you, sir, thank you, ma'am,' as he took his Christmas gift; a small package wrapped in red paper.

Adam nearly fainted but retained his composure and dignity, standing upright, but with head bowed with a brief nod. 'Thank you, sir, thank you, ma'am.' The words came out perfectly and he hardly heard Dr Russell say to him, 'Mr Granger tells me that you have done very well since you came here in the autumn.'

'Pardon, sir.' He really did not know how to respond. Not usually lost for words or nervous like this, he really did freeze just for that moment.

'The good doctor is congratulating you, Adam Warkin, on having done so well since you came to The Manor House,' said Mr Granger in his ever-so-slightly sarcastic, slow and louder voice.

'Have I?' said Adam. 'Thank you. I've done my best, sir. Done what I've been told.'

'You have certainly done that, so Mr Granger tells me.' It was the doctor speaking to him. 'And you seem to have learned a lot, and used your initiative.'

The moment had gone, before he had time to utter another 'Thank you', but he was pleased and felt very Christmassy all of a sudden.

No Christmas back home had ever been like this. Mrs Redman had given him a small gift for the past few years, and he tried to make something for his mother and father, when they were alive, but he had never been in such a beautiful house as this, never seen so many lights illuminating the space, and certainly never been given a gift wrapped in red paper. And this was where he now lived!

'There need be no more work, other than the essentials,' said Dr Russell to his butler and the gathered line-up, 'until the day after tomorrow.'

Mr Johnson thanked the doctor, on behalf of the staff, and the distribution of gifts was over. The family, with the mysterious three additional adults, had gone back into the sitting room and the line-up dispersed, with Freddie suggesting they go to their room first, before going down to the servants' hall for some drinks.

In the little bedroom at the top of the house, sitting on his bed, as Freddie was doing on his, Adam looked longingly at the wrapped gift he had been given, as Freddie began to open his.

'It's not Christmas until tomorrow,' said Adam. 'You can't open it now, can you?'

'I always do,' said Freddie, 'but you can save yours if you like.'

He didn't, and opened it straight away, just a few seconds behind his friend. His eyes nearly glazed over when, inside he found not just another very smart necktie, but two crisp cotton handkerchiefs, and a gold half sovereign.

'The doctor has given every member of staff a gold half sovereign!' At least that is what Adam told himself. Perhaps older members had been given more, but this, to him, was a glittering prize indeed. It was likely to be the best Christmas ever, and he determined, there and then, that he would save the money and definitely go to see Mrs Redman at Easter, if he were allowed a day or two away from the house.

As winter turned to spring in the following year, 1888, Adam still hoped that he might be able to return to Melton Ford and see Mrs Redman for a short visit.

He never, however, seemed to be able to find the right moment to ask. Mr Granger was not entirely approachable, but, Adam decided his moment would come and he was, after all, usually in Mr Ganger's good books.

It had not helped that during that winter, Mrs Russell had passed away, and so Adam had seen a rather more splendid funeral leave The Manor House than he had been able to afford his parents, a few years before. Horses with tall black plumes, a glass-sided hearse, mourners, all in deep black, and a chance to be informed whom some of the other adults were in the cortege.

There were two sons of Dr Russell, Mr Walter, and the elder Mr James, and some grandchildren of varying ages, even what could have been a great-grandchild. But, being all in black, Adam could never have remembered them individually. He stood alongside the other servants, heads bowed, as the carriages came past on their way to the local church, and the Russell's own burial plot.

He worked in the garden every day except Sundays. He also came to know other members of the household, and even one or two family members. Dr Russell, now in his seventies, and a widower, seldom came to Adam's part of the garden at all, but his son and heir, James, with his wife Lydia, sometimes walked in the garden and spoke to Adam.

Dr Russell's second son, Walter had been in the army for some twelve years and was now retired, living at The Manor House but having never married. He would sit in the garden and read on pleasant days, occasionally stopping Adam, as he passed by, perhaps with a wheelbarrow full of dead plants for composting.

Thus it was, that Adam got to know their names and who they were. He especially took to Mr Walter who had once told him of his exploits in the army some years before. Adam had paused, as he passed Mr Walter, reading, and perhaps glanced too longingly at the book he had in his hand.

'Do you read, er… Adam, isn't it?' said Walter Russell, stopping Adam in his tracks one February morning.

Yes, sir. Adam Warkin, sir. I didn't mean to stare at your book.'

'Don't worry about that. It's a very good read. You look as though you might be interested.'

'I read as often as I can, sir.' responded Adam, quickly removing his cap. 'I love to read. A good lady in the village where I was born taught me and, as often as I can obtain a book of my own, I will read at the end of the day when there is enough light. I have bought one or two volumes in the village but there is not too much to choose from.'

'Then you must read some of the books from the house,' Walter said. 'My father and brother would never object to anybody reading in the library. They are great believers in young men being educated, or even simply reading for the pleasure.'

'Do you think I could, sir?' rejoined Adam. 'I am not sure Mr

Granger would be very pleased about me going into the house.'

'Then I shall make sure he understands that you do it with our permission. Why not come now, to choose something to read?'

'Not now, sir, if it's all the same to you,' Adam was quick to respond. 'I am working until we have some tea about five o'clock but after that as it is quite dark by then, perhaps he won't object to me coming to the library.'

'Then five o'clock it is, or shall we say a quarter past?' And with that, Walter was up and away. Adam noticed that he was tall and slim, and, as he walked away, that he had a slight limp. 'A quarter past five, Adam. I shall see you there.'

Adam decided to tell Mr Granger, there and then, that he had been invited to the library.

'Mr Walter has invited you to the library?' said Mr Granger sounding very surprised. 'What on earth for?' Adam explained and was given permission but grudgingly.

'If you must, but I'm not sure I see the point. Hasn't got anything to do with your job here. But of course you must go if you've been summoned.' He almost spat the words out, as Adam explained the reason for his visit, as if there was something distasteful about books or reading.

'I don't hold with too much reading,' he said, 'But go if you must. Do not be late for supper at eight.' Then Mr Granger remembered something which arrested his thought train. 'Did Mr Walter mention mice?' he said.

'Not at all, sir,' responded Adam.

'Well maybe they're going to show you where the mice have been on that side of the house, and you'll get the job of cleaning up some of what they've left behind.' Mr Granger was strangely pleased that he had come up with what he thought was the real reason why Adam had been summoned to the library.

'I'm sure it wasn't that at all, sir…' began Adam, but his voice tailed off as he realised Mr Granger had gone, with his mind made up that nobody would encourage a garden boy to read, let alone invite them into the library. Adam, meanwhile was sure that he had not been invited to the library to sort out the mice!

Adam made sure his hands and his boots were spotless before he ventured towards the top of the back stairs. He opened the heavy padded door and found himself where he had received his Christmas present, two months earlier. He knew that the library was straight across the hall and proceeded with some trepidation.

'And where do you think you're going, young man?' rang out from the lungs of Mr Johnson, the butler.

'To the library, sir. The master's son, Mr Walter has asked me to…'

'Are your boots clean?' barked Mr Johnson.

'Absolutely, sir,' he began, just as Walter Russell appeared.

'Adam, there you are. Come along in. It's alright, Johnson.' And in they went, leaving Mr Johnson slightly bemused, hardly moving for several seconds before remembering where he himself had been going.

Inside the library, Adam thought it looked like a larger version of one of the bookshops in Weymouth which he had visited with Mrs Redman, but with no other customers and no cash till! He looked around, not knowing where to examine first, still clutching his cap.

'Now put your cap down here on the table and have a look around. There are books on travelling around the world, some books here on medicine and tropical diseases – they are mostly my father's – and along there you'll find several novels written by Mr Charles Dickens, the Bronte sisters and Mr William Makepeace Thackeray.' Adam was transfixed, but slowly began to move towards the travel books.

'There are so many books,' he began, utterly bemused, 'I wouldn't know where to start in here. I have read that one already,' he said, pointing to Mark Twain's '*Roughing It*' which Mrs Redman had introduced him to in her own home. 'But there are so many more.'

'Then you must come as often as you wish,' said Walter, encouraging him to browse shelves, high and low, take out any book he took a fancy to, and borrow it to read in his own room. 'I shall tell Johnson and Granger that you can come in here, with your hands and boots clean, of course, whenever your duties allow you to come and read, or borrow a book.

'And what about the mice, sir?' asked Adam. 'Mr Granger tells me that you may have been asking me to clean up after the signs of mice in the house.'

'Yes, we have had signs of mice indeed,' said Walter, 'but not so much now. We have certainly had plenty of unwelcome visits from the mice, but don't seem to be able to get rid of them completely. Don't you worry about them.'

'I can set a couple of traps, if you wish, sir,' said Adam. 'We used to do that at the blacksmith's and once at Mrs Redman's. I know how to make them, and I would need a few bits of cheese.'

'This is all very interesting,' said Walter. 'If you want to try that, please do. I'll see that you get some cheese from the kitchen.'

'No, don't do that, please.' Adam said quickly to him. 'I'll get the cheese, but I'll make sure I don't touch with my bare hands. The mice, or rats, if you have them, won't touch the cheese with human smells on. I like to fool them into thinking we haven't touched it first!'

'Sounds very clever to me,' said Walter almost warming to the subject. 'Anyway, you do that if you wish, but in the meantime have a look at the books. I'm going to get ready for dinner.'

'You're leaving me here on my own?' Adam hastily enquired. 'Thank you, sir.' With that, Walter was off, leaving the library door open, and Adam spoilt for choice.

A week or so later, and on his way to visit the library on a Sunday afternoon, Adam again met Mr Walter in the front hall.

'Good afternoon, young Adam. On your way to the library again?'

'Thank you, sir. Yes, I am.'

'Well, if you need anything, let me know.' said Walter.

'Thank you again, sir. Actually, there was something. I'm not sure how to ask,' he began.

'Well, just tell me, that's the best way.'

'I shouldn't be asking you, but I would like to get permission to go back to my village at Easter. Should I ask Mr Granger or go straight to Mr Johnson. Or maybe I should not ask at all!'

'Of course you should ask. It doesn't seem like you to be nervous.'

For all his newly acquired self-assurance, Adam was still the young boy at heart, unsure of himself in so many ways. 'I do enjoy my job here, sir, but nobody has ever mentioned anything about leave, or being allowed time off.'

'I'll ask Johnson,' said Walter, as he was walking away. 'Enjoy the library.'

'Thank you, sir, I will,' said Adam, and with that he was in amongst the great store of books, spoilt for choice again.

Two days later Adam was summoned to Mr Granger's machine shed.

'Seems as though you have the ear of Dr Russell's son, Mr Walter,' said Mr Granger. 'It seems like they're happy for you to go back to your village for a short visit, if I agree.'

'I would be very grateful,' said Adam. 'I'd like to visit Mrs Redman, who suggested that I come here to work for you.'

'You could have asked me, you know,' said Mr Granger.

'I realise that now,' Adam replied, 'but I was just not sure about whether it would be allowed at all.'

'Well, you never know if you don't ask. And I know Mrs Redman from some years ago, so you can take her a message from me. How about you go at Easter, perhaps on the Saturday, returning on Monday afternoon?'

Adam was delighted with that suggestion, and thanked Mr Granger profusely.

'In future, sir, I will only ask you.'

'Well,' he heard Mr Granger reply, 'Don't ask too often. But, well done. You have certainly proved your worth since you arrived here.'

This was almost as good as the Christmas gift and, when they next met, he thanked Mr Walter again for helping him to ask. Later he pondered for the second time, how it was that Mr Granger knew Mrs Redman, but the opportunity to ask had gone again.

The spring days got longer and longer. Adam sometimes spent an hour or so in the village with Freddie, and one or two of the other younger servants, on a Sunday mid-afternoon. That's where he learned to drink a little bit more than he should, but never getting intoxicated, especially if he spent the time laughing and talking along with an excellent meat pie.

Adam enjoyed these innocent outings. He learned a bit more about the village, and he most enjoyed sitting with Daisy, who was still as cheeky as ever, but sometimes even strolled back to the main house, with just Adam, very slowly, as if they were a pair, sharing stories about their upbringing.

They were never in any trouble when they got back to the house, always returning before their given time, just, entering by the garden gate which Adam now knew so well. Adam, it seemed, was treading his way with his position in the house very carefully and cleverly. He'd made a good start over the first few months and he was treading his way with Daisy even more carefully.

That was more than could be said for Freddie, who often crept out of the house, at other times, sometimes on a Sunday morning, when most of them were in church, and sometimes even during an evening, after the 8 o'clock meal. He was usually gone just for an hour or so, coming back and creeping in, later than he should.

Adam began to plan his trip back to Melton Ford. He needed money from his savings, he wanted to do some shopping and he checked the times of trains.

12

Continental visit

At about the same time, Her Majesty Queen Victoria's thoughts turned to travel, and plans were made for her to make another continental visit, as had become her custom in recent years. She had made occasional visits to her daughters, Vicky and Alice, in Germany, but, for sunshine and rest, the queen usually travelled to Italy or the South of France in the spring or early summer.

Supposedly travelling incognito, as The Countess of Balmoral, or The Countess of Lancaster, the Queen of Great Britain and Ireland was easily identifiable by everyone, with her enormous entourage of household and servants, and mountains of luggage, all labelled 'VR & I'.

Her wish to remain 'anonymous' was preposterous in the extreme, and, of course, she would have found it intolerable had she not been treated with the deference she always expected, despite insisting that she was indeed travelling 'incognito'!

Concealing her real identity was carefully planned so that Queen Victoria could safely, yet ostentatiously, travel through France and other parts of Europe without the encumbrance of having to submit to the protocol of making an 'official' or, worse still, a State Visit.

In 1888 her destination of preference was Italy, staying at

the *Villa Palmeiri* in Fiesole, near Florence. Her Majesty spent her days visiting local sights, talking with her ladies and enjoying the company of local dignitaries, and minor royals, who welcomed her to their homes or visited her by invitation.

Quite apart from Italy, Queen Victoria had somehow managed to make the French Riviera very popular indeed with British travellers. Since her first visit there, in 1882, she had turned a sleepy unknown corner of France into a joyful playground for the rich and their titled friends.

Prior to Victoria's first visit, a few English folk, who could afford it, had made their way there after contracting and recovering from tuberculosis. It was a place of convalescence. It was strange then, that Victoria, who had an abhorrence of illness and death, should come to love the area so much. Nevertheless the citrus groves and what she called the '*sunny flowery south*' proved irresistible to the Queen, who visited there many times, and attracted a following of tens of thousands of 'tourists' who popularised the Cote D'Azur, under the Mediterranean sun.

Now in her late sixties, the Queen enjoyed everything as if she were a seventeen year old. She rode donkey carts up medieval tracks and even took a fancy to one or more of the local teenage shepherds or goatherds, writing in her diary, even many years after being widowed, that '*the boys were very picturesque looking, wearing knee breeches, white stockings and leggings with large felt hats. Some are very handsome.*'

And Queen Victoria slummed it too, becoming much loved by the poorer locals where she stayed. She entertained a group of fishwives, when she stayed at Cimiez, and when they tried to kiss her on both cheeks, she declared them '*very friendly*' but offered them her hand instead.

She gave small gifts to local beggars telling her ladies, 'I know that I am sometimes exploited but it is better to make a mistake, in giving, than to be in error by not giving at all.' And she built a humble water trough for thirsty horses, on the high trail between Nice and Villefranche.

This year, in Italy for a change, she arrived on 24 March and was refreshed and delighted at the villa owned by the Dowager Countess of Crawford. She was visited by the King and Queen of Italy and presented with a painting of the villa by Hermann Corrodi, an artist who was already a favourite of The Prince and Princess of Wales. In fact Corrodi had given painting lessons to the Princess. Queen Victoria stayed for a month and returned to the villa twice more in the following six years.

13

A visit back home

Back in England, Adam, working in The Manor House gardens certainly did not have the luxury of a month-long visit anywhere, but was still delighted at having been given permission to travel back to Melton Ford for the Easter weekend. Despite such anticipation, and planning, he had found it impossible to get away, as planned, on the Saturday, so decided to leave it until the evening, before making his way to the station at East Hambley.

So it was, that he spent a chilly night in the station Waiting Room, and caught the first train, heading for Weymouth, on that Easter Sunday morning.

He took with him two small silver spoons, which he had bought from the pawn-shop in East Hambley, near to the railway station, for five shillings and sixpence each. He had them wrapped in soft tissue paper and was looking forward to giving them to Mrs Redman. Their cost just about equalled the ten shillings which she had given to him when he left the village.

He'd also treated himself to a small leather wallet, and even a small silver St Christopher medallion, which he put around his neck. It was almost the first time in his life he had ever bought anything for himself.

On the train on Easter Sunday morning Adam sat at a

window facing forwards, as was his preference, and was joined by a jolly young fellow in a check jacket and brown trousers, who had a great mop of brown curly hair, was carrying a small wicker hamper and was perhaps a little older than Adam's seventeen years. He sat opposite Adam and it took him no time at all to draw Adam into conversation.

'Where you off to, then?' he said without much introduction.

'Visiting a friend,' Adam replied.

'I've come all the way from London, me. Always enjoy going south, especially if the sun shines. The name's Arthur, by the way. I work in the markets at Covent Garden'

'Adam,' Adam offered, 'I work at one of the houses in East Hambley where I boarded the train.'

'Fancy a bite to eat?' offered Arthur and indicated his wicker hamper, but Adam declined politely, saying that he'd had a sandwich and a bottle of beer, which he'd already consumed, waiting at the station during the night.

'Come on,' said Arthur. 'I have plenty and you'll be hungry again before you get to… where is it you're going?'

'I'm getting off the train at the Halt near Melton Ford. It'll be about an hour.'

'Well take off your coat, relax and get one of these down you,' said Arthur proffering him a small pork pie. It looked very appetising. Adam succumbed, put his coat on the seat beside him and tucked into the pie. Arthur took a pie for himself, closed the lid of the hamper and put it on the seat beside Adam, then turned and spread his feet across the seat, leaning up against the window.

'Help yourself to anything in there,' he offered, although Adam was reluctant to take full advantage of his generosity.

'Why are you travelling today?'

'I have two days leave from the house where I work. I am visiting a friend.'

'Watch out for fools today,' he said. 'It being the first of April.'

'I hadn't even thought of it,' said Adam, remembering suddenly his days in the village when the children had tried to fool some adults with a trick or a joke on All Fool's Day. In all honesty, he wished that his destination would come soon.

Adam had with him his small, rather battered bag. In it were a few items he might need for the journey or for the stay at Mrs Redman's. There was a spare shirt, a couple of books which he'd been given permission to bring away from the house to read, his knife, a pencil, some socks and the two silver spoons wrapped in tissue paper.

He kept a very careful eye on it in the rack above his seat, as Arthur came across and sorted out a bottle of beer for himself from the hamper. Adam felt uncomfortable by the effusive presence of Arthur, without being able to pinpoint any actual fault in the young man. He was friendly and talkative.

'Perhaps,' thought Adam to himself, 'I am not at all sure of myself in strange company. Maybe I am still the innocent Adam, who left my village seven months ago.' Yet again, Adam's personal confidence was not quite as sharp as he would hope.

All too soon, although not soon enough for Adam, they approached the Halt where Adam wanted to leave the train, and he asked the conductor if the train could stop to let him off.

He extracted his coat from underneath Arthur's hamper, put it on and buttoned it, wishing the other young man farewell as the train slowed to a halt.

'All the best,' mouthed Arthur through the window, as Adam walked past the carriage and saw it slowly pulling away. 'And thanks.' The young man inside the carriage raised a bottle as if giving good cheer and then he was gone.

Adam walked briskly towards Mrs Redman's cottage. It was nearly midday, the sun was shining, and he was looking forward so much to seeing her. He took his jacket off again, feeling a little too warm wearing it, and folded it carefully, before hanging it across his arm. It was then that he noticed that his new wallet was missing.

He had a few coins in his trouser pocket, but the five pound note he had withdrawn from his savings, deposited with Mr Johnson, represented virtually all the money he had in the world and it was gone. He searched every pocket, there and then, on the village road, and searched again, delving into his trouser pockets, and then into the bag. He retraced his steps, all the way back to the station and on to the low platform, peering fruitlessly down the line into the void of the afternoon. It was gone.

That crisp white five pound note had been the first he had ever seen in his life. And he very quickly came to the conclusion that he had been the Fool of the Day to engage in conversation with Arthur, on the train, leaving his coat, even though it was so close to him, on the seat beside him, beneath, as he now remembered, Arthur's hamper.

He felt hollow and sick. He was angry and confused. How could he be so stupid? How could a jolly, chatterbox, on a train, rob him, whist he, Adam, was politely refusing most of his offers of food and drink? He was clenching his fists as he told

Mrs Redman, all the time wishing that this could have been the story of a longed-for journey, to see her, after a successful few months in service at The Manor House, instead of the story of a theft.

'It is indeed a horrible lesson to learn,' she said.

'Lesson?' said Adam. 'How is it a lesson?'

'All your life you have been surrounded by good people,' she began. 'Your parents, the reverend, the blacksmith who gave you some work, your friends in the village, your new friends at East Hambley and, dare I say, me, who has always been grateful for your friendship.'

Now he was confused again. 'You are grateful to me? It is I who will always be indebted to you.'

'That's as may be,' she came back at him. 'But you might also remember that, along the way, you played your part in the lives of others and they may be, in fact I suggest they are, even now, ever grateful that you counted among their friends. I, for one, always give thanks that you came to pick my apples and sweep the little barn, and, above all else, became my friend.'

'But you taught me to read.' Momentarily his mind was distracted from the loss of the five pound note. 'You showed me books and how to write a letter.'

'You taught yourself, once I gave you the letters and some of the rules! You were a keen learner and a bright young man. Somehow or other, you would have learned to read without me. And now you've been robbed.'

'Don't remind me,' he said. 'It's the worst thing that's ever happened to me.'

'Nonsense,' she said. 'I'm sorry to tell you that many more things, perhaps worse still may yet happen to you, as you go even further out into the world. But each time you travel along this path, or that, you will have learned something new as you have done today, and probably not make the same mistake again. A bit like reading!'

'But five pounds!'

'You will earn five pounds again, and in not so much time. Remember this, that if you remain honest and even cheerful, despite what sometimes happens along the way, you will always be somebody who is proud of himself and, may I say, a person whom I am proud to know.'

'Well, thank you,' he began. I suppose you're right. You usually are.'

'And remember this. That young… what was his name?'

'Arthur.'

'That young Arthur may have five pounds more than you now, and a hamper with food in, and you may have lost a few pounds, which you sweated to earn.' She almost laughed a little. 'But he will be a thief from now until his dying day.'

'Goodness me,' said Adam. 'I'm still not very pleased about it, but I left here last autumn without a five pound note, I've earned one, lost one, saved a bit more than that, which is with Mr Johnson, and I will earn it again.'

'That's the spirit,' Said Mrs Redman. 'Now, how about some tea?'

'You make the tea, and I have two silver spoons for us to stir in the milk. These,' he said as he produced the tissue paper package from his bag, 'are for you, from me.'

14

Hero to villain

After a night at Mrs Redman's, a splendid breakfast, and a brisk walk to his friend, Will, and Tom, the blacksmith, it was back on the path to the Halt and wait for the train to take him 'home'. Mrs Redman had given him another ten shillings which he had tried so hard to refuse, but she insisted and he was grateful.

On the train he mused over the long conversation they had had the previous evening, when the sun had finally set and the lamps ran down. Mrs Redman still intrigued him with her stories and her wisdom. 'She is a clever lady,' he thought to himself. 'And, perhaps, she has helped me to be a bit wiser too!'

Things moved quickly when he returned that Monday evening. There was an atmosphere in the house which he detected and did not much like.

'What's up?' he said to Freddie, as they sat on their beds that Monday evening.

'Things have gone missing from the house,' said Freddie. 'Some stuff from the dining room and the library.'

'Missing?' Adam came back to him. 'You mean stolen?'

'Looks like that. They've searched our room, and all the other top corridor rooms. Been asking about visitors and the like. Nobody from the garden is allowed inside the house on their own for the time being.'

It certainly was not quite the happy home that Adam had left on the Saturday afternoon, three days earlier. He was told that he could not go to the library under any circumstances.

'We're not picking on you, boy,' said the butler, Mr Johnson, when he came to the kitchen and summoned Adam in from the garden. 'It's just Dr Russell's orders.'

Working in the garden, in a never–ending cycle of tasks throughout the year, Adam became very useful and learned a great deal. He did get around to making mouse traps for the house, although was accompanied, when he set them in one or two rooms, including the library. He met Mr Walter a few times, when they passed each other in the kitchen garden as Adam was planting out crops for harvesting later in the year.

'Are you still reading, Adam?' said Mr Walter. 'I hope you are.'

'As often as I can, sir,' he replied, 'although I'm not allowed in the library at the moment.'

'Then I shall choose a book or two for you,' Walter replied. 'What would you like?'

'I'm not fussy, sir?' said Adam. 'Perhaps you could decide what you think might be interesting for me.'

'Well, what a responsibility!' said Walter, with tongue firmly in his cheek. 'Then you can blame me if they're boring, or if you've read them already!'

'Oh, no, not at all, sir. I wouldn't...' Adam was visibly embarrassed.

'I'm joking,' said Walter. 'Just leave it to me.'

The springtime came and went, one summer, then one year more and another. Nothing more was said about the missing items, and the rules were slowly relaxed, although the word amongst the staff was that things were still vanishing from the house.

Adam wrote to Mrs Redman at least once a month. He actually had nobody else to write to, but enjoyed telling her the news. He visited her again during the summer of 1890, having been given permission to be away for two days. It was the first time he had seen her in two years and she looked visibly older. He thought, perhaps, that he himself looked older too.

'You told me you loved silver,' said Adam, sitting in Mrs Redman's cottage again after an uneventful journey, 'so I found this for you.' He handed her a delicate silver trinket box which, on this occasion he had found in a small jewellery shop in West Hambley, the neighbouring village five miles from The Manor House.

'I think it's similar to the one you already have,' he said, as he stirred his tea with one of the silver spoons Mrs Redman had brought out specially.

'It isn't similar,' she said. 'Take a look. It is identical.'

Adam could hardly believe his eyes, when, looking at the two boxes he saw that they were indeed exactly the same.

'How can that happen?'

'Well,' Mrs Redman replied, 'I expect there were a lot of boxes. made to the same design. about the time my husband and I were given this one. It's not so surprising, but it's very good now to have a pair.' Adam was just that bit more pleased with the gift he had brought than he had expected to be.

By the following summer Adam would be twenty and enjoy a fair number of privileges, alongside his duties. His self confidence was growing by the day.

The springtime of 1891, however, had nearly brought everything in the house and garden, as well as in the south of England, to a standstill. Adam had been given permission to go home to Melton Ford for two full days, leaving The Manor House on Saturday 7 March. Easter was due much later in March again that year, but a visit at the beginning of March was considered quite permissible. He was due back to work on the Monday.

What nobody had anticipated was that on Monday the 9th, the south-west of England had been struck by a blizzard, so ferocious that some six thousand animals would die in snow drifts, or from being stranded and frozen to death.

Adam had enjoyed two beautiful, if cold, days with Mrs Redman, bought her a meal at the local hostelry and given her another small gift, which he had bought at the jewellers in West Hambley. This time it was an ornate fan, which she expressed her immediate delight in owning.

'You must not spend your hard-earned money on gifts for me,' she said as he handed her the gift, again wrapped up in tissue paper.

'But I enjoy choosing presents for you,' he said. 'In any case, I can never repay you for all you did to help me get started in life, when I left this village.'

'Nonsense,' she said, as she nearly always did, when he tried to pay her a compliment.

As he left Mrs Redman's, and the village, that morning to make his way back to his place of work Adam was soaked by the rain, even before arriving at the Halt outside the village. By the time he changed trains to get to East Hambley, the snow made visibility all but impossible, and as his journey got underway, there was nothing to see out of the windows whatever, except driving sleet.

That morning, violent gales had left dozens of ships floundering on the rocks along the Cornish coast, and Adam's train suddenly came to a jolting stop. Nothing happened for several long minutes. Passengers were straining to see up or down the line, which was at a bend, so from one side there was nothing to see.

From the windows on the other side, anybody could see that the locomotive was actually up against an enormous snow drift, which had prevented any further forward motion.

An eerie silence followed, with muted conversations between travellers, some of whom seemed unworried, whilst others jumped to all kinds of conclusions about being stuck there all night, without food or warmth. Warmth was actually what they were most in need of. It was freezing.

Back at The Manor House, everybody had been confined to the house, windows bolted, sheds and barns shut up. The rain and snow was lashing the entire estate, with rivers of slush forming quickly, and running through the yards. Boys were sent out to try to keep the snow away from the front door, but were fighting a losing battle and were allowed back in, to let the snow do its worst.

Passengers on Adam's train had all gathered into one carriage, as far as was possible, and were even pooling food, after an hour or two, as afternoon was giving way to early evening.

Adam was so cold. With his suit jacket being his most substantial garment, and most protective, he decided to open his bag and put on every other item of clothing he possessed. As darkness came, the entire train threatened to become a frozen tomb for the forty or so passengers, huddled together. They had shared what food they had and were still feeling very hungry. Some fell asleep on the floor, a couple of children were crying and the night passed very slowly indeed.

At first light next day, the Tuesday, Adam remembered that there had been a goods wagon attached to the train, which he had noticed when boarding. With one of the conductors, he made his way carefully through the carriages, one by one, until they were unable to go any further. They then knew that the goods wagon was next in the line of carriages. Adam had his bag with him, being reluctant to leave it behind, even though any thief, such as he had come across like Arthur three years earlier, would have nowhere to go!

'If we can get out here,' said Adam, 'can we get into the goods wagon?'

'Yes,' said the conductor, whom Adam had learned was Stuart. 'I can open it from the outside.'

They risked getting out through the end door of the carriage and down, into the very deep snow. The wind was biting through their outer garments and their feet were very quickly wet, but between them they managed to stride, carefully, the few yards towards the wagon, where Stuart was able to open the side door.

Once inside, they rummaged through piles of boxes and sacks, finding carrots, potatoes, and some turnips, some clothing, intended for shops at the end of the line, and some pots and pans in boxes. It did not take them long to put on some extra clothing. Ill-fitting though it may have been, it was entirely welcome, and it did not take long to distribute more of it to the other passengers.

'We could make soup,' said Adam. 'It looks as though we shall be stuck here for a while, but if we could make a fire, inside a pot, using a piece of metal grill, we could use some snow, with the vegetables and make something which would be, at least, warm even if it's not too tasty!'

The driver and fireman from the train's engine, just ahead of the closed goods wagon had arrived now, and the fireman agreed to get the fire going with some live coals. Adam seemed to take charge of clothing distribution, soup making, and the collection of any available dishes, cups or spoons.

He was in his element, and enjoying what might otherwise have been a deadly serious situation. He began to get everybody organised. The conductor went back to the rest of the passengers, as Adam began cutting up some vegetables with his knife and putting them in one of the pots, with handfuls of snow, gathered from just outside the wagon. The space around them warmed up considerably, as they made headway with the soup.

Two of the other male passengers had started to clear a slightly easier route from the carriage to the wagon, with the help of a shovel provided by the fireman, and before long some very weak, but hot, soup was being shared amongst the passengers, a motley looking crowd in the various outfits of jumpers, coats and blankets which they found in the goods wagon.

'It could do with a pinch of salt!' said one lady, who was travelling alone. She was ignored.

The blizzard continued for three days, moving eastwards and to the north. The wind was moving the snow, some springtime sun was helping it to melt, and, by the end of the Wednesday, it seemed that the train could push its way slowly through the snow and make some headway.

Adam did not consider himself by any means the hero of the hour, but a lot of grateful passengers hailed him and thanked him for helping them to get through a dangerous, very cold, and uncomfortable few days.

They arrived, eventually, on Thursday morning at East Hambley. As the conductor was unloading the Royal Mail bag to the local postmaster, Adam made as if to alight, but he was asked by the conductor, Stuart, to stay on the train until it reached Southampton. The southern half of Hampshire had not been nearly so affected by the great blizzard and the train made its way there safely, with Adam still on board.

'But I have to be back at my place of work,' said Adam. 'I should have been there on Monday.'

'Leave that to us,' said the station master. 'We have had a visit from your Mr Granger, at The Manor House, and he has agreed you can go back, when you are able to do so. In the meantime, the Railway Company would like you to visit Southampton.'

'I'm sure I don't understand,' said Adam, but went along with the plan. The journey along the remainder of the line was uneventful, and they arrived on Thursday afternoon, with all the remaining passengers still thanking Adam for some of the worst soup they had ever eaten in their lives!

The Station Master at Southampton was ready to greet him, and the train crew, along with one of the Directors of the Railway Company. And there, too, was Mr Walter, from The Manor House. To Adam it all seemed a bit unreal.

'Thanks to the marvel of the telephone,' said Sir Redmond Danby, the Railway Company Director, 'we have now heard of your efforts to keep everybody safe, young Adam Warkin.

'You are to be congratulated, even though you seem to have

masterminded your plan by raiding the goods wagon and utilising most of the contents!'

'I am so sorry,' began Adam. 'It was absolutely necess…'

'Nonsense,' said Sir Redmond. 'I am teasing you. The Railway Company will cover all the cost of what you had to use, to stay alive, and you, young man, will take this cheque for your pains.' He handed Adam a cheque for twenty pounds, which he took, staring at it in disbelief. Not only had nobody ever given him twenty pounds before in his life, but actually he wasn't sure of what a cheque was.

Thank you, sir,' he began again. And I am sorry, Mr Russell,' he said looking aside to Mr Walter, 'for not being back at work on Monday. I hope Mr Granger is not too angry.'

'You are doing an awful lot of worrying for a young man who has, just possibly, saved the lives of all the passengers on his train,' said Mr Walter. 'So now that the presentation is over, why don't we go into the town now? I shall book you and me into an hotel, and tomorrow we shall open you a bank account for that cheque you have, and return home. I have a carriage here for us to travel in.'

It was all very much beyond his wildest dreams. He'd never set foot in a hotel before, let alone contemplated staying in one. He ate a meal with Mr Walter, being served at the table in a manner which he only ever experienced with Mrs Redman, in the Tea Rooms in Weymouth, although this was better even than that. He slept the night in a sumptuous room, all to himself, very warm and very full-up, for the first time in several days.

The next morning, Mr Walter guided him through breakfast in the hotel restaurant, and they went together to The National

Provincial Bank in Southampton to open an account and deposit Adam's cheque. He received a bank book and receipt for his deposit and in the carriage on the way back to The Manor House in East Hambley, another first for Adam, Mr Walter explained how he could deposit or withdraw money from his own account at the bank. It was all quite a revelation.

Back at East Hambley the springtime continued with rather better weather than he had experienced on that fateful train journey home from his village.

He had learned about some of the new fangled machines, which were available to wealthy folk who had large gardens, and had made it his ambition to be the one who knew most about using them and even repairing them.

There were always large areas of grass which needed cutting, and a new steam lawn mower had arrived, which Adam took a shine to, and managed to master, also learning how to fix it, when it went wrong. His friend Freddie had moved to duties inside the house and, between them, they mastered the drum rotating washing machine and the wash boiler in the laundry as well.

Dr Russell's son, Walter, had earlier even authorised the purchase of a bicycle, for the younger members of staff to use, if errands were needed from the village. Adam and Freddie loved to be chosen to ride it, and of course, they loved to tinker with it, if it showed signs of being imperfect!

It was the bicycle that had taken him to West Hambley to find, and purchase, Mrs Redman's fan. The new young boot boy, Robert, was helping in the grounds, and Adam was given charge of him, to share a lot of what he knew about the garden.

The Christmas rituals were repeated every year, with the

usual packages, wrapped in red paper, and containing some very welcome items and a half sovereign. Adam had managed to save up another five pounds, and considerably more as the months went by.

The older brother of Mr Walter, Dr Russell's son, James had come to the house with his wife, Alice, and one of their sons, in the spring of 1891. The son, James Jnr, who was a young officer, on leave from the 29th Dorsetshire Regiment, with his uncle Walter, came across Adam reading in the garden, sitting near the greenhouses. They stopped.

'Now, here's a young man who could go far,' said Walter to his nephew.

Adam sprang to his feet, snatched off his cap and stood stock still.

'I'm having a break, sir.' said Adam. 'This is one of the books you sent to my room.' Adam looked at the young Mr James who was resplendent in his military uniform.

'Quite right too,' said Walter, 'sit yourself down. We don't want to disturb your break.' But they did anyway, and sat alongside him as Adam carefully closed the book and sat, gripping his cap between his knees

Despite sitting next to him, Adam could see that Mr James junior was an imposing young man. He was 28, very upright, with dark oily hair which extended into long sideburns on either side of his face. He had a smiley disposition, and spoke with a soft but commanding voice, in a very friendly manner towards Adam.

'How long have you been at the Manor House?' said the young officer.

'Since 1887, sir.' said Adam. 'So more than four years now, sir.'

'And this young man has probably read more books, from my father's library, than the two of us put together,' said Walter.

'That's very impressive,' said the young man. 'I'm Captain James Russell, Dr Russell's grandson.'

'Thank you, sir,' said Adam, 'I knew who you were when you came along.'

'What about these books then? What have you read?'

'I just love to read anything, sir.' Adam answered. 'Dr Russell's library is a treasure house of information'.

'I know,' said Walter, warming to the conversation, 'that young Adam, here, has borrowed novels and travel books, including all those volumes on the world around us, including Mr Darwin's *The Origin of Species* if you like! And he's borrowed some of the mechanical books. Is that right, Adam?'

'Yes, sir. I was so interested in the steam engine, and the new electric motors, and even the new tramways, sir. They're fascinating, and I love reading about how they work. The new lawn-mower, sir, I know how to keep it working efficiently. I've studied the drawings of the engines and motors and find myself absorbed by them,'

'So I have heard. I'm sure Mr Granger could hardly manage without you,' said James and started up as if to go.

'Have you been in the army, sir?' piped up Adam, quite out of the blue. 'or rather, should I say, are you in the army?'

'Absolutely,' said James. 'About eleven years. And what about you? How old are you?'

'Twenty last birthday, sir, and…' he hesitated.

'Yes?'

'I knew you were in Her Majesty's service, sir, and have seen you at the house. I wondered if… well, supposing somebody like me wanted to join the army, sir? What would I need to do? I don't suppose they'd have a gardener.'

'They'd certainly have somebody who reads books! These days you have to be able to read, even in the lowest ranks, before they accept you. And as for knowing about engines and the like, well that would be a bonus indeed. Why, are you considering leaving the Manor House?'

'I'm not really considering it, sir,' Adam replied, 'but you never know what the future might hold. A lady told me once that she had seen Her Majesty the Queen, and I have often wondered what it might be like to see Queen Victoria in person.'

'Well, I've only seen her once,' said James. 'She was in a carriage and I was on duty, at Windsor Castle, so she drove past at quite a speed, while I was standing to attention.'

'Perhaps I might consider it one day,' said Adam. 'I don't know what my future holds, but at the moment I am very happy here.'

The two gentlemen wished him well, and walked on. Adam's break was over, and he returned the book to a shelf in the pantry where he temporarily kept the books he was reading, and went out into the garden to carry on gathering some blooms for the house. 'Maybe I will think about leaving here one day,' he thought to himself, little knowing what would come next.

'You're to go straight to the main hall, and no dawdling.' It was a few days after his conversation with Captain James Jnr and Mr Walter, but he had the feeling this was nothing to do with them, or with borrowing books. Mr Granger was speaking and he looked none too pleased.

'Do you know why, sir?' said Adam and was immediately

pushed along, through the kitchen without much ceremony.

'Straight to the main hall, I said. Do as you're told.'

Adam was bemused, to say the least, but made his way up the stairs, towards the heavy padded door leading into the main hall. Mr Granger followed him. Adam's heart began to beat faster and he felt suddenly and unexpectedly scared.

He stood in the middle of the front hall, and faced Mr Walter and even the ancient Dr. Russell himself, as well as Mr Johnson, the butler, and now Mr Granger, who joined them. They all looked at Adam, who felt very small indeed.

'I'm amazed and disappointed.' said Mr Walter. 'Very disappointed indeed, even shocked.'

'At what, sir?' began Adam.

'Be quiet!' It was Mr Johnson, 'And speak, only if spoken to directly.'

'I have been in correspondence with your Mrs Redman in Melton Ford.' said Mr Granger. 'She's the lady who introduced you to The Mano…'

'Yes, sir, I know her…'

'Be quiet! I shan't tell you again,' came back Mr Johnson again.

'Sorry…'

We do not correspond a great deal.' said Mr Granger. 'I knew her late husband who worked here for a few years, so I keep in touch, just to be sure she is managing well in her older years. Do you know Mrs Redman, Adam Warkin?'

'Of course, sir. I knew her from a child. She taught me to read. I worked for her and helped her a lot. Has anything happened to her, sir?'

'Certainly not to her, but, of course, I know you have written to her, and visited her, when you have been given the privilege of being away from your duties for a day or two.'

'And I am very grateful, sir…' began Adam, before immediately shutting up.

'Did you,' began Mr Walter, 'visit her not long after you came to The Manor House, and take her a gift?'

'I did, sir. I took her two silver spoons. It was the least I could do as she had always been so generous to me. Is anything wrong?'

'Wrong!' Mr Granger came straight back in. 'Mrs Redman told me all about how you carefully wrapped them in tissue paper and gave them to her, as a 'gift" He almost spat the word 'gift'. 'I am so glad that we have kept in touch, even if so rarely.'

'And did you visit her again, a year later, and take another gift?'

'Yes, indeed, sir. I took her a small silver box for trinkets and the like.'

'Well, well. Out of the horse's mouth. I am so glad you have made it easy for us, and even more pleased that I kept in touch with Mrs Redman, otherwise the culprit involved in this affair would never have come to light. Mrs Redman happened to mention your gifts to me, in a letter, and has described them precisely. You stole those items from this house.'

'No, sir, I did n…'

'Be quiet!' came the immediate response. 'Things have gone missing, which we first discovered not long after you began your tenure here, which, I might remind you, was a great favour done to you, for the sake of your mentor, Mrs Redman.'

'But I boug…' began Adam, at which point Mr Johnson intervened with, 'You will go to your room, pack your things, and be ready to leave here in the morning.'

There was no more to be said. Adam was seething and angry. There was no way to respond and yet he knew that he had bought them in the nearby villages, at the pawnbrokers and at a jewellers. If they were stolen, it was certainly not he who had stolen them.

15

Clearing his name

'This is very odd,' said Freddie. 'You leaving us.'

'Not as odd as it seems to me,' Adam responded, feeling a mixture of anger and confusion about what had just happened. 'My Mrs Redman, I've told you about her, haven't I? Well, my Mrs Redman would never have told Mr Granger about the gifts I took her, if she had believed that I'd stolen them.'

'Can you prove you bought them fair and square?' said Freddie.

'I haven't got any proof that I bought the spoons. Wasn't even sure what he meant when he offered me a receipt! I know now, of course, and, once I realised what that meant, I did get a receipt for the silver box, and the fan. The man in the jewellers insisted, although goodness knows where they are now.'

Adam added, 'The trouble is, there doesn't seem to be any answering them 'upstairs'. They don't listen much. But I'll look.'

And look they did. There wasn't much of Adam's and Freddie's belongings in that room, but between them they made quite a mess of what they did possess; clothing, a couple of bags, uniform items which had to be kept clean, shoes and books, either Adam's or books from the library downstairs, where Adam had spent so much time.

Adam collected up three books, which did not belong to him, and began to work out how he could return them to the library, without being allowed anywhere near there. And sadly he could not find his father's large felt hat.

'I can take the books back for you,' Freddie offered. 'I am working in the house mostly now anyway, so I can get them back to the library.'

'I'm stopping up here in our room,' said Adam, 'But here are the ones belonging to Dr Russell.' He handed over three volumes to Freddie, including one on electric motors and engines, which he had so enjoyed mulling over. Freddie took them and made his way out, along the corridor and towards the stairs. He passed young Captain James, the doctor's grandson, as he began to descend the staircase.

'Can I get you anything, sir?' said Freddie. 'Are you alright?'

'Absolutely fine,' said the captain. 'Just tell me which room is young Adam's, the gardener.'

'The seventh one along there, sir. But it's in a bit of a mess. We've been looking for something.'

'Don't you worry about that,' said the captain. 'I'll find my way.'

When he knocked on the seventh door Adam answered furiously, 'What do you want?'

'May I come in?' he heard, as the door was pushed open.

'Oh! Sir, am I wanted again? Can I help you?' Adam scrambled to push some clothing to the side of the room, kicked his shoes under the bed and offered the Captain the one chair, once he'd removed a shirt from the back of it. 'I'm sorry it's such a…'

'Calm down,' said the young man. 'I'm not here to make any demands on you. Can I speak frankly with you?'

'Of course, sir.' Adam stood upright, with his back to the bed, not knowing quite how to appear the most deferential. 'I'm sorry it's such a mess.'

'Stop apologising about the mess. You should see my billet when we're away on manoeuvres. It's a wonder I can ever find where I am, let alone where anything else is. And, do sit down.'

'Thank you, sir,' said Adam as he sat on the bed, pushing more clothing to the foot end. 'Is there anything you want me to do?'

'Well, yes,' said the captain. 'In the privacy of this room, I want you to tell me how you got hold of the two spoons and the silver box.'

'I bought them, sir, honestly. I wanted to give Mrs Redman a gift and those spoons were the least I could do. I gave them to her when I had only been here a few months, and then last summer I bought the silver box and gave that to her, when I went on a visit. A few weeks ago I bought her a fan and took it to her in March, when there was the blizzard I got caught up in'

'Yes, I heard all about that. Very well done you, I say. You showed a lot of courage and initiative, so I hear. And your purchases? Is what you told them downstairs the truth, Granger and Johnson, and my grandfather?'

'Yes, sir, but it is difficult to get oneself heard. With respect, sir.'

'Oh, believe me! I understand that. I've been a child in this house,' said the captain. 'But those things, and others, seem to missing from the house. Mrs Redman described them precisely. She was not trying to incriminate you, of course, but quite innocently gave the perfect description of those items. So where did you get them... buy them from?'

Adam told him, at which the Captain asked, 'Can you ride a horse?'

'Not really had much opportunity, sir. Certainly never had a horse, but I can ride the bicycle which is in the machine shed.'

'Then tomorrow morning, you and I shall go and visit the places where you obtained the silver pieces. We shall look a comic pair, with me on a horse and you on a bicycle! I shall see you in the morning.'

Freddie had been told to take up some food and a drink to the top floor, and that Adam was not to come down to eat with the staff. He felt miserable and defeated, as he consumed some cold ham, boiled potatoes and a lukewarm cup of tea. But he had a meeting planned for the morning with Captain James which lifted his spirits.

The next morning a message was sent up to Adam's room to say he was wanted by the butler, but the message came back that he was not there.

'Why isn't he there?' demanded Mr Johnson. 'Where the hell is he?' He stormed through into the kitchen area, pushing aside several others on his way.

'Where is Warkin? he demanded of Mr Granger, 'Where is he?'

'He went out this morning, on the bicycle, with Captain James, about half an hour ago,' Mr Grainger replied.

'Why is he using that contraption? He has no right. I give permission for the use of the bicycle, and I didn't give it to him!'

'I think you'll find, Mr Johnson, that the bicycle belongs to the doctor and his family, not to you or me. Captain James came down with him, requested the use of the bicycle and off they went, with Captain James on horseback.'

'That's outrageous,' Mr Johnson spat out. 'Where have they gone?'

'That's hardly for me to say, or even for you to know, Mr Johnson, even if I did knew, which I don't.'

Mr Johnson slammed every door as he passed back through to his pantry. Meanwhile, the captain and Adam were several miles down the road, stopping off first at the pawn-brokers in East Hambley.

'It's three years ago,' said the man behind the counter, looking over his spectacles. 'Is that what you're telling me?'

'Yes, please, sir,' said Adam. 'Two silver spoons, I bought here. Please tell me you remember.'

'Oh, I remember, alright,' said the man. 'Clear as day. I offered you a receipt, but you said you didn't know what that meant, so you didn't take it. You seemed more concerned that they be wrapped in tissue paper.'

'Yes, that's right,' said Adam. 'You do remember.'

'Strange thing is, I kept the receipt, because I'd already written it out. It's a long time ago, but if you hang on here.'

'Oh, please,' said Adam, 'I would be very grateful.'

'Can you search out the receipt,' said Captain James, 'and we'll come back later?'

'Very well, that'll give me more time.' So the captain, and his bicycling friend, were off again, this time along the road to West Hambley, and along the main street until they reached the jewellers.

'You've lost the receipt?' said the girl behind the counter. 'I'll have to ask my father if he remembers you.'

'It was just last summer,' said Adam. 'I would be very grateful if I could get another.' Adam was doing all the talking, but he felt quite self-assured that the captain would assist, if he needed any help. The captain, meanwhile, was very impressed by the confidence of this young man and he kept thinking over what had happened, and what was happening now. This was not the behaviour of a thief.

'Here you are,' said the girl's father, looking in a heavy ledger, without any further ado. 'Twelve shillings and three pence for a silver trinket box, bought here in June 1890, on the thirteenth, and four shillings and four pence for an ornate fan bought in March this year, just before that dreadful blizzard, which nearly wiped us all out. It's a good job I remember you, young man, or at least your bicycle, which you seem so keen to keep an eye on.'

'Because it's not my bicycle,' said Adam. The man wrote out the receipts, put the original date on them and the word 'Copy' before handing them to Adam.

'Thank you, thank you so much.' And he made is if to leave, although the young captain held back.

'One more thing,' said James. 'If my young friend here bought the box and the fan from you, may I ask where you got them from?'

'That's easy,' said the man behind the counter.

'Oh, yes,' said his daughter, 'That's easy, because the man who brought them in has been in here more than once, with things to sell. Always says he was selling them for an elderly aunt, who needed the money.'

'And do you know his name?' said Captain James.

'Oh, no, sir!' said the jeweller. 'Don't really ask names for smaller items, and they was always smaller items; bit of silver, china, the fan, or a piece of cutlery. Sorry, sir, don't know his name.'

'Oh, well, never mind,' said the captain, as he and Adam made for the door. 'You've been very helpful.'

'Thank you very much.' said Adam, clutching his receipt as he went outside.

'But I do remember one thing,' said the girl almost as an afterthought. The captain turned at the door to listen. 'I remember he had a limp.'

Only the captain heard that last remark, and it took his breath away. He kept it to himself, as the pair set out on their journey home, looking, as Captain James had predicted, a comic pair, with one on a bicycle and one on a horse. They stopped in East Hambley to pick up the receipt, which the pawn-broker had found, and expressed their gratitude.

'Thank you so much, er Mr…?

'Trimblay,' said the man. 'Edwin Trimblay.'

'Well, thank you again,' said the captain as Adam left the shop. 'Er, just one more thing. How well do you remember whoever it was that brought in those spoons?'

'Oh, very well, indeed, sir. He has been in here quite a lot, offering things to pawn, sometimes redeeming them, but more often than not just selling them.'

'Does he have a limp?'

'He is not a very distinguished man, sir, and, yes, he does show a bit of a limp. He also wears pince-nez, just on the end of his nose, as if he does not really need them!' said Mr Trimblay. 'Oh, I remember him alright. And his hat.'

'His hat?' said the Captain.

'Nothing special,' said the man behind the counter, 'but he always wore a brown felt hat when he came in here.'

'Thank you,' said James, and they left the shop without

further ado.

'His name is…' began Mr Trimblay, but they had gone without hearing him.

Captain James and Adam made their way back to The Manor House, where James left his horse to the groom, and the bicycle outside on the gravel drive, as he took Adam in by the front door of the house and found Mr Johnson in the front hall.

'This is very irregular, sir,' said the butler. 'I think by now Warkin should have left the premises.'

'What is irregular, Johnson,' responded the captain, 'is that Adam here should have been summarily dismissed and accused of something he may not have done. Will you fetch my father and mother, and my uncle?'

'Sir.'

Adam stood slightly behind the captain, cap in hand, not knowing where his immediate future lay. Mr Granger, meantime, had heard about their return from the kitchen staff and came up to the front hall, looking decidedly displeased.

'Ah!' said the captain, pre-empting the man's complaint that Adam was still in the house. 'I wonder if you would be so good as to fetch me the letter, in which your Mrs Redman described the gifts which young Adam here took and gave to her?'

'Of course, sir,' said Mr Granger and he was gone again, through the padded door and down the back stairs, with a sidelong glance at Adam, who lowered his eyes. Mr Granger was still angry that Adam had seemingly been taken out of his charge that morning.

Captain Russell's father, James Snr, and his mother, Alice, and Uncle Walter arrived, with Johnson the butler. The small party went into the library, which Adam now knew so well, and Mr Granger returned with his letter. Adam felt very much the smallest person in the room.

'Read me the description, please, of the gifts which Adam took to your friend, Granger,' said the captain, which Mr Granger did, having found the correct part of the letter.

'It seems to me, sir,' said Mr Granger, when he had stopped reading, 'that those gifts were definitely taken from this house. Mrs Redman has described the silver items precisely.'

'Couldn't agree more,' said young James, at which point Adam felt his skin go cold, thinking that Captain James had deserted his cause. 'And may I ask, Uncle Walter, if these were the only things which have gone missing?'

'Good Lord, no,' said Walter Russell. 'There have been pieces of china, knick-knacks, silver mementoes, things from our late mother's room, even a book or two and maybe more, I suspect. The Housekeeper has made a list as things have gone missing.' Adam wondered if he was going to be accused of all these separate crimes.

'And yet,' the younger James continued, 'Adam here appears to have given only two gifts from our list to his friend; two silver teaspoons and a silver trinket box. I believe also, Adam, that you also gave your Mrs Redman a fan.'

'On another visit, yes, sir, I did.' said Adam.

'Which shows he must have taken them,' piped up the butler. 'Stands to reason. And there's been a fan missing.'

'It shows nothing of the kind,' James said replying to the butler. 'Johnson, I understand there has been a search made of the boy's room, and the other rooms on the top corridor?'

'Oh, yes, sir. All the servants' rooms have been gone through thoroughly.'

'And yet you found no trace of the other items Adam, or maybe somebody else, is supposed to have taken from the house?'

'Well, no, sir. But they could all be hidden anywhere.'

'Yes, I am sure they are,' said the young James. 'Adam will you tell us what the fan looked like which you gave to Mrs Redman?'

'What it looked like, sir? It looked like a fan,'

'Sheer insolence,' piped up Mr Johnson again.

'Be quiet, please,' said Walter Russell. 'Adam, did it have any decoration on it? What colour was it?'

'Oh, I see, sir,' said Adam, warming to the idea that Mr Johnson might be told to shut up. 'It was silk and a beautiful vivid green, sir, like one of Mrs Redman's dresses that I remember so well. And it had some white lace around its top edge and, like ivory, or bone handles and a little chain where it folded up.'

'That's very detailed,' said Walter.

'Thank you, sir,' said Adam. 'I chose it especially for her.'

'And, Johnson, has the Housekeeper mentioned any such item being missing from this house?'

'Well, no, sir. You might remember, sir, that your late mother did not go for green very much, so the housekeeper tells me.'

'And, mother,' James continued addressing Alice, 'have you lost a fan?'

'Certainly not,' replied his mother. 'I would have mentioned it before now, amongst all the other things which have been going astray.'

'So it would seem that young Adam here took items to his friend as gifts, which included some effects stolen from The Manor House. And yet another gift he took to Mrs Redman, has nothing to do with this house at all.'

'The fan could have been stolen from anywhere,' said Johnson again, very accusatively. He was determined not to be proven wrong, in laying the blame on this boy.

'Well,' continued young James, 'I can tell you that Adam, here, bought all those items, fair and square, and he can provide proof that he purchased them all, including the fan, which he took to Mrs Redman recently, about the time of the blizzard in March if you recall. He did not steal them from this house.'

'Proof?' intercepted Johnson. 'What proof? Those silver objects did come from this house.'

'I'll thank you, Johnson,' said Mr Walter, 'not to question my nephew's account of these things. I think the word 'proof' has only one meaning.'

'Thank you, Uncle Walter. The idea of proof is very easy to demonstrate,' said James, 'although it did involve us in a dash for the two villages nearby early this morning.'

'Adam, show my father and my uncle the receipts,' he continued, at which point Adam delved into his pocket and produced the receipts, holding them out for the senior gentlemen.

'That's why the bicycle was missing,' exclaimed Mr Granger.

'And I am not at all sure the boy should have left without permission,' said Johnson still hanging on to semblance of authority.

'He had my permission,' the captain told him firmly, 'and, if you look, there you will see that the tea spoons, the silver box and a fan were all bought honestly. They were purchased with Adam's own money.'

'But...' began Johnson.

'There is nothing more to say,' interrupted Mr Walter.

'There is just one more thing,' said young James. 'Adam was given permission by my uncle to come to this library and read, even to borrow books, some time ago. Do you really think he would have stolen books, when, time and again, he has borrowed and returned them? Even if some books are missing, I would consider it most unlikely that the very person given permission to come in here would have taken them. It would have been very foolish, and he had no need.'

Nobody said a word, except Mr Johnson, who began as if to speak but then thought better of it. Instead, Walter spoke up.

'Adam, you can, as far as I can see, return to your duties and for the time being we shall say no more about it. Somebody is responsible for taking things from this family home, but it would certainly appear not to be you.'

'Thank you, sir,' said Adam and for this, one of his few contributions to the conversation, he received a glaring and accusative look from Johnson. Mr Johnson, the butler, did not like to be wrong.

The group dispersed from the library, and Adam was given an hour to unpack his bag, settle back into his room and have some food and drink, before returning to the garden. Mr Granger was quietly pleased that he had regained the services of Adam Warkin. Adam, on the other hand, was not as pleased. To have been accused, so vehemently, of something he had not done left an unpleasant taste in his mouth. Almost the first such experience of his life.

16

Joining up

'Uncle Walter,' said Captain James as the group left the library. 'May I have a word?'

'Of course, my boy. What is it?'

The young James Russell rather uneasily told the story of the visits earlier to the jewellers and to the pawn-brokers.

'Are you telling me that the man who took the stolen items to the pawn-brokers, and to the jewellers, had a limp?'

'That's precisely what I'm telling you,' said the young captain to his uncle.

'And you think that could have been me?' Walter enquired.

'Of course I don't. And luckily young Adam didn't hear that particular detail.' James continued. 'But somebody with a limp went in there with property belonging to this family.'

'And what do you propose the family does about it?' enquired his uncle.

'I don't know, but there is one more thing I'd like to ask. You went to bring young Adam home after the blizzard didn't you?'

'I certainly did,' said his uncle, and the conversation between the two of them continued behind the closed doors of the library.

Her Majesty the Queen, meanwhile was having troubles of her own as regards missing property. Her Indian servant, who was Abdul Karim, affectionately called 'The Munshi' by the Queen, had been taken along on the trip to Italy, much to the consternation of the royal household, and even the Queen's family. None of them thought that a servant, even a personally favoured one, should accompany their mother so closely and be given rooms in the hotel, on the same floor as the Queen.

The Munshi's brother-in-law, one of his extended family who had been brought to England, and lived on the generosity of the Queen of England, had, in the meantime, been discovered trying to sell one of Victoria's brooches to a jeweller in Windsor. When confronted with the evidence Her Majesty had exploded.

'I refuse to believe any of you about my dear Munshi,' the queen had spat out. 'You are all against him and I believe that neither he nor his brother could have done any wrong, as you suggest.' There was never any answering the queen, when she was clearly so blinded by her affection for Abdul Karim.

'My dear friend tells me that the brooch had been found, and that it is customary, in his country, to keep property which one has the good fortune to find. There is nothing more to say on the matter.' And sure enough, nothing more was said.

Adam, meanwhile, had gone back to the garden, but it felt very unlike the friendly working atmosphere he had enjoyed for the past four years. Freddie, his friend was still working in the house, as a footman. Daisy was still sweet on him and their walks into the village resumed, all the more welcome, and pleasant, on summer evenings.

'Here you are,' said young Captain James one day a week or two after the library 'investigation' had taken place. I've been looking all over. And here you are in the engine shed.'

'Sorry, sir,' said Adam. 'I'm making sure the lawn mower works. Please be careful, sir, there's oil everywhere.'

'I'll be fine,' said James, and sat on a box, after carefully checking that it was relatively clean.

'Was there something, sir?' said Adam.

'Yes, actually there is something I need to ask you,' said James. 'How would you like to work for me, in the house?'

'Pardon, sir.'

'Work for me,' repeated James. 'We got on pretty well with our investigation, didn't we, making enquiries at the two shops in the villages? It wasn't much of a task, but we got the thing sorted out. And my uncle Walter has said some very complimentary things about you, being caught up in the blizzard in March, when you seem to have used a lot of initiative to save lives.'

'I don't know about that, sir,' said Adam. 'I just did what seemed obvious to me.'

'Well, anyway, whether you realise it or not, you did a great job,' continued James. 'I need a valet. Someone who can look after me, my uniforms, clothes, arrangements for each day, and so on, and my uncle, and my grandfather, Dr Russell, have agreed that you might be the best man for the job.'

'I don't know what to say, sir. I have not seen you grandfather since last Christmas, so I am not sure he even knows who I am! And it seems to me that I'm the last person Mr Johnson would want working in the house.'

'My grandfather is very weak, seldom comes out of his room now,' said James, 'and you can leave Johnson to us.'

'I'm not sure I'd be up to it,' said Adam, all the while hoping that he might indeed be up to it. 'Wouldn't know what to do.'

'You're still not at all sure of yourself are you? Did you say to me some while ago that you wee interested in the army?' said the captain.

'Well, yes,' said Adam. 'When I saw you, I wondered if I might be able to... at some time...'

'Well, let's get you sorted out for the house,' said James, 'and then later on we can think about your future and where that might lead you, or us.'

'Thank you, sir. What do I do now?'

'Well, you carry on here. I am sure Mr Granger needs that lawn mower fixing and perhaps, in the morning, you can come up to the house and we'll talk again.'

Captain James left, without saying another word, Adam carried on oiling the cogs of the lawn-mower and when evening came he suddenly felt rather more secure than he had done for some time.

Next morning, after breakfast when he was sitting in the servants' hall Mr Granger suddenly spoke to Adam.

'You're to go up to Captain James' room,' he said. 'Looks like we shall be losing you from the garden. It's a good job you've trained young Robert with plenty of your skills.'

'That was rather quicker than I thought,' said Adam to himself, as he found himself inside the house, again, this time asking Freddie the way to Captain James' room. Once outside the door he hesitated, then knocked.

'Come in,' said the voice he knew so well by now.

'Sir, you sent for me?'

'I certainly did,' said Captain James, who was standing by the window, fixing his cuff-links. 'I've asked Mrs Browne, the housekeeper to provide you with an indoor uniform, then all you need to do is wait for me to call. Between Mrs Browne,

Johnson and me your duties will become clear. And, you never know, it might give you even more time to read some of my grandfather's books!'

'Thank you, sir,' said Adam. 'Is there anything I can do now, before I go to find Mrs Browne?'

'Just tidy up a bit in here. I'm not very good at putting things away. Shoes for instance, and ties.'

'Leave it to me, sir, and what about the bed?' said Adam, as he held the door open for James to leave the room.

'Leave that. It's not for you to go making beds. Daisy will be up soon.' said James.

'There is just one more thing, sir,' Adam continued.

'And what's that?' James replied.

'My idea about joining the army someday. Would it seem very ungrateful if I asked you about it, now that you have just given me a job serving you?'

'Not at all,' said the captain. 'In fact, calling you up here to assist me could all be part of my double plan; to help you into the army if that's what you want...'

'Double plan?' enquired Adam.

'Yes, helping you, and finding out just who has been taking property from this house.'

Suddenly Captain James was gone, and Adam was left to tidy up, hoping he could spin it out long enough so that he'd be there when Daisy arrived to do the room.

In 1893, the following summer, Queen Victoria was visiting Italy again.

Now a frail seventy-four years of age, Her Majesty spent most of her time in England, in some degree of seclusion, at Windsor,

Balmoral or at Osborne House on the Isle of Wight. She was in Italy from March to April, although now she travelled to local places of interest far less than she had done in previous years.

A second visit from King Umberto of Italy had caused great excitement amongst her staff and ladies, and a drawing of Victoria and King Umberto sitting together at the *Villa Palmieri* had found its way into the *Illustrated London News* which is where Adam saw it, spread out on the table, in Captain James' billet in The Keep, his Dorchester Barracks.

For quite a lot had happened to Adam in these two years.

After his initial conversation with Captain James, Adam had found himself meeting up with Daisy quite often. In fact, they could time their duties carefully, without too much notice being taken, so that Adam and she were sorting out Captain James' room almost every day, at the same time. Then they went for walks together in the village, as they had done for some time, and always sat next to each other in the servants' hall for main meals.

By the end of 1892 Captain James had to return to his Regiment, in Dorchester, and he suggested that Adam accompany him.

Once in Dorchester it had been a simple sequence of events to encourage and advise Adam how to sign up in service of the Queen, for six years, and begin some basic training. He had volunteered to join the army, with the help and guidance of the captain, and was now being trained as a private in the 39th (Dorsetshire) Regiment of Foot.

Captain James, in the meantime, had not forgotten his double plan. Having enabled Adam to join the army in

Dorchester, he was now, at some time or other, determined to find out who the thief was at The Manor House.

The Keep
  Dorchester Barracks
  39th Regiment of Foot

12 February 1893

Dear Daisy,
  Thank you for saying that I could write to you. Such a lot has happened to me since I left The Manor House and I have never experienced anything like this in my short life. I travelled by train to Dorchester and arrived at The Keep, which is where the Dorsetshire regiments are stationed. Captain James helped me to volunteer and now I am in the 39th (Dorchester) Regiment of Foot.
  It is a bit crowded, sharing a long dormitory room with so many other boys about my age, and older men, all recruits and all being trained. Not at all like the little room I shared with Freddie at The Manor House.
  There is a lot of shouting and drill training, learning about different weapons and grenades, orienteering (that's finding your way, sometimes in the dark, really!) but I love the machines and engineering stuff and I seem to know quite a lot already, so I feel quite confident. Not that I've handled any weapons yet!
  I keep my part of the sleeping quarters neat and tidy so there was something to be said for all that advice from Mrs Browne the housekeeper and looking after the Captain. Some of the other men live in such a mess!
  Believe it or not, Captain James has carried on paying me as

his valet, and I get over to his billet to help him as much as I can. I also get one shilling and tuppence a day, so I am managing to save more than ever. It means that I now earn over ten shillings a week. Ten shillings used to seem to me like a complete fortune, which took for ever to save up, when I think back to leaving my village when I was fifteen.

I have had to learn how to look after Captain James' horse, Pharaoh, and love that horse now, as if it were my own. The Captain has showed and taught me such a lot.

You told me in your letter how Freddie seems to go to the village on his own quite a lot now. I'm sure he's fine. Perhaps he just likes being on his own, now that we three are not together. He is one of the most experienced members of the staff with you now, and must be very valuable to the house. And Mr Granger and Mr Johnson? I expect they are both well.

I don't miss any of them at all, except Freddie, but Daisy, I do miss our walks together down to the village and the little tea rooms – and the beer house – especially in the evenings, when I am sitting here with not much company. Some of the men drink rather too much, and then one or two get arrested and spend five days in confinement. I am so lucky to have Captain James to keep me occupied.

I will write again, when I can, but for now, I wish you a tender Good night,

Adam.

17

Solutions

'Adam,' said the Captain one evening in the late spring when they were together in James' billet room. Adam was buffing up the brass on the captain's belt, as well as polishing his shoes. James himself was reading a letter he had received from his father.

'Sir,' responded Adam.

'My father says that things still seem to be going missing from the house, and it seems obvious to me that somebody must be taking them to the jewellers or some dealer or other to get the cash for them.'

'I would think so too, sir,' said Adam. 'Daisy also tells me that Freddie goes off on his own quite a lot. I cannot believe that he would be….'

'Let's not jump to conclusions, Adam, but supposing you had permission to go back to The Manor House for a week or so and had a look around?'

'Go back, sir? That would be great, if it were allowed because I could see…'

'Yes, I know, you'd like to see Daisy,' James interrupted, 'and I'm sure Mr Granger could make use of you for a week, just to cover your reason for being there. But above all you would have time to keep your eyes and ears open.'

'Would the Battalion commander allow me to go?'

'I'll clear that somehow. I'll tell him that I need you there for a week to cover some family business. I'll write to my father and tell him you are coming, and that you need some time to yourself. He is as keen as anybody to find the root of these thefts.'

So in the early summer, Adam found himself on a train from Dorchester, returning to East Hambley, this time in uniform. He walked up to the house. Daisy was thrilled to see him and they spent the first evening, after supper, sitting and sharing what had happened to them both in the weeks since Adam had left.

Daisy showed him his own letter which she seemed to be carrying around with her all the time, and she showed him, too, the latest letter which she had started to write back to him, but never quite finished. She couldn't wait to tell him that she was now a lady's maid, to Mrs Russell, Alice, Mr James' mother.

Adam was back on the top floor, but in a room of his own. Young Robert, the new boy, had grown remarkably tall for his seventeen years, and now had Adam's old bed, sharing that room with Adam's first Manor House friend, Freddie. He was now twenty-six years old and a senior footman. They chatted into the night, after Daisy had been summoned to her mistress' room at about ten pm.

'Daisy tells me that you enjoy wandering off to the village on your own as often as you can,' said Adam casually, trying not to sound too inquisitive.

'Does she indeed?' said Freddie. 'Well, let's just say I have some personal business there. How about you and I go to the beer house tomorrow afternoon in East Hambley, and spend a good hour with a good pint?'

'That would be just fine,' said Adam, just as Daisy returned to the servant's dining room.

'Daisy, have you been telling Adam that I'm off on my own to the village?' said Freddie. Daisy was somewhat embarrassed, but Freddie laughed it off.

'It's nothing,' said Freddie, 'Don't you worry about me. I've got a secret trading business going on, which is going to make me rich!' He was clearly joking.

Adam laughed it off too, but began to think just what it might be that Freddie was up to. He was reluctant to think that Freddie might have some kind of sideline business – with property taken from the house.

The next day, as planned, being a Saturday, Freddie managed to get some time to himself and he, Adam and Robert wandered off to the village for a beer or two. Later, the three of them sat drinking during the early evening, and Daisy joined them too. It was a light-hearted and fun re-union, just like old times, and Adam shared with them some of his new experiences as an army recruit.

'I like my job here,' said Freddie. 'It is all I really want to do, although of course I am glad to have been promoted to working in the house, and maybe one day I shall be a butler.'

'I'm sure that's how it'll turn out for you,' said Adam and they sat back to enjoy their pints and each other's company. Adam was still thinking about Freddie's forays away from The Manor House, but did not want to question him.

The next day, being another Sunday, Adam was up early and said he was going for a walk. He walked towards the village, hoping that perhaps Freddie might appear at some point, but maybe also hoping that he might not. It was his earnest desire that Freddie was not up to no good! So he wandered on, hoping perhaps that Freddie would not appear.

The morning was clear and bright, with a slight breeze which kept him going. He was simply enjoying the walk, so when he reached East Hambley he carried on through the main street, and out again, on towards West Hambley.

He stopped for a drink, which he had brought with him in a flask, and also a bite to eat, which he had saved from breakfast. The morning was well advanced as he approached the outskirts of West Hambley, and sat on a seat, on the green, in the centre of the village, observing the comings and goings of local folk. A mother and two children passed by, a family who had clearly been to church, and two boys racing each other as Adam had done all those years ago with Will and his sister back in Melton Ford.

Suddenly, he was aware of Freddie approaching the village green, riding the bicycle from the machine shed at The Manor House. He was dressed with just a white shirt, no jacket, smart trousers, polished shoes and even a necktie. He was carrying a small packet and, to his surprise, Adam saw him come to a halt outside the jewellers. Freddie got off the bicycle, checked the package he was holding, leaned the machine up against the shop front window and went inside.

Adam was little short of aghast. Surely Freddie would not be bringing stolen items to the shop to try to sell. And yet, there he was, arriving, bicycling, carrying something, wrapped up, and vanishing into the shop. Adam was not at all sure what to do about it. He waited half an hour or so, but Freddie did not emerge. He decided to walk slowly back through the village and on, back to The Manor House.

It took him nearly an hour, at a very slow pace, to reach the other Hambley, where he stopped for another rest, a drink and, maybe, even to close his eyes for a few minutes.

It was then that he saw what he could hardly believe to be true. A tallish figure, with a long dark coat.

'Even in this warm weather,' said Adam to himself. 'It must be unbearable to be wearing that coat.' The man was making his way through the village. But what caught Adam's attention, all the more so, was a limp. And even more, to his surprise, he appeared to be wearing Adam's father's great floppy felt hat.

'So that's what happened to it!' he thought, not even considering yet how anybody could have got that hat from amongst his own possessions. Adam was transfixed, and, sure enough, the figure vanished into the pawn-brokers, limping over the threshold without a glance in either direction.

He waited. The figure did not emerge from the pawn-brokers, but who should appear, coming along on the bicycle, but Freddie. Adam stopped him in his tracks.

'Freddie, hello there, stop. Stop for a minute. I must talk to you,' said Adam to the somewhat surprised bicyclist.

'Hello! What are you doing here? Got time for another drink?' said Freddie, pulling up beside him.

'Well, yes,' said Adam, 'but I'd like to stick around here first, rather than go to the beer house.'

'Any reason?'

'Well,' said Adam, 'I'm keeping an eye on the pawn-brokers.'

'Really?' Freddie replied. 'Don't tell me, you and Captain Russell are still trying to find out where the missing stuff is going to and who's responsible?'

Adam replied, 'True enough. Between you and me, that's

why I have come home here for a week. And I have a confession to make,' he said, 'I hope you won't get angry by it.'

'Why would I do that?' said Freddie. 'What have you got to confess?'

'I came out for a long walk this morning just to take a look at the jewellers, in West Hambley, and saw you arriving and going in with a package. For a few minutes I thought that perhaps…'

'You didn't really think that I was taking stuff from the house to sell?' Freddie came back at him, with a note of anger and disbelief.

'Well, no, I didn't. At all,' said Adam, 'but the moment you arrived and went into the shop I didn't know what to think.'

'Well, you can rest assured it is not me responsible for the thefts from the house. I'm surprised you even began to think it.' Freddie was hurt and Adam was slightly annoyed with himself that he'd even seen him, let alone mentioned it.

'To be honest, I thought it was better to tell you I'd seen you than keep it to myself. Especially as I have never really thought it could be you. I know how happy you are working at The Manor House.'

'Yes, I am happy there, and well, I suppose there was no harm in you seeing me or telling me. If you really want to know…'

'No, I don't,' said Adam. 'It's probably none of my business but you can tell me some other time if you…' he broke off.

'Look, over there.' He pointed to the pawn-brokers. 'Just before you turned up I saw him going in to the pawn-brokers.'

'You mean the man coming out now? Goodness me! What a character.'

'Well,' said Adam, 'I saw him arrive about twenty minutes ago.'

'And what makes you think he is anything to do with The Manor House?' said Freddie.

'Because, believe it or not, he is wearing my hat. The one I seem to have lost from our room!'

'I remember,' said Freddie. 'So, whoever he is, may have taken some things from the top corridor as well.'

'We shall see. I'm going to follow him. You can ride the bicycle back and see if he comes anywhere near the house.'

They split up. Adam took the slow route back, keeping fifty yards or so behind the long dark coat. It was a casual walk, but just occasionally he had to dart behind a building or a tree, as the figure ahead of him slowed down or looked around him.

To his astonishment, but perhaps not so much to his surprise, the man went into the garden gate of The Manor House. It was then that Adam realised the anomaly, which puzzled him even more than the hat. The man was no longer limping. Adam did not dare to follow him straight in, but waited, hoping that perhaps Freddie might have seen him arrive from somewhere in the garden.

An hour or so later, at supper-time in the servants' dining room, Freddie and Adam sat together.

'You're not going to believe this,' said Freddie.

'Try me,' said Adam. 'I think I know what you're about to tell me.' He listened to the story of what happened to the man in the long coat, once he had arrived inside the gate.

'Well, he made his way around the side of the house and I lost him,' said Freddie, 'but he must have come into the house, surely?'

'I shall go and see Mr James Senior,' said Adam, 'first thing in the morning.'

That evening, in his room, he wrote to the Captain, but left out some of the final detail, which he hoped he would be would be able to complete the following day.

After breakfast on Monday morning Adam made it known that he would like to speak with Mr James and Mr Walter.

'And why would you want to see those good gentlemen?' said Mrs Browne, the housekeeper. 'Why indeed?'

'Young master Warkin seems to be wasting his time, back here at the house,' chipped in Mr Johnson, talking as if Adam were not even in the room. Then added very pointedly, 'I'm sure Mr James senior and Mr Walter are far too busy to see you.'

'Perhaps we should let them decide that,' said Adam.

'Damned impertinence,' said Johnson, 'I'll have none of it downstairs here among my staff! You'll stay down here and do as you're told, until you're called or needed.'

'I should perhaps remind you, Mr Johnson,' said Adam politely but firmly, 'that I no longer work for you 'down here'. I am a guest in the house, admittedly a below stairs guest, but here at the request of Captain James, and I am required by him to see his father and uncle at any time. I was merely asking as a courtesy.'

He stood up, and brushed past the housekeeper and the butler. Then he made his way upstairs, through the heavy door and across towards the library, just in time to see Mr James senior coming down the main staircase.

'May I have a word, sir?' said Adam, and proceeded to explain that it would be better, perhaps, if his brother were also present to hear what he had to say.

'Come into the drawing room. I shall order some coffee,'

said James, and pulled the bell cord before inviting Adam to sit down.

'Do you mind if I stand, sir?' said Adam.

'I certainly do mind,' James responded and insisted that Adam make himself comfortable, just as Mr Walter came into the room, followed by Johnson, whose face was like thunder as he spotted Adam.

'We'd like some coffee, Johnson,' said James. 'Please could you arrange for some to be brought up?'

'Of course, sir,' said Johnson. 'Would that be for the two of you, sir?'

'No, three,' Walter chipped in. 'Are you blind, Johnson? Or can you not see we have a guest?'

'Three it is, sir,' said Johnson as he turned his back on Adam and exited the room.

'Now then,' James began, 'what is it my son has sent you here for and what is it that is so important to tell us?'

During the coffee, which was brought into the room by Mrs Browne, Adam proceeded to tell the two men of his long walk the previous day, of seeing Freddie in West Hambley (as Freddie had given him leave to include his own outing in the narrative) and of seeing the mysterious gentleman going in to and coming out of the pawn-brokers.

'So, what was it that drew your attention to him?' said Walter. 'Why follow him?'

'Because he was wearing my hat, sir. A hat I thought I'd lost. In fact I have apparently lost it, sir, to him!'

'Anything else?' said James.

'Well, most intriguing of all, sir, was that he came back here to the house. Freddie was in the garden and watched him go to one of the side doors and then lost him, but he definitely came into this house.'

'And that's all you have at the present?' said Walter again. 'It seems he could be in cahoots with one of the staff, but who? And how do we find out who it is, without a major search, which could upset everyone in the house again.'

'There was just one other thing, sir,' said Adam. 'But I am reluctant to say it, sir.' It's a bit embarrassing.'

'Well, out with it, man,' said James. 'We're all keen to get to the bottom of this.'

'He had a limp, sir,' said Adam, then he glanced at Mr Walter, and immediately thought that it sounded like an accusation, as if his limp was a disability that should be noticed but never mentioned. He went red.

'But he wasn't limping all the time, sir,' Adam continued.

'Not a problem,' said Walter Russell. 'A man who can turn the limp on when it suits him! Strange indeed.'

'Well, well,' said James. 'Don't you worry about that. I'm pretty sure that my brother here is not the person responsible for the thefts, but I can tell you, Adam, that I already knew the apparent culprit had a limp.'

'Really, sir, you knew? I had no idea.'

'Absolutely,' said James. 'My son told me that's what the girl in the jewellers had said to him on the day you went to fetch the receipts. I'm sorry he did not tell you, but at the time, even we thought it was all a bit odd. I was hardly likely to point the finger at my own brother and tell you about it. My apologies, Adam, but, yes, we knew about the limp.

'Now, all we have to do is find him. We are a lot closer! Whoever he is, has gone to a lot of trouble to take stuff from this house, on a regular basis, and hide his identity, as of course he would.'

A knock on the door came, and Walter responded, 'Come in.' It was Freddie.

'Begging your pardon, sirs, but, Adam, this is yours, isn't it?' He held out the floppy felt hat which to Adam was instantly recognisable.

'Why, yes. Where did you find that?'

'Is this the hat you say you saw your mysterious figure wearing?' said James

'Certainly is,' said Adam. 'I'd know it anywhere.'

'Well,' Freddie continued, 'I'm sorry to say I just found it tucked in the cupboard where Robert and I keep our personal stuff, in the top floor bedroom.'

'Robert!' All three of the other men in the room almost said the name simultaneously. 'That's nonsense,' Adam continued.

'That's what I thought, but here it is,' said Freddie, 'large as life.'

'Call Robert up to his room.' said Walter, and Freddie left immediately to fetch him.

'What we need is another search,' said James. 'We have been on the lookout for some of the stolen things, but this time, maybe, we should be looking for that coat you say your mysterious figure was wearing. The three men left the sitting room and made their way up to the top floor. Adam had never been up the main staircase before, but ended up showing the other gentlemen the way to the top floor.

'This is it,' said Adam as they arrived at his old room. Within seconds Freddie and Robert came along the corridor too.

'We've come to have a look at some of your stuff, Robert,'

said Adam. 'Hope you don't mind, but it is important. Do you recognise this?' Mr Walter held out the felt hat.

'Have I done anything wrong, sir?' said Robert.

'I hope not,' said Walter and repeated, 'Do you recognise this?'

'No, sir,' said Robert. 'I've never seen that before.

'But it was found in your room,' said Adam, 'amongst your stuff.'

'Sorry, I have never seen that hat before,' said Robert.

'Have you been to the village lately?' said James.

'Only with Freddie, sir, and sometimes Daisy,' said Robert, 'although now Mr Adam is back home for a few days Daisy hasn't come at all. I did join them for a drink on Saturday, didn't I?'

'True enough,' said Adam, 'and you've not been to the village again since?'

'No, sir,' responded Robert. Adam seemed to be conducting this enquiry with some confidence and he continued to do so.

'Don't call me sir, Robert. There's no need for that. But,' he continued addressing James and Walter, 'would you mind if I conducted a little enquiry of my own? I will join you in the sitting room again, in a short while, if that's alright.'

'Go ahead,' said James, and the small group dispersed. James and Walter returned downstairs. Robert disappeared down the back stairs, followed by Freddie whom Adam called back.

'Freddie, come with me.'

'Yes, *sir*,' said Freddie, with his tongue firmly in his cheek, and a smile.

'And you can stop that,' said Adam. 'Come with me.'

Ten minutes later Adam and Freddie appeared at the door

of the sitting room again and knocked. They went in, Adam with a long dark coat over his arm.

'This, sir,' he began, 'is the coat I saw being worn by the figure who went into the pawn-brokers yesterday.'

'Where was it?' said Walter, hardly daring to ask.

'Under the bed… in Mr Johnson's room,' said Adam, hardly daring to reply.

'It certainly was, sir,' added Freddie. 'I was with Adam a few minutes ago, when we went into one or two other rooms on the top floor. Under the bed, rolled up.'

'You see,' began James, 'When we searched the house on other occasions, we were looking for objects that had been stolen. But how is it that the coat is in Johnson's room and the hat in your room, Freddie?'

'No idea, sir, but there's only one way to find out.' That was agreed. Adam suggested that the carriage might be useful and explained why. Freddie was despatched to ask the coachman to bring it round to the front. Freddie was also instructed to ask Johnson if he would attend Mr James and Mr Walter in the sitting room.

It was a very uncomfortable looking Johnson who arrived in the sitting room that morning. Above all, he hated the idea that Adam was in the room.

'Is this hat yours?' said Walter to his butler. 'We have just found it, and it is important to know whose it is.'

'Why, no, sir,' blustered Johnson, all the while glaring at Adam. 'Never seen that before.'

'And what about this?' said Walter, holding out the coat. 'We've found this too.'

Johnson couldn't contain himself. 'Have you been in my

room, Adam Warkin? Gentlemen, this is an outrage. I must protest.'

'Who said anything about it being in your room?' said James. 'We just said we had found it.' Johnson went beetroot red but stood his ground.

'We are all going out,' said James. 'Johnson, I think you'll find the carriage is at the front door. There's room for four of us. Wait for us there.'

Johnson sheepishly exited the room, followed by Adam and the two gentlemen of the house. They had, in the meantime, sent for Robert again who appeared through the heavy door into the main hall.

'Robert,' said Adam, 'Come with us.' The carriage filled up with Adam and Robert, accompanied by Mr James and Johnson, who was feeling more and more out of his depth in this strange foursome. Adam was carrying the coat and the hat. It took them a matter of minutes to reach the village and make their way to the pawn-brokers. Johnson had no alternative, but to comply with what was going on, although he knew what the outcome would be.

As they approached the pawn-brokers, Adam said to Robert, 'Have you ever been here?'

'No, sir, sorry, no, Adam,' blustered Robert, wishing he had not said 'sir' again and wondering what this was all about.

All four entered the shop, Johnson needing just a bit of encouragement, clearly reluctant to go in, but unable to do anything but go along with them.

'Can I help you, gentlemen?' began Mr Trimblay, before recognising a regular.

'Oh! Mr Warkin, nice to see you again. Nearly didn't

recognise you.'

'Pardon,' said Adam. 'I've only ever been in here a couple of times.'

'Not you, sir,' he said, then pointed at Johnson. 'Mr Warkin, you, sir. You seem to be managing without your glasses today.'

'My God,' said Adam. 'He's not only worn my hat, but has been using my name.'

Mr Johnson blanched and suddenly became very defensive. Perhaps the game was up!

'This foolish man must be mistaken. He doesn't know what he is talking about. He doesn't know me. How does he think he knows me?'

'Mr... er...?' began James Russell.

'Trimblay, sir.'

'Mr Trimblay, how do you recognise this man?' said James.

'He's quite a regular, sir. I thought you'd remember,' he said addressing himself to Johnson again. 'You bring in stuff that your elderly aunt wants to pawn or to sell. You must remember.'

Johnson was speechless.

'Of course he remembers,' said James. 'Adam, check the pockets of the coat.' Adam delved into both side pockets and came out with a pair of pince-nez.

'Those are yours, sir,' said Mr Trimblay . 'You usually wear them when you're in here, sir.' Johnson remained void of any semblance of speech.

'How often has this Mr... er 'Warkin' been in here?' said James.

'Dozens of times over the past few years, sir. I thought he was some kind of war veteran, what with his limp and all, and I just helped him out with cash for all his old aunt's stuff. And, sir, I don't know the other gentleman, sir, the tall young man,' he said, pointing at Robert.

'That's quite alright,' said James. 'I think the limp was put on to shift attention to somebody else! You've been very helpful. Johnson, I think you and I had better return to the house in the carriage. Adam, would you mind awfully walking back with Robert? I need to speak to Johnson on my own.'

'Not at all, sir,' said Adam. 'We'll be fine. We'll see you at the house.'

By the time Adam and Robert strolled into the side gate and through the garden to the kitchen and servants' dining room, not only did they know each other a little better, but the remainder of the staff were buzzing with gossip. A message came down for Adam to go up to the sitting room and to take Freddie with him.

They knocked on the door and went in, observing Mr Walter, Mr and Mrs James and even the elderly Dr Russell, in a bath chair, looking very frail.

'Come in, the pair of you,' said Walter. They stood side by side and could not help noticing the table, where the coffee had been, was now covered with items of silver, some porcelain ornaments, another fan and even a couple of pieces of jewellery.

'It seems that our Mr Johnson has been sifting off items for his own personal gain, for some time.' said Walter. 'When he conducted the searches of the house, some time ago, he carefully avoided searching his own room, or moved stuff around, so that it would not be noticed or found.

'He has come up with some fantastical story about it being one, or both, of you two, but in the end he admitted his guilt. He placed the hat in young Robert's stuff to try to shift the

131

blame to him, just as he seemed so pleased that the blame should be planted on you, Adam, a while ago.'

'Has he ever said why he tried to profit from your property, sir?' said Adam.

'Nothing that makes any sense to us.' said Walter. 'And now he's been told to pack his bags and go. That's quite a pity, after having been butler for about seven years. Now, Freddie, Dr Russell, my brother and I know you are still very young, how old are you?'

'Nearly twenty-six, sir.'

'Well, how do you think you would manage if I put you in charge of the rest of the staff for the time being?'

'Butler, sir?' said Freddie.

'Well, let's not get ahead of ourselves, but, yes, maybe you could take on the job of butler and see how we get on.' This time it was the doctor himself who had spoken. 'Your surname is Collins, isn't it?'

'Yes, sir. I don't know what to say, sir,' said Freddie not quite sure where to address his thanks.

'I know,' said Adam, suddenly very happy for his friend and brimming with his new-found confidence. 'I know that this is what Freddie has been aiming at ever since he came to work here, sir. He'll be very, very good if you give him this chance, sir.'

'Well, Collins, you'd better sort yourself out with Mrs Browne and with a uniform. I'll leave it to you, and Adam, to tell the remainder of the staff.'

'Thank you again, sir,' said Freddie, as they left. He was grinning from ear to ear and Adam knew that he would make a fine butler.

Once back in the servants' dining room, the word was out, everyone was pleased for Freddie, and even Mrs Browne accepted that Johnson had brought this on himself.

'Young Mr Freddie deserves this break,' she said. 'Who'd have believed it, eh? You just come along with me *Mr* Collins and we'll find you a proper suit to wear.'

As they left the room, Robert came up to Adam.

'That was the strangest morning I've ever experienced in this house,' he said, as he sat down next to Adam, who was contemplating returning to Dorchester.

'Strange indeed,' said Adam, 'oh, and by the way, I think you'd better call Freddie 'Sir' from now on.'

'I certainly will,' he said.

18

Overseas posting

Jasmine Cottage,
Melton Ford

1 July 1893

Dear Mr Granger,

I hope the gardens at The Manor House are as beautiful as ever.

I have had a letter from Adam, stationed in Dorset, telling me the news about the gifts he gave to me, apparently stolen from the house, and how he and Captain James, with help from James's father, eventually found the culprit. Fancy it being Mr Johnson! What an unexpected turn of events. I always knew it could never have been Adam, but whoever it turned out to be was bound to be such a surprise. One never knows.

As you know, I offered to return the spoons and the silver box to the family at The Manor House but I had a very nice letter from Mr James senior telling me that they wouldn't hear of such a thing. The items were bought in good faith and so, he said, I should keep them. I will treasure them always.

Of course I remember when we first met, all those years ago when we were so much younger. Life has taken some strange turns. And

now Master Adam is a grown man, 21 years old. He tells me that
he and Captain James are being posted overseas. No doubt I will
hear more of their adventures, at some time.

But for now,
Most sincerely, your friend,

Birgitta.

In Dorsetshire, in the barracks at The Keep, Adam had learned about the overseas posting from Captain James in July.

'I can hardly believe it, sir, that I am going to another country,' said Adam. 'What an adventure.'

'Well, we can put aside any ideas about adventures,' said the Captain, 'We may find it most uncomfortably hot, a lot of hard work and maybe not a little dangerous.'

'Well, anyway,' responded Adam, 'I am excited about travelling further afield. I will always remember when my friend Mrs Redman first took me to Weymouth. It felt like I was travelling to the end of the earth, but it was only an hour on the train.'

'How old were you then?' asked James.

'I was about thirteen or fourteen. Before my father died.'

'Well, you've travelled a long way since then, Adam,' said the Captain, 'In more ways than one. You've only done your first six months here. There is plenty more to learn and to see. Sergeant Mackenzie and other more experienced men will help you as you go along.'

'And now I feel as though it was worth buying my silver St Christopher medallion,' said Adam. James smiled and agreed.

Everything was new to Adam. The kit, the preparations and new sets of instructions, lessons with maps and, even later, with guns; it was quite a lot to take in, not to mention the difficulties the army had of feeding hundreds of troops a thousand miles from home.

'You will have rations,' said Sergeant Mackenzie when Adam was sitting in a large training room with about forty others. 'And it will be up to you to keep your rations safe and dry when we're out on the move.'

Sergeant Mackenzie was clearly a seasoned soldier. Built like a brick outhouse, he had a greying bristling moustache, not a great deal of hair under his cap, and a rosy red face. There was a hint of a paunch, but he was as fit as the proverbial fiddle. His feet were enormous, as was his voice, and he was hardly ever seen without his cane under his arm.

'What kind of rations, sergeant?' shouted out one of the recruits who'd also never been overseas before.

'It'll probably be week-old bread, hard cheese and even harder biscuits.'

'Sounds terrific, I don't think!' came the reply from the middle of the room.

'I don't need your smart-alec answers,' continued the Sergeant. 'And you might get some bully beef...'

'What's that, serg?' came a chorus of several voices.

'Beef in a tin,' said the sergeant.

'In a tin! Meat in a tin?' the chorus continued.

'Just shut up and listen,' said the sergeant. 'The British Army has been using it for years but you lot have obviously had it a lot easier where you come from. It might be called M&V, that's meat and veg to you lot, or it might be just a slab of meat that you can boil up with some water to make into a stew. It's called Machanochie Stew. I call it man-killer.'

The chorus of disapproval became louder than ever, as clearly few of the young men in his audience had ever heard of such things. The training continued, with some recruits ever more disbelieving of what they were hearing.

'Think yourselves lucky,' said the sergeant. 'My father, back in the 1850's, had shocking food when he was out in the Crimea and then they had pay for it themselves as well, taken out of their daily wages. You don't fancy paying for maggots, I suppose?'

Nobody fancied paying at all, let alone for food infested with living creatures, they all agreed, as the training and information session broke up. Later on that evening, Adam met up with another recruit in the mess after supper.

'Doesn't look as though we're going to be overfed,' said the boy as he sat down by Adam.

'Not exactly,' said Adam, as he shifted to make room on the bench seat. His new companion was not quite as tall as Adam. He looked thin but strong enough as far as Adam could see. He had a shock of strong black hair, cut short since he joined up, healthy red cheeks, strong weathered skin and brown eyes, He spoke with what Adam would find out later was a London accent.

'The name's Adam,' Adam offered.

'Joseph,' said his new companion, 'but everybody calls me Joe.'

'Still,' Joe continued, 'any food is better than none! Before I came here sometimes I had no food at all for days.'

'Really?' Adam was interested and continued, 'We were not very well off where I grew up in Dorset, but we usually had food. I suppose being in the country we always had vegetables or fruit.'

'Not in London, well, not too much, anyway, unless I could hang around Covent Garden and nick some,' said Joe. 'Suppose you had a mum and dad?'

'Doesn't everybody?' responded Adam without really thinking about what the alternatives could be.

'Oh, yeh!' said Joe, 'but my mum and dad slung me out when I was fourteen. That's five years ago. I lived on the streets, and on my wits, until I got caught stealing a bit of cash. Went to prison for six months, so at least I got fed there. That was the first time I'd ever slept in a bed!'

'That doesn't sound very good at all,' said Adam, doing an instant comparison with his own, relatively idyllic upbringing. 'Were you completely on your own?'

'Pretty much,' Joe replied, 'although I did have an older brother. Don't know what happened to him. He was into thieving as well and was called *The Rodent* by the locals. Nasty boy. He's probably in prison by now for all I know.'

'And what happened when you got out of prison?'

'I was drinking one evening in a pub, when a recruiting officer came in. Didn't take too much notice at first, but he plied me with spirits and suggested that the army might be a way out of a life of crime, not to mention hunger! So I joined up.'

'Could you read?' said Adam, interested in how he had been accepted into the Regiment.

'Just about,' said Joe. 'Enough to get me in, anyway. And now I'm quite pleased about it. I get two meals a day, clothing, and shelter and my own bed for the first time in my life! I'm happy. Still can't read very well.'

'I was happy too, until we heard about the bully beef and

the hard biscuits!' said Adam, half joking. 'I could help you with some reading if you like. I love reading.'

'Nah! You're alright,' said Joe. 'I'm okay as I am. I get by.'

'Well, you know where to find me,' said Adam. 'We're heading in the same direction very soon.'

Adam spent some of the evening later on with Captain James, sorting out his officer's freshly issued kit, polishing buckles and buttons and cleaning his revolver too which Adam had become quite adept at.

'Where exactly are we going, sir,' said Adam. 'Do you know? Everybody's talking about India.'

'I don't think so,' replied the captain, 'but wherever it is, you will find out soon enough. How are you getting on with the other men?'

'Really well, sir. There's a young recruit, younger than me actually, whose name is Joe and we've sort of paired up for meals and the like. We get on well. He's from London, another place I have never been to.'

'Good,' said James. 'Well, so far, you seem to be settling in, so here's hoping all goes well from here on. You're pleased you joined up?'

'Certainly am, sir,' said Adam. 'It was definitely time to move on.'

'Well, it will be time to move again soon,' said the captain. 'Tomorrow I understand you will all be getting some new kit and equipment.'

Sure enough, the next day Adam found himself in a line-up. Everybody in the regiment was kitted out for the journey, with additional underwear, shirts, tunics, belts, trousers and something called webbing. There was the most peculiar white hat, which the sergeant called a pith helmet, much to amusement of almost everybody who heard what it was called.

'We're definitely going somewhere hot,' said Joe as he found Adam in the queue. 'Look at this stuff. And what's this 'webbing' for?'

Everything was in a light stone coloured fabric which the boys soon learned was a variation of khaki, the brown uniforms worn overseas, and at home by so many British soldiers.

'You can bring your friend, Joe, over here to my billet, if you like,' said James to Adam then next day, 'after your evening meal. I'll show you how some of this stuff works.'

Captain James was supervising the distribution as the quartermaster and a couple of sergeants were handing stuff out. No sooner had he said that, than Adam and Joe were at the end of the line and being handed a rifle.

'Blimey,' said Joe. 'Never handled one of these before.'

'And you'll not handle it very much at all until tomorrow,' said the Sergeant. 'Get it back to your dorm, clean it up, get some of the grease off it and there'll be an instruction drill tomorrow, but without ammunition!'

Adam and Joe knocked on the Captain's door a few hours later and immediately heard, 'Come in.'

As they entered, Adam greeted the Captain, and introduced his friend.

'This is Joe, sir,' said Adam, 'is it okay if he joins us?'

'Yes, of course. I told you to bring him over.'

Joe suddenly looked very timid, almost suspicious. He'd never had any dealings with men in authority, other than being some kind of victim, or being accused of something. He was just a little envious of Adam's manner with the Captain.

'Thank you, er.. sir,' said Joe.

'Sit yourselves down, Joe you over there, Adam, on that other chair next to the table.'

Joe sat very precariously, almost on the edge of the seat, as James continued. 'Tomorrow you'll be told all about the Lee Enfield rifle you've been issued with. In the meantime, I might give you a few tips about the other bits and pieces you've been given, if that helps.'

'Yes, sir, thank you, sir,' said Joe. Adam just nodded in agreement.

'You see this white hat, the pith helmet,' said James, as he showed them the head gear which he had also received. 'Well it doesn't quite match the stone coloured or light brown kit you have to wear, the trousers and tunic and so on.'

'No, sir,' said Adam. 'Ours both look a bit brand new.'

'Well, when you get the chance, but maybe not before the first parade in your new kit, my advice is to stain it with some strong tea. Perhaps wait until we get to where we're being posted, then do it gradually and it will look a bit worn in.'

'To match the rest?' said Joe, suddenly animated.

'Dead right,' said James. 'And now, show me those gaiters.'

'The what?' said Adam.

'The gaiters, the webbing pieces. You've have two each.' James replied.

'Oh, these. Yes. We wondered what they were for.'

'I expect you'll be told at some point, but it's as well to know. When you've got your trousers on you don't want to leave the bottoms loose, as we might do in this country.'

'Why not, sir?' said Adam. Joe had now relaxed a little but was all ears.

'You really do not want to know what kind of flying or stinging creatures turn up in hot countries, such as where we're going, and the last thing you want is for any of them to be flying up your trouser leg!'

The two boys recoiled a little. 'Stingin'!' said Joe.

'Yes, you can get some very nasty little blighters in hot climates, so the webbing goes around the bottom of your leg, over the trousers, to stop anything flying up there.'

'That's good to know,' said Adam.

'Essential, I'd say,' said James. 'So now you're a little wiser.'

Their conversation continued for another forty-five minutes or so until James decided it was time for them to go.

'You'll probably be told a lot more stuff tomorrow and in the coming days,' said James, 'but that's enough to go on with for now.'

'Thank you, sir,' volunteered Joe.

'Thank you very much, sir,' said Adam. 'Is there anything else you want this evening before I go? Don't suppose you want a cup of tea? '

'No, thank you,' said James. 'You get going. I might have something a little stronger.'

'Fine, sir, see you tomorrow,' said Adam.

'Thank you, sir,' said Joe, beaming with something new to smile about. 'You're lucky to have somebody who seems to care about you,' said Joe, as they made their way back to their quarters.

'Fancy you knowing an officer like that?'

'Well, I do work for him as well,' said Adam, 'but yes, I am very lucky.'

After a good night's sleep, everybody was up and making

ready for a kit inspection by 6.30am. Adam was keen to do well and laid his kit out according to the regulations for an inspection.

He laid out the khaki single breasted tunic, sleeves folded in, one of the new shirts, folded to show the front only with buttons done up, the trousers folded according to regulation and gaiters alongside. He had all his bedding rolled or folded as he had done for the past six months, and had become very used to.

Personal hygiene equipment was shown, laid out as normal, and the rifle, cleaned the previous evening, as well as he could, all ready to be inspected. Finally the new pith helmet was placed on top of the inspection kit and a pair of dust-coloured boots, matching almost everything else, placed firmly at the foot of the bed.

Adam himself stood rock solid and stiffly upright as the Sergeant came down the dorm, passing from bed to bed, with occasional comments and quite a few grunts. One or two unfortunates had their kit upturned by the Sergeant, who told them in no uncertain terms to try setting it out again – '*this time properly!*'

It almost reminded Adam of his first Christmas in the hall at The Manor House, but now there would be no gift on its way and he hoped for no comment either.

The sergeant passed him by, checking very carefully and even lifting on or two items with his cane, before letting them drop again into their correct position.

'Well done, Warkin. Another good inspection for you. Now listen, you men,' he continued. 'Private Warkin has been here about six months, about the same length of time as most of you, some a bit longer, some not so long.

'His kit is pretty well perfectly laid out, so you might do well to have a look at it, especially if yours is not so good. After breakfast you can all go to the Lecture Hall by 09.30 hours and you'll learn a bit more about what this stuff is all for.' As the sergeant left, Adam was hugely embarrassed. He did not like to be held up as an example, and was on the point of apologising when Joe piped up.

'Well done, Adam. I'm glad my kit was not right next to yours! Mine looks like a grenade's gone off under it.'

'Sorry about that,' said Adam, as everybody relaxed, putting some stuff away in lockers and getting ready to go to breakfast.

'Don't apologise,' said another older soldier from further down the dormitory, who had been with the regiment for a few years. 'Just do the best you can, at all times. One day it'll save your life.'

'Thanks,' said Adam, as he and Joe made their way across the parade square to breakfast.

19

Weapons

Everybody was seated in the Lecture Hall by just before 9.30. This time it would be Captain James who would be doing most of the talking. The Sergeant brought everyone to attention as the Captain entered the room.

'Shun!' he shouted as the captain appeared. Everybody came to their feet and there was no movement, until Captain James was standing at the lectern.

'Thank you, everyone. At ease, sit down.' Captain James' manner was authoritative, without being aggressive, and his voice could be listened to easily. He continued, standing beside a map which showed Europe, Africa and the Far East.

'There is a Far Eastern protectorate, governed by the British, called Pehang. It's a part of Malaya.' Adam thought was probably the daftest place name he had ever heard. But then, he knew he had hardly been anywhere in the world, so he was fascinated to learn all things new. The Captain continued as Adam listened intently.

'In this territory, protected and governed by the British, there are pockets of resistance. The locals have their own systems of rule and rank, and the Sultans tend to co-operate with us to keep the peace. One of their leaders revels in the name of Abdul Rahman bin Tuanku Imam Nuh, which is a name you wouldn't want to write on your identity card too often.'

A ripple of laughter went around the room.

'He is known locally as Dato' Bahaman which is almost as bad! Now, three years ago, a British officer positioned a Police Station in the area, which had been locally administered by Dato', and our friend Dato', to put it mildly, was a bit put out. To keep the peace, the local Sultan tried to move Dato' on, while the issue of the Police Station was under investigation, but our friend objected and was demoted by the Sultan.

'Dato' and the Sultan were old buddies, who supported each other, so obviously Dato' took great offence at this and there followed a series of raids on British forces and settlements.

'The British were ambushed on the Semantan River in late 1891 and since then, power has swung from the locals under Dato' Bahaman and his friends, who want their autonomy to govern locally, and the British, with the support of the local Sultan. Between them they manage forestry, mining and local taxation. Somebody needs to go there and deliver a decisive blow to the rebels.'

'Why are the British governing Malaya, sir?' came a voice from half way up the hall.

'Good question,' replied the captain. 'Ours is not to reason why. Our political masters in Westminster seem to think, and have done so for about a hundred years, that the locals in India, and elsewhere, need governing or civilising, while we bring order to their chaos and help them to mine raw materials, and manufacture goods. Everybody benefits.'

'Not sure everyone does,' said a voice from about the same part of the room.

'What was that?' broke in the sergeant, who was sitting

alongside the Captain and suddenly stood up. 'Speak up if you have a comment.' There was silence.

'So we,' continued the captain, 'are to set sail in the next few days, to make our way to Malaya and Pehang, calling in to India on the way. Thanks to the opening of the Suez Canal in 1869, what might have taken six months to get there can now be done in a matter of weeks.'

'How is that, sir?' It was Joe, with an unexpected burst of vocal courage, but geographic naivety.

"Well, look at the map. It's Smith, isn't it?'

'Sir,' replied Joe, delighted that Captain Russell had remembered his name. The Captain replied using his cane to point at the map.

'Instead of having to sail the entire length of Africa to get around The Cape of Good Hope, here, and then all the way up again towards the Far East, India and so on, we can now cut through the Mediterranean Sea. From there, we sail down the Suez Canal and out into the Indian Ocean. Cuts about four thousand miles off the journey. And with the newer, faster warships and troop ships, all coal-powered, the length of the journey is decreased enormously.'

Adam was impressed by this knowledge, and pretty much overwhelmed by the distance he would now be travelling.

'That's all from me,' said Captain James. 'Sergeant Mackenzie will fill you in on other preparations.'

'Shun!' shouted the Sergeant, and every man in the room sprang to his feet. Captain James left them to it and the Sergeant continued.

'There'll be about six hundred of us on the ship. We shall embark at Portsmouth in the next few days and arrive at our final destination 'gawd knows when'!' There was a smattering of agreeable laughter and, just as the men thought they were free to go, he carried on.

'Now, you can go outside, but fetch your rifles first. I'll give you five minutes to form up.' The men scuttled off to the dorm area and fetched rifles, some grabbing a drink of water on the way. The sergeant was waiting for them on the parade ground, with a supply of materials as they all arrived, with their rifles.

'This,' said the sergeant, 'is your Lee Enfield rifle. I take it you've all had a good look at it? Have you?'

'Serg,' came back in unison.

'Well, this is the weapon that could save your life. It's modern and efficient. And we're lucky to have 'em. Don't you forget that. Now, you've all got to get to where you can see me, and my rifle, and where you can manipulate your own one.' There was a shuffling of feet, and gradually they closed in on the sergeant in a kind of semi-circle, with some kneeling at the front.

'It is your responsibility to look after this weapon with your life. If you lose it, or allow it to be stolen, it'll take you several years to pay for it out of the meagre wages we get. Understood?'

'Yes, serg,' came the unified response again.

'You will only be issued with ammunition from the quarter-master, if you are on guard duty or on patrol. We don't need it so much here in Britain, or in Dorchester, but out there you will.'

After about six months of training, drill, sleeping out in the open, orienteering and education it was time for learning how to use a weapon.

'Now this weapon is a piece of cake to clean, provided you

148

do it properly and regularly.'

The Sergeant carried on showing them how to remove the bolt, and then, with a piece of flannelette and a cord called a 'pull-through' how to clean the barrel of any carbon.

'Then,' continued the sergeant, 'you do it again with a clean piece of flannelette and a tiny amount of oil. Makes the barrel whistle clean. Got that?'

'Yes, serg.' replied the men, as they all managed, one by one, to remove the bolt and follow his example of cleaning the barrel. Adam was in his element

'Right,' continued Sergeant Mackenzie, 'We now proceed to clean the bolt itself, with a piece of flannelette and, if there's a large build up of carbon, you can use a bit of gauze, like this.' He showed them. The chamber was cleaned in much the same way.

'But,' said the sergeant, 'Whereas we would usually oil all the metal parts, we have to be careful in hot sticky climates, where dust can stick to metal and clog up everything that needs to move. That's called seizing up, and you do not want that to 'appen to your rifle. What don't we want to 'appen to your rifle?'

'We don't want the parts seizing up, serg!' came the response from the men, not quite in unison.

'And finally, you clean all the outside parts of the rifle with a cloth, get rid of any dirt or grime, and present your rifle in pristine condition, at all times. Clear?'

'Yes, serge.' came the predictable response. Everybody felt as thought they now knew all they needed to know about the Lee Enfield and were getting desperate for some lunch.

'This afternoon, we shall see about loading it up with

ammunition, and how to get your rifle inspected in a safe manner. We don't want you shooting your loveable sergeant now, do we, if I am inspecting your kit?'

There was muted, though hardly universal agreement among the men!

'Well, I haven't quite finished with you yet,' he continued, 'so line up again, and put your rifle down in front of you.'

They did as ordered and waited for more wisdom to flow. Adam and Joe found it all fascinating, and made sure that, unless told otherwise, they stood together. Learning with a friend was always easier

Adam just about had time to write to Daisy, before they were out on the parade ground again in the afternoon.

The Keep
Dorchester Barracks
39ᵗʰ Regiment of Foot

12 July 1893

Dear Daisy,

How are you? I hope everything is good at The Manor House and that Freddie is coping well with his new responsibilities. I am sure he is.

You wouldn't believe how far we are going to be travelling when we get sent to Malaya in a few days. Thousands of miles, in a ship across the Indian Ocean to a place called Pehang. The whole battalion, about 600 of us. You'll have to look it up if you want to know where it is exactly. Who would have ever thought that I, Adam from Melton Ford, would be travelling half way around the world. I wrote to my Mrs Redman and she replied. She said that she was not at all surprised that I was making my way in the world.

I wish you could be here with me, especially when there is some free time, and we could go walking or just sit and talk. Thank you for your letter, by the way. If you want to write to me, to the place we are being posted, it could take months for a letter to reach me and then to get a reply all the way back to you. They say that, not so long ago, if somebody wrote to their friend in India it could take more than a year to get a reply. But I will write, as soon as I know an address for you to write to, no matter how long it takes. I get the feeling we shall be there for a couple of years at least.

Enclosed here is a ten shilling note. I know it's not much but I'd like you to buy something for yourself. I am saving up like mad, and, who knows, maybe one day I will come back to East Hambley and we shall go somewhere really nice together. It may be a bit of a cheek to ask but, would you wait for me?

I hope so, but in the meantime, we have to get out on the Parade Ground again. I will post this tonight, and think of you reading it in a day or so. Don't know when I shall be able to write again or when you might get the letter.

May I send you my love! Hope you don't mind, it seems right.
God bless,
Yours affectionately,

Adam.

After a meagre lunch and half a pint of weak beer, Adam and Joe were out on the parade ground again.

It was a glorious day and Adam had difficulty in imagining how much hotter the weather could be than this in Pehang!

'Line up, you lot,' shouted Sergeant Mackenzie, 'Come on, make it snappy.'

The forty or so men shuffled about until they were in two lines facing the dining room. They had the sun in their eyes but the sergeant could see all of them quite clearly.

'Now, then,' he continued, 'Our enemies have all kinds of ways to see off the likes of you once we're out there in Penang, or whatever the wretched place is called. They've got lots of pointy things, knives, bayonets, even swords, most of them avoidable if you keep the enemy at arms length. But they might have hand grenades or rifles. So it's best to keep your head down during the day, and not light up any fags at night!

'Some of their banging nasties will deliver you an 'ell of a punch which could scatter your bones every which way from Penang to Portsmouth, but you won't feel a thing. And we'll give you an extra tot of rum before you go out - so it's not all bad.'

Adam and Joe glanced at each other. Was he joking? He didn't look the kind of man who suddenly made up jokes. Nothing sounded very good. Perhaps he was just being extra-careful. Adam had never thought of his own mortality before.

'Now then,' continued the sergeant. 'If you're sleeping out in the open on manoeuvres, the chances are you will wake up most days knee deep in a puddle of rainwater. When it rains out there you wouldn't want to know it! But being as how it's so hot most of the day in those climes, you'll dry out within the hour.

'You can put on anti-fly cream, but nobody knows really whether it repels them, attracts them, or even kills them. Maybe they love it! So you'll probably have to keep smacking them to death.'

There was no let-up in his dire warnings. But Adam and the others just listened and hoped he might be exaggerating.

'Now then, get your rifles and let's think about loading them, I want you all down at the far end of the range, across the road, with your rifle, and the Quartermaster will bring some ammunition. Keep your fingers crossed we're all still alive in an hour from now.'

'He really is the spirit of Christmas,' said Joe, as they collected their rifles and made their way across to the range. Adam laughed and assumed this was all part of the sergeant's brash method of keeping them well trained and safe.

'Now then, everybody here?' he began. 'Pay attention. I want you to pull the bolt to the rear and hold the weapon straight out in front of you. That's on the order, Port Arms. Get it?'

'Yes, serg,' they all said, in chorus, as each individual made sure they were doing the right thing.

'That shows me the gun has no ammunition in. Let's hope there isn't any! Try again,' said Mackenzie. 'Port Arms!'

Everybody pulled the bolt back and held the rifle out so that the sergeant could see that the magazine was empty.

'Good, so far,' said the sergeant. Now then, the magazine holds ten rounds before you have to re-load. For this exercise, you'll hear me give the order 'Load' which is when you can insert the magazine. Then all you have to do is look through the sight, and fire when the order comes. For this practice it'll be, 'At the target to your front, Fire!.'

Adam was feeling nervous now. The target was simply a canvas wall about seventy yards in front of them. This was just to get used to firing, but the rifle felt uncomfortably powerful in his hands just at that moment. Everybody was issued with a magazine and they were put into groups of eight, facing the target, and standing in front of the rest of the squad.

'This is for you eight. Got it?' said the sergeant when he made sure everybody else was safely well behind the firing line. Adam was in the first group alongside Joe.

'Load with a magazine. Load!' ordered the sergeant. 'And keep those guns facing the front! Nowhere else!' One or two were swivelling the thing around, while they struggled to load the magazine.

'You, idiot!' shouted Mackenzie at a young recruit three along in the row from Adam. 'Do you want to blow somebody's 'ead off?' 'Keep it steady and facing the front. Make up your mind whose side you're on.'

'Sorry, serg,' muttered the boy, holding a gun for the first time in his life.

'What's your name? Remind me.'

'Price, serg,' came the reply.

'Well keep that rifle facing forward or there'll be a price on your 'ead.'

'Serg.'

'Now, you're going to hear me say, 'At the target to your front, fire!' Then you can pull the trigger. Everybody okay with that?' There was no answer. They were all lining up the target wall in their sights.

'Fingers crossed,' thought the sergeant to himself, and then, louder, he ordered, 'At the target to your front, FIRE!'

The noise was deafening. The retort was instantaneous and Adam thought his shoulder had been flung out of joint. But he'd fired it, and suddenly all was calm again. The smoke cleared but the smell lingered.

The exercise continued throughout the afternoon. They got used to firing and re-loading with a charger, containing another five or ten rounds, they got slicker and quicker, and most of the recruits came away feeling confident they could look after themselves, and their weapon.

They learned how to fix bayonets to their Lee Enfield rifle, and eventually were sent away for another cleaning session. The day's work was pretty much over. Adam found Captain James and poured a couple of drinks for him, while he tidied his billet and made sure everything was in its proper place. He took a couple of messages across to other officers, while the Captain was poring over papers containing fresh orders, plans and maps.

'This,' thought Adam, 'is all becoming a bit real.'

It got more real than ever when, one morning in early September, they were told, during a drill session, that they were to have their kit bags and equipment ready to travel by the end of the day. The next day would be their departure.

The train took them to Southampton, and via a branch line from Eastleigh, on to Portsmouth early the next morning, each individual clutching his personal kit, and every man hoping against hope that he not forgotten anything. The inspection that morning had been more strict than usual, with a real dressing down for anybody with anything missing or out of place.

Adam had spent some of the evening helping James to pack his equipment and personal effects. Then James had invited him to have a drink, which they did together, and which Adam certainly appreciated. Without doubt, he had come a long way from being the young boy who had stood at the gate of The Manor House wondering how to get in. Now he was off on a six and a half thousand mile journey.

20

Embarkation

Embarkation at Portsmouth was a tedious business. Long queues of men, with kitbags strapped to their shoulders, or carried cumbersomely off the train, making their way along grey platforms, via gangways and listening out for instructions.

Adam and Joe managed to navigate their way slowly, but were not impressed by the organisation. The Lee Enfield rifles on their backs seemed to have a life of their own, twisting and getting caught in every available rope or railing, sometimes even other men's kit.

'Watch what you're doing, mate,' Adam heard and turned around to say 'sorry' thereby causing another poke in the ribs for another soldier ahead of him.

'Sorry, oh! Sorry again!'

'You're okay. Just take it easy,' came the reply. 'We're all in the same boat, or we will be if ever we get on it.'

They could see that officers, which presumably included Captain James, had been given a way through, by order of the captain or Chief Officer, straight on to the ship. The lot of all lower ranks was, however, predictably, to wait their turn.

The moment came, when they could see the length of the ship from where they were lining up. To Adam's eyes it was the largest vessel he had ever seen in his life.

It was painted predominantly white with a black stripe going the entire length of the hull. The boys presumed it was powered by engines and not sail, although it had three masts. There were two rows of port-holes, and they wondered in which part of this leviathan they would be accommodated. They didn't have long to wait, once the ship came completely into view.

'Keep going, you men,' called a voice just out of their view. 'Move along, and follow the others, don't dawdle.' For an instant, it was as if Adam was back to his first visit to The Manor House kitchen hearing Mr Granger barking orders. The young men, still wide-eyed at the size of the vessel they were boarding, crept forward and it looked even bigger, as they traipsed up the gangplank and into the hull.

The ceilings were a little lower than they were used to, although that didn't trouble Adam. The inside looked pretty sparse, at the deck level, where they had entered the ship, and, as they were shepherded forward, it soon became clear that this was not going to be a luxury journey.

'Down the stairs,' yelled a voice which seemed to be telling everybody the same thing. The crocodile of men descended, one by one, to a lower deck and were directed along to large rooms containing many single berths.

'Choose one of these and if you're lucky, you'll get to keep it for the duration of the voyage,' said the unnamed voice. 'Put your stuff on the berth and stay put until you're told anything different.'

Adam and Joe found two berths, one alongside the other and thought themselves quite lucky to have found anywhere at all, let alone next to each other. Everything around them seemed to be chaos and they could hear voices, somewhere in the distance, shouting similar orders.

They collapsed onto the beds, along with their kit, as there did not seem to be anywhere to put their kit bags, or other stuff.

'I'm staying put until we're told anything different,' said Joe.

'Me, too,' said Adam and they almost managed to relax, for about twenty minutes, wishing they had something to drink. Gradually the noise and movement died down and they heard another voice.

'All you men from the Dorchester regiment, make your way amidships, up two flights of the stairs and into the main mess towards the bow, that's the front!' For all he knew, Joe could have been listening to another language, but luckily Adam had done more reading and remembered travel books he had borrowed from the family library.

'Follow me,' he said to Joe, and several others followed to. It was a mixed bunch of men who made their way through the maze of accommodation and corridors, up stairs, turning this way and that before being led in the right direction to the main dining area, called the mess.

Adam thought he had navigated it quite well, but even he could not work out which was the front end of the ship or the back of it, once he had turned a couple of corners and gone up two flights of stairs. Most of the voices they heard were yelling insults, which were not helpful and directions which were.

At last, they found a few friendly faces of their officers, and Adam even recognised Captain James across the large space, where several hundred men were gathering. They were told to sit and everyone found a chair. Captain James spoke first.

'On the orders of the Colonel,' he said, 'Sergeant Mackenzie is now a Warrant Officer Class One, Regimental Sergeant Major.'

There was a murmur of approval, or in some cases disbelief, and surprise. Then the newly promoted Sergeant Major spoke.

'Every one of you should have found somewhere to berth by now,' he said. 'I just hope you remember where you came from.' He gave a snort of a laugh which some, who had not yet selected a berth, or navigated their way easily to the mess, found distinctly unamusing.

Most of the men would find it difficult to reverse the journey they had just made from the lower deck to this area, and find their way back again. Adam made something of an effort to try to recall it, while Joe, sitting next to him, just shrugged and smiled.

'This ship is called *HMS Malabar*. She is one of five, almost identical, ships in Her Majesty's service, carrying troops from England to India and sometimes on to Malaya.'

'Why is it called 'she', sergeant?' came a voice from across the room.

'All ships are called 'she', you ignorant man. And the chances are that this ship is the nearest thing you'll get to a female, in the next year or so, unless you want to end up in the medical room with a lot of discomfort… and on a charge!' That entire sentence came out of the sergeant in one long breath rising in intensity and generating a loud response from the room.

'To continue.' He reverted to his normal volume. 'These ships are nicknamed the 'Lobsterpots' meaning there is not a lot of room to move about, once we get about six hundred of you, plus officers, and some wives and daughters on board.'

Certain parts of the ships are out of bounds to you lot and I'll give you one guess as to which parts they might be. There'll be plenty of signs to show you where you can exercise and walk, and where you can't. Is that clear?'

'Serg',' came the response from them all.

'The ship was built in 1865, although I will admit that by the look of her she won't last much longer! Luckily, since the Suez Canal was built, we can get to India in less than ten weeks, instead of the six months it used to take.'

Joe suddenly felt very privileged that he was already aware of that, from the evening he and Adam had spent with Captain Russell.

'You have all got a place to sleep, and you might be interested to know that where you are is below the level of the water, called the waterline, but don't panic. It can't get in!

'We shall be travelling down the west coast of Spain, past the Rock of Gibraltar and into the Mediterranean Sea, from where we shall make for the British colony of Malta, to stay for a day or two and take on fresh water and more provisions. Then it'll be on through the Suez Canal, down the Red Sea and across the Indian Ocean.'

Most of the men were engrossed listening to the names of these places, having only ever heard them in school, or in books and stories. Some had never heard of them at all. Adam was so pleased that he had done a lot of reading in his life and was becoming very excited about the prospects of the voyage.

'This ship weighs in at six thousand tons, or thereabouts, and is three hundred and sixty feet long. But we don't want to lose you, do we? So you'll confine yourselves to your berth areas, this dining area, called the mess, and the top deck forecastle – pronounced fo'c'sle, which means the front end. Ships cannot use sail through the Suez Canal, which is why we have a very powerful engine, even though the ship has three masts and could use sail if needed.'

There were some men getting bored now, whilst others, including Adam, could not get enough of this stuff, which they found fascinating.

'You will be served a meal here in the lower-ranks mess at four pm and, in the meantime, I suggest you acclimatize yourselves to the ship and find your way around. And gawd help anybody who finds themselves in the wrong quarters. Dismiss.'

There was a general shuffling of chairs and Adam found himself being called over by Captain James.

'Sir,' he said as he came towards him.

'You got somewhere to berth?' said the captain as he caught sight of Joe, standing a little way off waiting for his friend.

'Yes, thank you, sir. We both have, though we don't have much room.'

'Frankly neither have I, but it's probably a bit better than you have. I want you to come with me and find your way to my cabin, then you'll know where to report if I need you. You'll have to wear this as an Officer's Batman.' And he gave Adam a small badge for his lapel.

'Yes, sir. Lead the way.'

'Sir,' piped up Joe. 'Do you mind if I tag along just this once? I don't think I would find my way back to our…?'

'Berth,' said Adam.

'Just this once,' said James, 'but stay close.'

Captain James Russell's cabin was certainly not luxurious. In fact it was very small, but it was private and had space for personal belongings, a cupboard at eye level and a space under the berth. Adam had taken careful note of the route to get there from the mess, and hoped he could work that out, from either his own berth, or other areas including the open deck which he'd not even yet been to see.

'There's not going to be any room in here for the both of us,' said James, 'So if you're going to tidy up or clean uniform brass-work, take stuff away for washing, or whatever, it'll either be you or me in here, but not likely the two of us.'

'I won't argue with that, sir,' said Adam. 'Don't worry, I'll just have to agree a time for me to be here, if I can, when you can open the door for me.' He and Joe made their farewells to the captain and went off to navigate their way back to their own berths.

They also managed to find their way up to the front of the ship out on to the deck just as she was casting off.

It was a majestic sight indeed, and Adam could feel the throb of the great seven hundred horse power engine turn the single screw, and take six thousand tons of steel hull slowly away from the quayside. It was like no other feeling he had ever experienced.

The other ships and buildings on the mainland slowly moved away and became smaller and smaller as the distance between them and *HMS Malabar* lengthened. Houses became models and people looked like scurrying ants, whilst the great ship, which was to be their home for several weeks, took them out into the Solent and around the Isle of Wight.

One person who was certainly not short of space, in which to live and breathe, was looking out of a sitting room window over the Solent towards Portsmouth as the ship glided out. Queen Victoria was alone, in Osborne House on the island, as the summer came towards its end.

At least, she was as alone as Her Majesty ever was. There were servants and the Royal Household always in attendance. And there was her daughter, Beatrice, Victoria's last child who had been just four years old when the Queen's beloved Albert died.

For the whole of Adam's life, and for ten years before even that, there had been a cloud hanging over the Queen as she tried to live in a state of perpetual mourning, whilst bringing up the nine children she and Albert had produced. Victoria had agreed that her youngest child, Beatrice, could be married to Prince Henry of Battenberg, provided that the couple stayed with her and did not move to Germany, which was Henry's birthplace. They agreed. It was their only option.

Sadly, having been married for just eight years, and producing four children, Prince Henry died of malaria which he had contracted whilst serving in the Ashanti wars on The Gold Coast of Africa. Beatrice was alone, with her four children and her grieving widowed mother.

Now the Queen was watching Adam, on his ship, as it glided past her favourite home. She was in the small four-roomed, virtually self-contained, personal apartment at Osborne where, forty years earlier, she and Albert used to stand and watch the moonlight shining on the waters of The Solent, and listen to nightingales singing in the trees below.

If only Adam had known who was observing his departure.

21

Malta

The ship was on its way to India and beyond, the sub-continent which had greatly influenced Queen Victoria in recent years, so much so, that just four years previously she had created the Durbar wing at Osborne House, to house her daughter and her family. The great Durbar Room itself was a masterpiece of Indian-style plaster work and carvings, which Victoria thought reflected perfectly on her relatively new status as Empress of India.

The connection between the boy on *HMS Malabar* and the Queen as the ship was sailing out would have been palpable had either party known the passage of the life of the other; Adam in his tiny personal space, serving his Queen and country, and the Queen herself, almost alone in her vast palace.

Also serving the Queen that summer were workmen in Osborne House, installing the new-fangled electric wiring in the sumptuous gold drawing room, specifically for the cut glass chandeliers. The contrast between Her lonely Majesty's home and the closely confined quarters of her overcrowded military troop ship could hardly have been starker. But they served the same great nation.

So, unaware of the anomaly of connection and contrast, the great ship and its passengers sailed slowly out of sight of

England, and all those on board gradually, indeed quite quickly, got used to the routines. The routine for eating and for lectures and training, the routine for exercising, for kit inspections, to make sure that at least what space they had was clean and tidy, and the routines for relaxing and taking advantage of the top deck to sit and watch the sea.

Adam knew it was Osborne House that they were passing in those few moments, and wondered, momentarily, if this might just be the closest he would ever get to copying Mrs Redman and actually seeing the Queen.

Joe was the first one to be violently sick. After about three days out, they had passed the tip of Cherbourg in France and then, with the vast Atlantic Ocean on their right, or to starboard as Adam and plenty of others now knew, and with The Bay of Biscay to their port side, they were in open water and feeling it.

Adam tried to persuade Joe to eat something, but it was virtually to no avail. The poor man was helpless, and even Adam felt queasy, partly having to deal with Joe and, in part, because there really was quite a swell on the sea as they headed for the Iberian peninsular.

Some men had been too ill to leave their berths, which did not contribute much to the comfort of the remainder. But, at least, not so many had actually been sick; they just thought they were going to die! And they didn't.

Adam's Captain James had fared pretty well, as had Adam himself.

'Perhaps,' he said to James, and then repeated himself, 'perhaps my St Christopher really does work!'

Adam was tucked away in James' tiny cabin polishing buckles

and buttons, putting stuff away in the limited space there was and conversing with James who stood at the door.

'We shall pass the Rock of Gibraltar soon,' said James, 'and head on into The Mediterranean Sea.'

'The Rock is British, isn't it, sir?' said Adam. 'Why is that?'

'When the King of Spain died childless in 1700 a war began to decide who would rule Spain, the French Bourbons or the Austrian Hapsburg families. The Hapsburg's eventually came out on top, and Britain was allowed to keep Gibraltar, for ever, as a kind of 'Thank-you' from The Treaty of Utrecht in 1713. The Spanish might not be so pleased in future about us British being on that tip of their nation, but for now, it stays with us!'

Adam pondered, considering all that he'd read about the British Empire, about India and South Africa, and now Gibraltar, and even Malta, where they were heading. 'Britain was a powerful nation, indeed,' he said to himself, 'but I wonder if it will be that way for ever.'

Joe got better. There were parades on the top deck, kit inspections daily by their sergeant who only missed one day, 'feeling a bit under the weather', he said. He'd agreed to let them off an inspection for one day 'as a privilege', so he said, but everybody knew he was flat out on his berth for twenty-four hours. 'Was that the sea or the drink?' was the topic of the evening.

There was advice about how to behave when they got to foreign climes and were mixing with locals of a different culture. There was plenty of sunshine, as they approached Gibraltar and passed by it into The Med.

Adam was talking to some friends, all perched on the railings of the ship, as they passed through the narrow strait.

'Years ago,' said Adam, 'These two points were considered

to be The Pillars of Hercules; the Rock on this, the European side and the Jebel Musa, on the African side, which is over there to the right.'

'Starboard,' corrected one of the others.

'Precisely,' said Adam. 'Now we all know what port and star-board mean.' He was trying not to sound too knowledgeable or 'clever' but everybody seemed to be listening. 'The Greeks and Phoenicians, coming from within the Mediterranean Sea, believed this was the limit of the known world, and that nobody should venture out any further.'

'In case they dropped off the edge of the world?' piped up Joe, now very much over his *mal de mer.*

'Precisely again,' Adam came back, 'although the other day I thought you might have preferred to drop off the ship altogether!'

'Very funny,' Joe replied. 'Actually you're right. God, I felt awful.'

Their voyage of discovery continued. They became a much closer bunch of comrades, within the confines of the ship and Joe's friendship with Adam strengthened every day.

The sergeant was addressing them all in the mess after one evening meal.

'We shall be in Malta the day after tomorrow. We should arrive early and be there for a day or two. If the officers in command think it suitable, and if you're not wanted for any other duties, you may be allowed ashore for eight hours. Of course you may not, so don't rely on it.

If you are allowed to leave the ship, there will be some pretty strict regulations regarding behaviour, especially relating to some of the ladies of Valetta who might be enthusiastic about meeting up with you!'

There was a vocal explosion of delight or disbelief, or surprise, depending on what everyone thought they heard or thought the Sergeant meant by it.

'Now for some rather more important information. On this ship we are also carrying two Maxim guns. We weren't sure if they would be available to us, but they were loaded on in Portsmouth, so as soon as we get to Pehang there will be additional training. They can see off a marauding tribe quicker than you can load a rifle or fix your bayonet'

'What does it do that's so special, Sergeant Major?'

The Sergeant Major continued. 'You've heard, maybe, about the Gatling gun, which fires sustained rounds of ammunition, but which has been found unreliable and sometimes dangerous, especially as it needs cranking to keep the firing going.

'Well, our military masters decided against bringing those out with us, but ordered the Maxims, two of which have arrived. They fire multiple rounds automatically, very quickly, and might I say, devastatingly, towards a charging enemy, without the need to crank it to keep it going.'

'Does it work?' came the predictable question from amongst the men.

'Does it work?' began the Sergeant Major sarcastically.' We shall wait and see won't we? But there have been stories of marauding crowds of thousands being held off by just five Maxims and a few men.'

Not everybody understood what he was talking about, but most relished the idea of such a weapon and couldn't wait to see it, or for the training. Adam, however, was just a little disturbed by the idea of a mechanical gun, firing hundreds of rounds into other people, be they enemy or not.

The ship duly arrived in Valetta, early in the morning two days later. Looking over the railings from the top deck of the ship, Adam and Joe could see clearly the bustle and activity going on below them. It was an enormous natural harbour, crowded with ships of all kinds, and clearly the hub of a busy city.

'That's quite something,' said Joe.

'I can hardly believe how far away we are from home,' said Adam, 'And yet there are horses, carts, stalls, crates and cranes, other boats and ships and hundreds of dock workers, just like Portsmouth.'

'But not quite the same,' Joe came back. 'Something is different.'

'Perhaps we shall be able to see for ourselves,' said Adam as they made their way down to the mess to await orders or information. The Sergeant Major gathered everyone together at midday and didn't pull any punches.

'The captain of this ship, Commander Arthur Dalrymple Fanshawe,' began Sergeant Major Mackenzie. There was a ripple of amusement at the name being almost spelled out.

'As I was saying, the Captain of this ship will give orders to set sail again by midday tomorrow. That does not mean that you can be out all night. It does mean that I will assemble you all at nine o'clock in the morning, and gawd help anybody who is not here, clean, tidy and ready to go. In the meantime, you can have eight hours, from the time you leave here until nine o'clock tonight. My advice is that you stay in small groups, and lay off the cheap drink.

'I do not want any of you laid up in a sick bay for the next two days, assuming you could even find your way back if you're intoxicated. I know I am probably talking to the deaf and the stupid, but Valetta is notorious for 'cheap entertainment.' He spat out the last two words as if they were poison.

Some of the assembled battalion of soldiers were more experienced than others, and took all of this with a pinch of salt. Some, like Adam and Joe, were suddenly both excited, and hesitant, about venturing out into a strange city in a new country. The meeting came to an end after a few more pieces of 'sensible' advice and they were dismissed.

The two boys made their way off the ship as soon as they could, and ventured out with one of the older men who had met them on the crowded berth deck.

'The name's Frank, Frank Lewis,' he said as they set foot on dry land. 'Do you two know where you're going?'

He was in his forties, still only a corporal, after quite a few years service. Slightly shorter than either Adam or Joe, with a bristling little moustache, small eyes and thinning grey hair, he paired up with them as they made their way to the gangplank.

'Not really. I'm Adam, by the way.'

'And my name's Joe,' his friend added.

'Don't suppose you know your way around Valetta?' said the corporal.

'Somewhere for a proper drink would be good enough for starters,' said Adam. And off they went, with Corporal Frank Lewis more or less leading the way and the two young soldiers, pleased they'd managed to find someone who knew the city, so he said.

It was very hot. The temperature in Valetta could reach the forties in high summer and this was towards the end of their summer. It was very crowded. There were any number of traders and hawkers, yelling about the value of their trinkets and baubles, but not much about the prices. It was very confusing.

There were extraordinarily steep steps up some streets from the harbour area, and Adam and Joe followed Frank like a couple of sheep. Frank told them some history as they climbed the steps

'The city has got these ancient fortifications which, despite all the best intentions, and their complete uselessness, have never been demolished.' He spluttered as they climbed.

'This island was a safe haven in the middle ages for crusaders coming or going to The Holy Land, or for safety if they'd been injured or become ill.'

'I've read about the Crusades,' said Adam.

'There isn't much you haven't read, is there?' Joe came back, half joking and half admiringly.

Eventually they found a café, with tables and chairs set out on the front pavement, and a middle-aged man clearly serving drinks. Some of the other men had got there first but there was a table free.

They were very soon sipping cold beer, which Frank offered to pay for from the coins in his pocket.

'We can use our English money here,' he told them. 'But this,' he continued, as he spread out some coins on the table, this is a *grano*. It's worth a third of a farthing.'

'A third of a farthing! That's twelve to a penny,' said Adam, quickly doing the maths and trying to work out how any coin could be so minimal in value.

'Your English pound is worth twelve of these Maltese *scudi*,' Frank continued, as he handed over a couple of slightly larger coins for the drinks. 'And a *scudi* is worth two hundred and forty *granos* or *grani*.

'Just like our pound is worth two hundred and forty pence. So all your English money here is worth about twelve times what it is at home.'

'In that case,' said Joe, 'I am buying the next drink.' He sorted out a few English pennies, and felt quite good about his sudden propulsion into local wealth.

Adam was looking into his purse. This was the purse he had found it necessary to buy, after Arthur had stolen his original wallet on the train during his first visit to see Mrs Redman. This purse he had managed to hold on to, and it contained a few English shillings.

'That means that if I have five shillings and six pence in here, that's sixty-six pence and every penny is worth twelve... what did you call them, Frank?'

'*Grani*,' said Frank as Adam calculated, using his piece of new-found knowledge.

'So I have seven hundred and ninety-two *grani*! I'm rich!'

'Not really,' said Frank, 'but your money will go a lot further here.'

'Adam,' said Joe. 'Tell me how much I've got.' He put down a five pound note and a few shillings on the table.

'Put that away!' Frank burst in. 'And keep it to yourself. You won't have it at all if you flash it about in a public place.' Joe quickly removed it and put away any plans to take it out again.

'Is *The Malabar* the worst ship you've ever been on, Frank?' ventured Adam.

'I've been around a few years and heard plenty of stories,' said Frank. 'Chances are this is not just the worst ship I've ever been on, but the worst ship ever put into service.'

'How come?' said Adam.

'Well, to tell the truth, it's just from what I have heard others say. And it's not all to do with *The Malabar*. Some of it is down to The War Office sending too many troops, and horses and wives...'

'Frank lumped those two groups – horses and wives - together in a strangely insulting fashion,' thought Adam.

Frank continued, 'Too many horses and wives packed into one journey. And sometimes it's down to the skipper, not caring too much about his passengers. However, judging from what I've heard tell, we've got it quite comfortable.'

'So what have you heard about other journeys?' asked Joe.

'Three or four years ago there were questions asked in The House of Commons about these long journeys, cramped conditions, dreadful cold, seasickness and even worse conditions for the horses below decks.'

'You don't have to tell me about sea sickness!' said Joe.

'Yours was just not being used to the sea,' replied Frank. 'I'm talking about sickness at sea, which was not taken care of. There were fourteen deaths on one return journey from India, on *The Malabar*, and all on account of too many invalids and sick people being loaded on at the outset. The number of individuals was within the War Office regulations, but the number of sick and injured was in excess so, of course, there was not enough medical help on board and fourteen died on the way home.

'I had a friend who was a farrier, and he said he thought the horses probably preferred death, down in the hold, to actually living in the mire and smells of below decks. Appalling, apparently'

'It all seems rather better now, although it is still not comfortable' said Adam.

'Dead right,' Frank continued. 'Would you believe that the worst conditions recorded were those in which the wives of men and officers had to live?'

'Captain Russell's cabin isn't exactly very big, but it is comfortable.' Adam offered.

'Maybe,' said Frank, 'But even until recently, all the women were berthed in one long cabin opening out on to a public room. Apparently, the arguments which could be heard were quite lively! And some had children with them! Things have changed since then. Despite what we might think, some officers have reported that these ships are now very well run, although they're getting a bit long in the tooth, probably due to be scrapped.'

Adam and Joe were keen to listen to the 'old' boy. He was still only in his forties, but they thought of him as old. However, they wanted to explore and they only had eight hours.

'We'll see you back at the ship this evening.' said Adam.

Take it easy,' replied Frank. 'Don't be fooled into buying rubbish.'

They smiled and went their way, climbing further away from the harbour. Almost everybody they saw seemed to be busy carting produce one way or another, towards their shops or stalls, or away from the harbour. The boys stopped to look at some jewellery and pottery, and were even tempted to buy a watch, but thought better of it. They kept their coins in their pockets.

There were beggars who seemed to be wearing no shoes at all, or with shoes that looked as though they had first been put on a hundred years earlier!

There were even one or two who seemed to be wearing army boots, but not necessarily of the correct size!

They made their way along the *Strada Reale* which was narrow, with overhanging balconies and upper floors, all leaning in, making it seem narrower still.

The two of them turned a corner occasionally, keeping the harbour behind them and were hoping to find somewhere else for a drink or a bite to eat.

Narrow streets still beckoned them, some with washing hanging out of windows, and wrinkled brown skinned men, and women, sitting outside open doors, usually on the doorstep, smoking or drinking. Adam had never seen anything like it, nor even imagined it. Joe was on the lookout for somewhere to buy a drink and at last spotted what seemed to be a café on a corner, which did not look too run down or uninviting.

The lady standing outside invited them to sit and offered olives and beer. Neither of them had any experience of olives before, and little knew what a staple of Mediterranean diet they were. But they loved them.

They managed to agree how many of their meagre supply of English coins would be sufficient, and were offered bread, more beer, some sliced meat and the most enormous tomato each. They were content, enjoying the heat, and each other's company, and even managed to order an additional beer each.

'We could just stay here for a few hours, Adam,' said Joe.

'Don't disagree with that,' Adam came back, 'It is very hot though, perhaps we could finish a couple of drinks and find some shade.

They agreed that staying put was fine for the moment, but, after less than an hour, the urge to move on and explore some more was too much. They paid for some more bread and olives, another tomato and two more bottles of beer. They waved a farewell 'thank-you' to the woman who had fed them, and headed on.

They even came across the one and only railway on Malta, which began its single line journey from Valetta at the station, where the two boys now found themselves. The train alongside the small platform looked inviting.

'I'm not suggesting we do, but I'd love to travel on that,' said Adam. 'How about we just follow the line for a short distance, find somewhere to sit and enjoy the view?' From where they now were they could see someway back the way they'd come, and could even make out the lighthouse out in the harbour.

Joe agreed it was a good plan and they made their way along the line, following the track for a short distance, until they reached a grassy bank, with a few trees which seemed to be inviting them to sit down and relax. They did just that and tucked into their olives. The beers were opened and they enjoyed the sunshine, under the shade of a tree.

It was late afternoon by now, but what happened next would have shocked and surprised them at any time.

They were approached by a small group of men who didn't look at all like needy beggars, or crew from their own ship, local fishermen or artisans. They didn't seem to be selling anything and, before either Joe or Adam had the chance to stand up, or formulate a question or a greeting, they were out cold.

The attack on the two of them had been sudden, violent and completely unchallenged. They knew nothing of it, other than the momentary fear that something was about to happen. And it did.

It was Adam who appeared to be coming round first. He was in the dark, he could feel movement, he could feel skin close to his and assumed it was Joe nearby, but still unconscious. He spoke his name,

'Joe.' Nothing. He tied to reach out perhaps to shake him awake. 'Joe!'

There was a stir, and as he came to he let out a short yelp that was lost by the other noise, around them, and the movement they now both felt. The noise was of hard wheels on gravel or stone. The movement meant that they were in the back of some cart, or wagon, and, yes, they felt it, they were tied up.

'What the f…' began Joe as he came to a little more. 'Oh! My head.'

'Ssh!' suggested Adam and quietly went on to ask if he felt okay.

'Where the hell are we, what are we doing here?' Joe began. 'Just where are we?'

'I've no idea, and wherever we are I suggest we stay quiet. Whoever is driving this bloody cart, or whatever it is, would clearly prefer it if we were unconscious so I suggest that for now we stay quiet.'

The movement continued and they trundled on for what seemed like hours. The two of them were trussed up and virtually unable to move. They tried to loosen some of the ties, but to no avail, so they conserved their energy and communicated very quietly if indeed there was anything to say. They were under some kind of tarpaulin, a heavy covering which allowed no light in, even assuming it was still light outside.

At long last the wagon seemed to stop. They heard voices, which were not speaking English, and it seemed like an unholy row was going on. Eventually the voices faded away. The two boys even heard the sound of men walking away, with what they assume was a horse, alongside them. Voices and noises faded. They were, apparently, alone, and after a very long pause, to be quite sure, began trying more energetically to loosen the ties they were trussed up with.

'I can just about…' began Adam as he strained at the rope around his wrist.

'Me, too,' Joe offered, as he too pushed and pulled at what might give way first. They both continued to struggle at what might be the weakest loop in their confinement, until all at once Joe yelled out loud.

'Done it!'

'Ssh!' said Adam again, although by now they had heard nothing but each other, for what seemed like hours. 'Can't be too careful about any noise we might make.'

'Sorry,' said Joe, but he continued to wriggle free, and gradually unravel himself from the ropes. It was still pitch black for them both, but somehow they acclimatised themselves to where they were, in relation to each other, until Joe felt he was able to pull at some of Adam's ties.

From then on it did not take them long, but, as they began to move to uncover themselves, what was obviously a two wheeled cart became unbalanced, with their weight towards the rear of it, and it tilted violently, tipping them both out on to the hard stone road beneath them.

'God, my bloody arm,' hissed Joe. 'Where in God's name are we?'

'Well, we're out of that thing,' said Adam, 'but as for where we are, I haven't a clue either and now I think my leg is bleeding.'

It was indeed pitch black outside, as well as inside their tarpaulin. They hadn't a clue about the time, about their whereabouts, their condition, other than feeling bruised and hurt, or the proximity of help or danger, whichever was the closer. After a few moments, it dawned on them that they were alone. They hardly dared to speak and, for a long while, could think of no better option than simply to sit and wait... and think.

22

Missing

'Where the hell are they?'

It was the bellowing voice of Sergeant Major Mackenzie addressing the gathered men, most of whom had returned by between eight and nine that evening. There had been a roll call and Privates Warkin and Smith were missing.

'Did any of you see them in the town?' Captain James Russell joined in the discussion, asking out loud. 'Anybody?'

'They went for a walk away from the front, sir,' said Corporal Frank Lewis. 'They seemed certain to stay together, as far as I could see. Wanted to see some shops and stuff.'

'And where were you, Corporal?' said Mackenzie.

'In a café, not far from the harbour, serg,' replied Frank. 'It all seemed very safe to me. They were in good spirits.'

Captain Russell came back into the conversation.

'It's now nearly ten o'clock. Can we look for them?'

'There's not much in the way of street lighting in Valetta, sir,' offered corporal Lewis. 'A few feeble gas lamps on some corners and in some cafés, but I've been told they're looking forward to getting electricity in Valetta next year sometime. It'll be almost pitch black, sir.'

'Well, 'next year' doesn't really help us, does it?' said Captain Russell.

'May I suggest six o'clock in the morning, sir?' said the sergeant major to Captain Russell. 'If they're not back, we will have an hour or two to send out some men to search. They could just be dead drunk and will make their way back at first light, even if that means being put on a charge.'

'Or they could be lost, or even in some kind of danger, but we'll not know that, unless we make an effort to look for him, for them,' the Captain corrected himself.

'But where the hell can they be?' repeated the sergeant major. 'Commander Fanshawe will not delay the departure of this ship, by even a few minutes, sir, if we've got the tide, so if they're not back that'll be it, sir. We leave without them.'

23

A way to get home

Out on a road, presumably somewhere on the island of Malta, two ragged figures sat and did what they could to nurse their wounds. Adam wrapped a handkerchief around his knee, while Joe cradled his own arm, which he hoped was just bruised and not broken.

They felt hungry and thirsty, but could hardly see their hands in front of their faces. If only there had been a moon, but there wasn't, and there seemed no point in trying to move on anywhere. At least they were dry, and alive.

The dawn came slowly. They slept a little, tried to get comfortable, leaning up against the upturned cart, and gradually they awoke as the early morning sun lit up the sky.

'My boots have gone!' said Adam. 'They've taken my damn boots. And, wait a minute, my wallet, of course, that's gone as well. Luckily I didn't have very many coins in it, but they've all gone. And how, in God's name are we going to get back to the ship?'

'So has my money gone,' said Joe, 'and my gold chain I had around my neck. .. and, of course, my boots.'

'Oh, God! My St Christopher. My silver St Christopher has gone too,' Adam realised, as he checked his neck. 'Damn them all.'

They sat, deflated for a good while, before either of them ventured the next enquiry.

'But did you,' began Adam, 'take any advice from the Sergeant Major about looking after your money?'

'Some of our money,' Joe added. 'Yes, I did, and, abracadabra!' Off came a sock and inside was his five pound note. 'You see? I put it there when we were sitting by the railway, after I'd flashed it about at the café.'

'Oh, yes. Well done,' said Adam, as he too removed a sock. 'Always let them steal a small amount and they won't look any further. 'Good advice,' he continued and pulled out of his sock three gold half sovereigns and, from inside the waistband of his trousers, a ten shilling note.

'That means we have just over seven English pounds between us, but we still don't know where we are. And the ship leaves this morning,' Adam announced.

'Doesn't look promising,' said Joe. 'Blimey, what a mess!'

At least they appeared safe, sitting on the ground by the wooden cart. They were not aware of any other person nearby, nor did anybody come anywhere near them, whilst they sat and pondered their situation.

'We can't tell which way we were brought here,' began Adam, 'The cart has pulled off the road so we don't know which way to walk, to try to get back to Valetta.'

'Why would people rob us and then just leave us here?' mused Joe. 'Doesn't make sense.'

'Maybe they will be back here during the morning. Maybe they themselves were frightened off, or just simply callous enough to leave us here while they went off to bed!'

'Charming,' said Joe. 'I could do with some breakfast.'

'The first thing to do is try to get back to the ship. We might make it; it's still very early and the ship doesn't go until midday.'

With their limited orientation skills, and some knowledge of the sun and the earth and its movements, between them they could see where the sun was coming up, which Adam calculated to be the East. If we knew where we were on the island, we would know whether Valetta was straight ahead, south, or...'

'Or not,' said Joe, not very helpfully.

'Okay, so we don't really know, but if we could see the sea, we'd at least be able to follow a coast road or something.'

'If only there was somebody to ask.' said Joe.

'I'm not at all sure I'd want to ask anybody within a stone's throw of where we are at the moment. We might be asking the very people who robbed us. Let's set out on this road, which is at least sloping downwards a bit, so maybe, eventually, it could come to the coast.'

Joe, having no reason to argue with that, got up and shook his arms as if to get the circulation going. In the meantime Adam got up, gingerly put his leg to the ground, testing it, and then put it firmly to the ground. He was fine. Although the handkerchief was blood stained, his leg wasn't getting any worse.

They started to walk away from the cart, turned right and proceeded along the dusty road, with the sun now on their right. They hoped it might lead to the sea, or better still to Valetta, especially if they could get there in time for the ship's departure.

They had in fact turned the wrong way and were heading up the east coast of the island, away from the harbour. With the sun on their right, the main body of the island was to their left, and Valetta behind them. But they appeared to be free from imminent danger, still confused as to why their attackers had left them.

'An apple tree,' said Adam suddenly. It was a chance to quench their thirst and eat something too, so they picked some, and stuffed what pockets they had full of apples, whilst eating one or two to be going on with. Nobody appeared to stop them and they felt that this might have been their first bit of luck in twelve hours.

The sun was rising higher, they were getting hotter, and they appeared to be no nearer anything they could identify which could help them.

They walked for over an hour. The sun was gaining height. They were losing hope.

After walking a long distance, which was not easy with no shoes, quite suddenly there was a solid white tower ahead of them. They had no idea what it was, or why it was there, but it seemed to be an omen. At least they were getting somewhere, even if they did not know where that was.

'Well, just look at that,' said Joe. 'Wonder if anybody lives near here. Wonder what it is.'

The two boys approached the white stone tower, which looked like some medieval watchtower, and, as they got nearer, they could suddenly see the sea to their right, a beautiful blue and still as a pond. There were boats, which they assumed were fishing boats, out almost as far as the horizon, and children playing on the sands beneath where they were.

'Let's keep going,' said Adam, just as a figure appeared from the road beyond the white tower, walking towards them. It was clearly a priest.

'We look a sorry sight,' thought Adam, at the same time hoping that perhaps the priest might speak a bit of English.

They got closer, and Adam and Joe stopped, to let the priest approach them.

'*Awguri?*' said the tall robed man coming towards them. '*Awguri?*'

'Sorry,' said Joe, turning to look at Adam.

'Pardon, sir, we are English.'

'English!' said the priest. 'English! Well, greetings. What are you doing here?'

'Can you give us some idea where we are?' continued Adam.

'And where we might get something to eat?' Joe added.

'English!' the man repeated. 'You English are always lost.'

'Yes, well we're sorry about that,' said Joe. 'Not exactly our fault.'

'Follow me,' said the priest and he passed them by and continued the way they had just come from. They turned, as he strode out along the road they had just travelled, but taking a fork in the road, down to their left. It was not easy following at his speed without shoes, but maybe he had not noticed they were barefoot.

The two boys had taken off their socks, each had put their money inside one of them, and tucked it down inside their trousers.

Suddenly they could see the sea again, ahead of them and down to the left. The sun was now not far from being directly above them. In a little more than ten minutes, or so it seemed to them, the priest turned through a gate, and headed for a pale orange stone church, set amongst gravestones and surrounded by palm trees and grass.

'Come in,' he said, as they made their way through the graveyard, following him but staying close together. 'Come in and follow me again.'

The church was cool and inviting. They looked around at some beautiful stained glass windows, not very much like the small grey church that Adam remembered in Melton Ford. The priest crossed himself, as he went through and across the central aisle. The boys casually did the same thing, but followed, nevertheless, all the while looking around them.

Soon their guide was out of a side-door, across a small garden and into a house. It was in the same orange stone, small and, Adam thought, not unlike Mrs Redman's cottage.

Once inside he noticed the differences. This was all stone floored, with large wooden pieces of furniture, white hessian curtains shielding the occupants from the sun, when it might be shining straight in through the windows, and a large oil-lamp suspended from the ceiling.

The two of them stood just inside the door.

'Excuse me, sir,' said Adam. 'I don't suppose you could tell us what time it is, or how far we are from Valetta Harbour?'

'Now why don't you just sit down and I'll find you some wine,' said the priest. 'You tell me you are lost, so, for now, you don't need to know where you are.'

'But, we do,' said Joe. 'We're supposed to be on a ship which leaves at midday, and if we're not on it, we'll probably be locked up for weeks!'

'Nobody's going to lock you up,' said the priest, so you might as well relax. It is almost the middle of the afternoon, or it will be in an hour or so, so your ship has gone without you, and in any case, Valetta is ten kilometres from here, so you would never have made it back, even if you had been walking in the right direction.'

'Dear God,' thought Adam. 'I can't think of anything worse. What will Captain James think?'

'Captain James?' said the priest

'He's sort of my boss, I'm his batman.'

'And I'm his friend,' said Joe, indicating Adam. 'That ship is going to India and Malaya, and we're supposed to be on it as members of Her Majesty Queen Victoria's army!'

'Well, you might still be in her army, but you most certainly will not get on that ship again for a couple of years, even if you waited here on Malta for it.'

'What on earth are we going to do?' said Adam.

'Well, first you are going to drink this,' said the priest, putting down glasses, and a bottle of red wine, 'And then you're going to eat something, before you tell me what you are doing in the town of St. Julian's, and looking at St George's Tower where I found you.'

The story came out fast and fluently from the two of them; the 'old' corporal who had taken them into the city; the drinks, the shops, the exploration and sitting down in the sun to drink some beer.

'And you were set upon and robbed?' said the priest.

'How do you know that?' said Joe.

'Isn't it pretty obvious?' came the reply. 'You have no shoes, you are ambling along, with no apparent destination, which is why you asked me where you were, and you followed me immediately because you had no other option.'

'Yes, that is pretty obvious, isn't it,' said Adam. 'So where are we? Can you show us a map or something?'

All the while, the priest had been in and out of the small room they were in, putting bread on the table, olives in a bowl central table was more bread, more olives, some cheese, fruit and a great pot of steaming coffee.

'I'm not sure we should be enjoying this quite as much as we are!' said Adam. 'Something tells me we are in big trouble with our Commanding Officer or with the ship's commander.'

'Well,' began Guiseppe, 'You're not likely to find out any time soon just how true that is. In the meantime, I suggest you enjoy some breakfast and make some plans.'

'That's precisely what we intend to do, eh? Joe?' Joe was slowly coming round, rubbing his eyes and still occasionally yawning.

'Sorry, I'm not quite with it yet.'

'This coffee is amazing,' said Adam, sipping a large cup, which had some milk and sugar added. 'I'm a bit surprised that you can get coffee at all on this island?'

'Why would you think that?' said Guiseppe.

'Well,' said Joe, 'It does seem like a bit of a posh drink.'

'Don't you believe it,' Guiseppe came back immediately. 'It might be expensive in northern Europe, I wouldn't know, but, would you believe that when coffee came to Europe, the first place it came to was Malta?'

'Really?' said Adam, who always enjoyed new knowledge.

'Yes,' continued their host. 'As long ago as 1565, there was the great siege of Malta. The Knights of St John had imprisoned many Turkish Muslims and they brought with them their favourite beverage which was coffee. It had been common in the eastern Islamic world for centuries. So Malta got coffee before it became common in the popular coffee houses of your country in the 18th century, or before it became the posh, after dinner beverage of Paris or London!'

and some fruit in front of them, as well. They tucked in eagerly.

'We don't know your name,' said Adam.

'And I don't know yours,' said the priest. 'I'm Don Guiseppi Scerri, and I'm in charge here at The Old Parish Church in St Julian's. Most people call me Guiseppe. It's the Italian version of the English name Joseph. Tuck in.'

'That's my name!' exclaimed Joe as he stood up to shake hands. 'Pleased to meet you, er… Guiseppe!'

'And I'm Adam.' Adam did the same. 'This fruit is delicious. Thank you.'

By now, the boys had settled into the uncomfortable, but inevitable truth, that their ship had gone without them. They sat with Guiseppe and told him some more about their own lives. He was interested in England, where he had been just once during his training for the priesthood, many years before.

He said he was lucky to have been there, because not all trainees had the chance to go to England, but of course living in Malta, and the church having one or two wealthy sponsors, gave him that opportunity all those years ago.

'And I don't get to practise my English too often.' he said.

They spent the evening under the light of the oil lamp, with the priest telling them that some soldiers and sailors are robbed in the city every time a ship comes in.

'Somebody is nearly always unlucky.' he said, 'And they leave you on the side of the road, miles from anywhere, so that at least they don't have bodies to get rid of, but the captain of the ship they come from, or their commanding officers, think they have deserted, so nobody comes looking. And you'll never find your attackers again.'

'Does anybody get caught?' enquired Joe, thinking of his

own 'profession' before he joined the military.

'Sometimes, but the level of poverty in Malta amongst some of the population is so great that young men think it is worth their while to steal, without murdering anybody. Even so, the penalties for stealing are very harsh. They get six months, or a year of hard labour, in this climate, even for a modest theft.'

'Not good,' said Joe, with just a hint of understanding of the plight of the very poor, or dispossessed.

'I'm sure the company would have come and looked for us,' said Adam.

'Don't be too sure. If they did, you were probably a valued man amongst the hundreds of others. Anyway, it's too late to worry about that now. You two are going to get a good night's sleep, I'm going to find you some shoes from the charity box collection of clothes we get from some who die, and in the morning you can decide what you might do next.'

The two of them were delighted to have fallen on the generosity and friendliness of Guiseppe, the priest. They did indeed need a good night's rest, and as they went upstairs in the little house, Adam found a small book, written in English, about St Julian's.

'May I borrow this?' he said.

'You certainly can,' said Guiseppe, 'but you'll not be able to read much up there. I've only got two candles at the moment, so you'll only have one, to share, and I'd rather you blew it out before you fall asleep and burn the place down.'

'Fair enough,' said Adam. 'I'll probably read it in the morning.'

'There's never any stopping you reading, is there?' said Joe, jokingly, but with just the barest hint of envy.

'Goodnight.' They all wished each other a good night's

Adam started reading the book under the light of the candle, whilst Joe was still trying to get himself comfortabl the little single bed, on the other side of the room. The pat saint of this town was indeed Saint Julian, Adam read, a known as Julian the Hospitaller, and also Julian the Poor, w was known and celebrated for his hospitality.

'We've certainly received hospitality,' Adam thought, as read on to himself. '*In 1854 the six hundred residents of St Julia appealed to the church authorities to make it a parish. The autho ities in Birkirkara had strongly objected but nearly forty years lat had relented so that St Julian's became a parish in 1891.*' 'Onl two years ago,' thought Adam. 'I'm glad they made it.'

He put the candle out, and as he fell asleep, Adam formu lated some ideas about what they could do, and where they might go. He had read travel books ever since arriving at The Manor House. He knew a lot about the shape of Europe and the major cities in different countries. But he had little idea of their relative sizes, or just how vast a country like France or even Italy was.

He drifted in and out of sleep, half worrying about what Captain James might think of him now, and where the two of them could go from here. The next thing he knew, there wa bright sunlight streaming in at the window. Guiseppe called up to ask if they'd like some coffee.

'Yes, please,' Adam called back. 'We'll be down straight away.

Adam roused Joe, who was pleased at the thought of some thing to drink, though he was not familiar very much witl coffee. They dressed and descended the narrow staircase, int the main room of the house, now awash with sunlight. On th

'That is extraordinary!' said Adam. 'Who would have thought it?'

'Who indeed?' piped up Joe at last. 'I don't care so much where it came from. I just think it is perfect and I like it a lot. Some of the stuff you can get in the markets in London are ditchwater compared to this. Excuse me.' And with that he piled his plate with more bread and olives, and cut off two slices of cheese.

'So what are you going to do?' Guiseppe asked.

'Joe and I have a little money, which was not stolen, and the first thing I want to do is to write to my Captain James, and to our Commanding Officer, no matter how long the letters take to arrive, to tell them what befell us. And I want to write to Daisy, to tell her where I am.'

'Can you send letters from Malta?' asked Joe.

'We are not living in the Middle Ages,' Guiseppe responded. 'We've had stamps for postage since 1860, admittedly only a half-penny yellow at first, for postage on the island, but we've had the Malta Post Office for nearly thirty years. The colour of our own stamps has changed to green and you can get them at The Police Station in St. Julian's.'

'Where can I buy some paper and envelopes?' Adam began.

'Don't you worry about any of that,' said Guiseppe. 'We have plenty here in the church, and ink too. Just eat your breakfast and then we'll sort you out some shoes to wear.'

'Thank you,' said both boys, as they sliced off more cheese and grabbed a nectarine each.

'Just what are we to do when we leave here?' said Joe to Adam, alarmed at what the future held for them both.

'Well, I don't fancy staying here and making a new life in

193

Malta,' said Adam, 'so we have to move on, somehow. I think we must find a way to get to Italy, and eventually through France and home, or a ship from Valetta going back to Britain. God knows how.'

'I hope he does,' said Joe, 'because I've no idea,' said Joe, 'so if you don't mind I'll tag along, and leave some of the decision making to you.'

'I'm no expert on survival in Europe,' said Adam, half jokingly and feeling extremely nervous, 'but I think between us we could take a stab at getting home and back to Dorchester to clear our names.'

The priest returned with several pairs of shoes, tucked under his arm, and slung around his neck. He was also carrying a brown wooden box with a handle at either end and, as he slid the base out from the main body of the box, he emptied about forty coins on to the table in front of them.

'What's this?' exclaimed Joe.

'Well it's not exactly Christmas,' said Guiseppe, 'You said you had some money but not much. All this lot has been donated by visitors over the past couple of years, so you might as well have it. It's a really odd mixture of coins,' he said as he slid them around the surface of the table. 'There's some English, some Italian, quite a few French francs, for some reason, and a few of our own coins in there. What have you got?'

Adam and Joe showed him their treasure. A five pound note and three gold half sovereigns all being not quite so safely guarded away, but by now simply in their pockets.

'You won't be able to change those very easily,' said the priest, 'But there is a small office of The Anglo-Maltese Bank in St Julian's where you can by some *scudi* and some Maltese-English money in smaller amounts.'

'I saw The Anglo-Maltese Bank in the *Strada Reale* in Valetta,' said Adam.

'You can go there if you prefer, but you can also have all of these coins too,' said Guiseppe.

'It looks like a lot of cash,' said Joe, 'Are you sure?'

'It probably doesn't amount to much. It was given for charitable purposes,' Guiseppe continued, 'and you certainly need something if you are going to survive when you leave here. Where will you go, by the way?'

Adam began to explain about wanting to get back to England as they began to try on the various shoes Guiseppe had brought in.

'You'll not get a ship from Valetta going in that direction now that we are approaching October,' said Guiseppe. 'Your best option is to get to Sicily, and work your way up through Italy. It's a very long way, but you have some money, and actually if you're careful, and offer yourselves for work along the way, you could make it without getting into too much trouble.'

It was quite a daunting thought, but both of them were resigned to a long journey that they hoped would get them back home, and even clear their names from any desertion charge. Joe quickly found a pair of shoes that fitted. The Priest went off to find some paper and ink and Adam too, eventually, found a pair of shoes that suited and fitted.

Malta

19 September 1893

Dear Captain Russell, Sir,

I don't know how to start this letter, sir, nor what to say in it, and I dread to think what you must think of me, and my friend, Joe Smith. During the eight hours shore leave, in Malta, we were set upon by some ruffians, near the railway station where we had gone to get a drink and sit down in the sun. They knocked us out cold, and the next thing we knew we were tied up and left to fend for ourselves, having been robbed. The ship had already gone by the time we knew where we were, or what time of day it was.

A kindly priest on the island has helped us to get ourselves on our feet again, literally, with some shoes of which we were also robbed, and we are making plans to try to get home.

Do not know when you might receive this, sir, or when we may meet again. Please don't think too harshly of me, or of us, sir,

I am, sir, your obedient servant,

Adam Warkin, Pte.

Malta

19 September 1893

Dear Daisy,

I am writing this to you from the island of Malta in the Mediterranean Sea where we docked for a day before we should have travelled on to the Far East. I found a friend among the men in my battalion but the pair of us were robbed, then trussed up, carried away, and the ship left without us.

We are okay, and not too badly hurt. I will certainly recover though what will happen to my military career heaven only knows. I just hope that if we can get back to England our story will be believed.

I wish I was with you. I wish you were nearer than you are but, now that we are going to try to get home to England, perhaps every day I shall be a little closer to you again.

We have virtually no money, but somehow I will see you again, although nobody knows, least of all me or my friend, Joe, when that will be.

> *Always in my thoughts, Daisy,*
> *With much affection,*

> *Yours, Adam.*

With their new shoes, and a few directions from Guiseppe, it would not take Adam and Joe long to get to St. Julian's and find the Police Station.

'You'd better go in the morning,' said Guiseppe. 'Most places close from about 1.00pm in the afternoon, for a very long afternoon *siesta*.' And once he had explained what that meant, Adam understood; it was all to do with the very hot strong afternoon sun.

The two boys chatted as they made their way to St. Julian's the next morning and, sure enough, they found their way, unlike a few days earlier when they had felt totally lost.

Everybody spoke some kind of English, some better than others, and Adam bought stamps, enough to get his letters to Malaysia and to Britain. He was told that his letter to Daisy would go by ship to Italy, then overland for most of the rest of the way. The man who sold him the stamps had no idea when, or if, his other letter would travel eastwards half way around the world.

Adam and Joe also managed to change their large denominations of money down to some coins, or paper money, less conspicuous and more convenient to spend. They had a little English money, from Guiseppe's charity box, which would be useable on Malta. In the bank they managed to get nearly one hundred and fifty Italian lire to the pound, which gave Joe seven hundred and fifty lire for his five pound note. He hoped he had not been cheated.

'I hope so, too,' said Adam. 'At least we are in a proper bank!'

Adam handed over two of his gold half sovereigns and was offered one hundred and fifty-seven lire. Their money came in *centesimi* copper coins, there being one hundred *centesimi* to each lire, as well as some silver and gold lire coins in various denominations ranging from one to twenty lire. They now had some useable currency, which could be spent locally, and their hope was that, somehow, it would see them through the start of a long journey home.

Joe and Adam stayed about a week with Guiseppe. They got quite used to his comfortable and welcoming home. The got very used to his food, and even had two or three delicious cooked meals. Joe helped Guiseppe with the food preparation and washing of dishes, but Guiseppe wouldn't let Adam do too much.

He thought the gash on his leg was a bit more serious than Adam had first thought. He dressed it every day, to avoid infection and insisted that he rest it for a few days, and maybe use the time to think about how to get home. The priest managed to borrow a rather out-of-date map of Europe from one of his parishioners and Adam spent hours pouring over it and making notes.

Adam had also thought about their plight, and what might happen if, and when, they managed to get back to their Dorchester barracks.

'Guiseppe?' he said, one morning. 'Would you mind if I wrote an account of what happened to us these past few days and how we found you, so that we could all sign it as a record of us being victims of a crime, and then stuck here in St Julian's?'

'Not at all,' he replied, 'although you make it sound like a prison sentence being here!'

'Sorry, I didn't mean 'stuck here' at all,' said Adam. 'It's just that, not so long ago, I was really in trouble not having receipts for some things I had bought in the village, near to where I worked. I just thought a signed account might be some kind of insurance against being accused of desertion.'

'Well, I can certainly sign it if you write it. And if you like we can write it on some of the Diocese note paper. It still does not mean that you will absolutely be believed, but it might help.'

Joe willingly agreed to the idea when he came in. He had been outside picking olives and some fruit. Joe was getting to like this rural life, but it was time to move on.

'I know some fishermen who might take you to Sicily,' said Guiseppe one day.

'Really?' said Adam. 'That would be amazing.'

'It will take a few days to know which boats might be going in that direction, and they won't do it for nothing!' said Guiseppe.

'Fair enough,' said Adam. 'Can we find out how much, so we know what to give them?'

'I'll do that,' said Guiseppe. 'One or two fishermen owe me. I'll call in a favour or two!'

Adam studied where they might be going.

Adam and Joe spent the next couple of days washing their clothes, helping Guiseppe with some chores, picking fruit and generally getting ready to travel. Guiseppe found them a couple of bags, in which to carry their belongings, and provided them with a spare shirt each and some socks.

They each had a not-entirely-satisfactory razor, but Guiseppe managed to get them sharpened for them. They were still wearing their uniform tunics, but had no real protection in case of rainfall or cold weather, which they hoped would not come their way.

Guiseppe introduced them to a local fisherman who owned a boat large enough for them, in which to travel to Sicily. He was a fierce looking individual, swarthy faced, jet black hair slicked back from his face and large green eyes. His chin was black with several days beard growth and his entire appearance reminded Adam of what could have been a Mediterranean pirate.

Adam thought all he needed was a cutlass and a Jolly Roger flag,

He hardly spoke any English. All four sat in Guiseppe's large sunny room one morning, with a hand-drawn map of Adam's.

'This is Louis,' said Guiseppe. 'He will take you from St George's Bay to Pozzallo, on the southern tip of Sicily.'

Jien nieħu miegħek fid-dgħajsa tiegħi,' repeated Louis,

'What's he say?' said Joe.

'He said he'll take you in his boat,' said Guiseppe.

Jien nieħu miegħek fid-dgħajsa tiegħi,' repeated Louis, *'għall fluss.'*

'And what's *'Gaul Floos'* when it's at home?' said Joe.

Louis said he will take you *for money,'* said Guiseppe. 'But then, we already anticipated that.'

'That's okay,' said Adam. 'The real question is, how much?'

'I spoke to Louis the other day.' said Guiseppe, 'and he told me he is going fishing the day after tomorrow. He goes almost every day, but it looks as though winds might be fair to take you across to Sicily then. He wants a hundred and fifty lire.'

'A hundred and fifty!' exclaimed Joe. 'That's about a fifth of my entire fortune as it stands at the moment!'

'It does sound a lot,' said Adam, 'But we have to get home, and this is a start.'

'*Mija u ħamsin*,' Louis came in. '*Mija u ħamsin*,'

'Yes, okay,' Guiseppe came in. 'Gentlemen, he says he wants a hundred and fifty because it is out of his way. That 's what he's thinking.'

'*Huwa Triq twila*,' Louis came back. 'Long way.'

'Tell him we'll pay him a hundred, and some English silver,' said Joe.

'Wait a minute!' said Adam.

'A hundred and some English silver,' repeated Joe.

'Silver?' said Louis. 'English?'

'So he does speak some English,' said Joe. 'One hundred lire.'

'And English silver?' said Louis.

'Yes. Good silver,' said Joe very slowly.

'What are you talking about?' said Adam, but he was stopped by Louis, thrusting out his hand to grab Joe, and shaking it firmly.

'Done!' said Joe.

'Good. Done,' said Louis and got up to go. 'Two days. *Jumejn*.'

'*Grazzi*,' said Guiseppe to Louis.

'*Grazzi*,' indeed, said Louis, and Adam followed suit. Louis was gone.

. 'What did you do that for?' said Adam. 'How are we going to give him some English silver? Have you brought a tea service with you?'

'Leave it to me,' said Joe and tapped his nose.

Guiseppe was equally nonplussed, but Adam trusted Joe, in a can't-do-much-else-about-it kind of way, and they carried on preparing for the start of their journey home.

Two days later, Guiseppe led them back towards the place where he had first found them, and carried on to St George's Bay a little further north. The weather was, predictably, fine and there was indeed a fresh breeze blowing as Louis had predicted.

As they approached the small harbour, the boys could see a beautiful brightly painted boat, with a single sail. It looked very sturdy, but was painted to look jolly, in bright yellow, with blue and red markings and stripes. Near the bow on either side an 'eye' was painted which could not be missed.

'What a splendid boat!' exclaimed Adam.

'Looks sea-worthy enough,' said Joe.

'Oh, it is,' said Guiseppe. 'Have no fears on that account. These are called *luzzu*. And the eyes are the Eyes of Osiris. These boats have been common here, probably since the time of the Phoenicians. They have a double ended hull, for sailing, or rowing, and can actually go out in all weathers. You'll be safe enough.'

Louis saw them coming and jumped down on to the quay. The boys approached carrying their bags and feeling slightly nervous about putting to sea in the *luzzu*. They had, after all, only been to sea once in a ship, carrying over eight hundred people, and Joe had been violently sick in that.

'English silver,' said Louis. 'English silver?'

'Yes, you'll be fine,' said Joe to the man who was going to get them to Italy.

'You have money?' said Louis. '*Għandek flus?*'

'He wants your money,' said Guiseppe. 'Have you one hundred lire?'

'I have it,' said Joe, 'but he's not getting it until we get to… where is it?'

'Pozzallo,' said Guiseppe, 'on the southern tip of Sicily.'

Joe wafted some ten-lire notes, from where he had them safely hidden away, and counted out ten. 'When we get to Pozzallo,' he said loudly. 'Pozzallo'

'One hundred,' said Louis, '*mija!*

'In Pozzallo,' insisted Joe and Louis seemed to understand. Adam was impressed, but still wondered about the English silver they had apparently promised.

'Come,' said Louis, and he ushered them to board the boat, on which were a couple of other sturdy men with oars.

'Take care, you two,' said Guiseppe, as he offered his hand to them. 'Just keep a careful watch out for each other.'

'We shall,' said Adam, 'Believe me, we shall. They shook hands almost violently.

'Thanks for all the food and… actually, thanks for finding us in the first place,' said Joe.

'Yes, thanks very much,' said Adam. 'Can't really thank you enough.'

'We go,' said Louis as Joe, too, shook Guiseppe's hand.

'Stay safe,' shouted Guiseppe, as their craft edged its way out of the harbour area. Adam and Joe were sat near the stern and one of Louis' friends was unfurling a sail, which picked up the breeze and they gathered pace.

'Don't know if we'll ever come back to visit you,' shouted Adam,' but really I would love to.'

'We shall see,' said Guiseppe, who could, by now, hardly be heard by the pair of innocent passengers, who had put their trust in a virtual stranger, and his friends, in a tiny boat heading out to sea.

No more words were spoken, as the boys made themselves comfortable. The men in the *luzzu* seemed to know what they were doing. There were folded up nets in the bottom of the boat, but no mention was made of fishing, and certainly nothing the men did indicated that they were looking for fish.

The further they got out to sea the more fearful both Adam and Joe felt, although neither said a word. The men seemed confident in what they were doing and, despite Adam and Joe's apprehension, there seemed no hint of a threat to the two English travellers.

24

Sicily

Once they were out on to the open sea, their boat did indeed seem very small indeed. They were completely at the mercy of the water around them, and Adam began to wonder if Joe had ever learned to swim, not that he ventured to ask. Perhaps it was better not to know.

They were completely at the mercy of the men rowing the boat and of Louis, who was sitting astern, acting as navigator. He seemed to know instinctively where to head for and, occasionally, the craft veered to the left maybe to pick up a current, Adam thought.

The boys didn't know it, but it was something over forty nautical miles across this part of the Mediterranean, to reach Pozzallo. Guiseppe had told them it would take at least half a day, if the wind was good, and the sea calm enough. The men with the oars soon stood the oars up and re-set the single sail, which seemed to boost their speed, although neither of the boys could really judge whether they were making good progress or not. They were, still, in the hands of Louis and his men.

No words were spoken until, quite suddenly, Joe nudged Adam's arm and pointed out ahead. There was land and what looked like a town, although it was still along way off. The boat headed for that spot and Adam inwardly heaved a sigh of relief, even though they weren't yet quite there.

Louis suddenly jumped up and hauled in the sail. The two men resumed rowing, but Louis stopped them, and they were becalmed, a few hundred yards off the shore.

'You have money,' said Louis. 'One hundred, *mija!*'

'We have to pay them,' Adam said, and Joe also knew that they could not hold off paying what they had promised. Joe took out the one hundred lire and offered it to Louis.

'English silver,' said Louis, and Joe immediately pointed to the shore just ahead of them.

'We land first,' he almost shouted. 'Sicily, Pozzallo, silver,' and he rubbed his thumb and forefinger together in a kind of gesture of promise. 'Sicily first.'

It worked. Louis took the cash and told the rowers to take them in to the harbour, where they found a safe place to disembark. As a fishing boat, there were no questions asked, nobody was there to question their arrival, and the two boys started to get out.

'English silver,' Louis insisted.

'Give me those coins that Father Guiseppe gave us,' said Joe to Adam, and the coins were duly fished out from a leather purse inside Adam's bag. He palmed a small quantity of them, and Joe fished around, pulling out two silver English sixpences, showing the Queen facing left with her hair tied back in a kind of bun.

'English silver,' said Joe to Louis. 'Look. Silver, Queen Victoria, English Queen.'

Louis' eyes lit up, as he took the two coins and looked, biting into one. He pointed to his two rowing friends.

'Three silvers,' he said. 'Three, *tlieta.*'

'Two,' said Joe, even as Adam was looking for a third sixpence.

'*Tlieta,*' said Louis. 'One, two three,' pointing to himself and the other two.

'Here,' said Adam, as he found a third. 'Silver for you.'

All three men smiled as Adam handed over the third silver sixpence and the men beamed. The bags were quickly thrown on to the harbour, alongside the two boys, and the boat pulled away.

'Thank you,' shouted Adam. 'Thank you.'

'Thank you, *grazzi,*' shouted the men in the boat, as they rowed away. Louis held up the money and the coins.

'English silver. Good.'

The boat went out of sight, as Adam and Joe stood and looked. Joe was smiling. Adam was impressed.

'That was a stroke of genius,' he said to Joe. 'You do realise, don't you. We have just given them some real silver, but it's only another 12 lire or so. Brilliant!'

'I just hoped you had two, or three, as it turned out, in that coin collection, but I thought I had seen sixpences in there, so kept quiet about it in case you didn't approve.'

'I would probably have questioned whether we'd get away with it, but we did, or you did. Brilliant! It seems that Queen Victoria, whom I've never seen, although I know somebody who has, has saved the day for us.'

'Not so much a collection of coins as a collection of cons!' said Joe, smiling to himself. 'My previous life, on the streets of London, may have its uses.'

'We're going to need all the cons, or tricks of your trade, we can muster if we are to get home before we reach old age!' Adam joked, and they picked up their bags and headed for the town. It was time to formulate another plan, but not until they had something to eat and a drink. Their next objective was to get to mainland Italy. The autumn was approaching.

It did not take them long to find a café on the street in Pozzallo, and by now they felt confident enough to ask for olives and wine, both of which appeared to be plentiful and cheap. They ordered bread and some ham, which they saw somebody else eating, and were able to point to. Gradually it dawned on them that they might need somewhere to stay the night.

The café had a room available. After a complicated piece of choreography, involving drawings and gestures, the proprietor, resplendent with both a very large apron and equally large moustache showed them upstairs to a room with two beds, but not much else.

'Twenty lire,' said the owner, '*Venti* lire,' at which point Joe took out some of his cash, being careful not to reveal how much he had in his possession.

'*Venti* lire,' said the owner which Adam thought sounded like twenty.

'Offer him twenty,' he said to Joe, which he did, and which the man took.

He was fully expecting the man to ask for another twenty from himself. But he didn't. He disappeared and returned quite soon with a big jug of wine, two glasses, and some more bread and olives.

'*Grazzi*,' said Adam, now confident that the word *grazzi* was very useful as an agreeable 'thank you'.

'S'good,' said the man as he made to leave them. '*Grazie*.' It was a slightly different word, but the difference did not register with Adam. The man pointed to the shutters at the window of the room. The shutters were closed, to keep the heat of the day out from the cool interior.

'Open, morning,' said the man. *'Mattina, aperta,'* he repeated, as he demonstrated opening the shutters. 'Morning.'

'Adam realised what he meant, from having stayed with Guiseppe for several days. The shutters could allow in a breeze or cool air early in the mornings, but needed to be closed at night, and for most of the hot sunny days.

'Open tomorrow,' said Adam, which seemed to satisfy the owner.

'*Grazie*,' said Joe as the door closed.

The evening was wearing on, and the two boys crashed out on the beds with tunics, shoes and socks thrown over the foot of the beds in glorious disarray. They had been pleased to find that the door locked from the inside, and duly turned the key. They were asleep within minutes, both of them with their bags safely tucked under the beds, but within touching distance.

Nothing more disturbed them until the morning light came through the shuttered window. Adam opened the shutters, to let some daylight in and then spent some time pouring over a map, which he had managed to draw before they left Malta.

'If we can get to Catania or Lentini on the east coast, believe it or not there is a train from there to the north and to Messina, which is only eight miles across from the mainland of Italy. So we need to get to Catania and then to Messina,' said Adam to Joe as he came to and sat up. 'I've no idea exactly how far it is but it looks like at least forty miles from here to Syracuse and then another sixty from there to Lentini.'

'We'd better get going then,' said Joe, as he sprang out of the bed. They managed to get some hot water, shaved rather precariously, then dressed and made ready to leave.

Downstairs, they were offered eggs, boiled, with more bread and hot coffee. It was a magnificent breakfast in the circumstances, and then in came Mr. Ashton, one Leopold Ashton.

'And just what are you two doing here in Pozzallo?' said the genial looking gentleman who approached them over their eggs and coffee.

Adam looked up. The man standing next to their table pulled up another chair and sat down with them. He looked distinguished in his appearance, with a light-weight linen suit and open necked shirt. He was clean-shaven, with auburn hair, well cut. His face was indeed genial, smiling and healthy looking. He looked at them kindly, with deep blue eyes.

'You look a very unlikely couple of visitors to Pozzallo.'

'Are you English?' said Joe, offering his hand as he put down his coffee cup.

'I most certainly am, although my wife is Sicilian. We live to the north of here, on a small estate near Catania at the foot of Mount Etna.'

'I've heard of Mount Etna,' said Adam, enthusiastically.

'Well, that's pretty well where I live,' said the gentleman, 'And, by the way, my name is Leopold Ashton. I produce olives and grapes as well as orchard produce, and sell it on the island wherever I can.'

'I'm Adam Warkin,' Adam offered, with his hand extended.

'And I'm Joe, Joe Smith,' said Joe. 'We're both stranded here. We're in the British Army, but we were robbed and knocked unconscious in Malta, and our ship left without us.'

'We're hoping to make our way home,' Adam said.

'You've got a long way to go!' said Leopold. 'You've managed to get into Italy, so I presume you want to get to the mainland and work your way through Italy to France?'

'That's right,' said Adam.

'And eventually home?'

'Right again. We know it's a long way, but we don't really have much choice.'

'And you stayed here last night?' Leopold asked.

'We did,' said Joe, 'and now I think we need to travel north. Adam, is that right?'

'Yes,' Adam replied. 'Mr Ashton, are you're down here to sell your produce?' Adam knew that Mount Etna was about eighty miles north of where they had spent the night.

'It absolutely is, and do call me Leo, everybody else does,' said Leopold, 'It's more a trip for getting orders, which I will bring down or send down later. People like the produce from the slopes of Mount Etna where the volcanic soil is very fertile and the harvests are rich in quality. There's always a demand for my olives, and most of my other produce.'

'When was the last time Mount Etna erupted?' said Adam.

'About the most serous recent eruption was in 1852,' said Leopold warming to his subject, 'But the land around the mountain is still eagerly sought after. It's been both a curse and a blessing, to local people, for generations.'

'But it is still worth living there?' asked Adam.

'Absolutely,' came the reply, 'On the one hand, violent outbursts of the volcano, throughout history, have destroyed large parts of Catania, whilst, on the other hand, the volcanic ashes yield fertile soil. In eighteen fifty-two it produced millions of cubic feet of lava and lahars covered more than three square miles of the volcano's flanks in lava flows.'

'*Lahars*?' said Adam, always eager for a new word or two.

'A lahars is the violent mud and lava flow coming down the mountain side, carrying everything with it in its path; ice, water, rock, vegetation. It can be truly terrifying. The last eruption flattened any timber-built houses and nearly destroyed the town of Zafferana.'

'Wow! exclaimed Joe. 'Sounds very dangerous.'

'But the mountain is still called *Mama Etna* by the locals, for the bounty it gives to our communities. Beautiful green pistachios, ruby-red strawberries, olives and wine providing almost all the income generated there,' continued Leopold.

'Hope there isn't an eruption due any time, if we're travelling that way north.' Joe sounded decidedly anxious.

'Is that the way you want to go?' said Leopold.

'It certainly is,' said Adam. 'Can you help us in any way?'

'Not today, but tomorrow I'm going about half way back, as far as Syracuse. I can give you a lift, if you want, in my *caretto*.'

'*Caretto*?' said Adam. 'Another word I haven't heard before.'

'It's my horse-drawn cart, and there's room for the three of us if you like,' said Leopold. 'And the following day, we should complete the journey back to my estate.'

'I'm sure we can stay one more night here,' said Joe. 'Can we ask the owner?'

'Well, you two sort that out, and I'll meet you here about this time tomorrow. As for today, I've got lots of people to see, and from whom I can hopefully confirm orders.'

'Thank you, er ..Leo,' said Adam. 'Much appreciated.'

'My pleasure,' Leo replied. 'Always nice to meet fellow

Englishmen.'

They confirmed with the café owner that they could keep the room, gave him another twenty lire, which seemed to please him, and looked around the town for most of the day, stopping to drink or just observe the locals.

'There's Leopold,' said Joe suddenly. Their new friend was passing them by, in the most lavishly decorated and colourful, horse-drawn cart. It was covered in gaily painted designs and scenes. It was a light, two wheeled cart, being drawn by one horse, with Leopold sat atop of the wagon, waving to them as he passed.

'See you tomorrow,' came the greeting. 'This is my *Caretto Siciliano*. A Sicilian Cart!'

'It's amazing,' said Adam back to him, admiring the extraordinary vehicle. 'Yes, we shall see you tomorrow.'

They ordered a splendid meal at their newly found temporary home that evening.

'You will have *arancini*,' suggested the owner. 'Typical food for Catania,' he continued. And he served them some stuffed rice-balls, coated in breadcrumbs and deep fried. They were shaped into cones and fascinated both Adam and Joe.

'Delicious,' indicated Joe, as he tucked into the *arancini*. 'Good shape!' He made a point with his two hands to show he admired the shape of them.

'Like Mount Etna, the mountain,' said the café owner. 'Typical food for Catania.' He was repeating himself now with his limited English, but the two boys enjoyed their meal, which came with bread, the ubiquitous olives and a carafe of wine.

The night passed, very hot, and not very comfortable, but they eventually slept, and were satisfied that they would be able to achieve the next leg of their long journey home tomorrow.

Morning brought them some more coffee, eggs and bread, and they made sure their bags were packed and ready after the morning meal. And they waited. It was a full hour and a half before Leopold appeared, looking less than pleased.

'Sorry to keep you waiting,' he began. 'It's not all gone according to plan, but I will tell you on the way.'

The two boys thanked their café owner, whose name they had never discovered, and mounted the *caretto* gingerly, storing their bags under the seat and taking their place beside Leopold. They were away, with a flick of the reins being held by Leo, and soon they were on the edge of the town, heading out to the countryside, which was yellow and green with vegetation, crops and the occasional wooden houses.

'Did anything go wrong with your business locally?' said Adam.

'It wasn't entirely straightforward,' began Leopold. 'In the past ten years, thousands of Sicilians have left the island, seeking a new life in America. Sicily has become somewhat industri-alised, especially in the west, near the capital of Palermo. So I have fewer and fewer people willing to pick the crops.

'The local people have never been rich. They are peasant stock, and usually satisfied with their lot in life, but other moves have been made amongst the islanders which threaten our way of life.'

The *caretto* was jogging along nicely and Adam was intrigued.

'So maybe your usual customers cannot buy so much of your produce?' he said.

'That's about it,' said Leopold, 'But there's more to it than that. Sicily's reputation as a food and wine paradise is in jeopardy.'

'Jeopardy?' said Joe, not wishing to be outdone in asking the meaning of new words!

'It means being in danger of being destroyed or changed beyond recognition,' said Adam. 'Threatened.'

'True,' said Leopold, as the horse in front of them continued along the coastal road, without needing any encouragement from the driver.

'It's several things,' continued Leopold. 'About thirteen years ago, in the autumn, and then again in the new year of 1880 and 1881, an aphid appeared on the island, a tiny insect that sucks the life out of plants and fruit, and in our case, out of the vines which produced the grapes. Called *Phylloxera*, it devastated entire crops and nobody seemed to be able to get rid of it. They tried sprays and destroying acres of vines, burning them, and thereby losing all the income from that crop. It would not go away.'

'That's terrible,' began Adam, not quite understanding the enormity of what the problem had caused.

'You can say that, and more,' said Leopold.

'What happened?' said Joe.

'In the following few years, some vineyards were wiped out. We were very lucky indeed. Mount Etna can boast some of Europe's oldest vines thanks to this soil that, in combination with this side of the island's being so close to the sea, has never played host to the scourge of *phylloxera*. I had a larger area to nurture, and other crops I could rely on.

'Gradually some people have introduced new vines from overseas. I've bought thousands of new vines, to play safe, and, only in the past year or two, have we managed to grow them without any bother from aphids. But the insect is still there, in some other parts of the island and we dread it spreading again. It could be fifty years before we are free of it completely.'

'So why do some of your regular customers not want to buy your produce?' Adam enquired. 'Are there fewer and fewer people living on Sicily?'

'That's one element of the problem. The aphids are not helping, and politics is looming large in Italy, particularly in Sicily.' Leopold did not know if he could explain the intricacies of how the population was shifting in its support for, or adherence to, old customs and systems of government.

'Let me try to put it in a nutshell,' said Leopold. 'Since 1889 there have been groups of workers, very dissatisfied with their working conditions, some on estates, where peasants working the land wanted better sharecropping and rental agreements. There was also unrest in some in mining and manufacturing industries.'

'And the groups got stronger?' said Adam, having heard back home about trades unions, and remembering the news he had read about disgruntled workers rioting in Trafalgar Square. 'And they made more demands?'

'All true,' said Leopold, 'and that is one of the reasons why the population has decreased. Thousands have decided they've had enough and have emigrated to The United States. There are less people eating my olives, or drinking my wine, and the people who grow the produce on my estate want higher and higher wages for their work.

'The crops are all mine by right. I produce them, I process them, I sell them and I pay all those who live on my estate for their time and their work, even when the harvest is not so good. But it seems some are groups coming together, called

216

Fasci, making a lot of trouble for landowners – and factory and mine owners.'

'Who speaks for the *Fasci*?' he asked.

'Whoever has the loudest voice, and, in some cases, whoever has the biggest club to beat the landowner with!' Leopold responded.

It took them almost the entire day to cover the thirty-eight miles or so to Syracuse. The sun was hot, even for late September. October was looming large, Adam thought, as it occurred to him that they had been away from England for nearly a month now.

'Did you find us in the café in Pozzallo by chance?' Adam suddenly enquired. The road stretched out before them, but clearly they had all had enough of politics for the time being.

'Not really,' said Leopold. 'I told you my wife was Sicilian, an Italian woman. Well, your café owner is her father. He is my father-in-law. He told you you had turned up, almost out of nowhere, and thought I might be the man to help. I just happened to be in the town on business.'

'That makes sense,' said Joe. 'And the owner could speak a bit of English, too.'

'My Italian has improved since our marriage, but we do speak English, a little, when we are together, such as at Christmas. His name is Luigi.'

'We really should have asked his name,' said Adam. 'What is Christmas like in Sicily?'

'Well, maybe you will find out, if you cannot get enough money to travel any further on from this island,' said Leopold.

'Is that an invitation?' Joe cheekily responded.

'Well, let's say that if you wanted a few weeks' working for me, you could stay with us. Luigi lives alone now in the café. He will come to our house for Christmas, and my wife, Anna, will cook for everybody. Then, perhaps, in the New Year, you will have saved some money for the train fare through the mainland of Italy.'

That all sounded very comforting to the two boys, although they had not realised just how long they might have to stretch out their homeward journey. The *caretto* clattered on and, by late afternoon, was approaching Syracuse. The sandy-coloured houses were visible in the distance and the deep green olive trees were becoming more abundant with olives, on either side of the road, as they got nearer.

'We cannot complete the journey home to Catania tonight,' said Leopold. 'I usually stay with a friend here, when I am travelling to and from home, so we shall have to see if there is room for you, or if we have to find another room to rent. Do you still have some money?'

'Oh, yes,' said Adam. 'In fact, Joe has more money than I have, but we're surviving this journey together, so there is certainly enough for another night's accommodation.'

'Good,' said Leo. He pulled the horse to the right and turned a corner off the main road. The *caretto* wheels ground into the stones of the road as it turned and sent dust flying up behind them. It was a maze of smaller streets, with some children playing and washing hanging from balconies.

Suddenly, he pulled the horse to a standstill by the side of a large house, where there was a middle-aged man, wearing grey trousers, a rough-looking striped shirt and braces, sitting on the doorstep. He was smoking a pipe.

'Roberto,' Leopold almost shouted at him. '*Roberto, saluti a te.*'

'*Saluti,*' responded Roberto, as he stood up and came to shake the hand of Leopold. A small boy, about nine years of age, suddenly appeared, and smiled at Leopold. He then took hold of the horse, very proficiently, Adam thought.

'*Amici,*' said Leopold, '*miei amici.* My 'friends' '

'*Saluti,*' Roberto addressed this word to the two boys. '*Mi chiamo Roberto.*'

'Adam,' said Adam, extending his hand.

Joe followed suit and said, 'Me, Joe.'

'*Benvenuto*, Joe *e* Adam.' Roberto managed the two new names very well.

Leopold had jumped down from the *caretto* by now, and the two men hugged, in a way which nether of the two boys had ever seen before. They seemed very pleased to see each other, although it did occur to Adam that Leopold must have stayed here a few days earlier, on his way to Pozzallo. They were clearly very good friends.

Words were spoken, which neither Adam nor Joe understood a word of until suddenly Leopold spoke.

'You can stay here with us for one night,' he said, 'And Roberto wants nothing for your board or meal.'

'You are a good friend,' said Joe. 'Thank you very much. *Grazie.*'

'*Grazie,*' said Adam and extended his hand again. Roberto suddenly grabbed Adam and gave him a bear hug that took him completely by surprise, and almost squeezed the breath out of him.

'*Benvenuto,*' said Roberto as he finally let go, and Adam rescued his bag from the *caretto*. The small boy then led the horse, and the *caretto,* away and disappeared around the side of the house. All four went inside the house and through to a cool courtyard leading out from the large downstairs room. And there they sat, for most of the evening, drinking some very good red wine and eating cheese and bread, olives and fruit.

At about eight o'clock, Roberto's wife, to whom they had not yet been introduced, brought out an enormous dish of spaghetti with anchovies and sardines. She was followed by the small boy.

'My wife, Sofia,' said Roberto. '*Mia moglie.*' Then he continued, 'This Adam,' pointing at Joe.

'No, I'm Adam,' said Adam, 'and this is Joe'

Sofia responded. 'Hello, hello,' but said nothing more.

'And this our son, Flavio,' said Roberto, very proudly, as the boy bowed to the guests.

Everybody tucked into the fish dish with considerable relish. Neither Joe nor Adam had experienced very much of spaghetti, or any kind of pasta in the past, but Adam felt very much at home, eating something entirely new to him, with his friend, Joe, and with Leopold, Roberto and his wife with their son.

Adam kept saying '*grazie*, this is good!' until the others laughed at his constant repetition.

The two older men, Roberto and Leopold, spent the rest of the evening talking, sometimes quite agitatedly with a conversation in which neither Adam nor Joe could participate. They were shown, by Flavio, to a room at the top of the house, which had one very small window in the eve of the roof. He bowed again and left them to get a night's sleep. It did not take them long to drift off into a peaceful slumber, after a day of being shaken on the *caretto*, under the hot Sicilian sun.

The following morning the two boys went downstairs when

they thought they heard the family moving about. Sure enough, Sofia was busying herself laying food on the table in the courtyard again; tomatoes, cheese and more bread with a steaming hot pot of coffee, and some pieces of fruit.

'You eat,' she said, as Roberto and Leopold also appeared. Adam could hardly believe that they were still being treated as honoured guests by complete strangers, and wondered if the same hospitality would apply in England were their situations reversed.

'We shall have to leave soon after breakfast,' said Leopold. 'We have about another forty miles to go to my estate and it would be good to arrive their sometime during the afternoon.' Everybody ate their fill, the boys gathered their bags and loaded them on to the *caretto* again, which Flavio had very efficiently brought around to the front of the house.

Adam glanced at Flavio, the boy who had bowed to them several times, but had not ventured to speak.

He saw himself, at about that age, skipping up and down the road in Melton Ford, racing his friends, Will and Helena, helping at the blacksmiths, and, above all, settling into Mrs Redman's armchair to learn to read and write. He pondered how far he had come since those days.

He was now a strapping, and good looking, young man in his early twenties, not quite six feet tall with hair cut short by the army barber, healthy and finding his way in the world. His eyes still sparkled.

Finding his way, stranded on a Mediterranean island, was not quite what he had anticipated, but he was here, with at least one good friend and he felt secure enough to believe that things would turn out right, in due course. Outside Roberto's house, young Flavio was holding the horse steady while bags were loaded in, and the travellers made their goodbyes.

'*Grazie*,' was on everybody's lips and several hugs were exchanged until finally Leopold said, 'Everybody on board, let's go. *Addio per ora*, Goodbye for now.'

'*Addio*,' said both Adam and Joe, quickly picking up what that meant. '*Addio, Flavio.*' They boy looked slightly embarrassed and smiled back, with the tiniest of waves.

Leopold steered the horse and *caretto* through the back streets, until they found themselves on the main coast road again, turning right to go further north. It was another clear and bright day, with the sun shining and rising slowly above them to their right. They had plenty of water and a journey of about forty miles ahead of them.

'You had plenty to talk about with your friend last night, Leo,' said Adam to Leopold.

'Plenty indeed,' he replied. 'The *Fasci* in the west of the island are gaining strength and power and influence. There have been strikes and violent incidents on some estates, and in factories. This past summer a drought did not help matters at all, and so much of the wheat crop has failed. It leads to terrible mistrust between the peasants, the landowners and local government.'

'And what about your estate?' said Adam.

'Some of the estates and factory owners in the west have appealed to the government, to bring in troops to calm the situation. Fortunately we, in the east of the island, have not seen too much of this and, on my own estate, I'd like to think that we have a good relationship with those who grow the crops an harvest them,'

'Why are the groups called *Fasci*?' ventured Joe.

'The word *Fascio* means a stick,' replied Leopold. 'If you have a single stick you can break it easily, but put a lot of sticks together, into a bundle, and nobody can break them.

'The *Fasci* consider themselves as bundles of unbreakable people, fighting for a greater share of the wealth of farming and manufacturing. But if there's been a bad harvest, as we had this year, with a terrible drought, and mass emigration, there is perhaps, not enough wealth to go around.'

Adam pondered all this information. Nobody knew how the year would end, or if any peaceful solution to the riots and killings in the west could be found.

'And what about staying with you and working for a while to save some money?' said Adam suddenly. 'Is that what you meant when we spoke yesterday?'

'Of course you can,' said Leo. 'The olive crop is ripe and any that are not picked will go to waste. I will never let that happen, if I can help it. The local people are harvesting the grapes, I hope! There is fruit also, and I hope we can make enough money to manage through to the next year.'

Of course it had never occurred to either Adam or Joe that a farmer has to sell what he grows, and look after the land, in order to survive from one year to the next. Adam knew all about growing fruit and foodstuff in the gardens at The Manor House, but they were hardly on any kind of breadline, and always had plenty to eat and plenty to spare. He could not envisage a situation in which the workers simply revolted against the very people who were paying them.

He thought, and drifted in and out of a shallow sleep, as the *caretto* trundled along, putting mile after mile behind them. In truth, all three of the passengers could have been asleep and the horse would have safely taken them to their destination. They all relaxed, in the warmth of the sun, and, one after the other, almost taking it in turns, they closed their eyes.

They were heading for Catania and Leopold's estate in almost the shadow of Mount Etna. Not long after midday, when they had stopped for a drink, and some bread and cheese, which had been provided by Roberto's wife, they were heading towards what looked like a small settlement or village when Adam became puzzled.

'What's that?' he said, pointing to the buildings across to their left. 'There. Looks like a fire.'

'That is a neighbour of mine,' said Leo. 'What on earth is going on?' And he pulled on the reins to steer the horse to the path on their left. The little group approached the house. It seemed that a barn had been burning, not the owner's house itself.

Leopold jumped down and simply left the horse to graze on some grass, as he ran towards the buildings. Adam and Joe were left there, wondering if it had been some kind of accident. Neither of them said a word.

After a short while, Leopold returned, jumped into the *caretto*, pulled the horse's head up from his grassy snack, and turned the vehicle around, making headway back to the main road.

There seemed to be some kind of urgency in the movement of the *caretto* now. It was as if Leopold wanted more speed, but did not want to wear out the poor horse. He just seemed to be encouraging it to get home.

'Was the fire deliberately set?' said Adam.

'Is your friend in serious trouble?' Joe enquired.

'One of the local branches of the Facisti have been making demands on my friend, who runs that estate, and the burning of an empty barn is a warning that they mean business,' Leopold was telling them.

'My friend has told me of strikes and arrests in the west. Now I just want to get home, to see if there is any unrest amongst the people on my estate. I just do not see how I am going to escape the problems and yet...'

'And yet you have always had good relations with those who live and work nearby to you,' Adam completed what he thought Leopold was trying to say.

'We have not long passed the town of Lentini,' said Leopold. 'That is where the train service to the north begins, which could eventually take you to Messina. From there you can get across to the Italian mainland. Maybe my friend has just been unlucky. Maybe, if the Fascisti had really meant business, his entire home would be in ashes by now.'

'Do you think we can still work for you?' said Joe. 'Maybe we can help in some way.' Leopold laughed, half heartedly.

'Who knows? If they haven't burnt down my house and my barns and set fire to my fields, maybe you two will be the only ones working this autumn.'

'And is the crop not yet all in?' Adam asked.

'This is September,' said Leopold. 'By now we should be harvesting all the grapes and all the olives. Millions of them. I hope it can be done, in which case I hope also that my workers and I can come to some kind of agreement about the estate. We have always got on so well, but political unrest does strange things to ordinary people.'

Nothing more was said for many miles, until during the

latter part of the afternoon Leopold pointed.

'We are passing the town of Catania,' he said. 'The railway comes through here too, and my estate is just about an hour away now. On the approach slopes to the mount itself.'

'See,' he said eventually. 'Over there, as the land rises to the left. Can you see a group of buildings and a large spread of fields?'

'Yes, indeed,' said Adam. 'Leo, do you mind if I ask you something else, or make some kind of suggestion?'

'When we get home, my friend.' Leo replied. 'I am eager to see my wife now.'

'Have you any children?' said Joe.

'Two,' said Leo, 'but they are older now. Our daughter Donna is recently married and went with her husband to Palermo, the capital of Sicily. Our son, Tony, is at the University of Catania, in a college learning agriculture and food. Ready to take over from me, maybe!'

Within half an hour the *caretto* had taken them off the main road, along dusty paths, through long lines of trees and vines, where Leopold had been pleased to wave to some workers harvesting grapes, who all greeted him. He seemed less than pleased, however and mumbled to himself something about there not being many people at work.

'Where is everybody?'

Eventually, they approached a large stone house and Leopold brought the *caretto* to a standstill, outside the front door. He jumped down and took the horses reins, telling the boys to alight and take their bags to the front door. Quite suddenly the lady of the house, as they thought she must be, emerged, wiping her hands on a large apron. She ran to hug Leopold.

'This is Anna,' he said to the boys. 'Anna, these are my two friends, whom I met in Pozzallo. They will stay with us for a while.'

'If that is okay,' said Adam quickly.

'Of course it is okay,' she replied instantly in slightly broken English. 'My husband is a good judge of character, so if you are friends of his you can be friend to me. Come.'

Leopold, by now, had released the horse from the *caretto* and led it across to the nearest gate, into a field, where it ran and jumped for a few moments, before finding a water trough and settling down to chew more grass.

'Come in, come in,' said Leopold. 'Don't stand on ceremony out here. Anna, has there been any trouble? We came across the burned out barn of one of our friends, near Catania, where some Fascisti had clearly been making their views known to the landowner.'

By now they had all entered the front door of the spacious house. The two boys put down their bags and followed Anna into the hall, a large airy room, where there was wine and fruit on a central table.

'Some men want to see you this evening.' she said. 'They are not angry, yet, but say that their local *Fasci* are demanding to know what concessions you will give them from this year's harvest. They will come at eight o'clock.'

Adam looked at Leopold whose face was almost ashen.

Everybody in the room knew that if Leopold could not come up with some ideas to appease the local people, then the mood of the peasants and workers on the estate could turn very ugly, and perhaps violent, very quickly. That was the impression Anna had clearly given to her husband.

The mood of the people of the west of Sicily was clearly spreading very quickly, and maybe, just maybe, Leopold had been given a stay of decision making by being away on business. But now the men were due to arrive at eight o'clock.

Anna had told them that the meal would be delayed until after the men had been. They had just over three hours before the meeting.

'I just hope we have a house to eat in after they have been,' said Leopold.

'May I make a suggestion?' said Adam.

'Of course,' Leo replied. 'We have only known each other for a few days, but you seem wise enough, even if you were stupid enough to get robbed in Malta!'

'We're very young, and I'm the stupid one,' said Joe quickly. 'Adam is clever.'

'I'm not so sure,' continued Adam, 'but if I may, I will make a suggestion. I know nothing of the desperation or the mood of the people who work for you on your land, but it seems you may have had very good relations over the years?'

'We have indeed,' said Leo.

'My father's family worked nearby,' said Anna, 'and when I met Leopold he was an Englishman abroad with plenty of money, who bought this estate, and together we have developed many friendships among the people.'

'I was lucky to inherit a very small fortune from an ancient aunt. I loved Italy and came to live here. You have met Anna's father in the café in Pozzallo. He is a wonderful man. Now, we don't know what will happen.' Leo did not have tears in his eyes, but he was talking as though some of this idyllic lifestyle was about to end.

'Please, may I?' Adam said. 'This may be the stupidest idea since time began, and since crops were first planted here a thousand years ago, but one never knows.

'A few years ago, when I was just seventeen, I was robbed on a train. The wretch took every penny I had, a full five pounds in English money, which was a fortune to me, and my leather wallet, which I had newly bought for a journey to see the lady who taught me to read.'

'Go on,' said Leo.

'Yes, please,' said Joe. 'I've never heard this.'

'Well, I thought it was the end of everything, until my good lady teacher told me that I would recover. I remember her saying, 'Well you earned five pounds, you've lost five pounds and you will earn five pounds again'! And I did.'

'If I lost my estate to a rampaging mob of fire-setters, it would be rather more difficult to replace,' said Leopold kindly.

'Agreed,' said Adam. 'A few years later, I lost my job on an estate in England, quite suddenly. Just thrown out because I had, allegedly, stolen some things, which I hadn't. My world collapsed around me, but I was rescued by some kind actions of others, and some good thinking and planning.'

'Where is this going?' said Joe.

'Well, maybe the stupidest idea of the year,' said Adam, 'is for you to offer the people on your estate the entire crop this year, for themselves.'

'I beg your pardon?' It was Leopold leaning forward, unbelieving.

'They are angry at the conditions of workers elsewhere, so they have heard. They think they are offered a bad deal every-where by landowners, so they have heard. Well, tell them the crop is theirs for this year, to make up for any years they have not been satisfied. Show them you are not just generous, but magnanimous. I lost everything, or so I thought. But it came right with time.'

'What would we live on?' said Anna.

'No, wait,' said Leopold, 'hear Adam out.'

'Where do you keep the transport for delivering crops, olives and so on to buyers? And machines for crushing olives, where are they?'

'They are in sheds and barns,' said Leo.

'Brick-built?' said Adam.

'Yes, almost all of them. And they can be locked, if this is going where I think it's going.'

'Precisely,' said Adam. 'Tell the men who come, that this year the entire crop is theirs, and that you will sell it for them. You only want payment from them for transport and the use of the equipment in your barns, which they do not have. Agree a small price for that. You must sound generous, but it could just take the wind out of their sails.

'It could give you the chance to retain the entire crop, admittedly not yours this year, but maintain your land and house, and, who knows, maybe some credit with the local people. I recovered my five pounds a lot quicker than I thought, and that theft on the train is now a distant memory.'

'It could just work.' said Leopold. 'Definitely, the daftest idea I have ever heard, but well worth making the gesture and deflating their demands by offering more than they are asking.'

'Genius!' said Joe.

'Not really,' said Adam. 'We shall see. It could only work for one year. Leo cannot give away his entire crop every year.'

'So what happens next year?' said Anna. 'Can we afford to give away all this year's crop, Leo?'

'Actually, yes.' he replied. 'But I agree with the question. Another year could bring another knife-edge situation. What do we do next year?'

'One year at a time,' said Adam. 'I read a story once. It was probably as daft as my idea. But I loved the story.'

'Come on then!' said Joe. 'Don't stop now.'

'A thousand years ago, a poor man, in a medieval village, was wrongly accused of a crime, and the king said that the man would be executed. The man was beside himself with fear, and sat in his dark dungeon cell, chained to the wall, awaiting his fate.'

'I think I know how he felt,' offered Leopold, half joking.

'The man asked to speak to the king's chamberlain,' Adam continued, 'and when the man arrived in the cell he told the prisoner to speak, and be quick about it! *If you let me out of here and into the King's service,* said the man, *I will look after His Majesty's white horse and within a year I will make the horse talk.*'

'Quite a story,' said Leopold. 'I'm intrigued'

'The chamberlain went back to the king, and told him that his prisoner could make his horse talk, within a year, so the king being a very proud man, and keen to outdo all his rivals, could not resist. Tell him that he can have one year's freedom, if he cares for my horse and teaches the horse to talk. *I will be the richest king in all the lands – with a talking horse.*'

'Maybe a year is all *we* need,' said Leo still listening intently.

'Well, the chamberlain went back to the prisoner,' continued Adam, 'unchained him from the wall, gave him good clothes to wear and brought him to the king. *So you can make my horse talk?* said the king, *and if you do, you shall have your freedom. If you fail, you will die.* '

All the other three in the room were now on the edge of their seats.

Adam continued, '*You're a fool*, said the chamberlain, *you'll never achieve this. It is impossible. It certainly looks like it*, said the man, now holding the king's horse and himself, dressed in a fine tunic. *But remember this. I do have a year. And in that year many things can happen. I might die. The king might die. The horse might die!*

The others were now amused and relaxed.

'*Or...*' said the man, '*... the horse might talk!*'

Everyone in the room laughed out loud. 'We shall give away this year's crop,' said Leopold, 'and see what another year brings. That is assuming, of course, that the men coming this evening will listen at all.' The atmosphere was lighter than it had been for nearly an hour, and Adam and Joe were invited to go upstairs, unpack their things and wash the dust off their faces.

'If I may ask,' said Adam. 'May we sit in with you? Perhaps they will think you have two English friends here, even if we won't understand a word you are saying. Just moral support, really.'

'I think that is a good idea, and I can confer with you, perhaps, even if I do not really need to! You are a wise young man.'

'Not really,' said Adam, 'but if it helps. And may I suggest that we offer food, and some wine? Always a good softener! Have you time to make any *arancini*. We had them at your father's café and they were so good.'

'I will,' said Anna, 'and perhaps some *cipollina.*'

'You'd certainly like those,' Leopold came in. 'Puff pastry with onion, tomato and *prosciutto* filling! Delicious.'

'Fantastic. Come on, Adam,' said Joe. 'Let's go and freshen up.'

'*Prosciutto*?' said Adam.

'It's just ham,' said Anna. 'But it is Sicilian ham!'

There were nearly three hours to go before the local men arrived. Some low tables were set, wine glasses and plates laid out and as many chairs as could be squeezed into the main room of the house. Somehow, the atmosphere seemed tense as the hour approached.

The first group of men arrived, several minutes early, and shuffled around outside the house. They were looking furtive, as if they did not want to be there on their own, and they cheered up with ever increasing volumes of conversation, as more and more arrived. Eventually, there were twenty-five or so, all dressed similarly.

The men were in black, grey or brown trousers, mostly ill-fitting with a belt or braces, and in some cases both. They wore rough fabric shirts, again grey or dark blue. Their clothing all seemed to be made from wool or linen.

The women were in wide skirts, predictably in dark blue, black or grey and blouses of lighter colours, with some embroidered decoration down the front. All the women wore white head scarves, covering the top of their heads, and tied under the chin.

Leopold went out to invite them in. He was somewhat rebuffed unceremoniously, as the men refused to budge from the front of the house. The women stayed at the back, and

Leopold again tried to welcome them into house. They would not budge, and clearly wanted to stay where they were, ready to speak.

Suddenly Anna and Adam appeared, Adam, taking a somewhat military pose, with his English army tunic buttoned up to the neck. They were both holding trays of drinks, which they started to offer around.

'*Entrare, prego,*' said Anna, '*Tutti, vieni, per favore.*' Which Adam took to mean, 'please come in.' Anna and Adam sidled towards the front door, with their trays of drinks, until one or two followed them in, quickly noticing the spread in the centre of the large room.

Almost unbelievably, they went straight back out and motioned their friends to come in! Inside, Joe, also with his military tunic looking very smart and constantly smiling, was shepherding everyone to a chair, and making sure the ladies got the pick of the seats.

'*Per favore,*' he said, having checked the simplest thing to say to the visitors.

The ice was broken, as Leopold came into the room and leaned against an old piano, which was covered in photographs. One of the men began very aggressively, clearly shouting his demands and addressing them directly to Leopold. Leo let him exhaust himself and never once tried to interrupt or stop him. Eventually the man exhausted himself, and one or two others piped up, with just a few waving a hand or even a fist in the air.

Adam and Joe, with Anna, stood near the door and said nothing until the shouting had died down. There had clearly been threats in amongst the voices shouting in the room but, at the same time, almost everybody was drinking their fill, being topped up by Joe, and eating from the centre table too.

At last it seemed as if they had run out of steam. Leopold then quite cleverly turned to Adam and spoke in English. It would not have mattered much what they said, but they decided between them that this was the right time to make an offer. In other parts of Italy the military had been brought in to quell disturbances, sometimes with disastrous results, but Adam and Joe did not look like 'the military', not quite.

Most of the men were puzzled as to what the two boys were doing there. They listened as Adam and Leopold eventually ceased their conversation. Perhaps they were relieved that there was no other military presence drafted in for this meeting.

It was then that Leo told them in their native language about his plan to bring in the complete crop, and hand over the proceeds of sales to them, entirely. He was clearly telling them that there would be a few deductions, for the use of transport and horses, machines and storage, but slowly the mood changed.

One man was quite obviously gesturing for some clarification, asking if Leopold really meant 'all' the proceeds of sales of the crop. Once or twice Leopold briefly stopped his conversation and came back to Adam in English, saying he thought they were coming round to accepting a peaceful offering for the current year.

Then it was back to the villagers, and somehow it quite suddenly turned into a handshaking festival, with everybody getting up, taking a bit more food, putting down their glass, or giving it back to Joe, shaking more hands, especially Leo's and Anna's and, one by one, leaving the house.

It was over. The crisis, if there was ever going to be one, had apparently been averted. Leopold stayed, and sat with two of the men, one of whom had been the first to arrive, and began making plans with pencil and paper. There were figures and signatures by the time they had finished, and the two men left, not exactly smiling, but in good spirits and with another flurry of handshaking.

'You may have saved our estate for one year at least, Adam,' said Leopold.

'Nonsense, not me,' said Adam, 'but so long as they are content at the moment, maybe you have saved your own estate.'

'Come and eat.' It was the voice of Anna at the door, inviting them into the dining room at the back of the house, which opened up on to a small courtyard. There was still enough light and sunshine to enjoy a meal before lights or candles had to be lit.

There was more wine, and the four of them enjoyed some lamb and rice, as well as Bolognese, which they were informed, was a small pizza, topped with tomato, *proscuitto* and a boiled egg, and then covered in puff pastry. Another new word for Adam,

Adam and Joe were eating like royalty! They had never experienced such tastes, or combinations of food. It was a revelation to them and they were loving every minutes of it.

'The main grape harvest we get here on the slopes of Mount Etna,' said Leopold, 'are *Nerello Mascalese* for red and *Carricante* for white wine. Tonight we shall have some more of both!' And they did.

25

Harvest

Everybody in the house slept well that night. The morning brought another glorious day of sunshine, and Leopold took Adam and Joe out to introduce them to the wonders and skills of olive and grape harvesting.

Leopold lent them a thick woolly cardigan each, and some trousers in the same woollen material as they had seen being worn by the men who came to the house. He, too, was similarly attired. All three had linen shirts and wore flat caps which reminded Adam of the little flat cap he had as a child.

'You'll need these,' he said. 'The sun may be shining but up on some of the slopes and the fields it can be almost Alpine.' They donned the new clothing, eagerly, and followed Leopold on a twenty minute walk to an olive grove. There was a man, nearby to where Leopold took them, who was carefully counting baskets of produce as they appeared.

Anna had packed them some *cannoli* and a bottle of wine in a kind of hamper, which were carefully put to one side for later. The faces of the other workers were tanned by the hot Sicilian sun and most were already there working when Leopold arrived with the two boys.

He exchanged some greetings with the local pickers, and the mood was quite clearly light-hearted. There were sideways glances when Leo was obviously introducing Adam and Joe, a bit of light laughter, but a mood of acceptance. Perhaps they were still wondering who these two young men were, who appeared last night to be wearing a uniform, and today were dressed for picking crops.

It did not take Adam and Joe long to get used to their methods, and they worked alongside the others methodically, tree by tree, with a small team at each, and every team progressing from one to the next. Some were up ladders, others were down below and there was also a great green mesh or netting spread out below to catch the falling olives.

They didn't want to miss any, not even one. There was some chatter, an occasional laugh at what the two boys assumed was a joke, but otherwise the day was punctuated only by the consistent rhythm of falling olives going plop into baskets, or into the netting. Adam and Joe hoped that the jokes were not at their expense, although both realised there was nothing much they could do about it anyway and it didn't bother them. They even laughed sometimes when the others did. Leopold stayed with them and joined in the picking.

'This handpicking method may be old fashioned, and time consuming,' he said to Adam and Joe, 'but the results are well worth the effort. We've been producing good quality olive oil for many years now, and the secret is to pick when the fruit is still on the trees, and not quite ripe. Would you believe, in some parts they are trying machines that will pick olives, or even waiting until the fruit falls to the ground? Ugh!' Clearly Leopold was unimpressed by such methods and, so it seemed, were the local people, who worked all day and left every tree behind them bare.

They stopped to eat the *cannoli* and drink some wine. Adam and Joe could not join in any of the conversation, but definitely enjoyed the joyous company of olive pickers, some of whom had been at the house the previous evening in a very different mood.

The olive harvesting continued for well over a week, and it was still not finished when Leo suggested they go to see the vines, as there was still plenty to pick there also.

Of course Adam and Joe had seen grapes in England, Adam at The Manor House when large dinner parties were being prepared, and Joe in Covent Garden, in London. But they had never seen the likes of these enormous bunches of glorious green grapes, by the hundreds of thousands, dripping from vines, hanging heavily and all ripe, ready to pick, and looking perfect. And black grapes, too, being brought in by the men and women, up and down the endless avenues of vines, which seemed to go on for ever. This was some estate.

'Aren't they wonderful?' said Leopold, as they explored the fields. 'Sicily is an island truly blessed by the sun, and cooled by gentle sea breezes, with this very special soil, giving us abundant harvests and renowned high-quality wine. These one hundred year-old *Carricante* and *Nerello Mascalese* vines sit on the southeast slopes of the volcano, which means they tend to be warmer than the rest of Etna and can generally be the first to be harvested each year.

'And how do they become wine?' asked Joe, knowing full well that they were crushed to extract juice, but never having thought about precisely how it was done.

'Well,' replied Leopold, 'it is simply a matter of pressing the fruit in these ancient *palmento*, or stone press-houses, with the great wooden presses inside, and then keeping the wine in storage tanks before it is taken away, and stored some more. We use metal tanks for white wine and old oak barrels for the reds. Then eventually it is bottled.' The two boys were impressed.

'The wonder of it all is just what God has granted us in the simple grape! From this one fruit, man has developed ways to make fruit juice or, with fermentation and the natural yeast which occurs in the skin of grapes, we have made beautiful wines, and some very strong wines at that. The wines can enhance our cooking, our meat, or sweet dishes!

'We have developed jams and jellies, we can make sour vinegar and we can dry them out to make raisins, and currants, which are then used in cooking and baking. Or we can pick a juicy grape off the vine and just eat it!'

'It certainly seems to be a valuable crop,' said Adam. 'I'd never thought of it before.'

'Grapes have huge quantities of vitamins and minerals, for a healthy diet,' continued Leopold, 'so it is little wonder how healthy Mediterranean people are!'

The two boys enjoyed their first day out in the vineyards, and among the olive groves. They watched, and eventually joined in, the snipping of great bunches of grapes from the vines and putting them into huge straw baskets ready to be taken away and eventually pressed.

They were exhilarated and exhausted by the time the sun began to set, and it was time to go back to the house. Once again, Anna had prepared some beautiful food for them to enjoy and a long evening was spent exchanging tales from their personal life stories.

To Adam and Joe the sheer amount of the harvest seemed

endless. The great vineyards spread over many acres, and literally millions of grapes and olives were gathered in, alongside some of the citrus fruits from the orchards as well.

'The harvest is all in,' announced Leopold one day. 'I have agreed with the men and their wives, hundreds of them in all over the estate, that they will share the value of the grape and olive crop. I will take a fee for their use of the presses, the *caretti*, the horses, and the barns. I will also pay you two much-needed gentlemen, as many others have left the estate recently, and we still have the citrus crop to collect. The estate workers seem satisfied and we seem to have avoided the catastrophe which we have read about, so sadly, in other parts of Sicily.' Adam hoped he was right.

The harvest season came and went. October turned to November. Everything was going well. Even Adam's wounded leg had now completely healed. It was approaching Christmas 1893 and Adam and Joe had earned some useful money, working for Leopold, but it was time to consider moving on.

26

Christmas

'But you must stay for Christmas,' said Leopold to them both. 'And then you can travel on after the New Year with a spring in your step and plans to conquer the remainder of Italy.'

They agreed, and so it was that they spent a Christmas unlike any other. Joe had never thought much of Christmas at all. He had spent most of his young adult life as a fugitive from the law, or as a young soldier, never having experienced the love of a close family of any level of wealth.

Adam, on the other hand, had enjoyed a few Christmases at The Manor House with the big tree and the regulation gifts given out in the hallway, always including the gold half-sovereign.

Now it was time to experience an Italian Christmas in the company of an Englishman abroad, with his Italian wife and, as it turned out, their son home from college and a married daughter with her husband, and his father-in-law, Luigi, the café owner whom they had met in Pozzallo.

There were no further crises for Leopold as November became December and he, along with Adam and Joe, spent time clearing out barns, cleaning farm machinery, delivering crops in various containers to local distributors, ready to be sent out to those who had agreed to buy the crop. Adam could not believe that Leo had any real financial problems, even with the agreement he had made with the estate workers for the current year.

They ate well and there was always plenty of food on the table, not at all as he remembered his own rather meagre meals with his mother and father years ago.

In the west of Sicily the politics of the Fascisti were making life very uncomfortable for the population, especially around Palermo, the capital. Leopold was speaking with Adam and Joe one evening to explain what was happening.

'Land owners, manufacturers and mine owners had asked the Prime Minister to intervene in some of the civil and industrial strife,' he explained, 'but Giovanni Giolitti had introduced relatively mild measures, being somewhat on the side of the protestors with his left wing views. This has led to more demands, more strikes and much more unrest.'

'Where might it end?' ventured Adam.

'Things have moved on, perhaps not for the better,' said Leopold. 'In late November Geolitti officially resigned as Prime Minister and three weeks of limbo followed, until a man named Crispi managed to form a government on the fifteenth of December.'

'And has he calmed the situation at all?' said Joe.

'Sorry to say, but no,' said Leo. 'Crispi's hard-line approach has led to the death of ninety-two peasants, who have lost their lives in clashes with the police and army. Government buildings have been burned, along with flour mills and bakeries that refused to lower their prices when taxes were lowered. It is all very ugly and I am glad that my daughter, and her husband, have managed to leave their home. They are on their way here for Christmas. Sadly we may not escape here in the east without similar things happening very soon.'

It all seemed very threatening to Adam and his friend, but then one day in December, Leopold suggested that the two boys might like to see the city of Catonia, and some shops. It was about an hour in the *caretto* and the three men spent a pleasant afternoon there.

Leopold went off to his bank and to buy supplies requested by Anna. Adam and Joe revelled in being able to shop and make purchases at some of the stalls and markets. They even bought some clothing, a couple of shirts each, trousers, which were not of a military hue, and Joe bought a woollen coat which suited him perfectly.

Adam suggested they might buy gifts for the family members for Christmas, something which had never bothered Joe in his few years spent in London, with no family, but he warmed to the idea and they spent a pleasant hour choosing small presents. It was good to have some cash to spend, even if it was not a fortune by any means, but they agreed on a tie each for Leopold, his son and son-in-law, whom they had never met, a smart coloured handkerchief for Luigi, who had fed them so well in Pozzallo, and bright coloured scarves for the ladies, Anna and her daughter.

The journey back to the Ashton estate was casual, with the horse ambling along, pulling the three men and their parcels and bags, through the late afternoon under the falling sun, with a very cool breeze, bringing the entire day to a very happy conclusion.

Christmas arrived, as did the remainder of Leopold's family.

His son, Tony arrived first, about two weeks before Christmas, followed by their daughter, Donna, and her husband a few days later. They had spent several days travelling, first from outside Palermo along the northern coast road in a hired *caretto*, then by train from Messina to Catania, where Leopold had picked them up for the final leg of the journey.

Luigi had closed down the café for Christmas, managing to get a ride to Lentini and then a short train ride to Catania, where he hired a man to bring him to the estate. They were all together by Tuesday the nineteenth of December.

The house was a crowded happy place. Adam and Joe fitted in well, helping in the house, assisting Anna in the kitchen and getting to know Toni, who was just a year or two younger than Adam and almost exactly the same as Joe's twenty-one years.

They went to the local Catholic church, just outside the estate on the road to Catania, on Sunday the twenty-fourth and again on Christmas day, all managing to squeeze into two vehicles, the *caretto* and one of the farm carts. The Ashton family, particularly Leopold, were not strict Catholics but Anna had been brought up in a traditional Italian family, who observed the yearly church calendar. She wanted to worship at Christmas, and Easter, and the rest of the family happily went along.

Adam and Joe were astonished at the enormous, colourful and crowded crib scene which greeted them in the large stone church. Joe was glad he had bought a new coat, and they both looked very smart as they arrived with the family on the Sunday.

Plenty of other worshippers recognised the two boys from the meeting that had been held at the estate house a few weeks earlier. Most of them smiled and greeted them with '*Bon Natali*' which the boys very quickly recognised must mean *Happy Christmas.*

They didn't understand a word of the services of worship on those two days, of course, but it didn't matter to them. They'd sat through drum-head services at the barracks in Dorchester back in England without understanding very much of those either, and they were in English!

Adam's memory took him back to his little church in Melton Ford where the reverend had been so kind to his mother and father, and to him when they died. It was a dull memory, perhaps because acts of worship there were not filled with much colour or movement. In this church, however, in Sicily, he was wide-eyed at the Nativity scene they saw as they arrived, and filled with warm joy at the singing by the enormous congregation. The model of the Nativity scene seemed to go on for ever, with lighted mini-caves, animals and figures representing all the major characters in the Birth of Jesus story, and plenty more besides.

The more one looked at it, the more entire creation seemed to grow outwards and upwards. There were huge pyramids of colour, Kings and shepherds, sheep, cattle, goats and even geese, a baby, a mother, tables laden with mini-creations of food items and everything illuminated by lamps and candles. It all gave the impression of a fantastical world, well worth celebrating.

Both Adam and Joe were entranced and lingered as long as they could, before all the family said it was time to go. Then it was back to the house, hearing children singing Christmas carols on the way, outside different homes, and once back indoors, a slice of *Panettone*, which the boys enjoyed very much.

This was a dry fruity sponge cake, which they consumed along with a drink of hot chocolate.

Back at the house, Christmas had begun almost as early as the eighth of December, when Anna began decorating the house with colourful objects, bags of sweets and lights. There was no Christmas tree as Adam would have recognised from the English tradition, but always plenty of food and drink.

'What about Father Christmas?' said Adam one evening to the gathered family. 'St Nicholas, or Santa Claus?'

'Ah, yes!' said Anna. 'I know what you mean. In Italy children can hardly restrain their excitement as they wait for the arrival of *La Befana*.'

'She is an ugly witch-like figure,' continued Tony, 'who distributes sweets to children who have been good, and a piece of coal to those who have not.'

'Sounds charming!' thought Adam.

'In Italy,' Adam learned from Leopold, 'the final '*natali*' celebration will come on Epiphany, the sixth of January.'

'This is when children would be given the extra gifts,' explained Anna. 'It is usually sweets, plus maybe the piece of coal.'

'Coal! I still cannot believe that,' said Joe open mouthed.

'Yes, indeed,' Tony joined in. 'The sweets are for all the good things the children have done during the year, but on the assumption that everybody does something a bit bad at least once a year, a piece of coal is included.'

'I just hope the children extract it before eating the sweets!' said Joe.

'In many poorer parts of Italy,' Leo continued, 'and in particular here in rural Sicily, a stick in a stocking was placed instead of coal, so you didn't have to worry too much. *La Befana* is depicted as an ugly hag riding on a broomstick, which is why everybody places great emphasis on sweeping the house clean every day during Christmas.'

'It's a good tradition,' Anna said. 'We do not want *La Befana*, with her broomstick, to stay any longer than she has to in our homes. Traditionally on Epiphany Eve the children leave a glass of wine and morsels of food for her before they go to bed.'

'Not unlike what some children do in England for Santa Claus,' said Adam who remembered his own meagre Christmases with his parents and Mrs Redman.

'And we have a Christmas song which the children sing. We have not sung it for years,' said Anna, 'but now is a good time to show our guests!' Then she started singing,

'La Befana vien di notte
Con le scarpe tutte rotte
Col vestito alla romana
Viva, Viva La Befana!'

'What does it all mean?' said Joe and Adam at the same time, laughing.

'Well, now,' said Leopold, 'I can help you there but I'm not much of a hand at singing. The English translation is,

The Befana comes by night
With her shoes all tattered and torn
She comes dressed in the Roman way
Long live the Befana!

Leopold collapsed and laughed at his own efforts to sing and translate.

'We have no young children here now,' said Anna, 'but we wish you much good fortune for this Christmas and for 1894.'

Serious eating in the Ashton home began on the twenty-fourth of December, and continued well into Christmas Day. The boys, Adam and Joe, realised that the local tradition was to give gifts on Christmas Eve, so they rushed to get the gifts they had bought and thoroughly enjoyed giving them to everybody in the family.

Joe could not remember when he had simply given and received gifts at any time in his life. Christmas Eve was truly joyful.

Leopold gifted the boys some extra money which he said he thought would be more useful to them in their quest to get home, than socks or useless trinkets. They were not in the least hesitant to accept it. Then it was back to eating and drinking. They had sweets and desserts, the like of which the boys had never seen, and there was *buccellati,* large round biscuits filled with almonds, pistachios and dried fruits.

'I don't think I shall ever eat again,' said Adam.

'Why do people say that,' said Leopold, 'when we all know we shall start again tomorrow?'

'Well I certainly will,' said Joe, 'and I haven't quite finished for tonight either.'

Adam and Joe made a good new friend of Tony, Leo's son. They exchanged stories of their individual lives, the poor boy from a village in England, the homeless young criminal, with no wish to remain so, who had joined the army, and the Italian boy with an English dad who had sent him to college.

They learned a lot about each other, their priorities and views on life. It is surprising how, at a young age, many young people cannot envisage any other life-style but their own. They have no extended life-map or anchor points in their life upon which to make judgements. They assume everybody has the same view as they do and the same priorities and values.

Tony's life at Catania University had shown Adam that there might be as many different views on life as there are people to share them, and now, meeting two men of his own age from England, his view of the world was wider still. Adam and Joe certainly had had their own eyes opened in the past year or two, in the British Army, and in the past month since getting lost in the Mediterranean.

'How are you going to get back to England?' said Tony, in surprisingly good English.

'After Christmas we must think seriously about the journey from here to the mainland of Italy,' said Adam. 'Then I hope we shall be able to afford to travel north and eventually through to France and home.'

'What will happen to you then?' said Tony.

'We will have to see,' Adam replied. 'The worst case is that we would be court marshalled for desertion, although if we can prove otherwise we may be lucky with a lesser charge.'

'I dread to think what the penalty is for desertion if proven,' said Joe.

'Well, don't think about it!' said Adam and Tony together almost in unison.

'I think I know which way my luck will go,' Joe said. 'I've always ended up on the wrong side of the law.'

'Well, let us hope that, eventually, we shall both end up on the same side and the right side,' said Adam. 'We have to get home, no matter what.'

'My father can give you a note of your contribution to the family fortunes for this year at least,' said Tony. 'Maybe, in the end, that could help prove that you were making your way back to Britain.'

'Of course,' said Adam. 'We'd be grateful for that, wouldn't we, Joe?'

'I am grateful for anything that helps us clear our names,' said Joe.

'We can also look at the railway system on the mainland,' said Tony. 'Some of Sicily's countryside is better served with rail links than even the mainland, especially the west coast up to Naples and Rome. North of Rome it is quite good.'

'I've looked at some maps, but actually but there is no certainty about where there may yet be railways. Knowing that would help.' Adam was determined to set out on the journey home knowing as much information as he could get hold of, but the family told him of many railway projects which had begun on the mainland, without knowing which were yet in operation.

When January arrived the family celebrated New Year with the traditional '*cenone*,' which Adam discovered meant literally a 'big dinner.' It was a pasta meal, not unlike what they now knew to called lasagne, and was supposed to bring good luck to the families who sat and ate together. It was enjoyed by everyone, together again for almost the last time this Christmas.

'Let us hope that our good fortune lasts into the New Year,' said Leopold. 'And you two, Adam and Joe, could do with some luck as well in getting home.'

'Thank you,' they both enjoined. '*Grazie*.'

The Christmas and New Year celebrations eventually came to an end. The two young men made ready to leave the Ashton family. Donna and her husband had already left to go back to their home in the north. Tony was actually looking forward to returning to his college life, but reluctant to leave his two new friends.

'Will you write to us when you eventually get home?' he said to Adam.

'I certainly will,' Adam replied, 'and maybe come to visit you again one day, probably one day a long way off!'

As they packed their things and made sure their money was safely tucked away out of the way of pickpockets, and, hopefully, more determined thieves, Adam had one more thing to do.

The Ashton Estate
   Catania
   Sicily

8*th* *January 1894*

Dear Daisy,

It seems to be taking for ever to get home, but we have been taken in and looked after by a Mr Ashton and his generous family here in Sicily.

Tomorrow we must set out to find our way to the mainland of Italy, then hopefully to France and home. I hope you are well, and I hope everybody at The Manor House had a good Christmas and that Freddie, Robert and the others are behaving themselves! Give my regards to Mr Granger and to the family.

I hope they have not heard from Captain James that I deserted, or anything like that, because we didn't. I would love to be together with you in a few weeks, but for now our plans have to be to get to Italy, and travel north.

With love, and much affection,

Yours, Adam.

27

Travel plans

While Adam and Joe were making plans to travel north and then homeward west, in another home, a long way away, an elderly lady was making plans to travel east and then south.

Queen Victoria was at Windsor, her Berkshire home, but not her favourite.

Her granddaughter, the Princess Victoria Melita of Saxe-Coburg and Gotha, a surname much beloved of the ageing Queen, had agreed to marry Ernest Louis, Grand Duke of Hesse. Victoria Melita was the third child and second daughter of Victoria's second son, Alfred, just one of a burgeoning bunch of grandchildren, and subsequently great-grandchildren, of Queen Victoria, the grandmother of Europe.

Victoria's first son, Bertie was, of course, heir to her throne. Her second son, Alfred became the heir to his uncle, Ernest II, Grand Duke of Saxe-Coburg and Gotha in Germany, the brother of the blessed Albert. He and his young family had lived, of all places, in Malta where he had served in The Royal Navy up to the previous year, 1893.

He was probably there when Adam had passed through on his ship, suffering the fateful consequence of getting robbed and knocked unconscious just outside Valetta. And it was in this same year, 1893, that Alfred had become a Grand Duke and moved to Coburg, when his uncle died. So it was his daughter, Princess Victoria Melita who was living in Coburg and was due to marry in April 1894 at Schloss Ehrenburg.

In her teens, the Princess had fallen in love with her maternal first cousin, Grand Duke Kirill Vladimirovich of Russia. The disapprobation of marriage, however, between first cousins of his faith, Orthodox Christianity, discouraged their romance, which was frowned upon by the Russian Tsar. Bowing to family pressure, Victoria was now to marry her Protestant paternal first cousin, Ernest Louis, Grand Duke of Hesse, following the wishes of their grandmother, Queen Victoria, who would honour the marriage with her presence.

Not wishing to waste a good European jaunt, the Queen decided that before the wedding in April, she would begin her continental wanderings, and re-visit the *Villa Fabbricotti*, in Florence, Italy, from mid March until the sixteenth of April, a month-long stay which was very much to her liking.

The grand entourage set sail from Portsmouth and trundled its way across Europe to Florence, with its tons of luggage and a multitude of attendants of the Royal Household.

28

Italy

Adam and Joe had packed their one bag each, and had no idea how they were to cover the vast distances which lay before them. Leopold gave them a lift in the *caretto* as far as Catania where they wished each other well.

It was the tenth of January, exactly a week after, unbeknown to Adam and Joe, that the new Prime Minister, Francesco Crispi had declared a state of siege throughout Sicily. Army reservists had been recalled and army general, Roberto Morra di Lavriano, had been dispatched to the north of the island with forty thousand troops. The old order had been restored through the use of extreme force, including summary executions.

None of this touched the two English travellers, who were not wearing uniform by now, but did have English Army identity cards safe and sound inside their pockets, and enough money to get them started.

They saw signs of the military on the roads, and even at the stations, but nothing like the unrest that Leopold had told them was unfolding in the north and around the capital. Maybe the St Christopher, even *in absentia*, was looking after Adam and his travelling companion.

The goodbyes, having mostly been completed at the house, were brief, as Adam wanted to find a Post Office to send his letter to Daisy before the train took them to Messina, on the northern tip of Sicily. There they hoped it would be easy to find a ferry boat for the eight mile crossing to Villa San Giovanni, on the mainland, or to Reggio Calabria, a slightly bigger town.

Indeed it was. There was a ferry boat which did not exactly fill them with confidence by the look of it, but then they remembered that they had made the journey from Malta to Sicily in a glorified canoe! The crossing was easy and took about an hour. Adam paid for both their fares with a few lire, in coins, and they landed on the mainland of Italy, in Reggio Calabria, safe and sound, but with nowhere to go and no clue as to how to proceed north.

'Let's find somewhere to drink and eat,' said Joe. 'At least once in the past sitting in a café landed us some luck. At least we shall not be hungry while we explore and make plans.'

'Good idea,' responded Adam, 'But look!' He had turned around and now showed Joe the view across the strait of Messina. 'You can see Mount Etna from here and somewhere down there, on the slopes, is our friend, Leopold, and his family.' It was a stunning view, which they now turned away from, as they walked from the ferry boat, towards a building and what appeared to be some shops along a wide thoroughfare.

There was a surprising amount of green open space between buildings and it did not take them long to find a café with outside tables. It was very inviting.

'*Vino, per favore,*' said Adam who had made some effort to acquire some very rudimentary Italian.

'*Si,*' said the girl. '*Vino rosso?* Er… red wine? You are English?'

'*Si,*' said Adam, 'Er… yes. *Grazie*'

The girl went away and came back with a bottle, two glasses

and a few small cakes. She put them down and waited.

'How much?' ventured Adam.

'*Quanto?*' said the girl and rubbed her fingers and thumb together to check what Adam was asking.

'*Quanto?*' said Adam. And pulled out a few coins.

'*Dodici,*' said the girl, and spread her five fingers, twice, and added two more fingers to indicate twelve. She then helped Adam find two five lire pieces and two ones. Both Adam and Joe thought that was a reasonable price and it did not make too big a hole in their new-found minor fortune of several hundred lire, which they had each earned in Sicily.

'Can we sleep here?' said Joe, indicating sleep with two palms of his hands against the side of his face.

'*Pensione?*' said the girl, at which point Adam recognised the word meaning a guest house, or something similar.

'*Si,*' he said. '*Pensione?*'

The girl pointed along the road, and indicated both left and right as if to say there were several places, It would have been too complicated to enter into a discussion about the relative excellence of different *pensione,* but the two boys, Adam and Joe, thanked her and settled down to eat their pieces of cake.

'Finding somewhere to eat and even to sleep is a good idea,' said Adam, 'but above all we must find out if there are trains. Let's walk and find someone to ask when we've finished here.'

They finished the bottle of wine, which was none too strong, but they did ask for some water before they left the café, which they thought they might need later. They filled a water bottle each, and went on their way.

The wide street was full of traffic, horse drawn carts and some carriages. They even noticed what look a bit like an omnibus, an open-sided carriage with half a dozen or so people inside, being drawn by a single horse with the driver sat on top of the vehicle.

There were, eventually, one or two buildings sporting the *pensione* sign and they stopped to evaluate them.

'Not sure I fancy staying at any of those!' said Joe.

'We have rather got used to being looked after,' said Adam. 'Still, we can enquire.' They chose a pale orange, stone building, with a black railing guiding them up four steps to a large brown front door. The temperature of the day was warm, without being hot. It was January, after all, but inside the *pensione* it was cooler still. There were some large pieces of furniture, some potted plants, and an elderly gentleman sitting behind a desk, dozing slowly off to sleep.

'Excuse me,' began Adam, softly.

'*Scusi?*' said the man, with the barest hint of a jolt out of his slumber.

'A room, for two?' said Adam, slowly. '*Per favore*'.

'*Scusi?*' said the man, at which point Joe took over and mimed sleeping again, the way he had with the waitress earlier. Then he pointed at himself and at Adam. The man thumbed carelessly through a book in front of him, took a pencil from a pot on the desk and wrote a number six on a piece of paper.

'*Venti lire,*' said the man, which Adam recognised as twenty and he produced a coin very carefully, not revealing any other money at all. The two of them were still impressed by the fact that one English pound was worth ninety lire, and that living and eating in southern Italy was apparently very cheap. They would hopefully have enough money on them to get home, if things carried on the way they had begun. If!

The man showed them up to a large room on the second floor, facing the front and from which they could view the street below. There followed more miming and muted discussions about eating which terminated in their believing a meal could be obtained at about seven o'clock.

'*Grazie*,' came from both Adam and Joe to which *prego* appeared to be the response from their hotelier. They managed to freshen up, and decided to walk to the town, for an hour, before eating. Luckily their room door locked from the outside and they took the key with them, as well as all their money on their persons.

There was still a fair amount of hustle and bustle going on, with stall holders and shopkeepers shouting, transacting deals, agreeing on prices and greeting each other with loud shouts and, eventually, big smiles.

Adam saw a wooden cart loaded with trinkets and a great variety of different objects. He looked, which may not have been the most sensible thing to do, as he then found it difficult to get away without the young man, by the cart, constantly thrusting different things in front of him and shouting what was obviously the word '*cheap*'.

'*Economico! Economico. Trente lire, trente lire.*'

Adam was having none of it, but did see two small leather purses with string-pull tops which took his fancy. Joe liked the look of a silver-looking pendant, but it was dangerous to show an interest.

'*Trente lire*,' continued the young man, who was actually not much more than a boy. '*Venti lire.*'

'I think he's dropped the price,' said Adam. 'Presumably if *venti* is twenty, then *trente* was thirty? Maybe I'll offer him fifteen.'

'Offer him ten,' said Joe, which Adam did. He rather fancied the two leather purses and would have been happy with fifteen.

'Ten,' shouted Joe very specifically, as he found a ten lire piece.

'*Quindici*,' said the boy, and indicated his five fingers, three times, to represent the price he wanted.

'No! Ten,' said Adam, as Joe, also was now offering ten lire for the pendant. They both made as if to walk away. '*Grazie*.' It worked.

'*Dieci, si dieci*,' said the boy holding out his hand for the cash. Presumably that meant ten.

Adam and Joe each gave him ten lire, and came away happy with their purchases. The boy, too, was happy in the end, and thanked them with handshakes and a smile.

'*Grazie, Grazie*.'

'That wasn't too difficult,' said Joe and Adam agreed.

'What do you want the purses for?' said Joe.

'I just like the look of them, said Adam, 'and they may come in handy. One never knows. I've been caught before.' There were other places to look at, including a magnificent white church building which they sadly thought that they did not have time to go into.

There were fruit and vegetable stalls, now slowly clearing away their produce into boxes. There were open-fronted shops, with large ladies just behind the counter, cooking flat pasta dishes which reminded the two travellers that it might be approaching time for their meal. They had carefully watched where they had walked, and now found their way back to the *pensione*.

The man behind the big desk got up as they came in to the

entrance lobby and gestured them to a back room. There was another woman, of considerable proportions, standing in what looked like the kitchen doorway, with a great white apron, her head covered in a similar scarf to those they had seen other women wearing in Sicily, knotted under the chin. In another part of the room were two other 'guests', as it appeared to Adam, already eating. They barely hinted at a greeting.

'Qui, here,' said the proprietor, indicating a table for them. The room was airy, and had French windows leading out to a courtyard, which Adam was learning appeared to be a very pleasant feature of most of the buildings he had visited in the Mediterranean area.

As they sat down the large lady at the kitchen door disappeared and very soon reappeared with a large bowl of spaghetti and what looked like meat balls and tomatoes. They smelt delicious and Joe indicated that they would like something to drink. Another bottle of *vino rosso* appeared, two glasses and a bowl of fruit. The boys were happy that they had found somewhere to sleep, something to eat and what appeared to be a safe haven for one night at least.

'We must find the railway station, which should not be too difficult,' said Adam as they ate. 'We need, if we can, to travel up the west coast of Italy, to Naples and then to Rome. If we can get there it should be easier in the north to get to the French border, but it could take us weeks.'

'So long as we have a plan,' Joe replied.

'I've got several,' confided Adam, with a twinkle in his eye.

They slept well in the room they had been given, and packed and dressed next morning ready to go down and, hopefully, get some breakfast. They were not disappointed. There was cheese, tomatoes, coffee, bread and olives. Both boys sated their appetites and stuffed whatever leftovers they could into the bags as well.

'You go and check that we've not left anything in the room,' said Adam to Joe, 'and I am going to have another look at the maps I brought from the Ashton's house, and maybe speak to the manager about rail travel, if I can get through to him.'

With that, Adam went out into the courtyard, beyond the dining room, in the hope of seeing the owner. In the far corner of the courtyard he was there, speaking with two boys, who both looked younger than Adam or Joe. It appeared to be casual enough, with the boys leaning against a table and the owner speaking openly with them of which, predictably, Adam understood not a word.

Adam had no time to waste. He spent a few minutes in the courtyard, looked at a map from his bag, until in due course, the conversation appeared to finish and the owner made as if to re-enter the house. Adam stopped him.

'Railway?' he said, pointing to his map. 'Railway to Naples?' He had drawn a small picture of a locomotive in the corer of the map. The owner looked.

'Ah! *Ferroiva*. Iron road,' he said. '*Ferroiva per Napoli.*'

'I think so,' said Adam to himself. 'Sounds about right. *Per favour.*'

The man quickly turned over Adam's map and, with Adam's pencil, drew a rough outline of the *pensione* pointing to 'this house' and continued with drawing a road outside, with arrows pointing this way and that, a square with a cross on, which could have been the church they saw the previous evening, then more arrows and, eventually, a cross with the word *ferrovia* written by it.

The task was complete. Adam thanked him profusely, as Joe re-appeared and the owner went back to speaking with the two young boys.

'I think I know where the railway is,' said Adam.

'Good, let's go. I am sure there is nothing left in the room.'

And with that the two travellers were on their way again. They thanked the owner, who shook their hands, and shouted '*Grazie*' to the woman still standing at the kitchen door. Then they were out in the street, Adam clutching his map, but fairly sure he knew which way to go.

After buying a bit more fruit and bread, plus a paper bag full of olives, Adam suddenly stopped Joe in his tracks.

'Here, take this,' He said, and handed Joe one of the two purses he had bought the previous day.

'What's this?' said Joe.

'Just take it, and make out as if it is valuable,' said Adam. 'And follow me.'

They went through the town, passed by the church they had seen the evening before, and walked further until what looked like railway sidings, and plenty of rolling stock, appeared ahead of them. They decided the station must be ahead of them. What happened next, happened very quickly but not entirely unexpectedly, at least for Adam.

A very imposing man in a black suit appeared in front of them, with one of the boys Adam had seen in the courtyard at the hotel behind him. He looked around, and, sure enough, the other boy was loitering a few yards behind them.

'You pay,' said the burly black-suited man as he stood in front of them.

'No!' said Joe as he began to side-step the man.

The man moved to block him and insisted. 'You English, pay now.'

'We have nothing, not much money,' said Adam unconvincingly, and not expecting him to understand or give up, as the three of them closed in a little.

'This is where you give them the purse,' whispered Adam from the side of his mouth. 'I thought we might be robbed here in the town, but did not think it would happen quite so quickly!'

Joe cottoned on to what Adam had done, and came back as the man kept repeating , 'Money!'

'Give him the purse, then run,' said Adam.

'Okay,' said Joe. 'I'll go to the left of the railway trucks, you go to the right. Keep going and we'll meet up in a few hundred yards. They won't chase both of us, if they bother to chase either of us!'

'Money!' said the man, and the boys made as if to resist them, but holding the purses, they extracted from their bags, tightly in their hands.

'You give.' said the man, as they 'reluctantly' handed over the purses. The man passed the purses to the two boys, with a deft movement, and they disappeared, whilst the man stood his ground and Adam and Joe walked on, and then broke into a run.

They did not stop until, having passed either side of a long line of railway trucks, they each found themselves on their own, and not sure which way to go. Adam came to halt and looked around. It appeared that the man and the boys had not given chase, and may have been satisfied with their 'takings'.

'Okay, for the time being,' thought Adam to himself, as he continued to look around and under the trucks in the sidings for Joe. Not quite five minutes went by until he heard a sound.

'Psst!' It was Joe, but where was he?

'Here,' came Joe's voice again, and as Adam looked up he saw him inside one of the trucks, under a tarpaulin, virtually hidden except for his face and a hand holding the covering up a little. 'Here, get in here.'

Adam climbed on to the wheel, and hauled himself into the truck beside Joe, where they sat and got their breath back, and gave a small smile of triumph.

'Okay, what was in the purses?' said Joe with a silent admiration that they were obviously worthless.

'There were three small coins in each, to make them rattle. two folded pieces of paper to make them rustle a bit, and quite a lot of gravel and small stones to make them weigh enough to feel good!' said Adam.

'I've been robbed enough times to want to make sure it doesn't happen any more than it has to, and that if it does, I am not the total loser!'

'Brilliant,' said Joe, 'I thought I was supposed to be the professional thief!'

'Maybe you are,' said Adam, 'but I am turning into a professional victim!'

'Well, they'll find out soon enough what's in the purses, so I suggest we stay here,' and that is precisely what they did. Sure enough, they suddenly heard shouts, without being able to discern what was being said, but it appeared to be the burly man, and his two juvenile accomplices. They were shouting at each other and the man sounded decidedly displeased. Adam and Joe lay low for a long time.

Eventually it seemed quiet, but they were not going to be fooled or take any chances. It was hot under the tarpaulin. They silently ate a bit of fruit and a few olives, then sipped from their water bottle, which they had filled before leaving the *pensione*.

They were not comfortable, but at least they were lying on sacks of some product which had a little give to it. Adam thought it might be flour or even sand. It was warm and the middle of the day was approaching, but they decided, silently, not to move. Better safe than sorry.

What awoke them from their semi-slumber was movement. They were suddenly aware that the truck had been shunted and was hooked up to another, and perhaps plenty of others for all they knew, and the whole lot were moving.

'Don't budge,' said Adam softly. 'This could be the free ride we would have liked, but did not expect!' The movement continued until they realised that that the train was gathering some speed.

'Supposing it is not going north,' said Joe. 'We'll be back where we started.'

'I doubt that,' Adam replied. 'From Reggio Calabri, where we landed from the ferry, trains can only really go north. There is hardly any more of Italy left to the south, certainly none with train services according to what I have learned. I suggest we just stay put.'

'Suits me,' said Joe and dug into another chunk of bread.

The train rattled on for several hours, so at least they were free of the two little urchins who had connived with the hotel owner and followed them to a place where they had tried to rob them. The afternoon came and went. They could sense it was getting dark, but they were reasonably comfortable, and as far as they knew were travelling in the right direction.

29

Salerno

When it stopped, it did so with a terribly jolt. Joe was half way through a gulp from his water bottle and spurted it everywhere. Adam laughed, as did Joe himself, and quickly put the top back on. They lay still for a while until they were fairly sure it was a real stop, and not just halted at a signal. It was Joe who first decided to look out.

'There's movement of men up towards the front of the train,' said Joe, as he peered out from under the tarpaulin. There's certainly no shouting or what appears to be instructions being given.'

They still waited, although by now they were fairly desperate to get out, and not a little hungry and thirsty, having exhausted all their supplies. It suddenly became quite dark and Adam suggested it would be safe to extricate themselves from the sacks and the tarpaulin. Gingerly they lifted up the cover, peered out again, and separately they climbed over the boarded sides and jumped to the ground.

There was a hint of light coming from beyond the front of the train, which they both assumed might well be buildings or a town settlement. They headed that way, and found no other people in the immediate vicinity.

The railway yard was deserted as they kept going, heading

for the lights. It wasn't too long before they came to a low-level railway platform, and there softly illuminated by a single lamp, left burning, was the word Salerno.

'I don't believe it,' said Adam. 'Salerno!'

'Meaning what?' Joe asked.

'If I'm right, and I think I am, we've been cooped up in that truck for well over two hundred miles, and if this is Salerno, we've covered a huge chunk of our journey north. That train must have been going at quite a speed.'

'Well, I think we knew it was,' said Joe, 'and I think the movement made both of us fall asleep for quite a long time during the journey.'

'Well,' repeated Adam, 'If I am right, we're well over half way to Rome. That is a huge leap for a single day!'

'Are we going to sleep on the road,' said Joe, 'or find somewhere as we did last night?'

'Let's keep going, but beware, I don't want to be the victim of another attempted robbery.' They walked on, heading for the lights and came into the town, looking for a *pensione* sign. Although it was now pretty dark, they could smell the sea. There were only the occasional lamps in late-night cafés and some bright room lights, where the blinds were still open. Luckily they had sensed these lights from the railway yard and headed in the right direction.

'*Pensione!*' said Joe, quite pleased with himself that he was the first to spot it.

'Looks okay,' said Adam. 'Worth a try.'

'*Al completo,*' said the woman behind the desk. She was tall, with very well coiffured hair, well dressed, and Adam still hoped that they had a room spare, although he had guessed what *al completo* meant.

'One room,' he indicated with one finger.

'*Al completo*,' she repeated. 'No room. *Niente Camere.*'

Adam tried again. '*Aqua?*' he said, hoping to fill the water bottles. 'We are English. Going to Rome.'

'*Aqua, si*,' she said, and came round to the front of the desk and ushered them to a table, and went away, quickly returning with a large bottle of water, and even a few biscuits.

'*Grazie*,' said Joe eagerly, '*Grazie.*'

The lady brought them a small road map, from which Adam could see that they were indeed in Salerno. He was delighted and pointed to the railway station. He hoped she would assume they had come to the town as paying passengers on a train, but of course had no idea which passenger trains, if any, had arrived that day. She was not apparently aware of any such dilemma in their demeanour, and obligingly put a small cross by two buildings shown on the map, which were nearby!

'*Pensione?*' she began. 'Here,' and she pointed, 'and here,' she pointed again. The two boys drank some of the water and filled their bottles with the remainder. The biscuits were very welcome and they offered some coins for the snack.

'*No! No!*' the woman responded, and they didn't argue.

Once out on the street again, Adam followed the woman's small map and they soon found a rather derelict-looking *pensione* which did not appeal in the slightest.

'Let's move on,' said Adam, 'and try the other one.'

'Seems a good move,' said Joe, 'although I hope the next one isn't worse.'

It apparently wasn't, and as they went into the front door the lobby was well lit, and had another distinguished, tall lady behind the desk. Adam showed her the map, as if to ask if they were at the guest house with the little cross by it, and her face lit up.

'*Buona*' she said, '*molte bene,*'which Adam took to be a good sign. Unbeknown to them, the woman recognised that they had come from her brother's guest house nearby, as her brother's wife had left a note on the map written in her own hand.

'*Camera?*' she said, which completely confused Adam. '*Una camera?*'

'*Camera?*' said Adam, looking slightly bewildered, 'Room? One room?'

'Yes, *si*,' she said, '*una camera*, one room. You are English?'

'Thank you, *Grazie*, yes,' spluttered Joe. The woman smiled and indicated for them to follow her. She went up a wide flight of stairs and took them to a large room, with two beds, and even a wash basin, not plumbed in, but with a large jug of water alongside. It was luxury, the like of which they had not seen since leaving the Ashtons.

'*Grazie*,' said Adam. '*Quanto*, how much?'

'*Trente*,' said the woman which Adam immediately knew meant thirty lire.

'It's thirty lire,' he said to Joe. 'I think it's worth it, and we have just had a two hundred mile journey for nothing, well, nothing apart from the few coins we donated to the local brigands!'

'Well worth it,' said Joe and brought out three ten lire coins, with his back to the lady at the door, turned and offered them to her. She accepted with a smile and invited them downstairs to eat.

'*Tu mangi?*' she said, and indicated the use of a knife and fork which brought a smile to both their faces.

'Ten minutes?' Adam said demonstrating with his fingers.

'*Ah! Si,*' she replied, and tapped a watch, hanging from a chain around her neck. 'Ten, *dieci minuti*'.

'I could get used to this Italian language,' said Joe, 'I think we're getting quite good at it.'

'Well, let's hope we won't need it for ever!' said Adam, smiling, but pleased that they were making themselves understood and were about to have a meal. They unpacked their bags, each put on another shirt and made their way downstairs to find the dining room, after making sure the room could be locked, and that they had the key.

The meal was sumptuous. There were more olives and a carafe of wine, just for starters, and then pasta, tomatoes, meat balls and even more wine. There was some fruit and more sweet biscuits. They were very full, and the lady seemed the most pleasant of hostesses. No man appeared that evening, although there were two other diners, in a far corner of the room, who did not communicate.

Both Adam and Joe hoped they were not being set up for another robbery or being softened up for any other form of crime upon their persons or their property. They felt quietly confident that the lady was friendly, as she certainly seemed to be.

Never in his wildest dreams, as a young boy in Dorset, did Adam think that one day, even before becoming twenty-three years old, he would be travelling in Europe, through Italy, and hopefully France, enjoying the food, spending their money and even using their language, albeit in a very simplistic way. France and Italy, Sicily and Malta were places he had only seen on maps, or read about with Mrs Redman, or at The Manor House.

Actually being in these places and having to fend for himself, travelling through them, virtually alone (although, he admitted to himself, with a good friend) was very much not part of the plan for his life, if he ever had a plan. Admittedly, he had come to be there by a chance of misfortune, but he had to admit there were some elements of their present situation he was thoroughly enjoying.

He only hoped the repercussions for having apparently 'deserted' would not be too serious, when they arrived back in England.

They slept well, and were up early to freshen up for the day, dress and pack their bags again. The had a breakfast, served by a young girl in a white headscarf and apron, which, again, was absolutely delicious and welcome. However, they did not quite know what to do next or how to continue their journey.

'We are English,' said Adam to the distinguished looking lady, who had shown them to their room, and was clearly the proprietor or his wife, although they had seen no sign of a man. She wore an elegant dress in a cotton print, had her hair tied up neatly behind her head, and her hands were beautifully smooth and white, with several rings adorning them.

'I know, you English,' she said with a smile. 'My husband, speak English, little,' she continued. 'He will be here, today. Five o'clock.'

Adam and Joe asked for some more coffee and sat down in the courtyard, with a view to making some more plans. They enjoyed the coffee and the morning sun, even if it was only the eleventh of January.

'From here, where do we go?' said Joe.

'We are in Salerno, here,' Adam indicated on his, by-now, rather crumpled map. We are not very far from Naples, perhaps thirty miles or so, where there might be a British representative or consular office.'

'A what?' said Joe who was getting out of his depth.

'It's like a representative of the British government abroad, like an Embassy, where they look after our people in other countries.'

'Is that in every country?' asked Joe, whose mind was expanding all the time.

'I think so,' said Adam. 'Maybe they will have some ideas about the best way home from here.'

'And may be they will have some ideas about how to lock up deserters!' said Joe.

'Not sure about that,' Adam added. 'It's virtually impossible for any message about our being missing to have been relayed from Malta to Naples, and anyway, why would they? They've no reason to suppose that we survived being missing, and then travelled north. We are just two travellers who can prove we are in the British Army with our identity cards, trying to get back to our barracks in Dorset.'

'Not sure how we explain not being with our regiment,' said Joe. 'We were hardly likely to have been given so much leave.'

'Maybe we just left the army and travelled,' said Adam.

'And got lost!'

'A bit far-fetched, maybe,' said Adam, 'but they may be able to advise us.'

'And how do we get to .. what is it? Naples?'

'Why don't we spend the day here, and see the lady's husband tonight? We can afford another night here. He may have some good advice – and in English.'

'Fair enough,' said Joe, and they stayed to finish their coffee, before exploring Salerno for part of the day, buying a couple of additional trinkets each; a silver pendant and a leather embossed bookmarker for Adam, and a man's leather bracelet and silver plated cigarette case for Joe. Joe did not think it could possibly be solid silver for the few pence that it cost.

They spent the afternoon at a café near the front, looking up at the *Forte de Canale* from the main coastal road, a very impressive fortress above a very impressive promenade, looking out over the sea. They were introduced to the delights of a pizza, which they saw somebody else eating at the café and asked for something similar for themselves.

The café owner brought them an enormous flat-bread pizza which he called *Margherita* topped with soft white mozzarella cheese, red tomatoes and green basil. He pointed out that the colours of the pizza matched the colours of the Italian flag, as he drew their attention, proudly, to the national standard flying above his café.

The afternoon wore on, with another bottle of wine being consumed, before they made their way back to the guest house with the elegant lady, hoping that they might soon meet her husband. Right on time, at five o'clock, he appeared in the lobby of the building where Adam and Joe were sitting and introduced himself.

30

Naples

'Stefano de Luca,' he said extending his hand. 'Good to meet with you, two English gentlemen.' In front of them stood a tall, imposing character.

Italian for Stephen, thought Adam, as he extended his hand too. Joe stood up and offered Stefano his seat.

'I am fine here,' he said, pulling up another chair. 'What are you doing in Salerno?'

His English was remarkably good, and Adam warmed to this gentleman, who appeared to be most interested in who they were. He was slim as well as tall with a slick of black hair and a clean-shaven chin. He wore a black suit, with some very elegant brown and white shoes, white shirt and no tie.

'We are travelling through Italy, northwards,' said Adam, 'hoping to get back to England on the little money we have left. We were stranded in Malta and then Sicily.'

'There were no ships back to England during the winter,' said Joe, 'So we thought overland would be our only way. We must, eventually, find our military base and report home.'

'You have a long way to go.' said Stefano. 'I was in England once when my father worked there in a famous London hotel. It is where I learned to speak English, although I am still not very good and don't get much chance to practise.'

'Your English is much better than our Italian,' said Adam.

'Much better,' said Joe, very impressed.

'Is there a British consulate or embassy in Salerno?' said Adam. 'Maybe that would help us.'

'Not in Salerno,' said Stefano, 'but tomorrow I am gong to Naples, about fifty kilometres from here, for supplies and to visit my bank. Why don't you come with me and you can find the consulate there?'

'We have been robbed a couple of times,' said Joe warily.

'Hope we don't sound suspicious,' added Adam, 'but we are trying to be very careful of our safety.'

'I will admit,' began Stefano. 'that Naples is probably the most dangerous city in Italy, and Italy is not very safe anyway! But you can either trust me or find your own way.

'I came here to meet you because my wife asked me to speak with you. You have alternatives, of course, but one of them is to hope that I am telling the truth and not leading you astray.'

'I think we should,' said Adam, wishing, for a brief moment, that he could speak with Joe without Stefano understanding. 'We do not have many alternatives, and it does look as though we could find somebody there who could advise us, and it may help us to get home.'

'Is our room vacant for one more night?' said Joe. 'It certainly was a superb room to stay in.'

'Of course,' said Stefano, 'and tonight you shall be our guests!'

'Goodness, me no!' said Adam. 'We couldn't ask for that.'

'I insist,' said the owner of the guest house, as his wife appeared and offered them drinks. Stefano continued, in fluent Italian, speaking to his wife and Adam presumed that he was telling them of the arrangement for one more night. She clapped her hands, delightedly and joined them with a drink for herself.

'What a fantastic couple!' said Joe as they got back to their room. 'Another night and nothing to pay!'

'Let's hope it's not too good to be true,' said Adam, 'although I do agree they seem a genuine couple. Perhaps not everybody in Italy is dishonest or a street brigand!'

All four of them ate together that night, another splendid meal, served by the young girl in the white headscarf, and they chatted into the evening, in the warm front parlour of the guest house, in a mixture of English and Italian, but to the relief of Adam and Joe, mostly in English. Even Stefano's wife joined in, when she could, and they learned that her name was Ilaria.

'Tomorrow, I shall use a cart for produce, with a horse, which I hire from the stables nearby,' said Stefano. 'We shall leave just after nine in the morning and there is room on the cart for you both, even if it is not very comfortable. It will take us about three hours, at just a steady trot. That way, the horse will be fit for the return journey, without you two.'

'We really are very grateful,' said Adam. 'Are you sure we should not be paying for tonight's accommodation?'

'It is not a problem,' said Stefano. 'We do not have many English people passing through here. I had a wonderful child-hood, or part of it anyway, in England, and now it is my pleasure for you to be my guests.'

Adam and Joe were up early next morning, well before break-fast time, and slipped out to where they had seen market stalls the day before. They bought a large bunch of colourful roses, from a flower stall, for Ilaria even though, Adam pondered, it was still January. In all Adam's years in the gardens at The Manor House, he had never seen such blooms at that time of year!

The breakfast was more than sufficient and indeed plentiful enough for them to pack some extra food for their journey, which Iliria encouraged. Stefano disappeared for half an hour while the boys readied themselves to travel, and he returned with a long open wooden cart drawn by a splendid chestnut horse, which he tethered to a post outside the building.

'Everybody ready?' he said as he came into the lobby area.

'Thank you so much,' said Joe to Iliria. She responded with a hug and a kiss on the cheek for them both.

'And *grazie*... for flowers,' she said.

All three of the men left, Adam and Joe carrying bags and climbing on to the front of the big wagon. They were off to Naples. Stefano steered the vehicle through the busy market area, which was more crowded now than an hour earlier, when Adam and Joe had gone to look for flowers. There were market traders and shopkeepers, some in dark clothes with white or grey shirts, but there were also some men and women in much more colourful attire.

Adam saw women wearing long blue skirts covered with red or bright green aprons, with white blouses and puff sleeves, trimmed with lace or frills. Some men wore trousers which ended buttoned at the knee, with white stockings and bright coloured waistcoats over white shirts. Many of the coloured clothing items had embroidered edges, or contrasting tape, stitched along the edges or hemlines.

Many graceful girls were carrying baskets over one or both arms filled with fruit, or bread, packages or vegetables. It was a vibrant and colourful scene, which both Adam and Joe took a last look at over their shoulders, as Stefano headed out of the town and along the coast road.

It was not a hot day but the sea to their left was a beautiful azure blue, rippling with sunlight. There was a breeze and, as they rode further and further into the countryside, there were bare rocks above the road, plenty of sandy-coloured houses where the land stretched out flat, some with folk sitting outside, some with washing hanging from little iron balconies, and all with their windows shuttered against the sun.

'January is one of our coldest months,' said Stefano, 'but even so we do not get frost or snow that you do in England.'

'This is very comfortable and pleasant,' said Adam, 'Do you get rain very often?'

'It is certainly possible, but let's hope not today. We have a long way to go,' Stefano replied. 'Do you know much about Italy?'

'Hardly anything at all,' said Joe, 'but I do like what we have experienced so far, except perhaps for somebody trying to steal from us.'

'You were lucky,' Stefano informed him. 'I also think you were clever. Since the unification of Italy, into one nation, thirty-three years ago, there has always been an undercurrent of brigands and thieves, gangs of men who want to control the areas where they live, as well as those who disagree with the government in the new capital, Rome.

'In some cases we even find the emergence of local heroes, who live beneath the law and become local legends, not always legends with a beneficial outcome for their own people. We look after our own.'

'That seems,' Adam said, 'as though they are anti-government and anti their own folk.'

'You have a famous legend, of a man who fought for the rights of the people against a tyrannical king,' said Stefano.

'Robin Hood,' Adam came back. 'He was probably not real, and probably not just one man, but he personified what the poor were going through.'

'And so it is with us,' Stefano continued, 'except that some of our powerful families pretend to protect others, and offer their services for extortionate amounts of money, so that they control villages and the local people aggressively.'

'Have you been troubled or threatened?' Joe asked, thinking how small and insignificant a thief he had been in London, on his own.

'I've been lucky, I think,' said Stefano. 'or maybe clever, like you. In Salerno we have peaceful people and maybe the gangs from other parts are biding their time!'

'What did you mean,' Adam asked, 'by the unification of Italy and the 'new' capital, Rome?'

'My goodness, I could spend the entire journey telling you the history of our country and its troubles.' Stefano began, 'but it is probably enough to tell you that Italy was a land of many provinces, and even kingdoms. Naples was the capital of Campania for many years.

'You had your Wars of the Roses in the fifteenth century, so we too had many troubles in Italy, between different regions, and centres of power, throughout the early eighteen hundreds. A movement calling themselves *Risorgimento*, or The Renewal, emerged, whose object was a single nation of Italy, under a strong monarchy. The power struggle went on for many years and through many disastrous battles.'

'Sounds as though you went through a lot,' said Joe.

'Sometimes it was terrible,' said Stefano, 'but a man named Garibaldi was a powerful influence and, cutting a very long story short, eventually Naples and this region of Campania became part of a unified nation, Italy. The proclamation of The Kingdom of Italy happened on 17th March 1861, which may yet one day become a national holiday.

'And would you believe, Naples became the first city on the Italian peninsula to have a railway in 1839!'

'We're very lucky,' 'said Adam, 'that the railway spread at least as far as Salerno from the south! But did the unification solve the problems?' asked Adam. 'Did everything settle down?'

'Goodness, no!' said Stefano. 'But, as in any revolution, there are pockets of resistance which keep their views and refuse to co-operate. And the real consequence of the years of unrest was emigration. Hundreds of thousands of Italians went to America, and are still going, every year, to find a new life in a new land.'

The cart trundled on, through miles of beautiful countryside, almost always with the sea in their sights to the west. The small group stopped to allow the horse to munch some grass while they drank and ate their food, packed carefully, by Ilaria, from breakfast.

'Did you know,' said Stefano, 'that in 1847 the famous English writer Edward Lear travelled throughout Calabria, where you travelled from three days ago? He was on foot, accompanied by a guide, and with a donkey to carry his luggage.'

'Of course,' said Adam, 'I have heard of him. 'He wrote *The*

Owl and the Pussycat .'

'The what?' said Joe.

'*The Owl and the Pussycat*,' said Adam. 'One day, I'll read it to you. It's a very famous poem for children.'

'He also wrote a travel diary, published as *Diary of a Voyage on Foot in Calabria* .' said Stefano. 'That, too, is quite famous. Your Mr Lear is quite a celebrated person in Italy.'

'If ever we get home and back to some kind of normality,' said Adam, 'I must be sure to find it and read it. It might be fascinating to read about places we've actually been to.'

'What do you suggest we do once we get to Naples?' enquired Adam of Stefano.

'It is entirely up to you,' said Stefano, 'but I think you could do a lot worse than to find the British Consulate and report to them. They can communicate with London, by telegraph these days, and maybe you will benefit from sending your story home in advance of actually getting there.'

'I think we need to earn some more money before setting out any further,' said Joe. 'We're not down to our last coins, by any means, but it is still a very long way to go.'

'What opportunities might there be to work for a few weeks in Naples?' said Adam. 'We are not too fussy about what we do, but it could help.'

'I'll have a word with my friends when we arrive at the markets,' Stefano replied. 'But I'm making no promises. Local people are not too keen on others arriving to work locally.'

'We'll have to take that chance,' said Adam, 'but thank you for suggesting you might ask.'

They arrived in the busy city of Naples, and Adam and Joe's eyes practically popped out of their heads. They had both seen

Dorchester and Portsmouth. Joe had experienced London in his early days, as Adam had experienced Weymouth, but nothing compared to the sunlit bustle of this great city by the sea. It was as if a great unified dance had been choreographed for the thousands of carriages, pedestrians and bicycles, all weaving in and out of each other, with organ music being generated on every street corner.

Most of the men, obviously at work on stalls or with barrows of produce, wore white shirts, and flat caps in grey, black, blue or brown were obviously the order of the day and possibly every day.

Horse-drawn cabs missed each other by inches and so many of the male population were also in black suits and ties that they might have been attending one vast funeral or wedding. There were women in flowing gowns, of many colours, clearly quite wealthy and sporting large flamboyant hats.

There were religious women, nuns, shrouded in black and going around in pairs. Messenger boys, in pale ill-fitting suits, were running and dodging the traffic, as they eagerly sought to deliver letter and notes from one office, or individual, to another. It was a riot, and framing it all was the sea, probably, even at this time of the year, more blue than it ought to be. Adam and Joe had never seen nor even imagined anything like it.

'We will go straight to my suppliers,' said Stefano. 'There we can find something more to eat and drink, and I can perhaps introduce you to a friend who may be able to find you somewhere to stay, and help you find the consulate.'

'Maybe even a temporary job,' added Joe.

'And maybe even a job,' said Stefano grinning. 'Okay, we shall see.'

The wagon weaved its way through the traffic, off the main road and into side streets where shop after shop was shaded by enormous exterior awnings, clearly meant to shield them from the blazing sun which hit the city for most of the year. Even today, it was still warm and most people were walking in the shade of the canvasses.

It did not take long to get to the large warehouse behind the busy streets which Stefano was aiming for. The wagon came to a halt and he jumped down, followed by Adam and Joe, who stood and stared at the boxes of produce piled high, crates with rattling bottles and great barrels being rolled along, or hoisted on to other vehicles. They gaped at the extraordinary activity going on around them.

'Come,' said Stefano, 'and we shall have some coffee.' He led them through a noisy hive of activity with porters and others sporting books and pencils, a few women carrying bundles of flowers or trays slung around their necks, and the ubiquitous messenger boys, darting to and fro, to find where their messages should go.

At the back of the warehouse they entered a large café-style room, filled with tables and chairs. As Stefano walked in and headed for a window seat, four men already sitting there stood up and greeted him with inelegant hugs and a kiss on each cheek. They exchanged words and Stefano indicated to the two boys that they should sit.

'These are my friends,' said Stefano rather pointedly to anyone in the room who would listen. Then he addressed Adam and Joe.

'Stay here. You can have coffee or wine, and some food, whatever you fancy. My friends will see you are well fed!' He almost laughed, but Adam and Joe felt assured that at least they would be safe there. Some others in the room smiled in their direction. Most were concentrating on their drink or a newspaper or both.

The man behind the counter preparing or serving food and drink could only be described as greasy. He had enormous hands, about three days growth of beard, wore black trousers and an enormous apron which reminded Adam of the first time he had met Mr Granger at The Manor House, although this one was white. At least it looked as if it should have been. The apron seemed to envelop him completely from neck to toe.

He came to Adam and Joe's table with a carafe of wine, a pot of coffee and some olives.

'*Pizza?*' he spoke gruffly, but only slightly obsequiously.

'*Grazie,*' said Adam, '*due Margherita.*' He indicated *two* with his fingers hoping he would be understood.

'S'good,' growled the 'apron' and he turned away, to return to the counter, then vanished through a curtain of hundreds of beads strung on to threads. It rattled as he went through it.

'Well, what have we hit upon here?' said Joe. 'It all seems safe enough and somehow everybody in here seems to accept us because we are friends of Stefano.'

'That is good enough for me,' said Adam, 'although frankly I'd rather be outside and looking around the city, or sitting by the sea.'

Their time in the café passed slowly. The 'apron' offered them some fruit and more coffee, and as one hour turned into two, Adam ventured to the door of the café and looked out at the activity in the warehouse. It was then he saw Stefano, across at a distance, talking with other men, exchanging packages, a hug or even a kiss before moving on to another part of the building, where Adam lost sight of him.

'I wonder if we shall be able to find some work for a week or two,' said Joe... when Adam returned to the table. 'I wouldn't mind working here as a porter or something.'

'Not sure I would,' said Adam. 'Somehow it all seems a bit threatening, and none too friendly. I hope I am wrong. I suppose it is hearing so many voices speaking a language I don't understand.'

Eventually Stefano returned.

'Have you been looked after?' said Stefano as he sat down.

'Absolutely,' Adam replied, 'although I would like to get away at some time, to find somewhere to stay when you return to Salerno, and maybe look for some work.'

'It is all arranged,' said Stefano to their astonishment. 'My brother, Carlo, lives in Naples and we do business together. He has a large house where you can stay. I can take you to the British Consulate in a little while, and maybe we can find you some work here.'

'Why would you do all that for us?' said Joe, who, through most of his short life had never experienced much altruism. 'That sounds amazing.' Stefano plunged his hand into his inside pocket and pulled out two twenty-five lire notes which he gave to the boys, one to each.

'Don't you worry about that. You are good English boys, trying to get home, and I remember England with much fondness when I was young.'

Adam took the note which had *Biglietto di Stato* printed on it, which Stefano told him actually meant 'Ticket of the State'.

'Thank you very much. You ought to be getting back soon.

You have along way to go. Have you done your business for today?'

'Almost,' said Stefano, as they rose from the chairs. He led them outside into the street which was still as busy as before. 'You two go for a breath of fresh air. I shall bring the wagon to the end of this street and meet you by the tall stone column, with what looks like a winged warrior on the top. It is a monument. You cannot miss it.'

'I hope we don't,' said Adam, although he felt confident that he had seen it on their way to the warehouse earlier.

'I saw it on the way here,' said Joe. 'It's a bit like Nelson's Column in London but not as big.'

'Exactly,' said Stefano, who remembered the great column which honoured England's hero, Lord Nelson, from when he was a boy in London, with his father. 'I'll meet you there in about thirty minutes.' Of course Adam had never seen Nelson's Column in London, but had seen pictures of it.

The street was crowded but they navigated their way through the carriages and the occasional omnibus. They kept to the walkway along each side of the street, as much as they could. Adam, quite suddenly, saw a sign saying '*Gelato Arlecchino*' where some people had formed a short queue, while others were walking away eating what looked deliciously like a tub of frozen fruit. One of them passed Adam, and he pulled Joe to the end of the queue.

'Two lire, that's really not very much money, is it?' he said to Joe. 'Let's try it.' Joe was game and they sorted out four lire between them. The coins were very small, but they passed them to the boy behind the brightly painted wheeled trolley when they got to the front, and were rewarded with two tubs of fruit flavoured ice, and a tiny wooden spatula. The ice was in three flavours, one of which was chocolate.

'Thank you,' said Adam as they paid the boy. '*Grazie.*'

'English?' said the boy. 'S'good. Ice cream! Naples Ice Cream, *Neopolitan!*'

'Ice cream, of course,' said Adam. He had seen some ice cream, made from the ice kept in the ice cellar, at The Manor House, but had seldom tasted any like this. Joe had never set eyes on anything like it and marvelled at the taste, the coldness and the texture.

'This is amazing,' he said, and Adam still wondered how so many people had just the tiniest bit of English with which to communicate, here in central Italy.

As he enjoyed the three flavours of '*Gelato Arlecchino*' it occurred to him that so many young men in England, from rich or aristocratic families, do undertake the Grand Tour of Europe, when they reach a certain age.

The places, where they spend money, on the continent, do accommodate these rich young men, with as much hospitality as their wealth will generate, and they leave behind a smattering of English for the locals to absorb.

They met Stefano, as planned, at the foot of the column as his wagon came to a halt. They climbed in and Stefano tugged on the reins to encourage the horse to pull away.

'The British Consulate is in the *Via Partenope*, right on the waterfront looking out over the sea,' said Stefano, as they rode through the traffic. 'It will not take long to get there.'

It was indeed a very impressive building and, as they drew up in front of it, Stefano made as if to make his way home from there.

'I have to leave you here,' he said. 'I have a long way to get home, and as you can see, the wagon is full and heavier for the horse to pull than it was this morning.'

'Thank you again,' said Adam. 'I am sure we can look after ourselves from here.'

'Over there, if you look,' said Stefano, 'there are several horse- drawn cabs. The first cab will wait for you. I have asked him to wait. Tell the driver of the first cab that you are friends of Stefano and Carlo de Luca, which he will guess anyway, and that you want to go to Carlo's house.

'Are you sure?' said Joe.

'Absolutely,' said Stefano. 'Trust me, I have many friends here in Naples, and they are happy to help two English travellers. Go in to the consulate first. Tell them how you got here, and who brought you and somebody will help you.'

'Thank you again,' said Adam as he pulled down his bag and made sure it was safely closed up.

'We will meet again,' said Stefano, and pulled on the reins as he waved them goodbye. The two boys stood and looked for a moment, then looked across the road at the cabs lined up. The driver of the first cab gave them a brief wave, almost a salute to acknowledge that he had seen them.

They turned and went into the Consulate, which was a large, cool, airy building with an enormous entrance hall. Adam looked around for some kind of reception desk, and made towards it with a confident step. Joe followed him.

Adam introduced himself and Joe, as travellers who had become stranded in Italy, making their way home to Britain. He told the young man on the desk some of their story, and particularly how they had been given one night's accommodation in Salerno, and even some cash by Stefano. The young man, on the desk, almost a boy, thought for a moment, went away, and very soon returned. He was dressed in a good blue, pinstriped suit with dark tie and winged-collared shirt.

'Can you come back on Monday?' he said very politely, 'at about this time, mid afternoon, when somebody will be here who can help you.'

'Yes, that's fine,' said Adam.

'You have somewhere to stay tonight, I understand, so will Monday be ok?'

'Yes, that is fine,' said Adam again and they made their way out of the building into the sun.

Just as they had been told, the cab driver seemed to know who they were, when they mentioned Stefano, and gestured them to get to the cab. He drove off through the traffic with Adam and Joe, of course, not knowing where they were going, but hoping, and trusting, that it would be Stefano's brother, Carlo's home.

The cab made its way out of the city centre, through the animated street life, which was still buzzing, and climbed away from the houses and shops. They had been travelling less than half an hour, Adam estimated about three miles, before the cab came to a halt outside an impressive house. Joe thought it was a mansion.

31

Working in Naples

'*Vomero*,' said the driver. 'Carlo de Luca'

He jumped down from his perch behind the passengers, helped them with their two bags and stood there. Adam was searching for some coins, which he refused, putting his hand up in front of them.

'*No*, no money,' he said. 'Tomorrow twelve o'clock,' he indicated on the hands of a watch he produced from his waistcoat. 'Twelve.'

'*Grazie*,' said Adam, putting away his money. The cab driver gave them the same salute he had given them in town, opposite the Consulate, and he was away. Adam and Joe hauled themselves up the short flight of stairs to a large front door and pulled a bell-ring.

The door was answered by a very smart lady, shorter than either Adam or Joe, but who looked very sophisticated. She was well dressed with a floral print dress, a short linen coat over the top and with dark brown hair, tied into a chignon, with a floral print ribbon trailing from it. She wore soft leather shoes, almost slippers.

'Come,' she said with a smile.

The boys slowly entered the 'mansion' and it was indeed, a splendid house. Another light and airy hallway, although not as big as the Consulate, of course, but with some marble pillars, very lightweight drapes hanging at the windows and dark wooden furniture placed on very comfortable-looking sheepskin rugs. A wide staircase began in the hallway and went up, before it divided, left and right, to an upper floor.

'What on earth are we doing here?' said Adam. 'This really doesn't feel right.'

'Well, as long as it lasts,' replied Joe obviously enjoying his new surroundings, 'let's enjoy it. *Grazie*, madam.'

'I show you room,' she said, and led the way upstairs to a spectacular room, and a bathroom just along nearby, which rather took Joe's breath away.

'My God,' Joe said. 'Who lives here?'

'Well, I rather hope it is Carlo, Stefano's brother,' said Adam, 'but it still doesn't feel right.'

They looked around the room, which had two enormous single beds, while the lady stayed at the door, after showing them the bathroom. She indicated that they can drink and eat downstairs.

'Eat, and drink,' she said and pointed downwards. '*Cinque minuti.*'

'*Grazie,*' said Adam, as she left. 'We seem to be doing nothing but eating and drinking other people's food and wine! And now we have more in five minutes'

They unpacked their bags. There was no key for the door, but Adam steeled himself to be positive and they went down the ornate staircase to find a dining room. The smell of pasta was very appealing, and along with tomatoes, cheese, olives and even more wine, they enjoyed their first meal in Stefano's brother's house.

The lady of the house, whose name they did not even know yet, left them to it and they sat looking out of the window at a beautiful garden.

'Either,' said Adam, 'we are being set up for the biggest fall yet in our fortunes, or this is a stroke of luck which will get us a long way towards home.'

'What do you mean?' said Joe as he enjoyed his third tomato.

'Well,' Adam continued quietly, as he looked around the room for any signs of the woman, 'how much have we heard about families who have great influence in this part of Italy? How much have we heard about gangs of brigands, and men who, so we're told, 'protect' other families and businesses?

'It's a big organisation, and apparently has some of the local government and others in their pockets. There's a lot of money involved, and there is an awful lot of money around us in this house!'

'Do you mean Stefano and his brother?' Joe ventured.

'And plenty of others,' said Adam. 'Think about it, we were not robbed or accosted on the road to Naples and there were just three of us...'

'And a horse,' joked Joe.

'And a horse! Agreed,' Adam smiled, 'but at the warehouse, we were greeted like old friends, along with Stefano, they stood up when we came in, and did you see the great wad of banknotes he came back to us with, before we went to the Consulate? He wasn't spending money. He was collecting it!'

'His wagon was full to the brim with produce, including wines and beers, and some boxes with no labels or obvious contents,' said Joe, warming to the possibility that they were being protected rather than set up as victims.

'And at the Consulate,' said Adam, 'the young man behind the reception greeted us with '*You have somewhere to stay tonight, I understand.*' Do you remember? How did he know that? I suppose Stefano could have told him. But why? And he's so friendly with the cab drivers that one of them is prepared to wait for us, asking for no fare, and promising to be back in the morning to pick us up. Only Queen Victoria gets that kind of door to door service, I think!

'So,' continued Adam, 'I repeat, either we are being set up for our biggest fall yet, or this is a stroke of luck which will get us a long way towards home.'

'Dear God, 'said Joe, 'I hope it's the lucky option. This is way above me in criminal activity!'

'And, if and when we get back to some kind of normality, travelling on or getting back to England, re-joining our regiment or whatever, might we unknowingly be mixed up in criminal activity, which could come back to bite us?'

'Or could we be arrested here for being involved or too close?' Joe wondered.

'Somehow I doubt that,' said Adam. 'Our dear 'uncles' Stefano, and Carlo, whom we haven't even met yet, would be rather more likely to be arrested than we would, and so far they have done nothing but look after us, feed us, protect us and house us. The protection comes with the friendship! Lucky us, I hope!'

'Which brings us back to our original question. What on earth are we doing here?' said Joe.

'Maybe we shall never quite know if our assumptions are correct, about the family and the brothers. But, for now, we can do no more than go with it, keep our eyes and ears peeled, be aware of our surroundings and… enjoy the pasta!'

'I'll drink to that,' said Joe, and he did.

They spent a cool night in sound sleep and the next morning they found a wonderful breakfast laid out for them, including a steaming pot of coffee. Quite suddenly, a plump little lady appeared wearing mostly sandy coloured linen, with a white apron, and indicated that she would do some washing for them.

'That's a real bonus,' said Adam as they agreed, and went upstairs to find clothing that needed laundering. The lady of the house was there to greet them when they came downstairs, and offered them two long white caftan-like garments while the 'laundry lady' took even the clothes they were wearing! Neither Adam nor Joe had ever seen such a piece of clothing but they soon found it was very comfortable and very cool to wear.

'My name is Rosa,' said the lady who had greeted them yesterday. 'My English is not good. Enjoy food?'

'*Grazie*, Yes,' said Adam quickly, 'very good.'

'*Grazie*,' Joe joined in.

'My husband comes soon' she said, then poured herself a coffee and vanished into what they boys thought was a kitchen.

'I hope her husband doesn't mind us being here,' said Joe.

'He shouldn't, should he?' Joe suggested. 'It was his brother, Stefano, who arranged for us to stay here, so he knows we're here.'

'I know, but I never ceased to be surprised by what comes next in our adventure!'

The next surprise came as 'the greasy apron' walked into the room, now much more smartly dressed than when they had seen him at the warehouse café the day before. He was shaved and wore a crisp white shirt. He was certainly no longer 'greasy'.

'Good morning,' he greeted them breezily. 'Hope you slept well.'

'You!' said Joe. 'Good morning. Are you Carlo, Stefano's brother?'

'Of course,' said Carlo, 'but we do not advertise it very much. I am his big brother by two years, and as you know, we spent a lot of time in London with our parents when we were young.'

'This is a surprise indeed,' said Adam, then added, 'Are you sure you did not mind us staying here last night?'

'Of course not,' said Carlo. 'Stefano told me all about you and tomorrow you must go to the Consulate to find out how to stay safe while you get home. And if you wish, you can take a short break here in Naples and work for some extra money.'

'But at the café,' said Adam, 'you looked as though you had nothing to do with Stefano.'

'We conduct the family's business together, but do not broadcast that we are related,' said Carlo. 'That way we can do deals and keep an eye on the markets, and the produce being loaded or unloaded. It wasn't me that made you your pizza! I never inherited my father's culinary skills. I leave that to Stefano and his hotel in Salerno. I just deliver the food to your to your table, while I have plenty of other business to attend to.'

'Well, that is certainly a surprise,' said Adam. 'And if we get some work, should we find somewhere to live in the city?'

'No. You stay here as our guests,' said Carlo. 'I will enjoy talking with you in the evenings. Joe, is it?' he said, indicating Joe who acknowledged that as being correct,

'Joe, you can come to the market place to work if you wish. You will not come to any harm there. It is about half an hour's walk, although you and I can travel together most days. Adam,

Stefano tells me that you worked as a gardener in a large English house.'

'That's right, said Adam. 'You certainly are well informed.'

'Good,' said Carlo, 'because at the University in Naples they have a beautiful Botanic Garden. They can offer you some work at this time, even though it is only the second week in January. There is plenty to do to prepare for the spring.'

'That sounds amazing,' said Adam. 'Will they employ me?'

'So many people have emigrated from southern Italy in the past ten years or more. Almost everywhere there are businesses, universities, shops and hospitals, trying to employ people and there are too few people to fill the tasks that need doing. The University is very old, at least six hundred years, and its Botanic Garden is famous, so you will be welcomed there if you have some horticultural skills.'

'I would love to see it,' said Adam.

'Today is Sunday,' said Carlo, 'so I think that the University, and most certainly the Consulate, will be closed. You can relax here, or go and see the shops and the sea. On Monday we shall go to the Consulate, then you must get a get a cab to take you to the University. It is not far, just east of the city, and I have a name for you to ask for when you arrive.'

'Thank you very much,' said Adam, as their prolonged breakfast came to an end.

Carlo continued, 'I've written the name of a contact at The University on the back of this card of mine, with our address on. Show this when you get to the Botanic Gardens on Monday, and to any cab driver too, who will not charge you for your journey, either to the Botanic Gardens, or back here to this house.'

'Adam looked on the back of the card, the front of which displayed Carlo's name and address. The reverse side showed a handwritten note , '*Università Naples, Giardino Botanico*'.

They enjoyed more conversation and coffee for nearly an hour and then returned to their rooms, to find some washing, already returned, and fresh clean clothes that they could change into. At no time did either of the boys bring up the subject of Carlo's 'business'.

At twelve o'clock they were outside waiting when the cab arrived. Carlo joined them for the trip into the city. It was there, just as Carlo had suggested, that they spent the day looking at shops and market stalls, the sea and the ships, coming and going, before making their way back to Carlo's house by asking a cab driver to take them.

There they spent another pleasant evening in conversation before retiring, in anticipation of their visit to the Consulate the next day.

At breakfast, Carlo began the conversation.

'Joe,' he began, 'after you two have been to the Consulate, find your way to the market warehouse, where you were yesterday, and find me in the café there.'

'Will do,' said Joe, who felt sure he knew the way up the wide main street to the warehouse.

'And, Adam,' continued Carlo. 'Take the cab and ask for the University Botanic Garden.'

'We seem to be saying an awful lot of thank-yous,' said Adam to Carlo, as he took the card.

'Never mind that for now. Let us go.'

At the Consulate, Adam and Joe went in as they had done on the Saturday, and found the young man at reception desk again.

'Good afternoon,' he said. 'Would you please sign this Visitors' Book and then wait a moment?' He vanished from around the front of the desk, across the hallway, and into another ground floor room behind a heavy door. The boys each signed the large leather-bound book on the desk, then waited, and decided to sit on one of the long leather-bound seats either side of the central staircase.

A few minutes passed and the slight young clerk emerged from the room into which he had vanished, took a quick look for Adam and Joe, then bound across and asked them to follow him. He went up the stairs, turned left, along a carpeted corridor and in through another door, which brought them to a room on the front of the building, which overlooked the harbour.

A distinguished looking spectacled gentleman, in a dark blue suit, winged collar on a white shirt, and polished shoes, gestured them to sit down in front of the desk at which he had been sitting.

'Thank you, Williams,' said the man behind the desk, and the young man made a polite 'thank you' and left.

'Well, what have you two been up to, that you find yourselves here in Naples with Army identity cards and not much else?'

'Who are we speaking with?' said Adam just slightly audaciously!

My name is Cadogen-Gower, Victor Cadogan-Gower of Her Majesty's Diplomatic Service. I am not the Ambassador, nor even the Consul in Naples, but I am a Consular Assistant and need to know who you are, and how you got here, as you do appear to be serving soldiers in Her Majesty's army.'

Adam began to explain the entire story, and even produced the modest, amateurish, affidavits, which he had folded up, from the priest in Malta and from Leopold Ashton. The story included having been set up and robbed, virtually twice. He explained that they had decided to try to make it home to England and their regiment, overland, because there were apparently no more ships from Valetta back to Britain in the winter.

'We have kept within the law,' explained Joe, as if that made much difference, 'although we accidentally did get a free train ride from Salerno to Naples, hiding from thieves, just as the goods train was about to depart!'

'I don't think we need add that to your record,' said Mr Cadogen-Gower, as he made a few notes.

'Our record?' Adam came in, leaning slightly forward. 'What kind of record?'

'Well, technically, you are deserters, if what you tell me is true, although I have no proof of that either way, even with your notes from kindly hosts along the way.' The Consular Assistant was looking over his glasses.

'We would hardly be here if we were trying to stay hidden, or attempting to start a new anonymous life, without reference to where we belong.' Adam was determined to state the case that they had done nothing wrong, except try to get home, which was not wrong.

'We are just trying to do the right thing, coming here,' said Joe almost pleading, but Adam restrained him from any further pleas!

'Can you give us an authority or 'safe passage' from here on through our journey and we will return to England and report to our barracks, as soon as we can?' said Adam. 'Unless, of course, you can pay our train fares all the way home from Naples.'

'That is not going to happen,' said the Assistant very firmly. 'There are telegraph messages which I can send and, hopefully, to which I may get some answers, but they take time, and if, as you say, your ship was on its way to India and further beyond, goodness knows when we might hear anything from them.'

'So what do we do, to stay on the right side of our own laws, or the rules of our army service?'

'Can you stay here in Naples?' said the Assistant.

'We certainly can, and can provide you with an address,' said Adam as he began to retrieve Carlo's card from his pocket. 'We are staying with...'

'Yes, there's no need for that,' said Mr Cadogen-Gower, 'I do actually know where you are staying. I was just asking if you are happy to stay put, while I try to communicate with London? There is a facility here for me to arrest you, and hold you, until I hear anything further to confirm your stories, but frankly, I'd rather not.'

'And, frankly, I'd definitely rather you didn't either,' said Adam glancing a sideways look at Joe, who was looking aghast. 'We'd prefer you didn't.'

'Fair enough,' said the Consular Assistant in Naples to Her Majesty's Ambassador in Rome. 'Fair enough. You stay with your Mr...'

'De Luca,' said Adam holding up the card.

'Yes, thank you. I don't really need to know his name. You stay with him, until further notice and when I can, I will provide you with proof of identity for you to continue your journeys to Britain. In the meantime, you must report here every Monday morning, as you have done today.

'If I get any news, or telegraph communication, I will let you know the next time you come, or I will get a message to you.'

'Thank you,' said Adam. 'Does that mean we are free to go now?'

'Just sign the book on the way out as you leave,' he said, then pressed a bell-push on his desk. Within seconds the young clerk from the front hall appeared at the door.

'You rang, sir?

'Please take Mr Smith and Mr Warkin down to the front hall, will you, Williams. They are leaving now,' said the Consular Assistant without even standing up.

'This way, please,' said the young man, and led them out into the corridor.

'You are English, and working in Italy?' said Adam as they descended the stairs.

'I am a very lucky man to get a job here in Naples,' replied the young man. 'Williams, Henry Williams, Harry to my friends.' He shook their hands as they reached the bottom of the stairs. 'I went to university in Cambridge and then found a job in the Diplomatic Service and was sent out here just six months ago.'

'Not entirely luck,' said Adam. 'You worked for your position.'

'Thank you very much,' said Harry, 'But I was still lucky. And what about you two?'

'Ours is quite a long story, as you know, but very different from yours,' Adam informed him, thinking of how he had grown up, without even going to school, and that Joe's background was a million miles from Harry's.

'Do you fancy a cup of coffee or a glass of wine?' said Harry as they finished signing the book ready to depart.

'Yes, that would be great,' Joe said quickly, before Adam had the chance to accept or decline.

'Well, follow me again,' he said, 'I am due a break about now.' He vanished into a room, behind the desk, and very quickly re-emerged, holding a dark wide-brimmed hat. He was followed by another, more elderly gentleman, who took up his position behind the reception desk.

'Thank you,' he said to the new arrival. 'I shall only be half an hour or so.'

The three young men went out into the January sun, which was not blazing hot, but sufficiently warm. He led them down across the main square in front of the Consulate, on to a promenade which ran along the sea front, before finding chairs and a table at a café, which overlooked the water.

'It is not encouraged for us to fraternize with clients at the Consulate,' said Harry, 'but you are English, and you're the only people of about my age I have seen in months. Everybody where I work seems to be doddering around in their dotage.'

'I am not sure of the meaning of all those words, Harry,' said Joe smiling at Adam, 'but I get the gist of it!'

They all three smiled; the young man from a Cambridge university background, the poor boy from Dorset, who almost taught himself to read and set out on his personal path to adulthood, and the ex-prisoner, who was pleased to have such a good friend as Adam, and who now sat talking with a young man with letters after his name!

It was a good half an hour, and at least two cups of coffee

each, before they got up for Harry to return to work, and for Adam and Joe to make their way to where they wanted to be next.

'I live in a small room in the Consulate,' said Harry. 'Drop by and say *hello* if you can, while you are still in Naples. It would be really good to catch up again while you are in the city.'

'Thanks,' said both Adam and Joe.

'Believe it or not, I am going to visit a university now,' said Adam and quickly explained his reasons.

'Well, I wish you well,' said Harry, at which point they separated. Adam went back across the square, to find a cab, and Joe made his way to the main street and back beyond the shops and the stalls, to find the warehouse. He even bought himself a flat cap, so as to merge into the universal appearance of almost all the workers he saw as he approached the warehouse.

'*Giardino Botanico, per favore*,' said Adam to the cab driver and showed him the card, which he examined both sides of.

'*Si, entra*,' said the driver which Adam took to mean okay, and 'get in', so he did.

The University was not far from the centre, away from the sea and, again, on a road rising away from the coast. He enjoyed the views of another part of Naples and very soon became aware of the most exotic gardens, and elegant buildings, as they approached the University campus.

'*Grazie*,' said Adam as he dismounted the cab. '*Grazie.*'

'*Si,*' said the driver, and pointed to a door across a green lawn, as he drove away.

Once inside the unlocked door, Adam found himself alone in a large well-lit room, with pot plants everywhere, and several elegant chairs. In every new situation where Adam found himself, he always made instant mental comparisons with his own home, Mrs Redman's sitting room, his tiny attic room at The Manor House or the barracks in Dorset. This was elegant indeed.

'*Buongiorno*,' said a voice. 'Good morning, Adam.'

'You know my name?' Adam replied, '… er… good morning, *buongiorno.*'

'Signor De Luca tells me you have been gardener,' said the voice which Adam now listened to more carefully, as a middle-aged man, wearing an open-neck shirt, brown trousers and brown boots, approached him. The man was slightly greying, but had a good head of hair, bright eyes and rosy cheeks, perhaps, Adam thought, from working in the open air in a country like Italy. He was an inch or two shorter than Adam.

'Yes, sir,' said Adam.

'Welcome,' said the voice. 'I am Georgio. Do you like our gardens?' He pointed through the large front windows.

'Very much,' replied Adam, as the man gestured him to follow. They toured the outside areas for half an hour, and then the greenhouses, before sitting down to eat some bread, olives, and wine.

It was a very comfortable meeting with few language problems, and finished up with Adam promising to come every day, as early as he could, for five days a week, and maybe sometimes on a Saturday. Georgio seemed to know, already, most of what Adam was promising to do, as if he had been informed earlier, and listened as Adam explained that he had to go to the Consulate on Mondays, as well as coming here to the gardens.

'S'good,' said Georgio. 'Maybe you walk back to the city?'

'Yes, if you show me the way,' said Adam. So Georgio drew

a small map and Adam was on his way, promising to see him the next day.

He did not meet Joe in the city centre, but made his way back to the De Luca's house where he freshened up, had some coffee and waited for Joe, who arrived in the early evening, very happy with what had befallen him during the afternoon.

They talked into the evening over another excellent meal, with Carlo and his wife sounding very happy that they had some work, telling them that they were happy for them both.

This arrangement, of working at the warehouse for Joe, and at the university gardens for Adam continued for several weeks, very successfully. They soon got to know the city centre, and some additional cafes, when they sometimes met after their day's work.

They duly reported to the Consulate every Monday and heard nothing new from Harry, or his boss, the Consular Assistant. The three of them, Harry, Adam and Joe, did occasionally meet for coffee and once or twice, on a Sunday, for ice creams and sweet cakes by the sea front.

32

Vesuvius

January became February and on Monday the 19th of February Harry met them at the front entrance, as usual, and told them that no communications had been received, as was the usual message on a Monday. They would have to wait, and work, another week.

Then, as the two boys made ready to go to work that morning, he unexpectedly, added, 'Would you like to see Mount Vesuvius?'

'Would I just? Yes!' said Adam, 'I've read so much about it, but is it dangerous?'

'Not at all,' said Harry, 'although admittedly it could be. One could be very unlucky and be stuck on the rim of the crater when it erupts, but there hasn't been even a small eruption for twenty years or more.'

'Can we get there?' said Adam who had been observing the view of the volcano across the Bay of Naples almost every day since arriving a month ago.

'Certainly,' said Harry. 'How about next Sunday? I can get some transport and we can make a day of it.'

'Agreed,' said both Adam and Joe. 'That will be amazing,' added Adam.

The following Sunday, they got to the Consulate before ten

o'clock and met Harry, who was now much more casually dressed, and was even sporting a flat cap, almost identical to Joe's. He was sitting on a small four-wheeled buggy, which had a single leather seat, with room for three across its width, and was being drawn by one grey horse, who looked happy just to wait for them. Harry looked very much in charge and comfortable sitting aboard the buggy.

'I have borrowed this for the day,' he said. 'Jump aboard.'

Adam and Joe climbed up to sit alongside Harry, who pulled on the reins to tell the horse to begin their day out.

'We have brought food and water,' said Joe. 'How far is it?'

'It's about six miles from here to Vesuvius, then we'll have to climb the track if you want to see the crater. And we could go on to Pompeii and see some of the ruins left by the eruption in 79AD, if you wanted to.'

Harry was almost having to shout above the noise of the wheels, and hundreds of other wheels, on the road, along with voices and even some music being played on street corners.

'This is simply amazing,' said Adam, thinking to himself, and not for the first time, how he could never have imagined himself doing anything of this kind, even a few months ago. He had read about Italy, Vesuvius, Pompeii and now, here he was, sightseeing along the very roads leading to the most famous and the only active volcano in Europe.

'Thank you for suggesting this trip.'

'A pleasure,' said Harry, as the horse picked up a little speed on the outskirts of the city. Within an hour they were on the lower slopes of Vesuvius.

Leaving the carriage with a small boy, who was happy to look after it for a lire or two, and the promise of one more a couple of hours later, the three intrepid climbers began the trek up to the summit of the mountain at about midday. They stopped half way up to take in the extraordinary view over the bay, and across to Naples itself.

'If this thing went up now,' said Harry, 'it could, at its worst, cover everything you can see with a layer of molten lava six feet thick. It would consume every living thing in its path and boil the sea.'

'Thanks for that,' said Joe rather timidly, 'and will it?'

'No,' said Harry. 'It has not erupted since 1872, and even that was not serious. The last eruption, which killed many, and destroyed so much, was over three hundred years ago, in 1631, when four thousand people died. There would always be warnings and rumbles if anything was likely to happen, so these days the local observatory would warn everybody for miles around.'

'Can that be accurate?' said Adam.

'Let's eat and drink a while, before we go to the top,' Harry said, almost ignoring the question. As they spread their food and drink for the mountain-side feast Harry continued.

'There can be no such thing as absolute accuracy, and maybe not even time for everyone to get away, if this thing were to explode seriously, as it has done once or twice in history. But we all know it is more dangerous to cross the road in Naples than it is to come up here and view the crater. The chances of anything untoward happening are very, very slim.'

Joe was almost satisfied, but still rather timid about what they were doing. Adam was agog with interest, and enthusiasm to get to the top.

Within an hour they reached the summit and peered in from

the rim of the crater.

'My God!' said Adam, with such language being very much unlike him, but he was mesmerised. 'It is bubbling and moving. There are patches of vivid flame red, peeking through the shifting rock. This is almost pre-historic barrenness, living and moving, as it has for thousands of years, before man even walked the earth!'

'Very poetic!' said Harry. 'You should write this down.'

'It's like a great mythological forge of Vulcan,' Adam continued, in poetic vein. 'Magnificently threatening! I've read that somewhere!' And he decided, there and then, that he must write to Daisy again, and perhaps even Mrs Redman. The little boy in Melton Ford, twenty years ago, would have thought this experience unimaginable.

The threesome made their way down the track and found the boy, with their buggy, waiting patiently. He was duly rewarded and they embarked on another hour long ride to Pompeii. Disembarking, they were surprised to find that they were almost alone amongst the ruins of the great city that had gradually been unearthed, following the seventeenth century eruption of Vesuvius.

'All the rich Europeans and young Englishmen come here in the spring and summer, some doing their Grand Tours of Europe, which have become less popular in recent years,' said Harry. 'In February there are few visitors. The site is looked after and protected, but we can see much of what has been excavated since the eruption in the 1630s.'

They did just that, with various exclamations of surprise and amazement at the petrified bodies of those who had been terrible victims of the first century cataclysmic eruption. Joe was somewhat confused and disgusted by what he imagined must have happened to those poor people. Adam, too, was very thoughtful and stupefied by the enormity of what that eruption had done.

'And it was not just Pompeii,' said Harry. 'Herculaneum, too, was destroyed, although it is Pompeii that everyone knows about.'

'Well, I didn't,' admitted Joe, 'but then I never went to school, and had a lot of other things to learn about where I lived!'

The day was perfect. Harry enjoyed the company of others of his age. Adam was completely bowled over by the things they had seen, and places they had visited. Joe was just very, very happy that he could have such a contented and trouble-free time, with food and drink, good company and lots to learn and laugh about.

That Sunday evening, back at the De Luca house, Adam sat down with a sharp pencil and some paper.

De Luca Household
  Vomero
  Naples, Italy

Sunday 25 February 1894

Dear Daisy,
It is weeks since I wrote to you, I know, and I am sorry for the delay and for taking such a long time to do this again. So many things have happened, and I hardly know where to begin. We have been robbed (that is my new friend Joe and I, who both missed

the ship when it let without us from Valetta). We have travelled
as far as central Italy to Naples which is beautiful and have even
climbed Mount Vesuvius which is a living volcano! ...

Adam wrote on and on, through several pages of narrative, with the occasional little drawing or map, and then wrote it all again, with some different detail to Mrs Redman.

De Luca Household
  Vomero
  Naples, Italy

Sunday 25 February 1894

Dear Mrs Redman,
  I can hardly believe that it has been at least two years since I saw
you last, let alone wrote to you and feel so ashamed at not having
got in touch before, with you, who taught me so much and put me
on the road to everything I have become. I do hope this letter gets
to you and, even more so, hope that you are well.
  How are things in Melton Ford? Do you see anything of my
friends there? Perhaps they too have moved away. One day I will
return and tell you so many stories, but in the meantime would
you believe that I am in Italy? ...

And so Adam continued, pouring out his story and his adventures, page after page, until they would barely cram into an envelope. He was determined to leave nothing out, and silently longed for the day, if ever, when he could return and meet Mrs Redman again... and, of course, Daisy.

33

On to Rome

The two young men, Adam and Joe, reported to The Consulate building on Monday the twenty-sixth of February, as usual on a Monday, and Harry, unexpectedly, asked them to wait. They were soon ushered up the stairs again, as they had been some weeks earlier, and into the large office of Mr Cadogen-Bower who did not stand up as they entered.

'Thank you, Williams,' said the Consular Assistant as Harry left the room. He did not invite the boys to sit.

'There have been some comings and goings, I can tell you,' he said, and, after a long pause, while he sorted out some papers and opened a file or two, he did indicate that the boys could take a chair.

'I have telegraphed the Admiralty in London and the Dorsetshire Regiment, to which you allege you are attached.'

'We are attached, sir, both of us,' said Adam, making it perfectly clear that there was no '*alleged*' about it.

'We joined up together, sir, in 1893,' Joe added.

'As you say. The Admiralty confirmed to me that their ship *H.M.S.Malabar* left Southampton in September last and called in at Valetta in Malta, at which point you failed to report back before the ship sailed. I have no doubt that you were in that Battalion, and that you sailed with the ship, because it is confirmed in the manifest of passengers.'

'Which is what we told you the last time we met,' said Adam.

'Which leaves us with the problem of your not reporting back in time for the ship to sail.' said Mr Cadogen-Bower, thumbing through several pages of telegraph messages.

'We were knocked unconscious and robbed, taken miles from the ship, dumped and left overnight, not knowing where we were.' Adam insisted.

'As you say,' repeated their interviewer, showing not an ounce of emotion whatever. 'However, what you do not know is that the ship stayed there for a couple more days, for provisions, and that you could have returned and reported for duty.'

'We certainly did not know that,' said Joe almost fiercely.

'I agree. You were not to know that, and what you also do not know is that messages had been received, in London, from as far away as India, informing the captain that the troops were not required in Malaya.

'Those messages, although they took weeks to arrive, were relayed to your commanding officer when the ship reached Aden, and it duly turned back, to return to Southampton. I do not know whether it remained in Malta once it reached there, to await finer weather, or whether it is yet back in England.'

'Can you help us to return to England?' said Adam more in hope than expectation.

'That is your responsibility, and I cannot guarantee you a fair welcome from your Regiment,' said The Consular Assistant. 'However, I have prepared a statement about your arrival here, your apparently genuine desire to return home, and to your barracks, and your regular reporting here, each week. If you can get back to Dorchester before Friday the 23rd of March, you may avoid a Court Marshall. It is a slow business travelling across Europe without much money.'

'You have no need to remind us of that,' said Adam. 'We have travelled a long way so far on a shoestring.'

'And been lucky,' came the reply, 'I genuinely hope your good luck continues, and that you can get home in due course to avoid any criminal or military charges against you.'

'Well, thank you,' said Joe.

'We are very grateful for you allowing us to stay in the city without being arrested, and work, and for the information you have just imparted. We shall do our level best to get back to England.'

'The written statements for you both are downstairs. Williams is preparing them for you, and you can collect them on your way out. I wish you well.' That last remark was as near as Mr Cadogen-Bower came to sounding as if he cared.

They went alone, out of his office, along the corridor and down the staircase, to find Harry waiting for them, with two brown envelopes in his hand.

'Look after these,' he said. 'They could be your 'keep-out-of-jail licences."

'Thanks for your friendship, and the days sitting by the sea,' said Joe.

'And suggesting the trip to Vesuvius,' added Adam. 'I think we shall be here for a few more days, and then must check out trains to the north, to Rome and on from there.'

'If you give me a day or two, I can give you some railway information,' said Harry, as he released the envelopes into their hands.

The two of them went to work as usual that day, and came

home in the evening, ready to tell their hosts that they would be moving on.

'I have a job for your both in the next few days,' said Carlo suddenly after the evening meal. 'I hope you don't mind, after you have been our guests for several weeks, that I claim an evening or so of your time, to assist me, with a special task which needs doing late this week.'

'Really?' Adam enquired. 'What kind of job?'

'I will tell you in a day or so. You are soldiers, you are strong and can help us load wagons. It has to be done at night, because there are bad people, who might want to stop us. But the business of mine and my brother needs just a little help from you two, perhaps on Thursday evening.'

Adam and Joe were almost speechless, frankly not knowing what to make of this request. Was it even, perhaps, an order? In their room later that evening, as they prepared for the night, their worries and confusion were out in the open.

'This is not something I want to do,' said Adam. 'If it involves Carlo and others being protected by us – he said *you are soldiers*! - then frankly I want nothing to do with it.'

'I don't think we can get out of it if we are living here,' said Joe. 'Maybe it is quite innocent.'

'A night-time outing for us to load up wagons? Why?' Adam insisted. 'Why us? Is there any likelihood that we or they might be arrested if the excursion is actually an illegal operation? Are they stealing somebody else's produce and loading it on to their own wagons. Do they need strong-arm help to fend of anybody who objects?'

They decided to sleep on it, but were very undecided about what to do when Thursday came. The next day dawned and, by the end of it, the news of the day and their circumstances became worse.

Adam went off to the university Botanic Garden, as usual, intending to tell them that he had to move on, away from Naples very soon. Joe turned up at the warehouse for a day's work there, as usual, and at some point in the middle of the afternoon was loading crates on to a wagon, when the wheels began to move.

No brake had been applied, the wagon moved slowly away from him, and everything he was holding, plus several crates he had just loaded on a few moments before, collapsed on top of him. His left arm was caught under several heavy boxes, full of produce, including a couple with a dozen large bottles of olive oil, and he was momentarily trapped.

He screamed at the shock of what had happened, and very soon was freed from the mêlée of boxes and bottles, but he had lost the feeling in his lower left arm.

A doctor was called to the warehouse. Carlo very soon appeared on the scene and told him not to worry; he would be taken care of. The doctor decided he may have broken his upper arm, the humerus bone, and that he should have it firmly strapped up, then return home.

A cab was called by Carlo, and instructions given to the driver to take Joe home, where Adam found him when he arrived home.

'How on earth…?' Adam began.

'Don't ask,' said Joe, but he told him anyway, what had happened.

'This makes my work on Thursday a little more difficult,' said Carlo after they had eaten. 'We shall go ahead anyway, and

Adam, I must call on your help, without the assistance of Joe.'

'I am a little unsure about doing night-time work,' said Adam just trying to introduce the idea of a refusal. 'Does it really need me? What will we actually be doing?'

'Trust me, I have many friends, but you are the one who I need for this particular job, on Thursday. We shall leave after dinner that evening.'

Adam refused to get involved in any further conversation, as clearly it would reveal nothing useful, and actually he did not really want to know any more details. He was forming another plan.

The next morning Joe stayed at the house with his arm tightly dressed by the doctor, and in a sling. He had been given some pain-killers and was relatively comfortable. Adam went off to work, as usual, but instead of going to the Botanic Garden made his way to the Consulate to meet up with Harry.

'Have you got time for a coffee, Harry?' he said, as he entered the lobby area.

'Give me ten minutes,' came the reply. 'I have something for you anyway. Where is Joe?'

Adam and he sat over a cup of coffee a few minutes later, looking out over the blue water, and Adam told him of Joe's accident. Then he listened and looked, as Harry showed him some details of trains leaving Naples for Rome, of which fortunately there were several to choose from. Then Adam told Harry what Carlo seemed to be suggesting, as a night-time 'works outing'.

'I would try to avoid it, at all costs.' said Harry. 'You must have got wind of the way in which business is conducted here in Naples, and elsewhere in the south of Italy. I do not need

to spell it out, but if you are being cajoled into a night-time…
I dare not call it a raid, but that's what it will be, if other men
are involved, and transport, and at night, then I would move
heaven and earth to have nothing to do with it.'

'Easier said than done,' said Adam. 'He does not seem to
want to take 'no' for an answer.'

'Then we must suggest something for you to do which will
pre-empt your helping your Mr Carlo,' said Harry. 'Believe me
if they are loading wagons late at night, then I can only believe
they are collecting produce, maybe hundreds of bottles of good
wine, from vineyards where the owners have no knowledge that
they are contributing to your Carlo's operations!'

'So you do mean a raid?' said Adam.

'They would call it *gathering in subscriptions* for protection
offered,' Harry suggested. 'And yet they do it at night, when
the owners are most vulnerable.'

'Does nobody stop them?' asked Adam almost incredulously.

'Oh! You don't know the half of it and could hardly even
guess at it. Even the police seem to make a good living from
the produce, and even from the manufactured items that the
likes of the De Luca's sell openly. Those who object find that
their 'subscriptions' go up. They are ruthless.

'Look here,' continued Harry, 'Can you have your bags
packed and be ready, when you finish your usual day's work
tomorrow? When do you finish? About four o'clock?'

'About then,' said Adam. 'I could get both our bags out of
the house in the morning, when going to work, then Joe would
have to find his own way, with his arm strapped up, but at least
with no bag to carry.'

'Bring both bags to the Consulate, in the morning, if you

wish. Make sure Joe can find his own way here.'

'He knows,' said Adam, 'we've been often enough.'

'Of course. When I finish work you can stay in the Consulate with me. I suggest you try to catch this train,' he said, indicating some detail on the written information he was offering Adam.

'You can lay low in the Consulate until it is time to leave for the station. We must get you to the railway in time to buy tickets and board the train, before you are missed from the De Luca house. I will have the buggy here, which I can use for a short journey, without anybody asking any questions.'

'Thank you so much,' said Adam, at which point they parted. Adam went to work, but left early and made no mention that he would not be back. They owed him for working on Monday, and most of Tuesday, but he would have to forego that small sum of money. Getting away from Naples was suddenly very important.

He spent the evening explaining plans for the next day to Joe, and they packed their bags.

The next morning, as luck would have it, Carlo left earlier than Adam had planned to leave, so the boys did not see him at all. Joe stayed in the house, which roused no suspicion, and Adam found his way out with two packed bags without Mrs De Carlo seeing him. He was nearly seen by the housekeeper, as she was sweeping the front porch, but Adam stayed inside, with the bags hidden until the front was clear.

He took a cab to the Consulate and Harry showed him up to his small room at the top. Adam was quite impressed; it was rather better than the small garret room Adam knew at The Manor House. Joe, meanwhile had left it until early afternoon, after a spot of lunch, to leave the house, so that he would not be missed until evening, and he too made his way to the Consulate. Harry directed him up to where Adam was relaxing.

'We shall leave by back door of the Consulate at six o'clock,' said Harry. 'The rear entrance is under the great staircase, but I will be here anyway to show you. The back exit is in a narrow street behind the building.'

'Thanks,' said Adam. 'We have with us all the money saved from working locally, so I hope it will cover the train fares.'

'Believe me, it will,' said Harry. 'Now, would you believe, somebody has already been here this morning, to the Consulate, asking after you, Adam!'

'What?' Adam could hardly believe his ears.

'Luckily,' Harry continued, 'I was on a break, so did not have to see them, nor they me. They have very long tentacles and very alert ears and eyes, your so-called friends. Somebody noticed very early that you were not at the Botanic Gardens. News travels fast amongst these people.'

'Then the sooner we get away the better,' said Joe. Suddenly he was scared.

Harry told them that yet another visitor came to the Consulate in the afternoon, enquiring after Adam, and then, it seemed, asking after Joe as well, who had been missed from the house. As luck would have it, Harry was again not at the front desk, so nobody lied, saying they knew nothing of the young men's whereabouts.

At just before six o'clock, after Harry had finished his shift at the front desk, and his work for the day, he returned to his room and said it was time to go. He gave Adam a hat but Joe was happy wearing his own flat cap. They went down the side stairs from Harry's room, along a corridor to the main staircase.

Having descended those stairs to the entrance hall, they doubled back on themselves, under the stairs and through another smaller lobby, piled with boxes and spare furniture, through to a set of double doors with frosted glass.

'Hold on here. I will check,' said Harry, and he went out into the street.

Moments later he returned and told them to follow. Outside the buggy was ready and waiting. They recalled the buggy from the Vesuvius day out, a rather more pleasant and relaxed journey than this was likely to be.

'Put these coats around you,' said Harry, and wear the hats. Then they pulled away, with their bags on their laps and Harry taking a route through side roads, rather than the main thoroughfares.

'I take it you have the train route suggestions,' said Harry, as they rode. Adam took out the piece of paper from his pocket and read.

'From Naples, we need to make sure the train goes to Casalnuovo, Cancello, Caserta, Cassino and Frosinone.'

'Most main line trains will be going that way, provided we get you on the correct one to start with.' said Harry. 'Now, you two get off and go through that gate, on to the waiting area, the platform, and make yourselves scarce, out of sight somewhere, till you see me coming. I'll be there in a moment.'

They had arrived at the side of the railway station, where Harry jumped down from the buggy and disappeared inside. Adam helped Joe down, and took both bags, as they made their way through to the platform. Inside the booking hall Harry saw two men, in dark suits, sitting waiting, but not, it would seem, for a train.

He went to the booking clerk and the two men got up, looked at him, watched him buy what presumably they thought was a single ticket for himself, then sat down again.

Harry appeared on the platform after, what seemed to Adam, like too many minutes! He looked for Adam, and found them almost hidden behind the building at the end of the station platform.

'Take these,' he said, and handed them two large paper travel vouchers. They will get you from here to Rome, even if you have to change trains. I have bought them as a Consulate requirement so you need not worry about your money.'

'But who has paid for them?' said Joe.

'Don't worry about that. Maybe one day in England you can buy me a meal at the Savoy in London.'

'I've pick-pocketed near there,' said Joe smiling, but he found himself being bustled along, as a train pulled in.

'Come on,' said Adam, and he picked up both bags again, and headed for the end of a carriage where there was a door opening.

'Good luck,' said Harry. 'Nice to have known you.'

'You too,' said Adam, as he leaned out of the open window, where they had boarded, and watched Harry step away from the train as it began to move.

'Get inside and don't be seen,' he said. Adam just caught sight of two men, in dark suits, coming out of the booking area and on to the platform. Adam darted back into the carriage. The two men ran a little as the train gathered a bit of speed, then stopped and just stared into the distance.

Harry, meanwhile, had doubled back, out of the side gate

and boarded his buggy, which he took at some speed back to where he had borrowed it, before returning to his room, silently wishing his two new friends all the luck they deserved.

'Timed it just right,' he said to himself. 'Most exciting thing I've done for months.'

On the train Adam and Joe found somewhere to sit, and Adam put their bags where they could see them. Joe's arm was still in a sling! After only about six miles, as they estimated, they saw the station sign for Casalunovo.

'Well, we're going the right way,' said Adam, hoping that the train would be going on further still. It was not even seven o'clock yet according to the station clock, so they sat tight. The train moved away slowly after a few minutes and they enjoyed some more scenery but no more seascapes, as the route took them inland.

The evening was drawing in with a sunset in view to their left and then behind them. It was then, after about twenty miles, that the train stopped and Adam heard loud voices which he drew to the attention of Joe.

'What are they saying, Joe?' said Adam.

'Caserta! Caserta! Il treno si ferma qui! Finisce qui,' came the voice, repeating itself as the station master walked the length of the platform.

'Sounds like 'finish',' said Joe.

'Yes, that's what I thought,' Adam confirmed. 'Let's sit for a minute or two, to make sure.' It was indeed where the train terminated for that evening, and a station official was walking through the train.

'Looks as if he wants tickets, like an inspector,' said Joe who had observed the man talking to somebody else, before that somebody else got up and left the train.

'*Bigliette, per favore?*' he said, as he came to them, before he realised they were not Italians.

'Do you mean tickets?' said Adam. 'Here,' and he proffered the paper voucher that Harry had given them. The man examined it.

'S'good, for Roma,' he said. 'You go Roma?'

'*Si,*' said Adam. 'We are English.'

'Yes, I understand,' said the inspector. 'You want go to Roma?

'*Si,*' said both Adam and Joe.

'Tomorrow,' said the inspector. '*Twelvo!*' and he indicated his watch, pointing to the twelve. 'Tomorrow. *Il treno si ferma qui,*' he said and even indicated 'sleeping' with his hands against the side of his face.

'*Grazie,*' said Adam and got up. 'Time to go,' he said to Joe. 'This train definitely finishes here. *Grazie, signore.*'

Once out into the street they were on the lookout for a *pensione* again. It did not take them long to find a choice of one or two, not far from the station, but they deferred the decision before deciding to eat.

'Tomorrow is the first of March,' said Adam, 'Thursday, the first of March, and according to *His Highness,* the Consular Assistant, we have to be back home in twenty-three days. We really don't want any set-backs, but we can afford a day or two here and there, and we do have money.'

'Until it runs out,' said Joe.

'We'll cross that bridge if we get anywhere near it,' said Adam. By now they were sitting inside a small café and drinking some coffee.

'*Pizza, per favore?*' said Adam to a waitress. '*Pizza per due?*'

He was getting quite good at some small samples of Italian! They sat and drank, ate olives and pizza for nearly an hour, and went off to find somewhere to stay for one night. It wasn't difficult.

'Sorry you're carrying both bags,' said Joe. 'I could actually manage mine with my left hand. This damned arm still hurts but I can carry something with the other one.'

'Don't worry,' said Adam. 'I have them both, one in each hand and they balance perfectly!'

'Well, thanks,' Joe said, 'but please tell me if I can help.'

'I don't think this place, Caserta, is exactly on the European Grand Tour list of top places!' said Adam, as they settled in to a perfectly comfortable room, with a basin and a jug ready to fill with hot water in the morning. They were on their way home – again.

The following morning, they decided they could afford one or two more items of clothing. They paid the quite insignificant bill at the *pensione* and toured the town, keeping their eye on the time, anticipating the twelve 'o clock train.

It was a successful shopping spree. Joe bought another jacket, this one linen and pale brown. Adam bought something slightly more substantial, and a hat. They both bought yet another shirt each and some personal underwear. The market stall holders thought all their Christmases had come at once.

Adam also bought some small items of some pottery, which appealed to him, and promised himself, that morning, that once in Rome or somewhere bigger than Caserta, he would find a post office and send small gifts to Daisy, and perhaps even Mrs Redman.

They were at the station well before twelve, and the train

came in on time. Adam checked that it was the train for Roma. Asking was not too difficult, and he was very sure they were on the right train by the time they settled in to their seats, and it pulled away.

'I think this may only take us as far as Cassino or a place called Frosinone,' said Adam. 'I spoke to one or two 'inspector' figures and they pointed to names on the list which Harry gave to us. They put thumbs up for Cassino, and I think they did the same for Frosinone, but I couldn't be sure. This train is certainly going in the right direction, but maybe not all the way to Rome today.'

'Well, I bought some bread and olives, and a bottle of wine while you were looking at pottery,' said Joe, so that took care of lunch for them, as the train rattled on in a north-easterly direction.

At Cassino they didn't know it, but they had travelled just shy of fifty miles since leaving Caserta. The train ground to a halt, there was lots of station activity but nobody seemed to be shouting for them to get off. The locomotive still had plenty of steam, judging by the amount of it belching out on to the platform, and new people were getting on the train, as well as some leaving, having arrived at their destination.

'I think we're okay for Frosinone,' said Adam, fairly sure of himself. 'Shall I ask again?'

'No harm in asking.' said Joe, so they waited for somebody to come along to the carriage they were in. Sure enough, before long there came a father-figure, tall and well dressed, along with a lanky teenage boy with a great shock of blond hair, and a girl, shorter and not very smiley! The man was holding a British magazine, *Punch*, under his arm, and was looking for somewhere for three of them to sit.

'Do you speak English?' ventured Adam as they came close.

'Good Lord, fancy hearing English on a train in the region of Lazio,' said the man.

'Stop, you two.' The two children came to a halt and all three of them noticed seats across the central aisle, opposite Adam and Joe.

'May we join you?'

'Of course,' said Joe. 'Those seats look free. Don't suppose you could tell us if this train continues from here to Frosinone?'

'It certainly does,' said the man, and then we're going to spend one night there, before the final eighty-five or so kilometres to Rome tomorrow.'

'Oh, thank you,' said Adam.

'That's what we wanted to hear. I feel better already!' added Joe.

'How unusual,' exclaimed the man again. 'I hardly ever meet English people on this train. How nice to meet you.'

'You too,' said Adam and there ensued a friendly conversation, which did not involve the children very much, who just sat and looked out of the windows. Adam and Joe discovered that he was Mr Edward Morgan with his children, travelling to Rome.

'Benjamin, Margaret, say 'hello' to these two new friends of ours,' said Mr Morgan, at which point there came a reluctant greeting from the two young people, from which it was impossible to decide whether they were very shy, or very insolent at being told to greet strangers. Adam and Joe returned their greetings, rather more enthusiastically and Adam continued.

'Are you looking forward to seeing Rome?'

'Yes, you are, aren't you,' broke in their father. 'They do travel quite a lot. I expect they're tired. I married an Italian girl. We met when I was at the university in Florence,' he said, 'and now we live in Bath and in Sorrento, although the children spend a lot of time in school in England where they live near grandparents. I am taking them to Rome for some sightseeing. The first time they have been to the capital.'

The children pressed their noses against the window and almost curled up into balls on the seats across the aisle.

'Rome's where we are aiming for,' said Adam. 'On our way home to England.'

'You two must have done quite a tour,' said Mr Morgan.

'You might not believe us if we told you how, and why, we come to be here,' said Joe.

'Let's just say we plan to be back in England before the end of the month.' Adam added. 'We are in the British Army, and have their blessing, sort of, to be here and making our way back through Europe!'

'*Sort of?*' said Mr Morgan. 'Well, I'm curious but I won't ask.'

'No, don't,' said Adam.

The journey continued smoothly. The two children, in railway hibernation, hardly moved and eventually the train pulled into Frosinone at the end of the afternoon. Again they could not know the detail, but they had now travelled about one hundred and sixty three kilometres from Naples, on a journey which had fortuitously proved uneventful.

They all three chatted about their lives, their fortune or misfortunes along the way, their childhoods and how Adam and Joe had managed since being robbed in Malta. They told the story of how Joe had broken his arm. Nobody mentioned

Joe ever having been in prison.

'That is extraordinary,' said the father of the two, who were now sleeping. We none of us knows what other people have experienced along the way. I was lucky to have been born into a wealthy family. I enjoyed learning Italian, and went to the university in Florence, where I met my wife. My mother and father still live in England, but I managed to find a job after university, studying marine biology, travelling a lot on the oceans of the world.

My wife and I had the children in Sorrento where we now live. They go to a boarding school in Hampshire, near where my parents live, and, well, here we are, taking a trip to Rome.

Joe was lost, gazing in disbelief and even Adam had his mouth open in amazement. Given the origins of these two young men which could possibly be summed up as poor, ignorant and criminal, the story of a family living in two places, in two countries, going to school far away from home, and travelling the world, huddled into the corner of a railway carriage, hardly communicating a word, did not make sense.

Adam did not express his interest or concern, but he did wonder at what life must be like for the two children.

'Where are you staying tonight?' said Mr Morgan.

'Absolutely do not know,' said Joe quickly. 'We're pretty good at finding some *pensione* or other.'

'I am already booked into an hotel,' said Mr Morgan. 'I could ask if they have rooms for you.'

'One room would be enough,' said Adam, 'but I doubt we could afford a hotel.'

'Let us see, shall we?' said Mr Morgan. 'Maybe you could be my guests for one night, if you would not mind the company of these two. Maybe you could bring them out of their shell!'

'They look very bored,' said Joe, which he said quite softly, not wishing to be heard by the children, or sounding too judgemental. 'Maybe they just need a bit of fun.'

The train was pulling into Frosinone, and all five of them got up to start picking up bags and coats. All the other passengers were getting off the train and Adam heard the now familiar '*Il treno si ferma qui!*' which he easily understood to mean that this was where the train terminated its journey.

As they left the station and came out into the evening sun, Adam was carrying both his and Joe's bags when Mr Morgan's son, Benjamin, offered to carry one of them.

'Thank you,' said Adam, 'That would help.'

'And thank you from me too,' added Joe, as they all walked towards the town. Mr Morgan seemed to know where he was going, so Adam and Joe simply went along. They came into the long road, the *Via Don Minzoni* and Adam saw a sign pointing to *Ufficio Postale, Poste Italiane* and pointed.

'That is a post office isn't it?' he said. 'I'd like to go there tomorrow if we have time.'

'Not a problem,' said Mr Morgan, and so they continued, until they came to the entrance steps of what looked like an hotel, which Adam quickly surmised they could not afford. 'I really don't think that…'

'… this is the kind of place which will accept us,' Joe said, finishing the sentence.

'Nonsense,' said Mr Morgan. 'Come on in, and let me speak to the front desk.'

They entered a beautiful entrance lobby, which smelled heavily and welcomingly of sweet flower blooms. A boy even came to take their bags from them, but Adam declined and thanked him for offering. Whether the boy understood, or not, he did not know.

The furniture was exquisite and they edged their way towards a long sofa, while Mr Morgan went to speak to a uniformed young man behind the desk.

'It is settled,' said Mr Morgan. 'You have a room on the second floor, with two beds for one night, and we shall meet for a meal at about eight. Is that alright with you two?'

'It's more than alright,' said Adam, 'It is more than we could have hoped for.'

'Well, we shall say no more then, and meet up to eat at eight o'clock.'

'After we've been to our rooms,' said Adam, 'we're going out for a walk. Would Benjamin and Margaret like to come with us?'

'Oh! Yes, please, father!' Suddenly they both came to life. 'May we go out with Adam and Joe?'

'Why not?' said their father. 'I'm sure you'll all be fine. But please be back in time to get ready to eat.'

'Absolutely.' said Adam. 'We'll meet you down here in ten minutes'.

The two, up-to-now, incommunicative children were off like a shot, finding their way, with their father, up to their room and within a few minutes re-appearing in the lobby eager to get out.

'Well, you two are keen,' said Adam.

'What's the rush?' Joe asked.

'Getting away from father, if we're honest,' said Benjamin. 'He talks of nothing but school, marine life, examinations and studying. Can we go?' The four of them walked out of the hotel and followed their noses, or actually Joe's nose. He seemed to be striding out ahead, sling and all, until they found a few shops and explored a side street, finding a beautiful river along the side of which ran another road.

'Even going to Rome,' continued Benjamin, 'is going to be traipsing around ancient sites, while he tells us the history of everything, without ever asking us what we'd like to do.'

'Wow,' said Adam. 'That is quite an agenda not to look forward to! You do know, don't know you that lots of children would give their eye teeth to be travelling like you two?'

'Never really thought about it,' said Benjamin. 'We just go where we're told.'

'Well, Benjamin, all we are doing is traipsing around now.' said Adam.

'This feels more like fun,' said Benjamin, 'And please call me Ben. We just hope that mother and father are both pleased with us at the end of each school year. We hardly ever see them.'

'And when we do, the only topic of conversation is school, or history, or sea life!' said Margaret.

'Right!' said Adam. 'Let's make this fun then. The first thing we are going to do is, hopefully, find some ice-cream! Then we shall sit and you can tell us about everything that you want to talk about.'

'Or you tell us more about you,' said Margaret. 'By the way, I am thirteen. Ben is fifteen. How old are you?'

'Twenty-three in July,' said Adam.

'And I'm nearly twenty-one,' said Joe.

They all continued a few yards further, until they saw a shop front offering ice-cream in small, edible, waffle-baskets. They were in their element, sitting by the river. Adam vanished after they had consumed the ice-creams, and was gone for several minutes, managing to buy some blank paper from a book-binding store. He returned to find the others deep in conservation.

'I don't understand,' said Ben, 'how you can survive in London without a mother or father to look after you? Who sends you to school or buys your clothes?'

'And, Adam,' said Margaret, 'you said you never went to school either but you did have a mother and father? How did you learn to read or calculate arithmetic, or learn about all the kings and queens of England?'

The discussion continued, with a variety of questions emanating from the two children. They found it almost impossible to believe what these two new friends had experienced in their relatively short lives, with no money, no parents for Adam beyond his teenage years, no rich grandparents or travel, clothing, toys or a guaranteed roof over their heads.

They were as astonished by the circumstances of Adam and Joe growing up, who seemed really nice, just as Adam and Joe had been amazed by the recounting of their privileged upbringing, which appeared to have bred a couple of sullen, ungrateful children.

There might still have been a long way to go in developing their new relationships, but it was a quarter to eight, by the big clock they could see from where they were sitting, so Adam suggested they retrace their steps to the hotel.

The meal was as nourishing and exquisite, as both Adam and Joe might have expected in such a place as this. The two children were articulate and happy, telling their father all about Adam and Joe, about living on the streets, the old forge in Melton Ford, living in one garret room, having no money, being robbed... and so it went on.

The two children were flowing with facts, literally spilling out information, which they found extraordinary and so far removed from any other 'knowledge' which they were ever required to commit to memory in their lives, with school, grandparents or with their father.

'Well, you've certainly made an impression on my two,' said Mr Morgan, as the meal was coming to an end.

'I'm sorry if you think we've told them rather too much for their own good,' said Adam. 'It was really nice to speak to them, hearing what they enjoy and what life for them at school and in England is like.'

'Maybe you have opened their eyes a little,' said their father. 'I doubt I shall be able to get them to sleep!'

'Well, I will certainly sleep,' said Joe, 'Would you excuse us?'

'Are you sure we should not be paying for our room?' said Adam, 'Not that I'm at all sure we could afford it!' he added.

'Not at all,' said Mr Morgan, as he rose to shake their hands. 'I think you may have done my little family a world of good today.' And with that, Adam and Joe wished Ben and Margaret goodnight and made their way to their own room. It was barely ten minutes before they were both sound asleep.

The morning of Friday 2nd March dawned with some pleasant sunshine, and, at breakfast, Mr Morgan told them that the Rome train would be leaving at half past eleven. He said it would only take two hours to cover the remaining fifty or so miles to the capital, and in the meantime Adam decided to write to Daisy and find his way back to The Post Office.

The two children, Ben and Margaret, were begging their father to let them go out with Joe, and Joe promised that no

337

harm would come to them in the town, and that he would be at the station with them by eleven. The three of them went off like scampering kittens, enjoying each other's incongruous company.

Adam retired to his room for half an hour, wrote a shorter letter than usual to Daisy, explaining that he had to catch a train, and that with any luck he would be back in England before the end of March. He then retrieved the little pots that he had bought in Caserta, chose two of them for Daisy and proceeded to find the Post Office.

He remembered where it was and, after some language problems, managed to purchase a very small wicker basket, which was packed with straw, then with the two small pots and Adam's letter. The man at the counter then wrapped it for him, in brown paper, and passed it to him to write an address on.

Miss Daisy Hill, The Manor House, East Hambley, Hampshire, England.

It was then time to go to the station, where he found Mr Morgan pacing up and down.

'Where are they? It's nearly eleven,' he said to Adam. 'Where have they got to?'

'They'll be here,' said Adam. 'As you say, it is not yet eleven o'clock.'

The train pulled into the station, although it was even then only just a few minutes after eleven. Clearly the train stayed there until it was time to leave. Mr Morgan had booked a small buggy cab to bring him and all their luggage, including Adam's and Joe's, to the station and was looking increasingly concerned. The minutes went by, until, a short distance away, they saw the two children, and a white sling, running towards them.

'Don't be cross with them,' said Joe. 'It is my fault but we mistimed the return walk!'

'Where have you been?' said Mr Morgan clearly not impressed.

'Oh! Father,' blurted out Margaret, 'we found a toy shop. It was amazing. And we found a toy with lots of puzzles, which we started playing with, until the man said we had to buy it, but we had no money and…'

'And we couldn't buy the puzzle game because Joe had no money either. But then of course, you see, Joe never has had any money, for his entire life, and…'

'Steady on,' said Joe, with a friendly smirk on his face. 'I may not be a wealthy man, but I've got a box at home with two whole pounds of your English money in it!' He was mocking himself, of course, and everyone laughed as they realised he was putting himself down.

'Father it was such fun, but we had to put the game away and run out of the shop!' said Margaret.

'Sorry, father,' said Ben, suddenly quite crestfallen, seeing that his father was not at all pleased. Mr Morgan looked at his watch, stood stock still for several seconds, and then let out the most enormous gust of laughter.

'What are you turning my children into?' he guffawed, patting Joe on the back, so that it nearly hurt the top of his arm. 'It looks as though they have never had so much fun in their lives. Judging by what they told me last night, after we went upstairs, you two have led a truly colourful life and I am glad that we met. But now we must get on this train.'

They made their way on to the platform area, and moved

along until they saw a carriage, which was mostly empty, taking their chances on finding seats. They climbed up into the carriage by the end door and walked through until they found seats, similar to those they had occupied the day before.

'Please may we sit with Joe and Adam?' said Margaret.

'Oh, please,' added Ben, as they sat down by a window and patted the seats next to them for Joe to sit on, alongside Adam.

The journey to Rome was one long animated conversation between the children and Joe and, to some extent, Adam and Mr Morgan, although all five of them joined in as one when they talked about the army, or the ship that brought them to Malta, or Adam's unfortunate experiences with the butler who stole the silver.

The children contributed, with descriptions of their school, or their Sorrento home, their grandparents' house and even their studies. It was as if the stopper had been taken out of the bottle, and the genie of conversational intercourse had been released.

'I have never seen them so talkative,' said Mr Morgan. 'It is wonderful to watch them with you two.'

'We've enjoyed being with them,' said Adam, 'but I am sorry to say we shall be moving on northwards once we get to the capital.'

'Why don't you spend three days with us?' Mr Morgan suggested.

'Oh, yes, father, please, let Joe and Adam stay with us in Rome,' pleaded Margaret, the younger child.

'We'd love that,' added Ben. 'Please, father, invite them to stay with us.'

'You can spare three days,' said Mr Morgan. 'Surely you

can allow just a short holiday break from your attempts to get home. The railway services to the north, and in France, are far superior to those in the south.'

'I'm not sure we can spare the time,' said Adam, 'although visiting Rome like a traveller, seeing the sights, does sound very appealing.'

'Let's do it,' said Joe. 'It does sound a very generous invitation.'

'I don't have a problem with the expense,' said Mr Morgan, 'and my two would learn so much more from you than they might if I tried to talk to them for days on end.'

'Perhaps we could all enjoy the city and learn a lot together,' said Adam, never one to turn down the chance to learn some more.

'That's settled then,' Mr Morgan decided, 'and I shall see about accommodation when we get to Rome.'

'Thank you, father,' said both Ben and Margaret in their own way. 'Now, Joe, tell us some more about living in London on your own!'

The five of them spent a glorious three days in Rome, with a very acceptable room, in Mr Morgan's hotel, with some splendid meals and above all, the opportunity to traipse around the city, like excited children, seeing all the sights.

They saw them all: the Roman Forum; The Coliseum; The Pantheon, Rome's best preserved building, which was a temple to Rome's pagan gods; the great Gladiator School and then, St Peter's Basilica, with its breathtaking approach across the Grand Square and, of course, The Sistine Chapel.

Somehow, even though Mr Morgan was flowing with historical or architectural information, the children didn't seem to mind as they usually had. Adam had read so much in his short life that he found himself able to embellish the raw detail of Mr Morgan's facts with stories, or word-pictures, of individuals who had once walked these streets, and worshipped, or been entertained, in these buildings.

They peppered the hours they spent in the sunshine in Rome with more ice-creams and sojourns by the River Tiber, eating bread or olives, pizza or sweet cakes, and drinking wine or fruit juices. It was an idyllic three days and Mr Morgan never stopped praising Adam and Joe for contributing to the best 'short holiday' he had ever known with his children.

'You must give me your address in Dorchester,' said Mr Morgan one day. 'I hope we can keep in touch when we all go home to where we live.'

'That would be very nice,' said Adam, and Joe agreed, as they all made their way back to the hotel, at the end of their third day.

At Rome Central Station on their final morning, Tuesday, the sixth of March, the parting was almost tearful.

'I cannot thank you enough,' said Mr Morgan, for the umpteenth time. 'You have made this stay in Rome a complete joy. I feel as though I know my children better now than I have ever done.'

'You just need to listen to them,' said Adam, hoping that did not sound too patronising. 'They have a lot to say, and a lot they want you to know.'

'I shall write to you,' said Joe to Ben and Margaret, 'although goodness knows when, and heaven knows how long letters might take!'

'Our train is in now,' said Mr Morgan. 'I wish you two all

the luck in the world. You deserve it.'

Thank-yous, handshakes and even a hug or two filled the next thirty seconds, and they were off. The two boys waved the train goodbye, before settling down to wait for their train taking them onwards.

Their next stop, Arezzo.

34

Arezzo

With his, now rather dog-eared, map of Italy, Adam could see they had quite a long journey to Arezzo, the stop to which their next train would take them.

'It looks like about a hundred and forty miles,' he said to Joe. 'I think that's as far as we'll get today.' They were sitting drinking coffee in the great piazza outside Roma Termini. 'And that,' said Adam pointing to a great stone obelisk standing in the square, 'is a memorial to Italian casualties in the battle of Dogali.'

'Where did that gem of information come from?' said Joe.

'It's surprising,' said Adam, 'to realise the extent of Mr Morgan's knowledge of Italy, when you and the children are eating ice-cream and talking to them about sleeping rough in London! The battle of Dogali was fought by the Italians against Ethiopia, only seven years ago. We know nothing, do we, of the history of other countries, when we are learning about our own?'

'I don't know much about the history of our own,' said Joe, resigned to the fact, yet again, that there was so much he didn't know.

'Well, here's one more fact for you,' said Adam. 'This railway station was begun when the Pope ruled this part of Italy, under papal rule, and was completed twenty years ago, in 1874, after the unification of Italy.'

'Now that I do recall us talking about,' said Joe, 'on the way to Naples on Stefano's wagon. Goodness me, I do know some Italian history!'

Their train arrived, and they had their travel voucher checked, which had only taken them as far as Rome. The man behind the ticket office desk looked at it and then charged them just fifty lire each, before he gave them a ticket to Florence, via Arezzo.

'Perhaps he thinks we are part of the Consular staff,' said Joe.

'I'm sure, 'said Adam, 'that the ticket to Florence should have been more than that, but you know what they say about a gift horse?'

'Don't think I do,' said Joe, so Adam told him.

The enjoyed the view from the train, and the bread and the cheese and the wine, which they had stuffed into their bags from a couple of market stalls in Rome, before they parted from the Morgan family. Eventually, the train pulled into Arezzo station and they found themselves in the province of Tuscany.

It was now time to fend for themselves again, maybe even find a way to earn a few hundred lire, before moving on and certainly find somewhere to sleep.

As the train pulled in, they saw that there appeared to be hundreds of goods wagons as well as their own passenger train. The goods' yards alongside the track spread for hundreds of yards, apparently in all directions. They were huge.

Adam and Joe left the train and tried to sense the main walking route to the town itself. Most people who had alighted were making their way up inclined roads, with nearly all roads on that town side, climbing away from the tracks. The boys decided to go that way, and the incline was indeed quite steep.

It certainly was a climb and soon they reached what they thought might be the centre of the town. They found themselves in a large square, the *Piazza Grande,* as it appeared on the walls of the buildings surrounding the Square. Dozens of people, some in families, were eating under the arcades which surrounded the square. It looked very 'Italian' thought Adam.

'This looks like the obvious place to get something to eat,' said Joe, to which Adam agreed, as he continued to look around the enormous square. He also was on the look-out for any signs of *pensione.* They found both and were soon tucking into a pizza *Marghareta,* with plenty of olives and another bottle of red wine. They had no difficulty getting what they wanted, but neither did they find anybody speaking English. It did not take them long to find a *pensione.*

'I think she is saying fifteen lire,' said Adam, after they had found a guest house and began negotiating the cost of a room, for at least one night. '*Quindici?*' he said to the woman, and counted out fifteen lire.

'*Si. Una notte,*' she said. So Adam smiled sweetly and hoped she meant 'one night'. They made their way to a room and settled in.

'One thing caught my eye at the railway station, while we were drifting through the surrounding area,' said Adam, as they crashed out onto the two beds in the room. 'There seemed to be dozens of workmen lining up, and dozens more being ticked off on some kind of register, by another man, with a large book.'

'Yes, I saw the great line of men,' said Joe. 'Do you think they were looking for work?'

'Each man in turn went forward into the goods yards, and looking a bit closer,' said Adam, 'I saw that they were unloading goods wagons, taking off hundreds of boxes, barrels, crates and bundles, and loading them into horse drawn carts. It was going to need a few hundred carts to take all the produce which was being unloaded from the long goods train.'

'Why don't we look a little closer in the morning?' said Joe 'Perhaps those men were being casually employed in the goods yard, day by day.'

'And even at this time in the afternoon!' said Adam. 'They must really need the men if they are taking them on all day.'

'Well, I'm going to rest here until dinner time and we shall see in the morning,' said Adam.

The two of them enjoyed another good evening meal. It was what they gradually learned during the evening was called *prosciutto*, with some creamy pasta and vegetables. There was a lot of signing and word-swapping during the evening meal, but gradually they picked up that this was a traditional meal for Tuscany, with the main base of the meal consisting of cured ham. They thoroughly enjoyed it, as they also did the breakfast the next morning.

They made sure that they could lock their bags inside the room and put what money they had safely on their persons, before making their way back to the station. On the way, Adam noticed that Joe had not put the sling on which he had been wearing for over a week, and commented.

'How's the arm?'

'I think I may have been lucky,' said Joe. 'The doctor they called in Naples said it was possibly broken, but maybe it was not quite that serious. I can move my fingers and the top of the arm is not so painful, though it has turned a funny colour. I could even carry my own bag with that arm if I had to, although I didn't tell you that yesterday. Sorry!'

'I forgive you,' said Adam, shoving Joe away in mock anger. 'Maybe you just cracked it, or maybe it was seriously bruised. I wonder if we could find a doctor to have a look at it.'

'If it doesn't cost too much!' said Joe.

They arrived in the area of the railway station and, sure enough, there were loads of men lining up, apparently being ticked off or noted in a book, as they proceeded into the goods yard, to be directed to unloading the dozens of railway wagons.

'Oh, well!' said Adam, 'here goes.' They both approached the end of the queue and tried to see what was going on as each man got to the book. Adam kept hearing '*un giorno*' which, if it was anything to do with *buon giorno* which they both knew meant good morning, probably meant one day, or one day's work.

Adam got to the head of the queue first and risked using the language.

'*Un giorno. Per favore,*' The man with the book looked up and smirked. Nobody was usually that polite.

'We are English. One day?' said Adam and Joe followed with, 'English.'

'*Un giorno?*' said the man and then, surprisingly, '*lavoro,* work?'

'*Si,*' said Adam with his fingers crossed. The man smiled, and shouted across to another. They were all middle aged working men, wearing dark or light brown trousers, with shirts and braces, and some with flat caps. Joe had worn his flat cap today. Maybe it helped.

'English!' The book-man attracted the attention of another worker, almost wearing a suit! It was too large for him, and he had a similar ill-fitting shirt with too large a neck and a dark red tie holding it together. He came across.

'English?' he said. 'You want work - *lavoro?*'

'*Si, Grazie, per favore*' said Adam.

'*Un giorno? Duo giorno, tre giorno?*'

Adam looked at Joe and asked him if they wanted one, two, or three days work?

'Three if they're offering?' Joe answered.

'*Tre,*' said Adam to the man standing in front of them.

'Come!' said the man and promptly showed them across to one of the railway wagons, where a team of men were unloading packages into waiting carts. A supervisor seemed to be making sure that the right amount of every product went into the correct wagons. 'This is Georgio,' he said. 'My name is, Matteo.'

'English,' said Matteo, as he apparently told the supervisor they were okay to work. The supervisor then took them to another loaded railway wagon, opened the sliding doors and hailed one of the waiting horse-drawn carts to come across. Nearby, a local man brought his cart across, and Adam and Joe very quickly began loading goods from one to the other.

'My name, Georgio,' he said. 'Hello,' and extended his hand. They already knew his name, shook hands and made themselves immediately useful unloading the wagon.

The work went on all day. They went from one goods wagon to another, loading up cart after cart, as instructed, sometimes with a specific number of boxes or crates, always with the supervisor ticking off on his lists which local purchasers had the right number of packages, or the correct amount of produce.

When it got to four o'clock, Adam and Joe were called across to Georgio and he indicated that they should come the next day, and that they would be paid then for two days. It was not difficult to understand and the two boys indicated their thanks and made their way up the steep incline towards the town again.

They asked along the way of any person who looked as though they might be helpful in finding a doctor, and one of the locals drew a small diagram of a snake, curling around a staff, then pointed along the road beyond the main square. It did not take them long to find the symbol above a door, so they went in.

'*Posso aiutarla*,' said a young man behind a large wooden counter, piled with bottles, boxes and paperwork, standing in front of a wall of shelves, filled completely with bottles containing liquids of every conceivable colour.

And so began the usual miming act of telling him that they were English, that Joe had an accident, hurt his arm, maybe broke it and that now they would appreciate some advice. The young man, tall and almost skinny inside his white coat, very attentive and wearing heavy-framed thick glasses, seemed to get the message, with his smattering of their language. He went to the end of the shelves and vanished through a wood panelled door.

'Come!' said a voice from behind the door, so in they went in and sat down in front of an elderly, white-haired, gentleman who was behind a desk, and who smiled benignly, and whom they thought they could trust instinctively.

'*Medico*, doctor,' said the young man and pointed to the

man behind the desk.

The elderly gentleman examined Joe's arm, pulled his fingers, twisted his wrist and flexed his arm, all the while enquiring about degrees of pain. They understood him, except for some detail, when he and the skinny young man from the front of the shop exchanged views or comments.

'Not broken,' said the elderly doctor. Then he drew a quick sketch of an arm, showing the bone inside the arm with a tiny hairline crack and lots of swelling, which Adam and Joe both understood as indicating bruising, or as the doctor called it '*livido*'.

'Arnica,' said the doctor and wrote the word on a piece of paper, giving it to the skinny assistant. The boys thanked the doctor, and followed the young man back into the shop, where he gave them a small pot filled with an ointment. He rubbed his own arm as if to demonstrate how to use it, then wrote down '10 lire' on the diagram which the doctor had provided. Joe handed over ten lire, in a single coin, and they left.

'*Grazie, Grazie*,' said Joe as they left to return to the main square.

They enjoyed yet another excellent meal of a local delicacy, followed by a long lazy sit down in the open, observing the local people. Some were in very drab working clothes and many, especially the women, in colourful traditional outfits of long skirts, blue or green covered with elaborate lace aprons, sometimes covering the entire front of the skirt. There were more head scarves and shawls, in bright colours, some with embroidered or braided edges. They sat drinking wine and eating sweet pieces of cake and passed away the evening, feeling quite good about their progress in getting home.

At the end of their third day working at the goods yard, Matteo gave them nine lire each, from a pouch hanging around his waist, like a short apron. It was hardly a fortune, but nine lire more than they had the day before. Adam mused over the fact that, at ninety lire to the pound, their ten lire was almost exactly two shillings, roughly two thirds of the soldiers wage he was getting back home.

They had no idea that even average wages for artisans, or working-class peasants in Italy, was barely two lire per day, actually less than the basic cost of living. Without knowing it, they had done rather well. Clearly the train company, or the local producers, would pay well for getting their stuff unloaded and into shops and factories.

'*Sabato, Lunedi*?' said Matteo. 'You work two days more, not Sunday,' he said hoping be would be understood. They understood.

'How about it?' said Joe, 'I am happy to stay here over two more days.' So they agreed and said 'yes'.

'*Sabato*, one o'clock finish,' said Matteo, which Adam understood to mean working only half a day on Saturday.

'*Si*,' he said, as both of them said their goodbyes and returned to the guest house. Their work on Saturday was the same, and the two of them then spent a very happy half day relaxing in the square, with wine and olives, good food and plenty of delicious fruit.

On Monday, they returned to the goods yard to work again and were greeted by Matteo, who had a very large 'henchman' by his side, whom the two boys took little notice of, at first. He really was a monster, with an enormous black leather belt, holding in his considerable waist, from which hung voluminous brown trousers. His white shirt was barely white, open necked with a red scarf tied around his neck. Predictably they unloaded railway wagons all day into waiting carts, and were looking forward to one more night in Arezzo, before completing the next leg of their journey to Florence.

At the end of Monday they assumed that Matteo would give them another nine lire, or perhaps a little less because Saturday had been only a half day. In fact he offered them a small copper two lire coin.

'Nine lire?' said Adam. Joe was looking furious.

'Two lire,' said Matteo, with his henchman hovering in the background.

'Why?' Joe came in. 'Why only two?'

'Tax,' said Matteo, without even a hint of irony or wanting to explain any further.

'Two lire and seven lire tax.'

Suddenly Joe became very acquiescent, and smiled a lot. 'Okay, thank you, sir. Thank you, *grazie.*'

'What are you saying?' said Adam. 'They're cheating us out of seven lire which is almost every 'penny' we need to live on! My god! Is everybody in Italy a crook?' Then he turned his attention again to Matteo. 'We worked two more days.' he said, 'Nine lire, *per favore.*'

'Thank you, *Grazie,*' said Matteo, dismissing them both, and, strangely, Joe did not argue. He shook Matteo's hand effusively, even energetically, and offered it also to his henchman.

'Looks like we cannot argue,' said Adam. Now he was the furious one, seething at having stayed on and received no more for it than a small copper coin, which would hardly buy them a glass of milk!

'Come on,' said Joe after he'd finished shaking hands and thanking everybody in sight. 'Good bye, *addio*.' He had learned the Italian for 'goodbye' somewhere along the way, and now used it to get them out of the railway yard without a fight. Then he almost dragged Adam away.

'Come on. Don't argue any more. Keep smiling,' Joe insisted, and they made their way away from the station for the fifth time in as many days.

When they got to the square, they stopped and found a table for a drink. Adam had hardly calmed down.

'We've been cheated,' he said. 'I would bet that there is no local tax. He simply underpaid us because he knew we probably wouldn't fight for our money, and we were moving on tomorrow anyway.'

'Precisely,' said Joe, 'which is why I negotiated an extra little bonus while I was shaking hands with him,' and with that he plonked four more coins on to the table which amounted to another forty lire.

'Where on earth… forty?' began Adam.

'Your career in gardening may have helped you in Naples,' he said, 'but my career in London comes to my rescue sometimes, when people try to cheat me.'

'It's very small change,' said Joe, 'but no more than we deserve.'

'It's forty lire!' said Adam, 'enough for one or two nights at a *pensione*. I'm not sure I approve. It is theft, after all.'

'Well I'll take my two back, then,' said Joe, starting to slide all the coins towards himself.

'No, no!' Adam retorted. 'I'll get over it.' And he retrieved his share of the loot.

The packed their bags that evening, slept soundly, and made their way to the station the next morning.

There was no apparent problem in passing the workers, who had reported that day at the goods yard, but then, Adam thought to himself, why should there be?

Their train was due to depart in a few minutes, when Joe suddenly said to Adam, 'Here, hold this,' and put his bag into Adam's spare hand. 'I'll be back.'

Joe ran off towards the men working at the yard, as Adam made his way onto the low station platform and stopped, near to a door where he thought there were seats. The guard's whistle blew and Adam kept the door open, beginning to sweat that he would have to go without Joe, or miss the train. A final blast of the whistle came and Joe rushed into view. Adam sprang onto the train, with Joe bounding in after him. The door was slammed, as the train picked up speed, and they went along the carriage to find two seats. There they sat down and both relaxed.

'What were you up to?' said Adam.

'I thought I'd give another friendly *addio* to Matteo,' said Joe, 'and collect a bit more *tax*!' He slammed another collection of coins onto his bag, which was across his lap in front of him, and looked up.

'They'd have murdered you for less!' said Adam. 'And I still disapprove, although, thinking about it,' he continued, as Joe scooped up the stash of coins, 'I think they owed us at least that much.'

'I'm not going back to my old ways, ever again, especially if I live in London again,' said Joe, 'but I'm not going to be cheated by people we worked for...'

'... in good faith,' said Adam.

'Whatever that means,' said Joe. 'People we worked for in an honest fashion, expecting a fair wage.'

'That's precisely what it means,' said Adam and they settled in, with their bags on a luggage rack and watched the country-side flash by, as they headed the last few miles into Florence.

35

Florence

The railway station in Florence was heaving with activity. As they left the train, once again they saw men unloading large crates, from a train on the adjoining platform, loading them into a very smart looking closed and 'crested' wagon, drawn by two horses. The crest was in gold on the dark green, painted and polished, wagon. Adam predictably had no idea whose it was.

Adam and Joe, with their bags safely with them, left the station and walked around to see the activity going on by the smart wagon being loaded up. They saw more identical vehicles, lined up, painted dark green, each with a groom standing by the horses.

'Well, what's going on here?' said Adam, fascinated by what appeared to be the grandeur of the activity. Very elegant pieces of furniture were being brought across from the railway platform, along with boxes and heavy swathes of fabric, covered with sheets and draped over the arms of porters.

'Somebody's moving house,' said Joe. 'Somebody with very good taste, and a lot of money.'

'So it seems,' added Adam as they got a little closer. It was then that they heard an English voice.

'Careful with that desk. It is very valuable,' said the voice, addressing two porters carrying a well wrapped piece of furniture. 'And that crate is for the bathroom.' Men in dark clothing, and green aprons, scurried around, packing the elegant wagons carefully and going back to check the train carriages were eventually empty.

'Excuse me,' said Adam to one of the men who was carrying a book and a pencil, 'may we ask whose property this is? You seem to be English. Is some English family coming to live here?'

'I can't speak to you now, sir. It's The Countess of Balmoral visiting Italy. Now move along, please, sir.'

Adam and Joe moved away, but were mesmerised by the sheer volume of goods and luggage items being loaded into the wagons. They enquired and discovered that the crest, on the side of each horse-drawn-wagon, was the family insignia of Count Giuseppe Fabricotti, who owned the fabulous *Villa Fabricotti* on Montughi Hill, near the city of Florence. This year it was his charming home where The Countess had chosen to stay for a month.

Something rang a bell in Adam's head but he could not be sure. He and Joe found their way from the *Piazza della Statzione*, outside the station, across to what they discovered quickly was the *Piazza dell'Unita Italiana*.

They both realised this was the square dedicated to the unification of Italy. They explored a little further, wanting some food and drink, as usual, and looking for what might be a reasonable *pensione* to stay the night.

'Look at that,' said Adam. 'Amerigo Vespucci.' He pointed to a road sign saying *Lungarno Amerigo Vespucci* running alongside the river through the city.

'Meaning?' said Joe.

'Amerigo Vespucci. I've read about him' said Adam. 'He was a merchant from this city of Florence, who first convinced the world that the new continent across the Atlantic was not Asia, but a completely different land-mass. He called it The New World. Everyone else started calling it America, after his name...'

'I get it,' said Joe. 'Amerigo, America!'

'Exactly,' said Adam, 'and look, these buildings along here all look a bit out of our class. Maybe we should go further away from the centre to find somewhere that looks a little cheaper.'

'There's a bridge there with buildings all along it,' said Joe pointing. They were walking toward the *Ponte Veccio,* which Adam had also read about somewhere, probably at The Manor House.

'I think most of the buildings on there are jewellers. Again, out of our price range,' said Adam as they continued walking.

They found a *pensione* where they could get a room for fifteen lire, including an evening meal and a breakfast. It was perfect, so they settled in and congratulated themselves in the dining room during the evening, with a bottle of red wine, that they had reached nearly as far as the north of Italy.

Adam could not get the activity at the railway station out of his mind, and determined that they should go the next day, to enquire some more. They would have to go to the railway anyway, to think about travelling further on to the north, and into France. The evening passed very pleasantly, with no mishaps of any kind, smiles from those around them in the dining room, and a cool night turning into a new warm day.

At breakfast, as they sat on an outside terrace, eating bread, fruit and drinking coffee, Adam noticed some locals at nearby tables reading *Il Tirreno,* a newspaper, and others reading a different daily, *La Nazione.* He could not understand a word, of course, but couldn't help noticing *Contessa di Balmoral* in amongst the headlines and bylines. Could it be? He hardly dared to think that it might be.

When one of the other guests left the terrace, he put the newspaper back into a rack and Adam immediately retrieved it.

'You're not telling me that you can read that?' said Joe to Adam.

'I can read it,' said Adam half jokingly, 'but I've no idea what it all means!'

He browsed the front page and turned over to find a grainy photograph of, impossible, of Queen Victoria, with the sub-heading *Contessa di Balmoral.* Then there were more words, of course, including the almost recognisable *'in arrivo'* and a date, *'Venerdi 16 Marzo'.*

'Joe,' he said, almost breathlessly, 'I think Queen Victoria is arriving in Florence in two days time, on Friday the sixteenth.'

'Why should she be coming here?' said Joe. 'Don't tell me it's to meet you and give us safe passage home!'

'If only,' Adam responded. 'Sorry to sound stupid, but many years ago a lady I knew, in fact I still know, said she had seen the queen arriving at Weymouth harbour and it struck me as, well, you know, a bit special.'

'I suppose it is a bit,' said Joe. 'I've never seen her in London, though I've seen troops of horsemen enough times, who may have been riding ahead of her.'

'Don't know why it has stuck in my mind, but supposing we were to see her on Friday, when she arrives at the station. It would be a bit of special thing for me, and I could write to tell my old lady in England that, now I had seen her too.'

'So we're staying here until Friday?' said Joe. 'I hope Her Majesty knows what expense we're going to, to catch a glimpse of her!'

'Thanks,' said Adam. 'It won't do our journey home any harm, will it?'

'I'll let you know, when we're late back for the end of March and we both get shot for desertion!' said Joe. 'Only joking! We'll make it.'

They asked if they could stay in their room until Friday, and had enough money for it, and more still, thanks to Joe's effusive goodbye's to Matteo in Arezzo! They spent two glorious days, sitting, eating and drinking, mostly by the river, or in the park, although Adam could not get it out of his head that the queen would be here, in the same city, sometime within forty-eight hours.

He wandered alone down to the station, just to soak up some more of the atmosphere. There was nothing particularly important about him seeing the Queen of England; it just seemed like completing the circle of Mrs Redman having seen her, all those years ago, he being so excited as a young boy, and now, possibly seeing her for himself. It would get the idea out of his system.

He watched, as more rich furniture and packages were unloaded from the train, in the sidings at the railway station, into the waiting wagons. Clearly, there were not enough wagons to do all the unloading in one day.

'Excuse me, sir,' he ventured, to a black suited gentleman who seemed to need to watch everything happening, but who was relaxed enough to know that all was going well. 'Excuse me, may I ask who all this is for?'

'There's hardly anybody else that these men would be going to all this trouble for, except her,' said the man who was obviously English.

'You mean the Countess of Balmoral?' said Adam.

'Well spotted,' said the black suit. 'Are you English?'

'Yes, indeed,' said Adam. 'Just travelling through Italy and here we are, hoping to get a glimpse of Her Majesty on Friday.' He thought it best not to admit to being a soldier, desperate to get back to Her Majesty's barracks at Dorchester by the end of March, for fear of criminal military charges!

'You'll be lucky,' said the man. 'I'm Henry, by the way, Henry Rochester, one of Her Majesty's, sorry, 'one of the *countess'* aides. It's good to meet another Englishman abroad.'

'Why Countess?' said Adam.

'If the old girl travels abroad as Queen of England, there have to be official receptions, and welcomes, military guards and all that paraphernalia. But if she travels as The Countess of Balmoral, she can just turn up, cross the red carpet, and drive into her holiday month!' he said.

'A month!' said Adam. 'Not a bad holiday. 'So she's obviously bringing a lot of stuff with her, but what's with all the furniture?'

Adam and Henry Rochester sat and chatted for a while, with Adam, wide-eyed and open-mouthed, at the lengths to which the Queen's staff and Household would go to, to make the visit comfortable and perfect for 'the old girl'.

He found Joe a little later, sitting by the River Arno, eating ice cream and bought himself one from a tiny kiosk nearby.

'You will not believe me!' he said to Joe, 'if I tell you what happens when the Queen travels here in Europe!'

'I probably won't, but you're going to tell me, aren't you?' Joe responded.

'She comes across from Dover to France, in the Royal Yacht, and then there is a special train, entirely for her, consisting of thirteen carriages, one of which is her bedroom!

'There are over eighty people travelling with her, all across France, and another train is sent in advance, with her furniture, clothing and personal effects, That's the train we saw yesterday being unloaded.'

'Well, the fare will cost her more than one lire per mile, I suspect,' said Joe.

'She is staying at *Villa Fabricotti* – for a month! – and then going to Germany, for the wedding of her granddaughter, the Princess Victoria Melissa to The Grand Duke of Hesse.'

'Bully beef for her!' said Joe, 'and who's running the country while she's away for a month or more?'

'Listen,' said Adam. 'All that stuff we saw being unloaded, is her own furniture!'

'That's great,' said Joe. 'Now she has two trains, and one of them she's not even on!'

'She prefers writing at her own desk, so she brings it with her, and sleeping in her own bed, brought from Balmoral, or somewhere. She has her daughter, the Princess Beatrice, with her all the time, and Beatrice's husband. She has chairs, curtains, cushions, covers, a sofa, a rocking chair, arm chairs, boxes of family photographs and baskets full of books! And God-knows what else, all brought in advance! And then they re-decorate the rooms she's going to be using to her favourite colours. It's extraordinary!'

'Well, God-knows indeed,' said Joe. 'It's nice to think that her daughter, and her husband, are all part of the fixtures she travels around with. I'm glad I'm just Joe Smith. And, as for re-decorating! Well, I'm happy if they put a pillow on my bed, with a clean cover and a jug for some water in the morning.'

'I agree,' said Adam, 'but it is amazing. I just could not get over all the things I was told at the station by one of her aides. She even brings her own donkey cart and an open carriage, a landau, because those are the ones she prefers to be taken out in.'

'Well I hope she doesn't mind using a local donkey!' said Joe. 'I don't mind if she has all this stuff, and preparation, going on around her. She's lived for over thirty years without her husband, as far as I know, so maybe she's entitled to a few home comforts. I wish Her Majesty, good health,' And with that he raised his ice cream and took another spoonful.

'On Friday,' said Adam, 'I am going to go to the station and try to get a glimpse, when she arrives.'

'I'll come too,' said Joe. 'It'll be fun, and something to tell everyone back home. Not that I have got anyone back home. Except you, and you're here!'

The remainder of the day was spent looking at the jewellery on *Il Ponte Veccio*, strolling around some more of the beautiful sights of Florence, and making their way slowly back to the *pensione*, for a meal and another night's rest.

Friday came. They packed their bags, paid their bill and made their way to the railway station to enquire about tickets to Milan, the next big city travelling north towards the French border. Once again, they man behind the ticket desk looked at their travel pass, which they'd been given at the consulate, and uttered not a word, as he passed them two vouchers to travel as far as the French border, this time asking for no money at all.

The two seasoned traveller uttered just the one word, '*Grazie!*'

It was then just a matter of waiting for the arrival of The Countess' train. Their train, on to Milan, and the Swiss border, was not due until the evening, so Adam hoped above hope that Her Majesty would arrive during the day.

They had bought and packed plenty of water, a bottle of wine each, some bread, a waxed paper bag of olives and some fruit, bought on their way to the station. The day was warm and pleasant, without being too hot, and Adam, along with his friend, took up a position near the station exit just to wait.

Activity began about midday, when a red carpet was brought out and unrolled from the main station entrance. Adam knew he was in the right spot, perched on a wall nearby with a clear view to the exit. Then it got rather crowded. Droves of people began to arrive, and were being corralled into groups, well away from the carpet, but right in front of Adam.

He was determined to be nearer or have a clearer view, so he got down from the perch and pushed his way towards the front of the gathering crowd. He was wishing, all the time, that he could exceed his height, of about five feet ten and a half inches.

Then a local band arrived and formed up, all sixteen of them, ready to play. They were all tall. They were an additional interruption to Adam's view of the carpet, and they caused the local stationmaster and his men to push the crowd back even further. Adam was losing any kind of view at all!

Joe was interested, but not that keen to see her. He had sat himself under a tree across the road, just to wait in the pleasant warmth of the mid-morning. Adam was now fearing that he would never get to see the arrival in any meaningful way, so he got to the edge of the road where there were carriages lining up, arriving one by one. He dodged between two of them and joined Joe on the other side of the road.

'Give me your hands, cupped like this,' said Adam, as he demonstrated that he wanted to get up the tree. Joe did it, and Adam clambered on to Joe's hands, catching a branch above himself and pulling upwards. He found the strength to pull, so that within seconds he had a new vantage point.

A train pulled in. Adam's heart was racing. The band was playing. Could this be the moment that he would see The Queen of England, in person, arriving and getting into a carriage? There was a flurry of activity at the doorway a few seconds after the train had come to a halt, and some uniformed men came out and went to stand, one each, against the doors of the carriages lined up. Adam could see, over the railway platform fence, that there were people getting out of the train, but of course, could not identify any one, or the one he was looking for. Would he see her?

No, he wouldn't; well, not quite. At the very moment that he believed she would emerge, a hefty-looking station official, in neat blue uniform stood beneath his tree, looked up and told him to get down.

'*Per favore!*' said Adam. '*Uno minuto!* Please.'

'*No!*' said the uniform, '*Scendere* – come!'

Adam delayed for as long as he could, feigning imminent danger, losing his balance or being scared to descend, but it was all to no avail.

'*Scendere!*' said the uniform. 'English, come down.'

Then, just as he began his descent, two white bonnets

appeared across the road, stepping out on to the red carpet, there was a bit of a cheer from the adjoining crowd. Adam saw a flash of bonnet, and swish of a black gown, indeed he saw both bonnets, and both gowns, which he assumed, in an instant, to be those of the Queen and Princess Beatrice.

A tall man followed quickly, *'Prince Henry of Battenberg?'* thought Adam. There was the slam of a carriage door, and the first landau was away, almost instantly blotting out Adam's view with the leaves of the trees, especially the one he was now jumping out of.

Did that count? Had he seen Queen Victoria? He told himself that he had, just, and in that moment, was content. He wanted to take in and commit to memory, all the details of that morning. He and Joe sat and waited for all the other passengers to emerge, to be loaded, in some cases, crowded, into the carriages behind the waiting horses, some open, some closed, and gradually the scene dispersed.

The crowds went away, the band stopped the music recital, the carpet was rolled up, and within minutes, nobody would ever have known who had passed that way a short while before.

'Happy now?' said Joe.

''Suppose that'll have to do. I will write to my Mrs Redman and tell her anyway. Thanks for coming down early and waiting.'

'No problem at all,' said Joe as they went off across the, now deserted and de-carpeted, concourse and into the station. The train for Milan would not be leaving until gone four o'clock, so they had more time to find something more substantial to eat, before sitting and waiting.

It was a comfortable train but the journey to Milan, via

Bologne, would take some time. Adam calculated, from his well-worn map, that it was about one hundred and eighty miles, so they settled in and enjoyed a beautiful sunset, and the countryside, as it changed colours with the approaching evening.

As night fell they became aware of the train travelling alongside less countryside, and more houses and buildings. Milan had long since become an industrialised area and a central hub for Italy's northern rail system. It was a slow approach, but eventually the carriage they were in jolted to a halt, clanging against the wagon ahead of it and they knew they had arrived.

36

France and home

'Let's enquire about forward tickets first thing in the morning,' said Adam, to which Joe willingly agreed. He didn't want the Countess of Balmoral, or anyone else for that matter, to encourage Adam to stay, just to see another red carpet arrival.

They hoped they still had enough lire, and some additional English money, to see them through the journey home. Gradually, the thought of staying anywhere else for long periods of time, earning some more cash, and delaying their arrival in Britain, had sapped their enthusiasm for Italy or the continent. It was now an all-out effort to repatriate themselves.

It was dark by now and the station was deserted. The two boys even decided not to bother to roam the streets looking for somewhere to stay, but settle down in one of the waiting rooms on the station and wait for the morning. They had eaten and drunk all the provisions they had brought from Naples, and subsequently fell asleep. Several hours later, as the sun came up, they woke, rather stiff, and hungry again.

Joe suggested they stay together, so they wandered off to find some more bread, fruit and maybe fill their water bottles. The morning was warm again, and the town was waking up, with market stalls being set up and shops opening their shutters. It did not take them long to stock up again, and they made their way back to the railway station.

'The ticket office is open now,' said Adam, so he approached the kiosk, where a yawning official was waiting for customers, while Joe looked after the bags. Once again, the mysterious paperwork given to them by Harry at the Consulate in Naples, worked its magic and Adam came back with two tickets in exchange for very little money.

The man at the ticket counter had written down all kinds of things in a book, on his side of the desk, and handed back the papers. Clearly, Harry had somehow managed to convince everyone who saw the vouchers, that the bill for the tickets should be settled by somebody else!

'There is a train from here in Milan via Geneva to Dijon, in France, and then an onward connection from there to Calais,' said Adam excitedly. 'It will be leaving here about eleven today, Saturday 17th March. We are on our way!'

It was not a fast train, but it would be going in the right direction so all they had to do was sit on it, and wait for it to take them where they needed to go! The total journey to the coast of France Adam calculated to be more than seven hundred miles. It could take another three days.

And so it did.

They had tickets, water and food. They managed to replace the water and bought more food, when the train stopped along the way, and they slept a lot, as the train rocked them in and out of wakefulness.

At roughly the half-way mark, in Dijon, it was necessary to change trains, but even there, with an hour and a half to spare for the connection to arrive, they simply crashed out on a waiting bench, in the hazy sunshine, clinging closely to their bags, and taking it in turns to keep a close eye on each other, for safety's sake.

In the spare time they had, they were able to exchange what Italian money they had left into French francs, and in what seemed like no time at all they were on another train and speeding towards the French coast.

Quite suddenly, their odyssey of adventure and indeed, survival, seemed to be nearing its end. They mused over their adventures, since leaving the ship in Malta, as they watched the French countryside flash by.

The kindly reverend in Malta, the crossing to Sicily and Christmas with Roberto and his family; their brush with organised crime in Salerno and Naples and then Harry, at the consulate, who seemed to have enjoyed giving them a crucial 'leg up' in their quest to get home.

In Calais, they left the train and found their way to the harbour, where, boats and ships, of all shapes and sizes, were clustered in the harbour area. Adam and Joe enjoyed a delightful fish meal, with a bottle of wine at one of the cafés near the sea front, and then decided to look for a boat. They wandered up and down until they heard an English voice.

'Hello,' said Joe to an elderly man standing near the gangplank of his paddle steamer. 'Are you English?'

'We certainly are,' replied the man. 'What are you two up to in Calais?'

'It's a long story,' replied Adam. 'We've been stuck on the continent for several months, and have to get back to our regiment in Dorchester. Are you going back to England any time soon?'

'In a couple of hours,' said the man, whom they now saw

was younger than they had first thought, slight but strong, but with prematurely grey hair, a moustache, a thick blue woollen roll-neck jumper and a sailor's cap.

'We bring the mail across every other day, and sometimes passengers, boxes and packages for companies, selling to each other between France and England. Sometimes we bring thirty or forty passengers, sometimes none, but there is always plenty of cargo and mail bags.'

'May we come back with you?' said Adam, assuming it would be a fairly straightforward arrangement.

'Have you got any papers?' said the man.

'We have out military identities and this,' said Adam offering the Naples consulate voucher. The man looked at them all, and declared that he could not understand the paper from the Consulate, but that the military identities would be sufficient. 'It'll cost your four shillings each,' he said.

'I think we can manage that,' said Adam. 'Would you take French francs? I think what you're asking is about three francs or less. Can we say five francs for the both of us?'

'That'll do fine,' said the man, and told them he would be casting off in two hours, about two o'clock.

Adam and Joe used the time to find a small shop near the harbour which sold stationery, home and general goods, and even stamps, although Joe didn't buy any. Adam bought a couple of sheets of paper and two envelopes, then sat down near the harbour entrance.

Calais harbour

Tuesday 20 March 1894

Dear Daisy,

At the time of writing this we have made it to Calais, in France, and looking forward to being in England in a few hours. My friend, Joe and I have found our way all the way up through Italy, and across France. There is so much to tell you and I hope that you might soon receive the two little pots I bought for you in Caserta and sent to The Manor House from a place called Frosinone.

When we are safely back in Dorchester I shall write to you again and perhaps you could write to me there.

Thinking of you a lot, my dearest, Daisy,

Adam.

Then Adam and Joe just sat on the harbour wall and waited, keeping their eye on the paddle steamer, which would take them 'home'. The slight, grey haired man, who appeared to be the owner, came and sat with them.

'We're just waiting for the tide, now,' he said. 'My name is Albert, by the way. My dear mother named me after the queen's husband as I was born just about the time he died.'

'Nothing like being reminded of somebody else's death every time you have a birthday!' said Joe.

'Exactly,' he responded, 'but I don't mind.'

'And how long have you been going back and forth, on your steamer here?'

'About twelve years. Since I was about twenty-one,' he said.

'My age,' said Joe. 'And were you always on boats as you grew up?'

'Grew up in Folkestone, loved messing around on boats and got a job as a deck hand when I was only fourteen. Saved up a lot, and eventually went half shares in this old tug,' he said, pointing to his boat, named '*The Little Empress*'.

'You must be a good sailor,' said Adam. 'My friend, Joe here, is nearly always sick at sea.'

'Well, we shall see, shan't we?' said Joe, not entirely keen on being reminded of it.

'You have to be pretty skilled to get in and out of here,' said Albert. 'They are gradually building a proper deep water harbour, but until then, we have to wait for tides to get going, or even to come in, and it is very tricky navigating your way into Calais.'

'So will it be better when there is a harbour built?' said Adam.

'Absolutely,' said Albert, 'and on the other side they're thinking of building deep harbour facilities, for naval ships, so we shall get a good berth and much easier docking, all at the Royal Navy's expense!'

'You seem to have a queue building up,' said Joe, looking at the array of people with all kinds of carrying bags, carpet bags, suitcases and some with nothing at all, waiting to board *The Little Empress*.

'Why the name?' said Joe, always interested in everything around him, and curious too, as he had been from a child.

'Ferry boats have come a long way, since the early days of everybody sitting on a chilly deck, and being sailed across at the mercy of wind and rain, then waiting for the tide, before being able to land people on the beaches.

'Now they are building bigger steam ships, with passenger rooms and all sorts. Some of the bigger ones have been named after queens and empresses, so when I got my little tug I called her *The Little Empress*.

'You can sit inside, out of the elements, if you can find room, and half way through the two hour crossing, we might even make you a cup of tea.'

'Oh! Now that would be heaven,' said Adam. 'A cup of tea. That would help us to feel as if we were really home.'

'Right indeed,' said Joe. Captain Albert, with his sailor's cap and his thick blue jumper, got up and strolled towards the boat.

'We're just waiting for the flow of the tide,' he shouted at the queue, before turning again to Adam and Joe. 'Come along you two, I'll find you a couple of chairs in my little passenger cabin,' so they by-passed the queue and went aboard.

They went aboard and, sure enough, Albert showed them into an enclosed cabin, with some tables and chairs, with windows either side, which the two of them found very comfortable.

'We should take about two hours,' said Albert again, 'but, as I said, it is always tricky navigating out of Calais, and into Dover. One day the big harbours will be finished and there will be even bigger ferries going back and forth every day. Anyway, we're off now, so I will make sure you get a hot cup of tea. I'll be on the bridge.'

They left the continent of mainland Europe behind, after their long adventurous journey, and sat back to enjoy a day, which was cloudy but with occasional shafts of sunlight filtering through. The boat gathered speed and headed into the waves, on its way to the white cliffs and the English town of Dover.

'Oh! God, I hate ships!' Joe suddenly moaned, as he put his head down on the table, resting on his folded arms.

'Not sick again?' said Adam. 'Here, eat something, it helps, sit up, take a sip of tea.'

'I can't,' came the reply. 'Oh, God! I feel awful. And we've only just…' He did not finish the sentence before gasping and dropping his head again on to his arms. 'Ugh!'

Adam fished out of his own bag, a paper carrier that some of the fruit had been in, and put it into Joe's hand. 'If you have to be sick, use this, rather than the floor,' he said. 'I can still see the French coast easily, so we've a way to go.'

'Thanks, ugh!' was all he got in reply.

After drinking a very welcome cup of the captain's tea, Adam went out on to the open deck. There he enjoyed the spray of the sea, the gulls circling above and, unlike Joe, the sway of the boat as it ploughed into each successive wave, and furrowed a way through the English Channel to England's coast.

The two hours passed and, fortunately, Joe had managed to fall asleep with his head in his arms. The captain, and his small crew, took their craft carefully towards the beach and managed successfully to tie it up against a small jetty, which meant that the passengers, of which there were just about the twenty or so Adam had seen queuing up, were able to disembark. Adam woke Joe and virtually lifted him out of the seat.

'Come on, we're here. We're home. You'll feel better the moment we step on to dry land, provided you can keep your balance on that jetty!'

'That's very reassuring,' was all Joe managed to get out, but he did manage to stand, and walk, and together they set foot on the pavements of Dover, their long journey home almost ended.

'Why is it,' said Joe, 'that as soon as you set foot on firm land, the sea-sickness goes?'

'Don't know,' said Adam. 'Maybe because the sickness is all in the mind!'

'I can assure you the sickness was not in my mind. Anywhere but!' said Joe.

They made sure their bags were secure and followed directions to the railway station. It would seem, from maps and enquiries they made there, that the only way to get to Dorchester would be by train to Waterloo, on a South Eastern Railway line, travelling into London, and then out on a London and South Western line train. From that train they might have to change again to get to Dorchester.

'I've never been to London,' said Adam.

'At last, there's something I know that you don't,' said Joe, 'not that we'll be there for long. We'll be going into Waterloo station and then out again, from a different platform.'

'I am certainly going to come back to London one day,' Adam insisted. 'It's never bothered me much before, but having seen some of Rome and other amazing cities, I've a hankering to see our capital, and maybe take Daisy.'

'You'll have to introduce me to this Daisy of yours,' said Joe.

'I think I am going to ask her to marry me, before I introduce her to you!' Adam laughed as he said that, but he certainly would like to have made plans, there and then, to see Daisy.

They had arrived at a ticket sales kiosk, showed their military identities, and rather hoped they would be given some special treatment in the purchase of two single third class tickets to London. They need not have worried too much. The single fare, third class, now the only class available other than First Class, which they did not even consider, was just four shillings each.

'That's okay,' said Joe. 'We have some English money and a few extras also from the reverend's collection of coins in Malta.'

'It's less than a penny per mile,' said Adam. 'Four shillings, forty eight pence, about sixty or seventy miles. Maybe we did get a special rate for military identity.'

Joe paid for two tickets and they went off to look for something to eat, before boarding the train, which would leave about forty-five minutes later.

'Maybe we should begin to think about how we are going to present ourselves at the barracks in Dorchester,' said Adam. 'Up to now it has been a very distant thought, but quite suddenly it is a bit close.'

'Or too close for comfort,' added Joe. 'It could be very nasty if nobody believes our stories, or believes the efforts we have made to get home.'

'Maybe they will simply say we took too long,' said Adam, 'although come to think of it, we did have an understanding from the Consulate in Naples, judging from the telegraph messages, they had received from England, that we should aim to be home by the 23rd of March. Today is only Tuesday 20th March, so we should be back in Dorchester by tomorrow.'

'I think we have done rather well!' said Joe. By now they were sipping at two mugs of tea from a café on the railway approach, and waiting for two sandwiches, which they had requested. Adam meanwhile had just thought of his letter to Daisy.

'Is there a Post Office nearby?' he said to one of the porters.

'Round the corner, mate,' said the porter. 'Out there and round to the left.'

'Save my sandwich,' he said to Joe. 'I shan't be a few minutes.'

He ran off, hoped he would find the Post Office quickly and that it would be open. He was not disappointed and it took him barely a few seconds to be served with a stamp, which he affixed to his letter to Daisy, and passed it across the counter to be collected by the end of the day.

He returned to his mug of tea, and the waiting sandwiches, by which time it was almost time to board the train. It didn't take them long to finish the tea, walk to the platform and seek out a place to sit. Joe had discovered, while Adam was at the Post Office, that the train would take just under a couple of hours.

'We'll be in London at just about night fall,' said Joe. 'The only places I have ever slept in London have nearly all been doorways and alleyways. Sorry I don't know anybody who could put us up for the night.'

'Then we shall spend one more night on a railway station,' said Adam. 'It won't hurt us, and we can get the first train tomorrow, which will get us to Dorchester, or at least well on the way.'

The train pulled out of Dover and gathered speed. An inspector came along quite soon to check their tickets, and struck up a conversation, asking how two privates in the Queen's army could be travelling alone back from France.

'You probably would not believe us if we told you!' said Adam.

37

Dorchester

Sometime, during the mid afternoon of Wednesday, the twenty-first of March 1894, two dishevelled, dusty, hungry, and certainly unexpected young men, arrived at the gate of the barracks in Dorchester;

Adam, aged twenty-three, was looking reasonably self-assured, probably the smarter of the two, with what was now quite a rugged complexion, and standing quite upright;

Joe, aged twenty-one, slightly shorter than Adam, was less self-assured. However, he was still holding his ground, knowing that they were in the right place, in good time, but still overwhelmed by the thought of what might happen next. They were greeted, half-heartedly, by a sergeant, whom they did not recognise, and to whom they offered their military identities.

'You're not telling me you belong in here?' said the sergeant. 'Look at the state of you, long hair, unshaven and with your dress a complete shambles.'

'It's a long story, sergeant,' said Adam, 'but I can assure you we belong here, and indeed I think you will find that we are expected. We're even two days early.'

'Wait here,' said the sergeant, and vanished across the parade ground and into the block flying the regimental colours from the roof.

'I've absolutely no idea what we're going to say,' said Joe, suddenly gripped by a fear of the authority, to which they had returned to subject themselves.

'We shall tell the story, and tell the truth,' said Adam, as they saw the sergeant reappear out from the front door of the building. His attitude had somewhat changed.

'Follow me, you two and look sharp,' he said. Then he shut the front gate, wrapped a chain around it temporarily, and marched ahead of them, across to the far side of the building, around the side and in through a smaller door, which led immediately down a flight of stone steps. Behind him, Adam and Joe were almost marching, although somehow out of practice! They still had their bags held tightly, and descended the stairway, only a few feet behind the sergeant.

'In here!' he said, and ushered them into a cell with two bunk beds.

'We're not prisoners,' said Adam. 'We are genuine members of Her Majesty's army in Dorchester, reporting for duty, in good time, after a traumatic journey to get here!'

'Get in!' said the sergeant. 'I don't know what happens next, but these are my orders. Somebody else will be down to see you shortly.'

'And what is shortly?' said Joe, 'Ten minutes, ten days, or maybe we'll be forgotten about and just left here!'

'If you are privates in the regiment, and I am not saying you're not,' said the sergeant, 'then maybe you'd like to remember who you're talking to, and act your rank. Somebody will be down shortly, and if it makes you feel any better, I'll bring you some water and some biscuits.'

'Sounds a bit like bread and water... sergeant!' said Joe,

trying to recover his composure, but agreeing to honour his rank at the same time.

'As I said, just settle down here for a while, and somebody will come.'

As they had no choice, they entered the cell while the sergeant closed the door. However, he did not lock it. It would have been the height of foolishness to take advantage of that, and walk. Maybe this was a test, just to be sure they were who they said they were, and that they deserved a proper 'welcome' for a proper return to duty, whatever that might entail.

They consumed the jug of water, which came with two mugs and some biscuits, as promised, and waited. It was cooler in this cell than any temperature they had experienced for the past few months. The temperature during the month of March in England, sitting in a concrete cell, was not as comfortable as March in southern Europe.

And it wasn't just the air temperature that was different. Suddenly they felt more at risk, vulnerable and unsure of what might come next. They felt more fear than they had done in almost every situation in which they'd found themselves for the past few months. They were not longer in control .

It was just about two hours before they saw a face they did know. Corporal Frank Lewis, with whom they had ventured off the ship in Malta, now a sergeant himself, entered the cell and the two boys, Adam and Joe stood up. The sergeant saluted and they returned it instantly. Normality was resuming.

'Sit down, you two,' said Frank, which they did, all three of them and Frank let out a huge gasp of air, almost a yawn, but definitely a resigned exhalation of breath.

'Well, what the bloody hell happened to you two? Did you

382

jump ship and decide not to come back, or what?'

'Corporal,' said Adam, which caused a sudden short cough from Frank, who pointed to his stripes.

'Sorry, sergeant,' said Adam. 'We certainly did not jump ship. Somebody jumped us. On the day of that shore leave, after we left you in the town centre, we were exploring the shops a little, sitting enjoying the sun and were suddenly attacked, and overwhelmed, by some local lads who robbed us, and, would you believe, tied us up, took us in a donkey cart or something, God knows how many miles, and dumped us. We did not know where we were and, in any case, we were spark out for hours.'

'The next day,' Joe came in, 'we woke up, tried to free ourselves, which we eventually did and, as Adam says, we didn't know where we were, or which way Valetta might be.'

'We were on a roadside somewhere, tied up in the back of a cart, covered with a tarpaulin and completely disorientated.' Adam added.

'Dis… orri… what?' said Frank the sergeant.

'Yes, dis… orri… what?' added Joe.

'We did not know where we were,' said Adam. 'We have spent nearly six months, literally, finding our way and sometimes even having to earn our fare home. Look. These are statements from the priest in Malta, one of our friends in Sicily, who employed us, and the British Consul in Naples, all confirming where we were what we were doing and what we were aiming for.'

He handed over the affidavits to Frank, who did not look very closely at them, but folded them, stood up and said he would be back.

Adam and Joe rested on the bunk beds and just waited. They had no other choice and, in any case, were now feeling exhausted, having achieved their goal of actually getting back to their barracks. It was as if their future now rested in the hands of others, and not their own, as had been the case for many months.

As evening was approaching, they were told they had to spend one night here. The messenger was a corporal, whom they recognised from their few days on the ship back in September. He did not recognise them. He gave them blankets, two pillows, a meal which looked surprisingly appetising, with some more water and a cheery smile.

'Cheer up, you two,' said the corporal. 'You're not being locked in, but the orders are that you stay here tonight. There are lavatories down the corridor there, to the right, and in the morning you'll be taken up to see some of the officers. The building is locked but the cell isn't, on the orders of the major. You'd be advised to stay put and just look upon this as your billet for tonight.'

'We will,' said Adam. 'I'm not going anywhere. Don't suppose you know if Captain James Russell is in the barracks anywhere?'

'We don't have a Captain James Russell,' said the corporal, 'but we do now have Major James Russell. He was promoted when we returned to England, a month or so ago.' Suddenly Adam was very interested. Joe was still crashed out on his bunk.

'Why did you return to England?' said Adam.

'It was a saga and a half, that was,' said the Corporal. 'It would have taken us another few weeks to get from India to Malaya, even using steam power, but somehow, telegraph messages had been sent from England to Bombay, on the Indian west coast, and there were rumours of a plague beginning there, so nobody was allowed off the ship.

'They managed to get supplies, by calling in to Mormugao two days further down the coast from Bombay, then we were turned round and told to return home.'

'That is quite a saga,' said Adam.

'Glad we weren't with you in India,' chipped in Joe.

'You'll find out tomorrow whether you'd have rather been with us or roaming around Europe, when you should have been with your regiment.' The corporal left them to eat and, in due course, to sleep. The door was left ajar.

There was no rude awakening the next morning. Adam and Joe had already been awake for more than an hour when the Corporal, whom they'd seen the day before, brought them some water, in a jug, a bowl, two small towels, two mugs of tea and some bread, butter and even some jam.

'They're going to see you upstairs at ten o'clock,' said the Corporal. 'Before that you can go to the stores and get your uniform sorted out, or replaced. You need to be properly dressed before the officers see you.'

'Can we leave our own bags here?' said Joe.

'Yes, this cell is reserved for you until you're allowed back in the barrack accommodation, always assuming you will be allowed back.'

'Is there a danger that we won't?' added Adam.

'Not up to me. You just have to explain yourselves upstairs, I suppose. I'll be back at five to ten. Have you got a watch?'

'No,' said Joe, 'But if we go straight to the stores in a few minutes, we can get uniforms sorted and check the clock up there. Then we'll be ready well in time.'

'Good idea,' said the corporal. 'Good Luck!' He went away with a cheery smile, which made a positive impression on Adam and Joe, although, of course, they had no idea what the outcome of 'going upstairs' would be.

The door to a large wood-panelled room was opened ahead of them, by the corporal, on the dot of ten o'clock. He ushered them in, Adam first and Joe following up closely. They stood, side by side, in front of a long table, behind which sat just three senior officers. By now they had washed, shaved, eaten, and been kitted out to look at least one hundred percent better than they did when they arrived at the gates the day before.

Adam and Joe stood to attention and saluted.

'At ease,' said the commanding officer, at which point Adam suddenly recognised a face he knew

Sitting to the left of two colonels, of the First and Second Brigades of the Dorchester Regiment, was Major James Russell. His head was lowered and he was thumbing through papers. Adam was determined not to catch his eye. Adam and Joe came to the ease position, but remained very alert, with eyes straight forward. One of the colonels spoke first and indeed, conducted the interview.

'Not sure if we should be welcoming you two back into the fold, or hounding you out of the army altogether.' He spoke very gruffly, and from under a bristling moustache, and through pierced lips. 'You have been missing since *HMS Malabar* set sail from Valetta, in Malta, last September.

'You should have reported back for duty onto that ship, on the evening before it set sail. You did not, and the following morning, despite sending out personnel to look for you, and waiting for you with the gangplank down until the very last possible moment, you failed to report. Private Warkin, is that substantially correct?'

'Yes, sir.'

'Smith?'

'Yes, sir'.

'Right,' the colonel continued. 'This is not a Court Martial. If that were to happen, this room would be filled almost to the brim with all kinds of military personnel and lawyers, and you two would be standing in a dock.

'This is,' and he paused as if he could not quite believe he was saying it himself.

'This is… a Regimental Disciplinary Hearing. I am Colonel Fisher, your Battalion commanding officer, as I suspect you know. This is Colonel Trenchard, and sitting to our left, your right, is Major James Russell, from your Battalion. If we decide, here in this room, that you are in serious breach of the military code of Her Majesty's Army, you will be put under lock and key, to await a Court Martial. The charge would then be desertion, and the penalty for desertion, you do not want me to remind you of in this room.'

Adam and Joe stood stock still. There was a slight wavering in both the bodies, and the minds, of them both. They tried to look completely 'at ease' but concentrating fully to what was going on. They said nothing.

'Do you understand?' said the colonel.

'Sir!'

'Sir!'

'I have here your military identities, which you seem to have carried with you everywhere since you er… disappeared. I also have statements from three different people you seem to have solicited throughout your journeys in Italy.'

'Sir,' Adam ventured, as if to confirm what he had said was correct.

'Right,' the colonel continued. 'I can appreciate that if you had intended to desert the army, you would not have retained your identity cards so carefully. I presume you would have disposed of them, and adopted new identities. Can you explain, therefore, in simple terms, where you were when the ship left without you, and why you ventured from the harbour through Malta, as it seems you did, to Sicily, the length of Italy and home overland? Warkin?'

Adam stood his ground and, referring to Joe occasionally to suggest that his friend could provide a detail or two, he retold the entire story, from their decision not to return to the harbour, having learned that it had almost certainly sailed without them, by the time they recovered from the first assault, and their decision to make their way home together.

He told how they had earned money on the way, been robbed again, but nevertheless decided to collect 'proof' of their activities and intentions, throughout the long journey home, hence the affidavits which were now being looked at by both Colonels. Adam related their time in Naples, and the suggestion of the British Consul there to telegraph London leading to, as he believed, the Regiment being aware of their existence and that they were indeed making for a return home.

'I got a job in a market, sir,' said Joe, 'until I went and broke my arm, or thought I had.'

'Thank you, Smith.' said the colonel. 'This all seems a very clear train of thought on your part. How did you know the geography of Europe, find accommodation, work, trains and so on? How did you even know which way to go? It says on your records, both of you, that you never went to school.'

'I've been very lucky, sir,' said Adam, 'throughout my life and in many ways. I was taught to read by a lady in my village, when I was growing up, and then had the good fortune to work for a gentleman and his family where I was a gardener for some years. They were kind enough to allow me the use of their library ,and I never stopped reading, learning, being inquisitive about everything, so much so that...'

'That's enough,' said the colonel. 'Strangely, I do know about your apparent thirst for knowledge. I believe you already know Major Russell here?'

'I have had the honour, sir, to serve Captain, my apologies, *Major* Russell, and will always be entirely grateful to him for his kindness to me in so many ways...' The colonel moved, as if to interrupt him, but Adam finished what he wanted to say.

'... whatever may be the outcome of this hearing, sir.'

'Good man!' muttered Joe, completely under his breath. Completely. He never moved a muscle.

'Now, you two will return to the cell you occupied last night,' said the Colonel again. 'You will know, before the end of today, my decision, our decision.'

Back in the cell Adam and Joe enjoyed a lunch of cold ham with some potatoes, and spinach, a jug of water and a rather stodgy pudding which was nevertheless sweet and filling.

They waited, sitting on the bunks with backs to the wall, speaking softly and, for nearly an hour after the lunch, re-visiting their various outings and adventures of the past few months.

'Cannot believe that we have climbed Mount Vesuvius,' said

Joe. 'The kind of thing I might never have done had I stayed in London.'

'In fact the kind of thing we might never had done, had we stayed on the ship!' joked Adam. 'If the hearing this morning believes us, and we don't get locked up for life, or worse, then we certainly have some things to remember.'

Nothing was said then for almost another hour, until they heard footsteps on the concrete floor of the corridor outside. Their hearts missed a beat, wanting to know the outcome of the hearing, but dreading the arrival of a decision. They were surprised by who it was. There was a knock on the door.

'Mind if I come in?' said Major James Russell. The boys leapt to their feet and stood to attention.

'Sit down, Adam, Joe,' said James. 'Relax.'

Adam was simply at loss as to how to respond to this visit. As they sat down, he looked at the floor, then at his feet, then at the wall. He glanced in the direction of the newly promoted major and their eyes met for a split second, but Adam was immediately consumed with embarrassment, and bowed his head to the ground again.

'Cheer up, Adam,' said the major. 'Aren't you going to say 'hello' at least?'

'I'm not sure whether you would ever agree to speak to me again,' said Adam, eyes still firmly fixed on his own boots.

'Okay,' said the major again. 'I think I know how you feel, and what you mean. Let's make this official, and then we can clear the air. Stand up, the pair of you.'

Adam and Joe immediately sprang to their feet again, stood to attention and faced the wall behind Major Russell.

'Sir,' came from both privates.

'Now, stand at ease,' said the major, which they did in one sharp click of each left foot. 'Your presentation of yourselves this morning was exemplary. You were polite, neat, tidy, definitely contrite and clear in offering reasons for nearly six months absence. You should be proud of yourselves, having done that.'

'Thank you, sir,' said Adam, followed immediately by Joe.

'You both, as it were, cleared the path, both behind you and ahead of you, in your attempts to get home, after your original mishap of being knocked unconscious. Obviously, the statements you collected along the way helped, but there was one more document that probably swung it in your favour.'

'In our favour, sir?' said Joe.

'Be quiet, Joe,' said Adam.

'Yes, in your favour,' said the major. 'And that was the letter you sent me from Malta, on 19th September last. Had our ship gone on to Malaya, I might never have received that letter, even now. However, it was here waiting for me, when we returned to Dorchester, and your obvious intention to find a way home, within days of being stranded swayed the colonels this morning.'

'Swayed them?' muttered Adam.

'Be quiet, Adam,' said Joe, returning the admonition.

'You will be called back to the hearing in a few minutes. I wouldn't make too many plans, in your head, about going on leave, but you can rest assured that you are not going to be put in front of a Court Martial. Now sit down, the pair of you.'

'Sir,' said Adam. 'Writing to you seemed obvious to me. We were appalled by the situation we got ourselves into. I wrote to Mrs Redman my friend, and to Daisy, at The Manor House too. I am so glad I wrote to you.'

'Yes, well so am I,' said Major Russell, as he himself then stood up. The boys stood with him. 'Sit down, and wait to be called upstairs. Adam, I shall see you later, I hope. I have not had anything like such a good batman as you for six months!' With that he was gone; no chance to make a comment, or a reply. Apparently no more thanks required. The ice was broken,

In front of the panel of colonels, less than an hour after their face to face meeting with the major, Adam and Joe saluted, stood to attention again, and were left in that stance.

'The Disciplinary Hearing Panel have closely considered, and studied, the details of your prolonged absence from duty,' Colonel Fisher began. ' We are convinced, beyond reasonable doubt, that it was never your original intention to absent yourselves from duty, and that you made every reasonable effort to return to Dorchester, albeit taking a little over six months to do so. Circumstances, beyond your control, would appear to have been the prime reason for your original absence.'

So far, the two young men had discerned no reason to dread the remainder of the 'verdict'. Colonel Fisher continued.

'We have therefore decided to allow your service with the regiment to be considered as continuous, and without break. You may resume your duties, subject to the loss of six months wages and being confined to these barracks, until the first of June. There will be no custodial element to this decision. Have you anything to say?'

'Thank you, sir, for your consideration of our situation, sir, and for the deliberations of the panel. We are most grateful, and look forward to resuming our proper duties, sir.'

There was a moment's silence, and then.

'What he said, sirs!' said Joe. 'The same from me, sir.'

'Dismiss!' Adam and Joe, in perfect unison, saluted, did an about turn and marched from the room. They went immediately to their cell, collected such other belongings as they had in their two bags and went to the sleeping quarters to find where they would be that night. There was some additional kit already on their two beds, which needed sorting and putting into lockers, before they went to find the orders for the day and report to their company.

Perhaps the outcome of their hearing was never in doubt. They had not purposely absconded from either their duties or the army, but it was always going to be 'touch and go' whether there would be any compassion at all, in the verdict announced, after a six month absence. They were pleased, relieved and almost delighted.

'We probably knew we'd not get six months pay backdated,' said Joe,' but we earned plenty on our way home!'

'I've still got some French francs and a few lire coins, which will not be of much use now. We're hardly likely to be taking a holiday any time soon, and most likely never to the continent. I shall save my few coins as souvenirs.' Adam and Joe were looking at notice boards and, even on their first day back, were finding their feet as members of the Dorchester Regiment and their particular company again.

Within a few days, Major James Russell had approached Adam again to seek out his opinion about resuming duties as a batman.

'Surely you've got a servant and don't need me,' said Adam, who had seriously had no thoughts of that particular privilege being revived.

'He's not too keen, although he was to start with,' said James.

'He does not mind relinquishing the post, and spending more time with his mates, than polishing my boots!'

'When can I start?' said Adam. 'Or start again?'

'Come over tomorrow evening,' was the reply. 'I'll let him know this evening, and, provided he hasn't changed his mind, the job is yours – again!'

Everything seemed to be falling back into place. Sometimes, amongst the various parades, inspections, training sessions and orienteering exercises, it was as if they'd never been away. The memories of Malta, Sicily, and mainland Europe were fading into the past. The two of them would, however, never be the same, even if they were now confined to barracks for another two months or so.

38

Return to East Hambley

A dam enquired of the major, one evening, whether he might be permitted to visit The Manor House at the end of their confinement, for a short summer visit.

'I think I can guess why,' said the major one evening. 'Have you written to Daisy since you got back?'

'I posted a letter to her from Dover, when we got off the boat that brought us across the channel,' said Adam, 'and I am halfway through writing her another letter now. I would just like to know if I might promise her a visit from me. When I am able to leave the barracks again, that would be my first choice for a trip outside of Dorchester. But I do need to know whether I'd be welcome at The Manor House.'

'Of course you'd be welcome,' Major James responded instinctively. 'And you can be assured that Daisy is still there, dare I say, waiting for you. She's a lady's maid now to my mother. My uncle, Walter still lives at The Manor House and you might know that our father, Dr Russell is now in his mid-seventies. A very venerable old man.'

'I'm sure he is,' said Adam. 'and Mr Granger, and Freddie, and Mrs Browne, and young Robert?'

'We have been very lucky with staff at home these past couple of years, but you will have to wait until you get there to see for yourself,' the major concluded.

'I cannot wait,' said Adam, and went about the rest of that day, that week, that month, content that June would soon come.

By the time it came, as the summer began to spread its warmth over the south of England, Adam was feeling very optimistic about a trip to his old place of work. He had written to Daisy twice and even to Mrs Redman, and received a reply from both Daisy herself and the old lady in Melton Ford.

Mrs Redman still occupied her little cottage and, now in her fifties, still tended her orchard, and her garden, with much care. She was as excited as anyone, hearing about Adam's adventures with Joe and possibly seeing Adam again before long.

Being paid again, one shilling and tuppence per day, plus what he was earning from Major Russell, and considering there had been no outings to the shops or bars in Dorchester, Adam soon found his personal nest-egg of savings had grown considerably.

The opportunity came at last. Being granted three days leave in early July, Adam waited desperately for the Friday of that week to arrive and, now, legally, and with permission, left the confines of the barracks at last. He made his way to Dorchester station and, once on the Southampton train, was constantly on the lookout for the little railway stop at East Hambley.

Arriving there, it was a brisk walk, such as he had made first at the age of sixteen, to pass by the big gates and enter at the wooden garden gate, pass through the vegetable patches, alongside the greenhouses, and make a tentative knock at the kitchen door.

Such was the welcome and the excitement generated at the

door and in the kitchen, that, once or twice, Adam thought he might stop breathing. Clearly, Daisy had told the others of his misfortunes and his good fortune. The questions came thick and fast, and Mrs Browne, now much friendlier than Adam remembered her being, very quickly placed a tray of tea, with several cups and saucers, and a plate of cakes in front of him.

'You tuck into that, my lad,' she said, but it was not tea and cakes that Adam had made the journey for. 'You tuck into those cakes, we'll all have a cup of tea with you, and I shall go and see where Daisy is.' That is what Adam wanted to hear, so he agreed to field all their questions and wait for Daisy to be free to come down.

Robert, whom Adam remembered as the 'new' garden boy was quite shy, standing back a little from those gathered around Adam. Mr Granger made an appearance and slapped Adam heartily on the back.

'You've done well, my boy!' he said. 'We've never had anybody here, since you left, who quite knew how to repair the lawn mower engine. We've even had to get somebody in.'

'Sorry I cannot stay long enough to show Robert,' said Adam, 'or teach him.'

Freddie appeared at the door and bounded in, rather belying his elevated status as butler, flung his arms around Adam and then stood back, and offered his hand to this smart young member of Her Majesty's army.

'Welcome home,' he said. 'We've missed you this past year.'

'Has it only been a year?' said Adam. 'I feel as though I've been around the world and back, but... Where is Daisy?'

'She'll be down in a minute,' said Freddie. 'Just laying out her mistress's clothes for later this evening.'

'So, how have you been getting on with your new position?' said Adam to Freddie, sipping his second cup of tea.

'He's been doing just fine,' chipped in Mrs Browne. 'Mr Collins is a proper gent, who gets things done and gets them done efficiently, with no bullying or threats.'

'I could do a bit of bullying if you like, Mrs Browne,' said Freddie, chirpily, and with a false bang on the table.

'You'll get nothing more done than you do now,' she replied. 'I'm rushed off my feet as it is, but we all get along fine.'

'Daisy tells me you've been to Italy and goodness knows where else,' said Freddie. 'You could tell us all about it, if we had a walk to the pub in the village. How long are you here for?'

'I'll pass on the walk to the village with you, if you don't mind, at least as my first priority!' said Adam smiling.

'Of course! Stupid of me,' said Freddie. 'Oh! and by the way, she's here.'

Adam looked up, and there, just inside the door, looking demure, as beautiful as ever in his eyes, and just a little unsure of herself, was Daisy. In just a year she had blossomed into a beautiful young woman, different even from what he remembered a year ago, and so unlike the cheeky young thing, who made fun of him waiting at the wrong gates seven years ago.

Adam bounced out of his seat, and, ignoring all others in the room, came to Daisy, with both arms outstretched. He grabbed both her hands, which were also offered to him, and they stood there, with the remainder of the large kitchen now just swirling around them in a haze. They were simply staring into each other's eyes, as they stretched and then embraced, without kissing, but with such joy that neither of them could quite breathe for a few seconds, before letting go again. Each of them was simply looking at the other.

'There'll be no talking to those two for half an hour or more,' said Mrs Browne.

'I don't think they'd hear us if we tried,' Freddie added. 'Why don't you two go into the garden. There's plenty of space out there. The sun is shining, you can find a bench to sit on, and catch up stories. If any of the family come along, I am sure they'll not mind. I'll make sure they know that you're back, Adam.'

'Thank you, sir,' said Daisy to Freddie the butler, but he had no time to acknowledge her polite thanks. Adam whisked her away and found the bench, where he had sat and talked to James Russell and his father and uncle, when he had been just a garden boy.

'I've been waiting for this moment,' he said, 'and there were times in the past seven or eight months when I thought I might never see you again.'

'I've still got all your letters,' she said. 'And I still read them whenever I can.'

'Well, now you don't need a letter. We are here together, although I only have tomorrow, and Sunday until the mid-afternoon. I dare not be back late. The last time I was delayed returning after leave I was gone for six months!'

'Well, two days is just fine by me,' said Daisy. 'Tomorrow morning I have the morning off. When the mistress heard you were coming, she said I could spend Saturday morning with you.'

'In that case, we are going shopping,' said Adam. They sat there for nearly an hour, exchanging stories and dreams, jokes and memories, until finally it was time for the evening meal for the staff. Freddie told Adam that he had a room prepared for him on the top floor.

'Just like old times,' he said.

'Just as I remember it,' said Adam, when he took his small bag up to the top corridor.

That Saturday morning in July at The Manor House dawned as a bright sunny day. The house seemed quite relaxed, with no large family events happening that day, breakfast was jovial and noisy, as Adam regaled the staff with several stories of his adventures in Italy. He was wearing his smart army uniform and certainly knew how to tell a story. Freddie and Robert were keen to engage Adam in conversation.

'Don't know what I would have done,' said Robert. 'It sounds to me like you are real survivor, sir.'

'Well, I think we were lucky, as well as trying to be clever.' Adam replied. 'Anybody in our position would certainly have to think on their feet. Now, if you don't mind, Mr Freddie Collins, I'd like to take Daisy to the village and perhaps we could meet later on for a pint of ale.'

'Perfect.' said Freddie. 'Of course Daisy can go. I'll meet you, this afternoon, perhaps about four?'

'Ready, Daisy?' She was, and with a bright and pretty yellow day dress, and bonnet, plus a shawl around her shoulders, she and Adam walked through the gardens, and out of the wooden gate, to enjoy the walk to the village. They looked in windows and enjoyed swapping opinions on the value or quality of chinaware, various kinds of shoes, even food in the grocery store. Then they passed the pawn shop.

'Coming in?' said Adam, stopping near the doorway.

'Nothing in there that I can afford,' said Daisy.

'Well, perhaps not,' Adam replied, 'but maybe I can.' The pair of them stopped outside the little shop for several minutes. Adam took Daisy's hand and spoke very gently.

'Daisy, I may not be much of a catch for a clever lady's maid like you, but ever since we first met, at the gates of The Manor House, I have admired you. I became devoted to you before I ever joined the army, and since then, being without you for well over a year, I have come to realise that I would find it difficult to think of a future without you.' And right there, outside the shop, he dropped to one knee.

'What are you doing?' whispered Daisy. 'Get up.'

'Will you marry me?'

'Marry you?' Daisy blushed, and smiled, laughed and stepped back before brushing her eye. 'Are you serious?'

'Of course I'm serious,' Adam came back. 'I have absolutely no idea how it might work out with me in Dorchester, marrying a lady's maid in East Hambley. We would need your father's permission, presumably, and I think I need my Commanding Officer's permission. But all that is by the way. My question is still, will you marry me?'

'Me, a wife. Fancy that!' she said.

'Is that a Yes?' he said, coming back up to his full height. 'Is that your answer? If we can sort out any problems, or getting permission, or whatever it takes, will you marry me?'

'Yes, I will, of course I will. I'd love to be your wife. I'd be so proud.'

'Don't know if I'm very much to be proud of,' said Adam, 'but come on...' and he almost dragged her into the pawn shop.

'Where are we going?' she exclaimed, by which time they

were in and the elderly jeweller recognised Adam from the incidents of the past.

'Goodness me,' he said. 'What a smart young man. And such a pretty lady with you too.'

'Good morning,' said Adam. 'I'd like to buy an engagement ring that I can afford.' Daisy was blushing uncontrollably, but Adam held her hand firmly and they looked at several rings, with tiny diamonds, on gold bands in little red or blue boxes.

'I don't know what to say,' said Daisy. 'Nobody's ever bought me a ring before!'

'I should hope not,' said Adam, 'but look at these, and see if you like one of them. For instance,' he picked up one delicate band with just one stone in, 'how much is this?'

The jeweller looked closely at it, raised a small magnifying glass to his eye and looked at it. 'That's a beautiful, but very small, real diamond,' he said. 'Less than one tenth of a carat, but well cut and elegant, isn't it?'

'It's beautiful,' said Daisy.

'I can let you have that, seeing as I know you,' said the jeweller in his friendly voice, 'for just about four pounds.'

'Four whole pounds!' said Daisy. 'That's almost half a year's wages.'

'Well, it's a good job it's not you who's buying it,' said Adam. 'Do you like it?'

'I love it, but…'

'I think we'll have that one,' said Adam. 'Listen, Daisy,' said Adam, 'I have never wanted anybody to be my wife but you, it's always been you, and I didn't really mean to propose to you in a shop! But, well, I have to go back to The Keep in Dorset tomorrow, so let's get this done.'

Adam hesitated, before offering some well-earned cash that he'd been saving for weeks, from his wages and the extra allowance he earned from Major James, alongside any meagre savings he had returned home with in March, which all came to just about four pounds.

'Don't suppose you'd take three pounds fifteen shillings?' said Adam, quietly, to the jeweller.

'No, but I'll take three pounds, ten shillings! Seeing as it's you, and you're such a smart young man, and you make a lovely couple!'

'That's ridiculous,' said Adam, 'but it is really kind of you. I do appreciate it.'

'You look after that young lady,' said the jeweller. 'She looks very proud of you. Don't you let her down. And the ten shillings discount is my little present to you both.'

'I won't ever let her down,' said Adam, and he took the ring, and placed it on Daisy, third finger, left hand. She wiped away a tear while Adam turned and handed over the money.

'Best three pounds ten shillings I ever spent,' he said. Then, right there in the shop, with the jeweller watching, he planted a loving kiss on Daisy's lips which she was only half expecting.

It took several seconds for her to recover, but immediately reciprocated the romantic gesture with a long warm kiss of her own. Adam was engaged to be married!

39

Betrothed

They walked away from the shop, hand in hand, with Adam feeling the little diamond on his fiancé's hand. He was also feeling a little light-headed. What had he just done? Probably the best move he'd ever made in his life, but it was a big decision nevertheless. They had tea in the village, chatted animatedly and then, for several minutes, didn't speak a word. They just looked at each other before thinking of something else to say.

'Who do we tell first?'

'You must write to your parents,' said Adam. 'I will ask about getting married when I get back to Dorset. I know there are some married quarters at The Keep and in the barracks accommodation, but let's just enjoy the moment for now and sort out the answers to all our questions later.'

'Yes, let's enjoy the moment,' she said, 'although goodness knows what Freddie and the others will say back at the house.'

'We'll find out in an hour or so. We ought to be getting back. I'm coming out again for a pint of ale with Freddie later on.'

'Well, that's typical!' Daisy said. 'You married men are all the same, gallivanting off to the pub while we women stay at home!' Luckily for Adam, she smiled, even laughed, as she said it. They laughed and smiled and chatted a lot more on the long walk back to the house.

Daisy held out her hand over the long kitchen table in the staff quarters. The others, including some of the downstairs maids, Robert, Mr Granger, Freddie and Mrs Browne were staring in disbelief.

'That's amazing,' said Freddie. 'Adam, you sly old thing, no wonder you made a beeline for here as soon as you had some leave. A real diamond!'

'I know she is! I never had any other intention in coming here,' said Adam, 'although it's good to see you all again, of course! Now, when are we going out for this drink?'

Daisy and Adam went through the remainder of the day in a bit of a trance, Daisy particularly.

Adam went to the village again, this time with Freddie and they sat out on the green in two large wooden chairs, with Adam telling yet more stories about the past year.

It was a glorious weekend for Adam. Daisy promised to write to her parents, who lived in Southampton, where her father worked at the docks. Adam promised that he would bring up the subject of being a married soldier, when he got back to Dorchester.

They then spent as many moments as they could in the garden or the kitchen, just looking at each other, thinking up new ideas and relishing all the moments spent together.

When the time came to return to Dorchester, Mr James Russell senior kindly offered to take Adam to the railway halt in his small carriage. Adam was grateful and not a little embarrassed.

'Well, you're not employed here any more,' said Walter. 'You have served my son well, and perhaps we can consider you a friend of the family.'

'That is very kind indeed,' said Adam.

And, have I heard correctly that you have proposed marriage to Daisy, my wife's maid?' said Mr James.

'Indeed,' said Adam, 'that is true. I am as pleased as punch that she has accepted me, although there are no more detailed plans at the moment.'

'Well, I am sure my brother and I, together with father will want to help in any way we can. It is a big adventure for you, although I am not sure what my wife will think about you taking Daisy away from her. My brother never married, and even our son, your Major James, has never shown any inclination to marry, although he is now thirty years old.'

'He has been a professional soldier for some years,' said Adam, 'and a very fine one too. Perhaps he will marry at a later time in life.' Adam felt honoured to be talking to Mr James senior about the family, and confident, too, that he could hold his own in such a conversation. Long gone was the little boy, or even the young man, too nervous even to speak to his employer.

He thanked Major James' father for the lift, caught the train as planned, and returned to the Keep in Dorchester, well in time for the evening meal and an evening sharing his news with Joe. He made the short walk across to Major James' quarters and did not, at first, bring up the subject of his intended marriage.

'I hope you had a good weekend,' said the Major, as Adam was fussing around in Major James' room, almost on the point of leaving.

'Almost as good as it could be,' said Adam,

'Meaning?' said James and so Adam told him.

'I've proposed marriage to Daisy, but I do not want it to be public, until I have obtained your permission, or Daisy has told her parents. It was all a bit sudden, but I could not wait another day, and I had no idea when my next leave to see her might be.'

'It's not my permission you need,' said James. 'It is the colonel's, your commanding officer. If you get official permission, then your wife can come here and there are some married quarters available, with even some provision for her living allowance, alongside your wages.

'That is amazing,' said Adam. 'I had no idea.'

'But that's only granted to about six percent of un-commissioned soldiers. Now I will tell you something even more amazing. It was my father, Dr William Russell, when he was a war correspondent during the Crimean war, who brought the attention of the government of the day to the terrible state of soldiers' accommodation in English barracks.'

'Really?' said Adam. 'I always thought what a great man he was, without really knowing why.'

'Eventually, after many years of acrimonious discussions about money, the Cardwell Reforms brought in the wages you now get, soldiers not having to pay for their own food, and even some equipment, proper living quarters, with sanitation. That was not so many years ago, between 1870 and 1881.'

'When I was ten,' said Adam.

'In those reforms there was provision made for married soldiers' quarters. If you marry without the commanding officer's permission, you get nowhere to live as a pair, and no allowance for her, so it is far better to seek permission.'

'I will. It seems the obvious thing to do,' said Adam. 'That's the military rules we live by, so perhaps, the sooner I ask the better.'

'I agree,' said the major and they parted as the evening darkness closed in.

Adam wrote to his commanding officer a formal request to get married, at some unspecified date in the future, if he and his wife could be considered to occupy one of the married quarters. He wrote to Daisy again, and again, almost once a week, although there were a lot of lectures, drill training and manoeuvres in the south-west of England in which to take part.

He wrote to Mrs Redman and told her all that had happened to him in the past year, plus the news of his proposal, and expressing the wish that he might come and see her sometime soon.

Adam also received a reply from his commanding officer after a week or two.

Pte. Warkin A.

Permission for you to marry and thereby obtain married quarters with the Regiment is denied. The decision as to whether you marry in the meantime is your own to make.

Allocation of quarters for you and your wife would fall outside the quota we have available. This situation is unlikely to change until 1896 when one or more married non-commissioned men are due to retire.

I regret this is not perhaps the reply you would have wished for, but you are free to make a further request at some time in the future.

Signed,
  Fisher P, Colonel

1 August 1894

Adam showed the note to Major James.

'I am not surprised,' he said, 'married quarters are like hens' teeth at The Keep here in Dorchester. You can decide to get married and live separately, for the time being, in which case you would have to rent a room for Daisy in the town, or wait. Are you asking my advice?'

'I'm listening, sir,' said Adam.

'Wait,' the major replied. 'Between you and me, I can tell you that at least one company of our Battalion, maybe both, is being deployed to Ireland sometime soon, for a period of six months, or even a year. That is not yet common knowledge so keep it under your hat.'

'A year, maybe!' said Adam.

'Well, it's not so long in a way. It's been about a year since you joined up. A year soon goes by, and six months is hardly any time if we are busy. You can write to Daisy and, better still, you can save up quite a lot of your income for your wedding, and for starting a new life.

'One of the married quarters might become available sooner than you think, but whatever happens, you'd be better off living as you are now and waiting for a good place to live in than getting married too soon and then living apart, and paying out for a rented place.'

'Very sensible,' said Adam, 'but not quite what I had planned.'

'You're in the army,' the major came back, 'probably best not to plan too much. As long as you are in, let the army make the plans. You won't regret waiting, although you may hate the thought of it.'

'Sometimes, I just hate being sensible! I'm going to write to

Daisy. Can I tell her about Ireland?'

'You can put it in the letter, but don't post it until we have all been told officially,' said the major.

'Thank you, sir,' Adam replied and went back to his own barrack to think how to tell, or ask, Daisy to wait.

He did not have to wait long for the parade which revealed the plans for their deployment. It was to be a year in Ireland, starting in October. Everybody could take a three day weekend leave, just before they travelled, and Adam immediately thought of adding to the letter he'd already written, before posting it.

The Keep,
Dorchester Regiment

8 August 1894

My dear Daisy,

I can picture the ring on your finger as I write this letter. I wish I was there to hold the hand it adorns. Better still, I wish I were holding your hand in East Hambley church and marrying you today. That, however, is not to be, just yet.

Much as I hate the idea, I have to ask you to wait for our wedding to take place. As a soldier I do not have the freedom simply to up sticks and come to you, but we do have our wages, and we can save up for the wedding of our dreams – well nearly all our dreams! In the meantime I can come to see you in September, for two or three days, and then we shall all be going to Ireland for a year!

The time will pass, but in the meantime I have managed to get a photograph of me, which I am enclosing with this letter. Keep it safe, and perhaps we can find a way to get a picture of you when

I come 'home' for a weekend.

I have not written for a week or two because I have been wait-ing for permission to post this letter, once our tour of Ireland was confirmed. We leave in October, but I will see you before then.

Until that day, and our other great day, yet to be confirmed !!, I remain,

Your loving fiancé

Adam xxx

The time between writing the letter and being able to visit Daisy again passed quickly and, in mid-September, Adam boarded the train again, heading for The Manor House. This time he was with Major Russell, also going home on weekend leave.

They enjoyed the train journey together with Adam filling in some more details of his Italian adventure, much to James' amusement.

Once 'home', Adam and Daisy spent as much time together as they could and even discussed all manner of plans for their future. It was exciting just making them. They hoped for living quarters at The Keep in two years time; they thought about a wedding day and even the daunting thought of being parents one day.

'I'm sorry that it seems better to wait for a wedding, rather than rush into it and have nowhere to live, and still be sepa-rated,' said Adam.

'That's alright,' said Daisy. 'For the moment, I am happy to wear your ring and read your letters. My father would like to meet you at some time, but that can wait. And Mrs Russell will need to find a new lady's maid, so we have given her plenty of time. To be honest, I shall be sorry to leave here when the time comes.'

'Of course you will,' said Adam, 'and rightly so. This family are good employers.'

Just how good her employers were, Daisy and Adam were close to finding out. After the evening meal on the Saturday of Adam's weekend visit, Mr Walter Russell called in on the staff dining room. Everybody stood up and he spoke very quietly, thanking them for that evening's splendid dinner.

'Please sit down,' he said. 'May I have a word with my wife's maid, Armstrong, and young Adam, our weekend visitor?' The pair of them blanched and stood up. 'Would you mind coming to the drawing room?' he said and left, presuming them to be following him.

'Now what is up?' said Daisy to Adam, as they ascended the back stairs. Adam remembered the extraordinarily unpleasant day, when he had been summoned, and accused of theft. Daisy recalled being 'promoted' to learning the skills of being a lady's maid, but this was different. They had been summoned together.

They knocked and entered. Inside, and sitting, were Mr James Russell senior, and his wife Alice, Major James home for the weekend as Adam was, Mr Walter and even the elderly Dr Russell in some kind of bath chair. He was alert, and smiling. All the men were drinking whisky. It was a pleasant family gathering which Adam and Daisy had been invited to join.

'You called us, sir?' said Adam, addressing Walter, although he was not the most senior member of the family in the room. Both Adam and Daisy were nervous, but had no idea why they should be.

'Please sit down,' said James indicating two spare chairs. They did so and sat very upright.

'First of all, relax. Nothing is wrong,' said Walter. 'Adam, would you like a whisky?' How completely out of the blue was that?

Not so long ago he was the one serving or bringing up new bottles from the cellar. Now he was being invited to 'have a drink'!

'And Daisy,' Walter continued, 'just this once, how about a small glass of champagne?'

'Oh, no, sir! I don't think I should.' She glanced across at Mrs Russell, who jumped into the conversation, feeling for Daisy's embarrassment.

'Well, Daisy, I think you should,' she said. 'You know this is a celebration?'

'A celebration?' ventured Adam, with only the slightest of a feeling that this gathering was about him and Daisy.

'Absolutely,' said Major James. 'My family, Adam, are delighted to have heard about your engagement to each other. So, here is your whisky, Adam, and, Daisy, drink this.' He offered her a flute of champagne. She blushed and looked sideways at Adam, who took the champagne and handed it to his fiancé. Adam was delighted to have been asked up to the family gathering and raised his glass to the others in the room. He might be sleeping in the top corridor with Freddie and the others, but he was actually a guest of the family, not an employee.

'Now,' began Mr James senior, 'when are you getting married and where? Have you made any plans?'

'Not too many, sir,' said Adam, who now took on the role

of spokesman for him and Daisy. Daisy was holding the champagne flute very tightly and sipping from it. 'We have to wait, until 1896, to be considered for married quarters at The Keep, so it gives us time to save up for all kinds of things.'

'Splendid,' said Mr James. 'What about a church? Anything settled?'

'We hope that we might be able to be married in the church here, in East Hambley, as Daisy lives in the parish, as did I for a while, and then, perhaps, just enjoy some cold ham, like a modest meal and some beers at the pub in the village. Perhaps you would allow Freddie and some of the others to join us…'

'Good,' said the senior Mr James. 'All that is what we hoped you would say. We would like you to get married in the church locally, of course. But your wedding breakfast can be here at the house, with a splendid meal, and an evening reception. Daisy, your parents could join us for a day or two. Adam, you could invite some of your company to be with you on your special day.'

'We could hardly ask for so much,' began Adam. 'We could not bear even half the cost of such a…'

'Nonsense,' Major James jumped in. 'You didn't ask for it. We are offering it, We'd love to have it here. Haven't had a wedding at The Manor House for years, and this would be our gift to you two, who have served the family so well. Any ideas for a date?'

'Well, sir,' said Adam. 'My birthday is the 22nd of July. I shall be twenty five in 1896.'

'The perfect day,' Mr James senior came back in. 'July the 22nd, in two years from now, it shall be. Frankly I can't wait.'

'Well, neither can we,' said Daisy very softly, and almost

cheekily under her breath. She smiled and the entire room burst into laughter. The drinks glasses were re-filled.

Adam and Daisy were in a hazy mist of joy for the remainder of the weekend, but on Sunday morning Adam found himself seated in the garden, when Mr James senior came by during a casual walk after church. Adam stood up.

'Sit down, man,' James began. 'You're a guest in our house, and we do thank you for your most pleasant news, and for allowing us to be part of your celebration, both now and in two years time.'

'Well, I am most grateful for being allowed to stay as a guest, let alone contemplating the wonderful gesture you have made to make our wedding just perfect.'

'You're more than welcome. We simply can't wait,' James replied.

'May I ask you a question?' Adam began. 'Tell me if it is none of my business, but there is something that has intrigued me for a long time, and you may know the answer.' He was remarkably confident now and enjoyed being treated as a guest not the garden boy.

'Go ahead,' said James.

'I was born and brought up in my little village and had the good fortune to meet up and befriend my Mrs Redman. I owe her everything, really, apart from the love my mother and father gave me before they died. She taught me to read, to be confident, to be honest and inquisitive!'

'She sounds a treasure,' said James.

'She certainly was, and still is. I would love her to come to our wedding...'

'Well have no qualms about that,' said James. 'She will be

invited anyway, if you wish her to be. She already knows our head gardener Mr Granger.'

'Well, that is my question,' said Adam, 'and thank you for suggesting that she can be invited. How does Mrs Redman know Mr Granger? It was she who first suggested I apply here, to Mr Granger, for a job, but I have never established in my own mind how they knew each other. Do you know?'

'I think I know the bare bones of it,' said Mr James. 'I'm happy to tell you what I know, but maybe you should have asked Mr Granger himself while you were working here.'

'I was young, and he was not always the easiest person to talk to,' Adam replied.

'Anyway,' James continued. 'Something like thirty years ago, Jonathan Redman was a valet to the doctor here at The Manor House. That's how he knew Mr Granger, who himself was very young then and working in the garden.'

'The garden-boy like I was!' said Adam.

'Absolutely. Jonathan Redman worked for our family, man and boy, for many years, faithfully working his way up. One day he went with the doctor, as his valet, to a splendid house in Hampshire, sometime in the 1860s. Quite by chance, he met there a lady's maid, or at any rate, a maid to a real aristocrat, something like that. They fell in love and out of the blue, presumably after writing to each other for months, they announced that they wanted to get married. Not only that, but they were leaving their jobs in service and moving to a Dorset village to start a small business in fruit and vegetables.'

'That's my Mrs Redman, in Melton Ford,' said Adam.

'Must be,' Mr James continued. 'I don't know much else, except that they were given a small pension by their employers.

Jonathan died quite young and left Mrs Redman as a young widow.'

'So it was Jonathan knowing Mr Granger, when he worked here, which led to Mr Granger knowing Mrs Redman and keeping in touch?'

'Precisely,' said Mr James. 'He's always, sort of, looked out for her. And we shall be delighted to see her again if she can make the journey here for your wedding.'

'I'd love that,' said Adam, as Mr James made his excuses about being late for lunch and left Adam, sitting in the garden, contemplating his future, again, and with much pleasure.

40

Ireland

Back at the barracks, in Dorchester, there was a great deal of preparation going on for their forthcoming tour of Ireland.

They were going to the army camp at The Curragh, in County Kildare, and were likely to be there for a year, hopefully not much longer.

There was some new kit, plenty of new equipment and lectures on the kind of tasks they would be undertaking. One evening Adam and Joe were having a late night drink of cocoa, before retiring, just a few days before their departure.

'Do you understand all the information we've been listening to about Ireland?' said Joe. 'Not sure I do.'

'For several hundred years there's been bit of a running dispute as to whether Ireland is part of the United Kingdom,' said Adam. 'I've read all kinds of stuff and the discussions do get very complicated and heated.'

'Surely Ireland is part of Britain?' said Joe.

'Not necessarily, if you're Irish,' said Adam. 'For a start, many Irish have always been Catholic, Roman Catholic, for generations and the law of the land, as I understand it, said that Catholics could not hold public office, become mayors or members of parliament, or even go to a university. By the time some of these restrictions were lifted, about sixty years ago, and the penalties for refusing to take Church of England communion were abolished, it was a bit late for some Irish folk.'

'What do you mean?' said Joe.

'Thanks to what had happened over these few hundred years, since the Stuarts ruled as monarchs, nearly all landowners in Ireland had English roots and English, Church of England, sympathies. The Irish Catholics were gradually losing control of what they considered their homeland. Hardly any Irish Catholics actually owned the land they were working on. It all belonged to Anglican English families or their descendents.'

'They wanted to govern themselves?' Joe asked, already knowing the answer.

'They did, 'Adam came back. 'In 1870, only three percent of Irish farmers actually owned the land they lived on. Simply being tenants, they were at the mercy of landowners. Mr Gladstone…'

'He was Prime Minister while we were in Italy,' said Joe.

'He certainly was. Well, he introduced the Land Act and gave tenant farmers the right to buy the land they worked on, a step towards the aim of governing themselves, and not being subject to the Parliament in Westminster. Of course, it is all a lot more complicated than that, but, as far as the army is concerned, we simply have to keep the peace and train the locals.'

'Because?' said Joe.

'Apparently, after the Crimean War in the 1850s, it was realised that the army needed more space, more training, more proper barracks and so on, so all the accommodation at Aldershot was built. The Keep, where we are based, was upgraded, and a great open tract of land in Ireland was acquired for the development of barracks at The Curragh, where we are going.'

'And our job?'

'Don't you listen to any of the lectures?' said Adam. 'We shall be training local soldiers, who might then be part of the British Army, going out to the Sudan, or Egypt or South Africa. Or we might be keeping the peace locally if any troubles flare up'.

'Such as?' said Joe. 'I'm not sure I want to fight people who are actually British.'

'Let's hope, then,' said Adam, 'that there won't be any aggressive peace keeping! A man named Charles Stuart Parnell was campaigning for Irish Home Rule, and that story probably has a long way to run yet. But sometimes there are outbreaks of troubles and our job is to calm them down. Let's hope, as you say, that we don't come into contact with our own citizens, even though some of them don't want to be British.'

'Complicated!' said Joe.

'Indeed it is,' I don't think we've heard the last of Home Rule campaigning, although Mr Parnell himself died three years ago. Fortunately, we are soldiers, not politicians.'

'Not a good thought at all,' said Joe again, 'fighting your own people.'

'Let me read you this,' said Adam, as he got out a newspaper cutting, which he had read earlier and kept. He read it to Joe. 'This is from a young soldier named Michael McDonough who enlisted in the Connaught Rangers…'

'The Connaught Rangers?' said Joe.

'An Irish line of Infantry in the British Army,' said Adam. 'Some of the very people we are going to Ireland to train. Michael McDonough said, '*I am fully willing to leave my home and to go into the interiors of Africa to fight voluntarily for Queen Victoria and, as far as there is life in my bones and breath in my body, I will not let any foreign invasion tramp on Queen's land. However, if her, or her leaders, ever turns with cruelty on the Irish race, I will be the first to raise my sword to fight against her. I will have plenty of Irishmen at my side, for they are known to be the bravest race in the world.'*

'That,' said Joe, 'is quite a statement.'

'It very much is,' said Adam, 'and it's true for all of us. We don't want to be fighting, ever, against our own. Let's hope it never comes to that. The Connaught Rangers have been nicknamed The Devil's Own. I don't fancy coming up against them at all!'

'It's time we packed it in and got some sleep,' said Joe and they made their way back to the barrack room to do precisely that. It was now only a few days before their departure and on the way back Adam spoke again.

'I'll tell you one more choice piece of information about The Curragh camp where we are going,'

'What's that?' said Joe, 'I'm all ears.'

'When Queen Victoria's son, our Prince Albert Edward, Prince of Wales was desperate to be allowed to join the army back in 1861, the Queen and Prince Albert relented and allowed him to join in, or at least watch the manoeuvres in Ireland at The Curragh.'

'Fair enough,' said Joe.

'Until His Royal Highness started acting like a playboy, and got himself involved with an actress, called Nellie Clifden, and spent three nights with her. And this was despite there being a guard on the Prince, which was supposed to be keeping him in line and out of trouble!'

'Saucy devil,' said Joe.

'The Queen was appalled,' said Adam, 'and The Prince Consort travelled to Cambridge, where the heir was at university, now returned from Ireland, to see the young Prince of Wales. He arrived in the pouring rain, soaked to the skin! Two weeks later he was dead. The Queen, as we know, has worn black ever since and, if we can believe the gossips, she has always blamed The Prince of Wales for the Prince Consort's death.'

'Well, on that happy note,' said Joe as they arrived at the barrack hut, 'I wish you goodnight.'

The next day dawned to a flurry of even more activity. The journey to Ireland and indeed a complete year spent in Ireland were successful for the Regiment, and Adam's company. Adam wrote to Daisy many times, some longer and some shorter 'notes', written during busy weeks with local duties, training and keeping the peace, although there had been no real dramas of that kind. After a year, Adam was pleased to be back in England.

Adam himself came out of the year as a Lance Corporal, with his first stripe. He was proud and grateful. He had a tiny bit more income and Major James was the first to congratulate him.

'You'll be too busy to look after me,' said the Major, half tongue in cheek.

'Never too busy, for you, sir,' Adam replied. 'It is a pleasure and an honour.'

Back in Dorchester, after a year, Adam could not wait to see Daisy. On the whole, the army did a good job in Ireland, despite the continuous undercurrent of disaffection with the British. Adam was indeed pleased to be back in England.

41

London

'How about a trip to London?' said Joe, one day in November.

'Don't know about that,' said Adam. 'We've been away a year, I haven't seen Daisy, and we get married in abut eight or nine month's time. I think I should see her first, and keep saving up for our wedding.'

'That's okay,' said Joe. 'But we do have a complete week's leave now we're back in Dorchester. I could show you St Paul's Cathedral, the Tower of London and the fantastic new Tower Bridge, which opens up in the middle to allow ships through. It has not long been opened. You could buy something nice for Daisy, and then go straight to her before you come back to Dorchester.'

'I read about that bridge in a newspaper,' said Adam. 'The Prince and Princess of Wales opened it officially just last year. I'd love to see it.'

They made an application for their week's leave and Major James even suggested that a good friend of his grandfather's might give them a room for a couple of nights on London.

'Really, sir?' said Adam one evening.

'Why not?' said the Major. 'What are friends for? Leave it to me.'

Their application for a week in November was approved, and the major gave Adam the address of his grandfather's friend, who had a large house in Sydenham, south London. Adam wrote to Daisy to say he would be in London from Tuesday to Friday morning of the following week, with Joe, and that he had permission to visit The Manor House for the weekend.

He was even offered a room for Joe at The Manor House, over the weekend, and could not wait to show his friend where he had worked from the age of sixteen.

They prepared for their week-long leave, withdrawing some money from their savings at the Dorchester barracks, packing a small suitcase each and buying tickets to London for the following Tuesday. Adam could hardly believe he was going to visit London, and with a Londoner!

The two of them arrived at Waterloo during the late morning, and Adam was astonished to see the size of London as they approached the city. He had noticed it before, coming in from Dover with Adam many months ago, but this was different. It was almost winter. It was cold and the first thing Adam noticed was the smell and the darkness, even during the day.

'London is covered in soot,' said Joe as they alighted the train and found somewhere to have some hot tea and a bite to eat. 'An 'undred years of burning coal fires, in the grates of all the houses has left a great pall of smoke hanging over London for almost half the year.'

'It's horrible,' Adam added, thinking of the beautiful clean air of his home village, The Manor House in Dorset and even, perhaps, Italy and those beautiful cities on the sea coast.

'And the smell? I know exactly what that is. I've lived in the country long enough to know the smell of horses, but there are so many of them.'

As they left the station, Adam was astonished to see literally hundreds of horse-drawn carriages, carts, wagons, delivery drays, milling from left to right, in an almost choreographed formation of traffic. Pedestrians were running between them, to cross the roads.

'I think I'd be killed trying to cross the road anywhere,' said Adam.

'Oh! You get used to it,' Joe added. 'Come on. I can tell you that there are about three hundred thousand horses in London, and a thousand tons of horse-dung is collected, every day, by the twelve and thirteen year-old dung-boys. I used to do it for a while, but pick-pocketing got better returns, until I got caught.'

'At least in the country there is somewhere to put it!' said Adam. 'And look, I've never seen one of those before, although I have read about them.' There, weaving its way in and out of the horse-drawn traffic, was an automobile. Adam was transfixed. It was a vehicle, other than a train, going along under its own 'steam'. He had never seen one, other than in pictures. Adam had read that they were what Karl Benz, in Germany, called his '*motorwagen*' invention.

'That is amazing,' he said, as Joe urged him on to find their way across to Victoria.

'Tonight we must find your boss's friend's house,' he said. 'It's a train ride to Sydenham, but at least it will be cleaner air out there.' And so it was.

They arrived later in the afternoon and knocked politely on the front door. A maid answered and ushered them in. They were not quite sure of what kind of welcome they might receive. They still thought of themselves as 'staff' rather than in any way deserving of guest status, but the lady of the house was most welcoming and invited them into the front sitting room, while a young man in footman's livery took their cases.

'This is very kind of you,' said Adam. 'We really are most grateful.'

'Nonsense,' said their hostess, Mrs Elizabeth Treves, whose name the boys already knew from the Major. 'It is our pleasure.'

She was elegant, tall, with a considerable amount of dark brown hair, gathered up into a very smart style, with a fawn dress, embroidered with brown frogging, and a beautiful smile. Her father and the old Dr Russell had been professional friends, many years ago, and Elizabeth herself had married a Dr Treves before settling in London. 'Now let us get some tea, and dinner will be at eight o'clock.' She pulled the bell cord.

'Oh!' said Adam. 'We weren't expecting to impose upon you for our meals. We can go out to eat.' Joe was sitting on a sofa with his knees close together, grasping his cap over them.

'Well, you can do that tomorrow,' she said. 'Tonight you eat with us. In fact it is only with two of us. My husband is away for a few days and my daughter, Enid, will be home soon.'

'That is very kind,' repeated Adam, with Joe muttering a 'thank-you' also. They enjoyed the tea, which arrived carried by a footman, and Adam gave as much 'news' as he could of the Russell family to Mrs Treves.

'Now, Richard will show you to your room. You can freshen up. Please use the downstairs rooms as you wish, and I will see you at dinner.'

It was almost too much. Adam could not quite cope with another man carrying his suitcase upstairs, and his embarrassment was all the more magnified when he later discovered night clothing laid out on the bed, and all his other belongings safely stored away in the chest of drawers.

'Blimey,' said Joe. 'You know some mighty posh people.'

'I don't know them at all, which is why I feel such a fraud,' said Adam. 'but, I suppose we must be grateful and be on our best behaviour.'

The evening meal was a decidedly pleasant experience, not in the least uncomfortable for Adam or Joe, who held their own in conversation admirably. They discovered that, Hetty, the younger daughter, was away at school and Enid, the elder, worked in a London bank and was engaged to be married in March the following year.

'A bit like me,' said Adam. 'I'm getting married in July.' He was duly congratulated by Mrs Treves. 'In fact, when we leave your house and London, we are going to The Manor House for the weekend where my fiancée works.'

'I remember The Manor House,' said Elizabeth. 'I was taken there many years ago by my father, when he and Dr Russell were colleagues. They trained together, as doctors, and both of them had very successful careers. Then I went and married a doctor too,' she said. Adam was happy to tell her of his origins, about being a gardener, then a soldier and batman to Major Russell. Joe was less forthcoming about his origins.

The evening went very smoothly, considering how hesitant the boys had been to be served at the table for dinner in such a house. In fact they relaxed and thoroughly enjoyed it. After breakfast the next morning, leaving their uniforms behind, and smartly dressed for the day, they made their way to what they now knew to be Crystal Palace station to get to London.

'Oh, my God, 'said Adam, suddenly. '*The* Crystal Palace,'

'Right first time,' said Joe, as they saw the magnificent glass frontage of the exquisite building, on Sydenham Hill, ahead of them. 'Maybe we could find the time to go and see it, but for now, we're off to London.'

'I read a lot about why it was built, for the Great Exhibition, twenty years before I was born, and then how they transported the entire building here a couple of years later. It is beautiful.'

'Off we go,' said Joe, who felt on this occasion that he was the leader of the two of them. London was his patch. Victoria was rather less than half an hour away and they came out into the streets of the capital, with Adam still agog at the number of horse-drawn vehicles, cabs, omnibuses, men on horseback and private carriages clogging the thoroughfare. He saw the very occasional automobile and enjoyed the great throng which filled Victoria and Belgravia.

Joe showed Adam Buckingham Palace, just around the corner from the station, where Adam just stood and stared. How often had he pictured the queen, being driven in or out of the palace, ever since Mrs Redman told him that she had seen her in Weymouth.

'Come on,' said Joe, 'we'll walk down to Trafalgar Square, then along the Strand, and eventually to Tower Bridge. It's quite a walk. London is bigger than Dorchester!'

Adam was in his element and offered to buy Joe some tea and cakes. Joe knew of a couple of places nearby, from his early days in the city and before long they were seated in a coffee house, which fortunately offered them tea as an alternative.

'Psst!' came a hissing noise from the door of the café. 'Psst. Joseph.'

The two young men took no notice, but one or two other

customers were attracted to the noise. Suddenly the door opened completely, and a young man walked in and sat himself down between Adam and Joe. Adam immediately recognised the check jacket and the great mop of unruly brown hair.

'Psst! Joseph. It's me. What are you doing here?'

'Oh, my God!' said Joe.

'Oh, my God,' said Adam. 'You!'

'Pardon?' said the young man. 'Do I know you?'

'Adam,' said Joe, 'this is my brother. The one I told you about. Haven't seen him for years. What brings you right here, right now?'

'I thought you'd be locked up by now, Joseph,' said the young man with the check jacket, at which Adam was still staring, in disbelief.

'Adam, you remember I told you about my brother, nicknamed *The Rodent*. Well this is…?'

'I know exactly who he is,' said Adam, who stood up and, for a moment, towered over the check jacket and the hair.

'What?' said both Joe and the newcomer. 'What are you talking about?'

'Your name is Arthur, isn't it?' said Adam. 'Arthur Smith, the sneaky thief on the Weymouth train, eight years ago, who robbed me of almost my last penny, when I was just sixteen. How could I forget you?'

'Oh! Good grief,' said Arthur, 'was that you? I don't really remember…'

'Well, you've probably robbed so many people,' said Adam, still towering over him. 'I'd be surprised if you could remember any of them.'

'Adam,' said Joe quietly. 'Do you want to sit down?'

429

'Of course,' Adam replied.

'Look, I'm sorry,' said Arthur. 'It was a long time ago, and I expect I was desperate.'

'You weren't that desperate! You had a hamper, and food...'

'Yes, okay, I really am sorry. I've moved on a bit since then.'

'Arthur,' said Joe, 'this is Adam, my very closest friend. We've been through a lot together, and we're both in the army in Dorchester. Any chance, Adam, you wouldn't mind letting him sit with us for a cup of tea?'

'Of course,' Adam replied, 'Actually, it's fine. My good friend from the village where I grew up taught me that maybe holding a grudge for ever brings no rewards. If you are Joe's brother, then let's enjoy some tea together. But I still think that you owe me five pounds!'

'Sorry about that,' said Arthur. 'Don't have five pounds on me. Don't have five pounds to my name.'

They ordered more tea, and Arthur explained that he had not really been able to leave his life of petty crime behind. He still existed on stealing, pick pocketing, even burglary.

'Well, you haven't moved on much then, have you?' said Adam.

'At the moment I am not actually on the run, or anything like that. But I live in a hostel in Southwark which is horrible. Full of old men drinking too much.'

'I wish we'd stayed together,' said Joe. 'I've been in the army for a few years now. Regular income, a bed, food, clothing and travel.'

'You always were the clever one,' said Arthur. 'Well, thanks for the tea. Mind if I sit here with you for a while?'

'You're welcome,' said Adam. 'I hope you might be able to

find a job sometime.'

'So do I,' said Arthur, 'but it is difficult without references.'

In fact, all three of them stayed together for the remainder of the day, seeing St. Paul's Cathedral, The Tower of London and Tower Bridge, which was a revelation.

'Wish we could have seen the bridge open,' said Adam, as they slowly made their way back to Victoria. 'What a day. Thanks, Joe.'

'Let's get an omnibus from here,' said Joe, as they reached The Mansion House, where The Lord Mayor of London lived. They had walked the length of King William Street, and the bus took them by Cannon Street, Ludgate Hill, Fleet Street and the Strand, before they found themselves back in Trafalgar Square.

'Fantastic,' said Adam.

'First time I've been on an omnibus and paid!' said Arthur, who was still with them and clearly enjoying his day with his brother.

'Well actually, Arthur, you didn't pay,' said Joe, 'I did. Come on, let's find somewhere to eat.'

Adam's couple of days in London passed pleasantly, even successfully, despite meeting the young man who had robbed him eight years earlier. He managed to find some shops, around Piccadilly and Regent Street, on their second day, and bought Daisy a splendid blue silk scarf, to match her eyes, and a pair of white kidskin gloves.

The goodbyes to Arthur, who had met with them every day, came as they arrived at Victoria on the Friday morning. They walked down to Westminster and across the river to Waterloo station.

Joe had given Arthur some money to help him out a bit.

Adam bought the teas for all of them on their second full day, and actually was quite pleased to have met Joe's *Rodent* brother. It somehow exorcised that unpleasant memory.

'One day, I'll pay you back the five pounds,' said Arthur. 'Promise.'

'I'll believe it when I see it,' said Adam and, with that, he and Joe shook Arthur's hand, picked up their bags and began the journey from Waterloo to East Hambley. They arrived during the Friday afternoon and found that Major James had also managed to get away from the barracks, and was at home.

'We have had a splendid few days in London, sir,' said Adam. 'and thank you so much for suggesting our superb accommodation.'

'I am pleased for you,' said the major, having met them in the garden.

Adam met Daisy that first evening and was sorry that they could not take a walk to the village as the weather was so cold, and it was dark by about seven o'clock. They spent the evening in the butler's sitting room, at Freddie's invitation, and all three were still there long after the others had retired to bed. Adam had given Daisy the gifts he'd brought from London.

'These are wonderful,' said Daisy. 'The softest leather I've ever felt apart from the mistress' gloves. Never thought I would own a pair like it. And the scarf is beautiful. Is it silk?'

'Of course!' said Adam. 'Nothing but the finest for you. But that's the last present you're getting until we get married. We have to save up.'

'I'm saving nearly all my wages,' said Daisy, and the three of them sat there until nearly midnight, swapping stories of The Manor House or London, comfortable in each other's company.

Major James used his grandfather's landau to get to the railway station on the Sunday afternoon, taking Adam and Joe along with him.

'Thank you, sir,' said Joe as they got down from the carriage. 'Can I help you with your bag?'

'I'm fine,' said Major James. They waited together for the train to arrive, at which point the Major went into a first class carriage, with a book to read, leaving Joe and Adam with their third class seats.

Back at the barracks in Dorchester, it was a return to the routine of army life and for Adam, a lot of planning for his marriage and hoping that there would be some married quarters available the following summer.

42

A setback and two weddings

As the spring and summer of the following year approached, the trees surrounding the parade ground became greener, some blossoming and providing lots of colour. The air became warmer for parades and training manoeuvres.

Adam was promoted to a full corporal and Joe earned himself a lance-corporal stripe, as some new recruits arrived at the barracks. Adam noted carefully that some men, who had been in the army for nearly twenty years, were soon to retire.

He learned from Major James Russell that some of the older men had been in the second Afghan War back in 1878. Some had even transferred from the Royal Engineers having been involved in the Anglo-Zulu War. Luckily, none of them had been at the Battle of Isandlwana, from which nobody came out alive. Just a very few came home from the battle of Rourkes Drift, which took place the next day, the twenty-third of January 1879. No less than twelve Victoria Crosses had been won in those two days, most posthumously.

Adam was now ready to write and ask again about married quarters and this time received a more positive answer.

Cpl Warkin A.
Permission for you to marry, in the summer of 1896, as a

Corporal in this Regiment is hereby granted. There is still no guarantee that you can be allocated married quarters accommodation, although we have every reason to believe that rooms will be available to you by July or August. In any case, your wife can expect to receive a married woman's allowance, once your Marriage Certificate is examined here on the camp. You will be granted one week and one day's leave around the time of your nuptials.

We have every hope that allocation of quarters for you and your wife, as a married couple will fall within the quota we have available. I trust you will understand that this is still not a guaranteed offer until the War Office confirm.

Signed,
Fisher P, Colonel

12 December 1895

Adam made another visit to The Manor House, with the Major, over Christmas, and began to look forward to the next year. Then it was simply a count-down to his and Daisy's big day for the twenty-second of July. He knew that Daisy was making arrangements, with Mrs Browne at the Manor House, for a wedding breakfast menu and that Freddie was helping with invitations. Even Robert was getting very excited and asked if he could be responsible for ushering the guests to their seats on the day.

'I have a feeling you will be an invited guest,' said Freddie, 'but even so, I am sure you can be of great help to Adam and Daisy. Maybe I will be ushering guests too!'

The family were being superbly generous and, while Adam was still earning his keep as a serving soldier in Dorchester, the excitement was building up in East Hambley.

'Now listen, Daisy,' said Mrs Browne one afternoon in February, 'I have some very nimble fingers when it comes to sewing, so how about you and I just sit down and we'll sort out what you want to look like on your big day.'

Daisy was beside herself with excitement and couldn't wait to sit down with the Housekeeper and decide what she was going to wear. Her father, in Southampton, had given her an allowance, so she knew what she could spend. He and Daisy's mother had been invited to The Manor House for two days at Easter, in order to meet Adam, and Adam himself had requested those two days for leave to visit 'home'.

The countdown was going very smoothly. At least, that was, until just after Easter.

Adam developed severe headaches and a feeling of sickness on Monday the 13th of April, a week after Easter. He was confined to his barrack room space and transferred to the hospital wing, where there were a dozen beds and a medical orderly. Major James was acutely worried and visited him as often as he could. There seemed no logical reason for him to have become so ill, and the military doctor began to think the worst. He monitored his symptoms carefully and kept in close touch with Major James.

'He has developed a rose coloured rash on the lower half of his body,' said the doctor to Major James. 'He has a temperature, is breathless and won't eat. I'm almost afraid to tell you what it might be.'

'I'm going to get in touch with a family friend, who is a doctor in London,' said James and went away to send a telegram to Dr Treves and another to The Manor House.' Adam, meanwhile, was debilitated and feeling extremely ill.

Daisy was beside herself with worry and waited, day by day, for news of Adam. Dr Treves very obligingly travelled to Dorchester and met with Major Russell. He entered the hospital wing and met there with the nurse in charge and with Major Russell.

'Dr Treves, Frederick,' said James, 'how good of you to come. I am most grateful that you have agreed to see Adam, my batman and a good servant to the Russell family.' James was facing the eminent doctor friend of his family who was not a tall man, with thinning black hair and a drooping moustache. He wore a stiff white collar and a very elegant dark grey suit.

'It is not a problem,' said the doctor, 'Can anybody tell me where Adam might have been in the past three weeks?'

'We were on a manoeuvre in north Dartmoor, near Oakhampton nearly a month ago' said James. 'The men were out on the moor in small groups, some maybe even on their own overnight.'

'I need to know what he may have drunk or eaten,' said the doctor. 'Has anybody else become ill?'

'Not as far as I know,' said James, but he spoke too soon.

There was indeed another young soldier, who had been admitted the day after Adam, exhibiting the same symptoms. Major James made enquiries about the manoeuvres and discovered that he and Adam had been together in the same small platoon.

Adam's symptoms persisted. They managed to glean from him that he, and at least one other soldier on Dartmoor, had drunk from a water barrel alongside a farmstead, with a very run-down cottage. Fears grew but Major James sent telegrams to Daisy at The Manor House to try to allay her fears. Dr Treves confirmed that this appeared to be a case of typhoid.

Adams temperature did not fall much below one hundred degrees Fahrenheit and James and the doctor, who had taken rooms nearby in Dorchester, maintained a vigil by his bedside. Dr Treves very kindly also monitored the other sick young soldier. Joe was permitted to visit briefly, but not stay. There was a constant effort being made to reduce his temperature. Nothing seemed to reduce the symptoms, and the rash did not go away.

'This is uncanny,' said Dr Treves. 'Just over twenty years ago, in 1871, Dr Sir William Gull was treating The Prince of Wales for typhoid. He appeared to be getting worse as the date approached, which was the anniversary of The Prince Consort's death. The Queen was beside herself. Adam seems to be going through the same sequence of symptoms.'

'Uncanny indeed.' said the major. 'And 1871 is the year of Adam's birth,' said James, then added, 'Is this typhoid?'

'Indeed it is,' said the doctor, 'but these days it is less likely to be fatal. It is important to keep the patient, and his surroundings, scrupulously clean. It is still very serious and decidedly nasty for the patient. He needs antipyretic drugs to lower the febrile temperature. He will be more susceptible to pain, probably won't eat, but he can get through this. He is strong.'

Adam had a fearful night on Sunday the 3rd of May, almost delirious and shouting, screaming and crying through the hours from about ten o'clock through to the morning. It was a dark night indeed.

The next day Dr Treves stayed close by for several hours but Adam seemed peaceful enough.

'I have to return to London,' said the doctor. 'There are other patients to see, and my partner there cannot see to them all. There is not much more I can do here.'

'One more night,' pleaded James. 'The delirium last night could take Adam one way or the other, is that what you are saying?'

'I am,' said the doctor. 'We shall see.'

Dawn broke on the morning of Tuesday the 4th of May. Miraculously, Adam had slept through the night and Major James found him awake and smiling weakly.

'It seems the worst is over,' said Dr Treves. 'There is a considerable abatement of the gravity of his condition. And now I really must return to London. Get him to eat something, light and easy to digest. He must keep drinking. He will now get better.'

Adam could hardly remember a thing about his illness. The temperature dropped, he sat up and ate a healthy lunch that day. The danger had passed.

'You are a lucky young man,' said Major James to the patient. 'I am not sure you fully understand how serious your condition was. Dr Treves was almost despairing of you two nights ago.'

'Dr Treves came to see me!' said Adam, almost unbelieving, 'He is a very eminent doctor in London. Why would he come to see me?'

'Because he is a family friend and I asked him to,' said the Major, 'Now you, finish that drink, and relax.'

It took another fortnight of rest, and a gradual return to normality, before Adam could go back to his billet, alongside Joe and the others. He learned that the other young soldier, who had exhibited the same typhoid symptoms, had also been lucky enough to come through it. The officers of the Company made a note about what advice they should give to young men on manoeuvres, about drinking water from anything other than a clean source or a mountain stream!

Adam wrote to Daisy to tell her about his illness, of which she already knew as she had been fretting over it for more than a week. She cried to herself as she read his letter, and, almost in disbelief at his kind thoughts for her, showed the letter to Mrs Browne.

'He's apologising for being ill and causing me so much worry!' she said. 'Can you believe that?'

'Your Adam is a good man,' said Mrs Browne. 'And we can thank the Lord above that he's come through this.'

In Dorchester, one evening in June, as Adam and Joe sat with a drink each Adam spoke.

'Would you be my best man for the wedding?'

'Would I?' said Joe. 'Try'n stop me! I thought you'd never ask!'

'You'll have to make a speech, but not too many tawdry details about our escapades in Italy. Don't want you going on for hours!'

'No Italian stories at all,' said Joe. 'Just five minutes, maximum.'

'Four would be fine,' said Adam. He then wrote to Freddie, at The Manor House, and asked if you he would organise two or three ushers for the day, which was precisely what Freddie had been expecting.

I am sorry not to ask you to be my best man,' wrote Adam, *'but Joe and I have been together for a few years now and I'd like him standing by my side.'*

Freddie wrote back to say he would be honoured to organise some of the logistics for the day.

'It'll be the biggest event we have seen in The Manor House for years,' he wrote. *'And I will be proud to do what you ask. Just one thing more, Adam. May I bring my young lady friend to the wedding?'*

Now, at last, Adam realised why Freddie went off, quite often, on his own, to the jewellers in West Hambley!

Adam wrote to Daisy almost every day, and some of the finer details were put in place as the weeks went by. Adam decided to get married in the dress uniform of his Regiment, and then discovered, to his great delight, that one of the married quarters would almost certainly be available for him after the end of July. Everything was falling into place.

He wrote to Mrs Redman, to make sure she would be coming to the wedding, and discovered that she had already been invited by Daisy, with Mr Granger's help providing the address. It was all very exciting for everyone involved.

'Joe,' said Adam, on another evening as the big day drew closer, 'Are you still in touch with Arthur?'

'Yes,' said Joe. 'I am pleased to have got his address at the hostel and have written a couple of times. Even his writing is getting better as time has gone by!'

'Invite him to our wedding,' said Adam, surprising Joe completely.

'Really?' Joe responded. 'Why?'

'Don't know, really,' said Adam. 'Regardless of what happened when I was sixteen, we did get on well in London, didn't we? Maybe he doesn't get the chance to be with you very often, and maybe, just maybe, having a day out like the wedding day will encourage him even more to stay out of trouble.'

'I know he's tried very hard not to get into any scrapes with the law, although he tells me he almost got mixed up with a couple of idiots who were going to break into Marlborough House, along the Mall in London.'

'What a fool,' said Adam. 'Why would he do that?'

'Apparently the Prince and Princess of Wales were away in Sandringham, as usual, for the summer, and it seemed a good idea to my brother. Then he managed to get a job, as a porter in Covent Garden, stuck with it, and abandoned the other two. They went ahead and got caught. Arthur was rather pleased with himself.'

'Well, that is a good reason to invite him,' said Adam. 'Please do, and send him the money for the fare, as well as instructions on how to get here on the day. He's quite good at travelling on trains heading for Weymouth, so he'll probably bring his trusty hamper!'

The morning of Wednesday the 22nd of July came, with glorious sunshine from the moment the day began. Adam was at The Manor House in one of the main house bedrooms allocated to him, to his great surprise, when he had arrived two days earlier.

Joe was in one of the top floor bedrooms. Daisy's Mum and Dad were in a guest house in the village. The family were all gathered at the house the day before the wedding, which is where Adam first met Daisy's parents. They got on remarkably well and Adam, Daisy, Joe and Daisy's father went to the church for a rehearsal.

Just about a hundred miles away, in London, another family had gathered, preparing for their great wedding on that very same day. On a slightly larger scale than Adam's, Queen Victoria's granddaughter, the Princess Maud, youngest daughter of the Prince and Princess of Wales was marrying her first cousin, Prince Carl of Denmark. She was twenty-six.

Prince Carl was the second son of his Danish father and Swedish mother. This was a family gathering indeed, with most of the royalty of Europe, relations and descendents of Victoria, gathered in the Private Chapel at Buckingham Palace, to witness the marriage of the beautiful girl who became, later, the Queen of Norway alongside this new husband, renamed King Haakon VII.

The dress had been designed by the Royal Female School of Art. It was made from white satin, manufactured in Spitalfields, London, with chiffon and flowers at the skirt hem, and a long train bordered with orange blossoms. The waist was embroidered with silver and diamonds. Maud wore her mother's wedding veil.

She wore minimal jewellery, with a choker on her neck and some bracelets; she also wore flowers on her head instead of a tiara. Her bouquet was a mix of white jasmine, orange blossom and German myrtle.

Her dear grandmother, the queen, sat throughout the ceremony, dressed in black as always but with gold embroidery glistening across and down the front of the gown. She, too, wore a lace veil, but with the adornment of a diamond tiara. Standing behind the Queen were the bride's mother and father, and the bridegroom's parents also, Princess Alexandra's eldest brother, Crown Prince Frederick of Denmark, and Princess Louise of Sweden. The room was a treasure trove of sashes, medals and orders, together with thousands of precious stones glittering and lighting up the room.

Queen Victoria herself wrote in her diary that night, '*After the Benediction, Maud came forward to her parents & then to me & I kissed both her & the Bridegroom*'.

Every bride deserves her wedding day to be the day she will never forget, and, on that same day, Daisy Armstrong, at twenty-five years of age, was no exception. There was no 'royal' dress designer or fabulous family jewels but she felt like a princess that morning. By nine o'clock Daisy was in an upstairs room, with Mrs Alice Russell and the Housekeeper.

'I feel such a fraud,' she said, 'standing here dressed like this in your room, madam.'

'Nonsense,' said Mrs Russell, 'we are all having such a wonderful time. It has been so exciting helping you to prepare for today and we could not think of a nicer couple for it to happen to.'

Dr Russell, senior, and Walter had arranged with Freddie to bring in a few extra staff from the hotel at West Hambley, so there were no onerous duties for most of the staff on that special day.

Mrs Redman had arrived the day before the wedding and had a most tender reunion with both Adam and Mr Granger. She looked amazing and Adam could not help thinking that she looked younger now than when he had last seen her. She was ecstatically happy for Adam. He introduced Daisy, and Joe, to her and was almost lost for words describing what an influence she had been on his life.

At a quarter to one, Adam and Joe left to walk to the church nearby. At one-o'clock precisely Daisy, resplendent in her white gown, with flowers in her hair and a veil covering her face, stepped out of the Russell family phaeton, accompanied by her father, and entered the crowded church. Only the elderly and fragile Dr Russell excused himself and stayed back at the house.

Adam, looking every inch the dashing hero of any nineteenth century romantic novel, was standing to the left of Joe both wearing their dress uniforms, at the front of the church. Freddie and Robert were hugely proud of the way they had shepherded the congregation into their places, and fully expected the same degree of perfect organisation when they got back to the house.

Mrs Redman was majestic, in her favourite green with an enormous hat, sitting in pride of place among the Russell family and household, equally divided, left and right, between the bride and groom's acquaintances. Joe's brother, Arthur, was preening himself continuously, sartorially glowing in a suit of brown and cream check, still hardly able to believe he had been invited to such an occasion.

Adam's eyes sparkled but became clouded over with small tears as he turned and looked at Daisy, approaching him down the aisle, on the arm of her father. She looked to him like a floating dream, almost beyond belief, yet coming closer and more real, until she reached out her arm and gave her bouquet to the one waiting bridesmaid. Adam took her hand into his and, in due course, they placed a delicate band of gold on each other's third finger, left hand.

The next fifteen minutes were rather a blur to the pair of them, as they could hardly take their eyes of one another and had to be reminded, more than once, to repeat the words they had hardly heard. Outside the church the rose petals filled the air as they emerged into the sunshine. It was the perfect picture.

The phaeton took them back to the house, at the head of a

glorious and joyous procession of walkers and small carriages, where everything had been organised to perfection.

At the end of the meal Joe excelled himself. He had taken some advice from Major James, and one or two others in the Battalion back at Dorchester, then probably ignored most of it and spoke both eloquently and amusingly for just four minutes.

'I have to say I am feeling really nervous about giving the Best Man's speech.

'We all know I am supposed to be singing the bridegroom's praises, but I can't sing, so I won't. And if anybody here, this afternoon, is feeling nervous, apprehensive or even sick at the thought of what's coming next, then you're probably the one who's just married Adam! Now, Daisy, I want you to put your hand flat on the table in front of you. Adam, place your hand on top of Daisy's. Now look, everyone, that's probably the last time Adam is going to have the upper hand!'

His four minutes were nearly up, but he wasn't finished yet.

'Ladies and gentlemen, and my Lords, if there are any, I wrote down a few days ago every good feature that I would like to find in a life-long friend; loyalty, courage, good humour and brotherly love. And the longer the list became, the more I realised that I had already found that friend. It was my friend, Adam.

'And now, for him with his beautiful wife, I ask you to raise a glass of this splendid champagne, paid for by the Russell family – Adam and Daisy!'

'Adam and Daisy' the toast was repeated around the room and was heard along with the clinking of glasses and the laughter. Joe had done his job to perfection and Adam smiled, looked along to him and mouthed his most grateful, 'Thank you'.

'And this,' said Joe, 'is for you, Adam, from my brother, Arthur, and me.' Joe handed him a small gift which Adam opened, and found inside a silver St Christopher and a five pound note.

Daisy and Joe spent their first night in the sumptuous bedroom Adam had been given the night before. After breakfast, on the following morning, the phaeton took them to the station and they made their way to London where Adam had booked three nights, until Sunday the 26th, in a hotel near The Crystal Palace in Sydenham.

They were sublimely happy in that July summer and, all too soon, came the Sunday morning when they had to make their way back, first to The Manor House. There was still no definite offer of married quarters accommodation, so Adam went back to Dorchester to wait for the time when Daisy could join him.

He sat on the train from East Hambley and lived through that memorable day when he had married Daisy, just hoping and praying that she would be able to join him soon.

43

Diamond Jubilee

'You will never believe this,' said Joe to Adam a few days after returning to Dorchester.

'Not unless you tell me,' said Adam.

'Your Mr James senior, Major Russell's father, only went and offered my brother, Arthur, a job on their small estate.'

'That is incredible,' said Adam, 'but it's good, isn't it? Did he accept?'

'I think he did,' said Joe, 'and I am delighted. He liked the feel of the countryside. You know he often took a train to the coast.'

'And robbed people on the way!' said Adam.

'Be that as it may, or be that as it was! At The Manor House they are growing much more now, in the land around the house, and selling it locally. Your Mr Granger, so Arthur tells me, has taken him on as a picker and a packer, sounds a bit odd! But the job is his permanently, if he wishes to stay. Maybe he's turned a corner.'

'I'd be really pleased, if he has,' Adam replied, 'Anything has to be better than that hostel which he hated. And now for my news.'

'What has happened?' asked Joe

'I've got accommodation confirmed from the first of August.

Daisy can come here and I'll be moving in with her, away from this billet.'

'I'll miss you!' said Joe.

'Well, I'll still be on parade,' said Adam, 'so you won't get rid of me, but think of it, me, a married man living on the camp.'

Daisy made the journey, with her few personal belongings and some really rather splendid wedding presents, accompanied by Robert, who did all the heavy carrying for her. She arrived on Monday the 3rd of August. Robert stayed one night, on the sofa in their one living room, and returned to The Manor House the next day.

Adam and Daisy unpacked some boxes and made the one bedroom, one living room, one small kitchen, and a bathroom, look very comfortable. They arranged some ornaments and cushions, put away spare bed linen, hung clothes in the one wardrobe and made some tea. Then they sat looking out of their front window, wrapped in each other's arms before realising they had nothing to eat for the evening, necessitating a shopping trip.

The news, which soon filtered through to all ranks on the camp, was of the forthcoming jubilee of Her Majesty the Queen. On the 23rd of September, less than two months after Daisy came to join Adam in the married quarters, Queen Victoria surpassed her grandfather, King George the Third, as the longest reigning monarch in British history. Then in 1897, just a few months away, she would have been on the throne for sixty years.

That following year would bring with it the Diamond Jubilee, and it was soon explained that most of the standing army in Britain, and thousands of overseas troops, from the

Empire and the Colonies, would be coming to London to take their part in the celebrations. At the suggestion of Colonial Secretary, Joseph Chamberlain, it was to be a Festival of the British Empire.

The Queen was very much in favour of such a decision, as inviting only Colonial representation meant that she would not have to invite some Heads of State from less friendly or unpleasant nations. Most especially she would not invite her grandson, Kaiser Wilhelm the second of Germany, who would almost certainly be troublesome.

Adam began to wonder where he might fit into all this. If the Regiment were to go to London, to be part of the procession, or the guard, he might, at last, get to see the Queen in person, up closer than just glimpsing a bonnet as he believed he had done in Naples.

Christmas came to Dorchester that year with Adam and Daisy decorating their little living room with a small tree. They invited Joe to join them for Christmas lunch, on the twenty-fifth, a week after the regimental lunch for non-commissioned men on the camp.

In the New Year, Joe became a full corporal with his second stripe. Adam was still on very good terms with Major Russell but had decided to suggest that he find another batman, now that he was spending most of his spare time with Daisy. Joe was very agreeable to being asked to take on the role. Once again, Adam and Joe were settled in their way of life, with regular wages and food, a job and the promise of a great celebration in the summer.

Another springtime came and went and Adam was delighted to discover that he, with the two battalions at Dorchester, would be going to London in June, for the magnificent parade, which was to be held on the 22nd.

There was still no indication of the role they would play, but being a part of such an event was something to anticipate with relish. Daisy said that she would come to London too, and perhaps stay in the little hotel in Sydenham, so as to be near London and, perhaps, join the crowds who would line the route.

There was little or no let up in the preparations for the Jubilee. The number of orders which came through about smartness, shining buttons, perfect appearance, deportment, outstanding drill alignment and much more, seemed never ending.

Then came the journey to London in early June. Enormous marquees had been erected in Hyde Park to accommodate the thousands of troops, British, Irish and Colonial. The barracks in London were full to capacity, and some high ranking officers were given hotel rooms.

There were rehearsals, but the day itself surpassed the expectations of everyone involved. The procession, which took more than an hour and a half to pass any one spot, did not include Adam and his battalion.

They were stationed at the roadside, on Ludgate Hill, approaching St Paul's Cathedral, spaced out along where the Queen would pass by. Along the roadside they formed a human fence of soldiers, with bayonets protruding like pikes, walling off the entire route of the six mile processional journey.

'Was this,' thought Adam to himself, 'going to be the day he saw the Queen?'

The morning of Tuesday the 22nd of June dawned none too

promisingly, in fact quite overcast. It was cold, but the sun was there and promised to emerge as the day went by, as indeed it did.

Nothing could have prepared Adam or Joe, nor any of their young soldier comrades, for the spectacle that was to pass their eyes. The whole of London, as it seemed, was festooned in red, white and blue.

There were flowers, banners and rosettes covering every available space on the fronts of buildings, balconies and rooftops. Great stands had been built along the route, with tickets for seats changing hands at extraordinary prices. Vendors, with trays and boxes of goods, hawked their wares to all who had pennies to spare, for souvenir flags, mugs and programmes of the carriage procession.

Individual homeowners, and office managers, had rented out floor space, with access to windows and a view of the procession. Daisy discovered, from the newspapers, that after the Service of Thanksgiving at St Paul's, the procession would pass along the broad arc of the Borough Road, where some of the Queen's poorest subjects lived. She managed to find a place, on the steps of Saint George's Church, with her bag of sandwiches and drink, and waited patiently for the magnificent display of the procession to appear,

Unbeknown to Adam, and most others, this was to be the first great Royal occasion in history which would be recorded, in part, by moving cinematograph cameras, forty of them, stationed along the route by different operators from different 'film' companies. Her Majesty's appearance, her carriage and her troops, would be captured on film for all time. It was also the first time that the word 'diamond' had been used to elevate the sixtieth anniversary to this high level.

It was to be jubilee field day for pickpockets too, although on that day, no such small-fry crime, generating a watch or wallet or two, could compare with the theft in transit of a £300,000 diamond, intended as a Jubilee gift to the Queen, from the Nizam of Hyderabad. It was, without doubt, a diamond day for someone!

The procession itself contained fifty thousand troops and was in two halves. The first, that of the colonial troops, had paraded past Buckingham Palace while the Queen herself was sitting at breakfast. The other, of the home forces, was headed by Captain Oswald Ames who, at six foot eight, was said to be the tallest man in the British Army. And, by all accounts, the stupidest.

Adam stood his ground, when positioned, not far from St Paul's Cathedral steps, where the Queen's carriage was to be halted. There she would stay inside the carriage, being, at seventy-eight, too old and infirm to climb the steps to the front door of the cathedral. The Colonial troops passed by, then the home forces. The crowds behind Adam cheered and waved. It was indeed a splendid day for all the nation.

Then one by one, the seventeen carriage procession, carrying the royal family, children and grandchildren of the Queen, and leaders of the Dominions, came into view and passed by. Their occupants alighted and moved up the outside steps approaching the Cathedral.

Finally a roar, of almost alarming magnitude, hit the ears of all those standing behind Adam telling him, and them, that the queen was at hand.

Before she had left the Palace, Victoria had pressed an electric button, which sent a telegraph message to all the Dominion countries across her vast British Empire which read;

'From my heart I thank my beloved people.
May God bless them. V.R. & I.'

Then, at 11.15am, the roar of a cannon being fired was heard, which announced the Monarch's departure from Buckingham Palace, and even the cannon itself must have shattered the clouds above, because that was the moment the sun came out.

Adam, Joe, and every one of his company, came to attention, knowing that the queen was almost in view. Bands were playing, crowds were cheering, children were laughing and screaming, hardly able to wait those few more minutes, even though there was so much to see.

Then came the confused shouts, and a scream from behind where Adam was standing. Adam was instantly confused and bewildered. They had been told to keep the crowds under control, at the same time as facing outwards in front of the crowds, on the pavements, to guard the procession and the monarch. But the scuffling going on behind him could not be ignored.

'Help us, please,' came the voice of a boy. Adam turned from his post and became aware of a woman who had fallen to the ground. Another young man immediately next to her asked for help. It was he who spoke.

'My sister has been robbed, and then she fell,' he said. 'Can you help?'

Every bone in Adam's body wanted to help the boy and his sister. Every instinct was to stand erect, and stay at his post, as part of the roadside guard. He turned, knelt down to help the woman and did his best to allay the fears of her brother.

'She has fainted,' said Adam. 'Give her some space here, please. Has anybody some smelling salts?' Nearby another, more mature, woman came through and she too knelt down to help Adam's 'patient'.

'Leave her to me, young man,' she said, and opened her shoulder bag.

Adam stood up, to resume his position in the roadside guard, and watched, in disbelief, as the queen's carriage, already past him, turned into the front of the cathedral, on to a large open space covered in sand to allow the horses and carriage wheels to get some grip.

He had missed his view of her, again! She was holding a white parasol which unsurprisingly obscured what he could just about glimpse of the occupants of the carriage. The queen was sitting opposite her daughter-in-law, the Princess of Wales. Once again, Adam had not seen the queen, but merely a bonnet or a sunshade.

He stood to attention.

The short service outside the Cathedral was conducted by the Archbishop of London and The Bishop of London, each in rich copes and holding ornate crosiers, while Her Majesty stayed in the carriage.

The vast crowds, who were enjoying the 'bank' holiday, as this day had been declared, could not contain their enthusiasm, but those surrounding the cathedral remained silent, for the most part, while the choir sang a Te Deum and chanted The Lord's Prayer beautifully. The Archbishop recited the special Jubilee prayer and the Bishop called for '*three cheers for Her Majesty*' from the steps of the great building. The crowd erupted.

As the carriage pulled away, it went around the cathedral forecourt in the opposite direction to where Adam was on duty. He saw the parasol disappear as her carriage, and all the others, continued on their six mile progress, to the great excitement of the hundreds of thousands waiting to see the spectacle.

It was a long journey, through some of the poorer streets of south-east London and the queen arrived back at the palace tired but elated. It was quarter to two, and she had been sitting in the carriage for well over three hours.

Queen Victoria wrote in her journal that night, '*A never to be forgotten day. No one ever, I believe, has met with such an ovation as was given to me, passing through those six miles of streets. The crowds were quite indescribable and their enthusiasm truly marvellous and deeply touching. The cheering was quite deafening, and every face seemed to be filled with real joy. I was much moved and gratified.*'

The cheering and singing went on well into the night, in the streets and pubs of the nation, aided, no doubt, by the extension of the opening hours until two-thirty am.

To Victoria, and everyone in London celebrating the Diamond Jubilee, it must have seemed as if the sun would indeed never set on the British Empire. Adam, however, had many conflicting thoughts, as he remembered his few days in Malta, and as he had now watched the thousands of Colonial troops passing by, dressed in their finery.

'I still cannot get my head to understand why,' he said to Joe that night in their temporary billet under canvas in Hyde Park, 'why we, the British, own so much of the world and why Victoria is Queen of millions of subjects all over the globe. Do we have the right to 'own' such vast tracts of other people's nations and call them our own, with varying degrees of smugness, dressed up in judicial, military and religious finery?'

'Maybe one day it will all change,' said Joe. 'Things do change, but not overnight.'

That evening, at the magnificent state banquet at Buckingham Palace, Her Majesty the Queen sat next to The Archduke Ferdinand of Austria. Unbeknown to them all, within a mere seventeen years, the world would change indeed, dramatically and tragically.

44

A new home, a new Warkin

Daisy's miscarriage of her first child, in 1898, really shook both her, and Adam, to the core. It brought them closer together and they listened carefully to the midwife, and the army doctor, about the fragility of life, especially when bearing a child.

'We will have others,' said Adam. 'My mother and father lost two siblings of mine, before I came along, and survived.' He knew that would not be of much comfort to Daisy, and suddenly wished he had not said 'two'.

'Well, I'm glad their third one came through and lived,' said Daisy, 'otherwise you would not be here now, holding my hand. Perhaps next time?'

Sadly, it was not to be and in 1899, even though Daisy gave birth to a beautiful baby boy, he survived for just seventeen days. He was weak and pale, but loved by his parents so much. They were distraught. His tiny cot, in the married accommodation bedroom, remained empty.

Adam, only then, began to re-think his life and career path and came to a decision which would take a little while, and a stroke of good fortune, to fulfil.

'Someday soon, sir,' he had said to Major James, after the death of their baby son, 'I must consider leaving the army. I have served seven years and would like to give my wife, and perhaps, hopefully, a child, the chance to live in rather different surroundings than an army barracks. Daisy is happy enough, but maybe we need the countryside that she is used to, not the military atmosphere that we live in now. I hope you are not offended, sir.'

'Good Lord, no,' said the major. 'You must do what you think is best. I wonder if there might be room for you back at East Hambley, to earn a living there somehow.'

'I'm certainly on the lookout, sir,' Adam replied, 'but I would not ask you to make any special effort on my behalf. Your family have done so much for us.'

'Well, we shall see what might come up' said the major.

Adam began corresponding with some of the helpful and interesting people he and Joe had met on their travels.

He got in touch with the Ashton family in Sicily, who told them that he had saved the family business, but that all his land was now a co-operative, jointly owned and run by his former tenants. He was happy and pleased to be relieved of the stress of previous years.

The Morgan father and children, whom they had met on the train to Rome, were thriving with Edward's children now maturing and enjoying a whole new relationship with their father.

Harry from the Naples Consulate, also wrote back with a friendly and encouraging letter, wishing Adam and Joe well, and exchanging the news that he was now in London, at the Home Office. He hoped they could meet up one day.

All of Adam's correspondents shared, vicariously, in the joy of his marriage to Daisy, but expressed their sadness at the loss of their offspring. Everybody wished the newly married couple much happiness and more joyous news in the future..

In the early autumn of that year a letter arrive for Major James. He already knew that Dr Frederick Treves and his wife, in London, were on very good terms with The Princess of Wales. Dr Treves worked at the renowned London Hospital, where he had specialised in abdominal surgery. He also befriended the now famous Joseph Merrick, dubbed, rather cruelly, The Elephant Man.

Dr. Treves had invited Her Royal Highness to visit Mr Merrick and, not only had she done so, but she made at least one repeat visit and always sent Mr Merrick a Christmas card, until his death in eighteen-ninety.

Sydenham

12 September 1899

Dear James,

We have been honoured to be invited to Marlborough House to dine with Their Royal Highnesses the Prince and Princess of Wales. I would not bother you with such news, other than because we met there, the Warden of Windsor Great Park, another guest, and heard of an opening that may be of interest to young Warkin, your batman, or is he your ex-batman now?

When he and his friend stayed at our house he regaled Elizabeth and Enid with his stories of having worked for you in the gardens, and also of working in the University Botanic Gardens in Naples, admittedly for a very short time. I thought he seemed an intelligent and ambitious young man when he became sick, and I met him in Dorchester, although perhaps not committed to soldiering for a lifetime.

Would you tell him to write to me, if he is interested in a change of career at sometime, and I will forward any useful information to Windsor.

Truly, your friend,

Frederick.

Major James knew that their family friend, Dr Treves was an outstanding doctor, and surgeon. Any suggestion from him about an opening for Adam was not to be ignored. What neither James nor Dr. Treves himself knew was that three years later, in 1902, Frederick Treves would save the life of Edward, by then the new King, when he nearly died, with a burst appendix, on the eve of his Coronation. That was all in the future, of course, but in having his life saved by Dr Treves, Adam was in good company. Now, it seemed, the good doctor might help Adam even more.

'I don't know what to say, sir,' said Adam to Major James. 'This is incredible news for me.'

'Well, just take it easy, think about writing and, if you wish, show me the letter before you send it.' said the major.

He sat down that same night, with a pen and some ink, and wrote to Dr Treves. He showed the letter to James the next day, who thought it was a splendid and intelligent letter, seeking new employment in Windsor Great Park, and not boasting about his horticultural skills too much.

He then bit the bullet and told his commanding officer about wishing to leave the army. He was entitled to do so, after seven years, with a very small pension, but his mind was made up and he waited for any news from London or Windsor.

It came within a month, and Adam opened a very elegant envelope one morning at home, before reporting to the main barracks building at The Keep for duty. He had been invited to Windsor, almost beyond belief, to meet the Warden and one other at the Great Park.

Things moved rapidly from then, and he found himself getting the train from Waterloo in London to Windsor within a week. He had been granted a day or two leave, to make the enquiries about a change in direction for his life. Not for a long time, had Adam felt anything like this degree of excitement. This time it was not just to improve himself, but to give a better life to Daisy and, hopefully, a family.

Meeting with one or two apparently important people in Windsor was daunting, but not too much so, for Adam. He was quite able to hold a conversation and present recommendations and references from his commanding officer.

There was another glowing report from Major Russell and a further one from The Manor House, from where Mr Granger had written to support Adam in any future search for employment. How different from the first day he had met Mr Granger, when he was ridiculed for waiting at the wrong gate, and the occasion when he and Freddie had first met.

He was questioned about his ability to manage a large garden, a variety of plants, a rose garden, herbaceous borders and provide regular blooms for a large household. He was asked how he would manage junior staff and maintain a healthy kitchen garden throughout the course of a year.

What he was also told at Windsor almost left him reeling. This offer was not actually for a position at Windsor, where there was no current need for a gardener or a young Ranger. It was a position for Osborne House on the Isle of Wight; the favourite home of Her Majesty the Queen.

He had been brought to Windsor, and was being told the very least that he needed to know, for purposes of security. But the position was offered him, if he would like to consider it.

This was heady stuff. If he accepted, there would be a small cottage on the estate, for him and Daisy. He would still, in effect, be in the service of Her Majesty and, after considering the offer, which was now in writing, he returned home and told Daisy what had happened, discussing it at length together.

'It could be perfect,' she said. 'It is what you're good at. And maybe we could continue to try to start our family there. Seems a little too good to be true'

'Well, it is true,' he replied, 'and maybe I'll get to see the queen!'

'You and your pipe dreams!' said Daisy, and continued, 'How many people have you helped and guided along the way these past twenty eight years? A lot of people you come into contact with seem to find some happiness because you have befriended them.'

'Nonsense,' Adam replied. 'I'm hardly that important to anybody.'

'Well, I tell you it's true,' she said. 'There's Mrs Redman, who has always sung your praises, Freddie, Joe, your Army companion and his brother Arthur, who's even got a job now!'

'Okay, I've been lucky enough to find some good friends,' he said.

'You've done more than that. From what you tell me, the family in Sicily, that Mr Morgan, and even possibly Harry you met at the Consulate; they're all delighted to have known you. And even the famous Dr Treves and his family. You must have made quite an impression on them for them to think of you, with the introduction to a new position.'

'Yes, I have been very fortunate,' said Adam, and this extraordinary conversation with Daisy continued, as they celebrated their last Christmas in the barracks and heralded in the new century on the first of January 1900.

Adam spoke with Major Russell, made all the correct moves to allow his release from the army. He was allowed a four days leave in February, to visit the Osborne estate, even when the Queen was in residence. He took Daisy with him, met the Master of the Household there and looked over the cottage.

It was perfection. Daisy was quite teary eyed when she examined the beautiful little living room and sitting room downstairs, which were even carpeted. They climbed to view the two bedrooms above, with their exquisite pieces wooden furniture, chintz curtains and views over the green lawns towards the house and the sea beyond.

They moved in on the 1st March and Adam made every effort to come to an understanding of the size of the estate, and the formal gardens, which had been designed by Prince Albert, forty-five years earlier. The work was strenuous and complex.

There were young men who came in from the surrounding villages as daily workers, as well as live-in garden staff. There was one other senior grounds-man, who was responsible to Adam and supervised the parkland with its extensive network of paths and driveways, totalling twenty one miles in all.

It was a beautiful estate for Adam to oversee, and along the way Daisy became pregnant, for the third time, in April, 1900.

They were ecstatic and timid about the possibility of another terrible loss, but all went well as the months went by. The eminent Dr Treves even offered to come to the Isle of Wight to assist Daisy, and said in a letter that he was to be telegrammed instantly, if there were any problems or if Adam needed help.

Adam replied, with profuse thanks, and said that all their fingers were crossed for a successful outcome this time. Even Sir James Reid, the queen's personal physician, who was almost in permanent attendance on the ageing queen, came to see Daisy during her nine months of waiting.

'This is indeed an honour,' said Adam, as he welcomed the gentleman doctor into the cottage.

'It's quite alright,' said Sir James, 'and my pleasure. My good friend, Dr Treves in London, has told me of your unfortunate experience with childbirth, and the newborn infant who died. Please feel free to call upon me at the house if you need anything.'

Adam's world had changed beyond recognition. But as the summertime approached, he was reminded of an incongruous link with his own past, when the senior grounds-man, the short and stocky Mr David Price came to see him. David's shock of bright ginger hair was tamed under a wide brimmed straw hat and he began speaking with Adam one afternoon, over some tea at the cottage.

'Forty-seven years ago,' he said, 'the Prince Consort re-designed so much of this estate after the house had been completed. He built stables for sixty horses and several carriages. He also had built the Swiss Cottage for the children of the day, his and the queen's brood of nine children. It was used by the little ones, as the older ones were grown up before the youngest was even born. Now it is in disrepair, hardly ever used, and run over with mice.'

'Grief,' said Adam. 'It's like being back in the village of my birth. I used to get rid of mice all the time. Can I have a look?'

'Of course,' said David. 'Any time you like, and if you have any ideas about getting rid of them, let me know.'

'I don't think it will be that difficult,' said Adam. 'We need a cat and some traps. I'll go and have a look tomorrow.'

One afternoon, out amongst the shrubs and flowering plants in the July sunshine, while he was supervising two young apprentice gardeners, Adam became aware of activity along the path, towards the big house. There, unmistakably, was a nurse, several black-suited gentlemen, two elegant ladies dressed in fine purple or navy blue gowns, also carrying parasols, and a wheelchair in the midst of them.

It was, without doubt, the queen being taken out into the sun for a short period of 'exercise', although the wheelchair afforded her very little of that. The old lady was now just about eighty-one, and almost blind. She was also almost completely surrounded by the attendants and virtually invisible. Adam stood his ground and wondered how long she would be out in the fresh air. The small party turned away at the next pathway junction, and walked back towards the house. Adam could only chalk up another brief glimpse!

Adam kept up a constant flow of correspondence with Major Russell and Mrs Redman, as well as Freddie and Joe. He even continued to hear from the Ashtons and Mr Morgan's son, Benjamin. His life was full of the things he loved most, including his beautiful and now rather larger wife, still thankfully in good health, the gardens and the flower and fruit, where his talents shone and the delightful home, which now felt entirely their own.

They invited Mrs Redman to stay with them for Christmas 1900, and she made the journey across to the Isle of Wight, much to the delight of Adam and Daisy. They invited Joe, too, who could have slept on the couch downstairs, but he and most of the regiment had been sent to South Africa, where the war between Britain and the two Afrikaner republics had begun in 1899.

Adam was allowed to cut down a small fir tree for their celebration and had organised a much larger tree to be felled for the main house.

Daisy was near to her time now, and Mrs Redman decided to stay on at their invitation. January came in with some wild weather, and plenty of comings and goings at Osborne House. There was not so much to do in the gardens during the winter. Adam had made an amazing job of ridding the Swiss Cottage of mice, and a few rats. The queen, according to rumour and some bulletins, was sinking fast. It was just a matter of time.

And her time came, on the same day as Daisy's.

'Osborne House, January 22nd, 1901, 6.45pm.
Her Majesty breathed her last at 6.30pm
surrounded by her children and grandchildren.'

Gone, quite suddenly, in that moment, were the days when a great sovereign rode amongst her people, as she had done in 1897, and when all was as golden as that golden sovereign herself, who had given the nation peace, security and might.

On the morning of that same day, at about half past six, just twelve short hours before the momentous death of the queen, Daisy gave birth to a perfect baby boy. The local doctor was there, a midwife and Mrs Redman who was beside herself with joy. She had seen Adam, the new and overjoyed father, grow up from the little waif, who ran along the street, into this fine young man of whom she felt inordinately proud.

'Why do I feel so proud of you?' she almost wept. 'I'm not even your mother!'

'Well, you are to me,' said Adam, and they took it in turns to cradle the baby while Daisy rested.

Word reached the great house of the birth of a baby on the estate. The entire family, even including the Kaiser from Germany, had gathered around the queen's bed, as she lay dying. But Alexandra, the Princess of Wales was, as always, entranced by the news of a baby born so close to that auspicious moment, and on the estate. She decided to pay the cottage a visit.

The next morning panic broke out in the royal household. Nobody knew how to organise a Monarch's funeral. There had not been one since 1837 and nobody alive had the slightest idea of what to do. The Lord Chamberlain's office and the Earl Marshall's office, in London, were in chaos.

There was no such panic or chaos in the little Warkin household, at least until they were told that Princess Alexandra, the Princess of Wales, wanted to come and pay her respects. She was to arrive on the twenty-fourth of January at eleven in the morning, and Mrs Redman, Adam and the wife of one of the gardeners, scurried around to make the downstairs rooms perfect. Daisy would be in the main sitting room, dressed, and with her baby in its crib brought downstairs.

'Can this be happening to me?' wrote Adam in a letter to Freddie, and similarly to Major James, at The Manor House. 'I keep wanting somebody to pinch me.'

An equerry arrived an hour before their special guest. He gave no detailed instructions and tried to allay any fears they might have about etiquette, or being overwhelmed by such a visitor. 'Just be yourselves,' he said, 'Her Majesty has requested no special fuss to be made during her visit.'

'Her Majesty?' said Adam, suddenly coming to the obvious conclusion. This was not a visit by The Princess of Wales. For two days now, Alexandra had been the Queen of England, alongside her husband, the new King Edward VII.

It didn't help, or calm the nerves, for him to come to that realisation. On the dot of eleven she arrived, in a small carriage, dressed in black, and Adam met her at the door to save the trouble of ringing the little bell. Adam gave her the bow of his head, as he had learned to do at The Manor House all those years ago, at Christmastime.

'Welcome, Your Majesty. You do us a great honour,' he offered.

'The pleasure is entirely mine,' she said, 'and thank you for your welcome.' Her clipped, and somewhat treble voice surprised Adam, but he was nevertheless bowled over by her friendliness. 'Now where's this baby of yours?'

'Come this way. Ma'am,' said Adam, as he led her into the cottage. Her rather large black hat only just made it through the door. 'May I introduce Daisy, my wife?' Daisy made as if to move.

'Don't get up!' said the queen. 'Perhaps you will allow me to sit next to you.'

Adam pulled up a chair and the queen sat, upright and smiling.

'Thank you,' she said. 'Now, Mr Warkin, I have heard so much about you from my friend Dr Treves, in London. You seem to have travelled a long way in your short life, and, may I say, come a long way too to your present position.'

'I've been very lucky in most things, ma'am,' he said.

'And from humble beginnings,' she added.

'True, ma'am. And if you have no objection, I would like to introduce you to the lady who made all this possible. She taught me to read and took me under her wing when both my parents died.'

'Of course we must meet her,' said Alexandra as Adam went from the room to the small kitchen, where Mrs Redman was making some tea.

'Absolutely not,' she said to Adam. 'You don't want me in there. Her Majesty has come to see you, not me.'

'I insist,' said Adam, and he practically, but carefully, dragged her into the sitting room.

'Your Majesty, may I introduce my friend and life-long mentor, Mrs Redman. Mrs Redman went down into a low curtsey, with her head bowed. She almost looked as if she did not want to get up.

'I am charmed,' said the queen. 'And may I say that whatever you have done for this young man has truly been of great value to him...'

She stopped in her tracks and looked into the eyes of Mrs Redman, who tried to avert her gaze without seeming to be impolite.

'Gustasson?' said the queen. 'Is this you, Birgitta? Can it possibly be you?'

'I'm afraid it is, Ma'am.' said the now upright, Mrs Redman. 'I do apologise for even being here. I had no idea that her late Majesty would be dying, or that Daisy's baby would be born now, let alone that you would be visiting them.'

'Of course you wouldn't know,' said the queen. 'Can my dear friend have another chair?' Adam sprang into action to find another chair from the next door room and positioned it by the queen.

Dear friend?' he mumbled to himself. 'Just what has Mrs Redman not been telling me all these years?' The two ladies continued to exchange news and information over the tea cups, for half an hour, as Adam and his wife tried, but could barely follow what was going on. They took no part in the conversation, most of which was being conducted in Danish! The morning concluded with the queen asking some delightful questions of them both.

'Dear Adam and Daisy,' said Queen Alexandra, using their forenames for the first time, 'my good friend, Birgitta here, tells me that you have asked her to be a godmother to your darling baby boy.'

'That's true, ma'am,' said Adam, 'and she has kindly agreed. There's nobody else I would rather have perform that role.'

'Well, I hope there maybe,' said the queen smiling, 'because, with your permission, I would also like to be a godmother to your son.'

Does one refuse the Queen of England? Or does one simply faint on the spot?

'Your Majesty...' Adam began.

'We would be delighted if you would,' said Daisy. 'And, having listened to the conversation this morning, I hope you will allow us, Mrs Redman, Birgitta, to call our baby Jonathan, after your late husband. If Adam agrees.'

If Adam agrees! Adam was feeling quite light-headed as the queen rose from her chair, kissed both Daisy and Mrs Redman lightly on the cheek and touched the baby's head with her kid-gloved hand. She shook Adam's hand as she turned to leave.

Adam could hardly think of another word to say as she left the cottage, got into her carriage and said her goodbyes.

'Thank you, Your Majesty,' said Adam. 'Thank you so much.'

'I will see you again,' said the queen, 'but probably not for a while. We have a funeral to attend. Perhaps you would allow somebody to stand in for me at baby Jonathan's baptism, but I will see you again.' And she was gone.

Back in house, Mrs Redman held her fingers to Adam's lips. 'Now before you start firing questions at me,' she said. 'Let us have some more tea and I will tell you what you obviously want to know.'

'You told me you had seen the queen once in Weymouth!' said a flabbergasted Adam. 'Now it turns out you practically knew her.'

'Not true,' said Mrs Redman, 'and by the way, do you think you could now begin to call me Birgitta? You are grown up now. It is my name and I have so missed people using it until today.'

Over a fresh pot of tea, the story was revealed.

45

Thirty-seven years earlier

'In 1863,' Birgitta began, 'the young Prince of Wales married the Princess Alexandra of Denmark. Queen Victoria had insisted that he settle down with a wife and I was, at the time, a lady's maid to Alexandra in Denmark. My parents, and my grandparents, had worked for the family for three generations, but their family was Royal only for some twelve years before that. It was a long story.'

'So you came over to England when Princess Alexandra married the Prince of Wales?' said Adam. 'What was the princess' family name?'

'*Schleswig-Holstein-Sonderburg-Glücksburg.*' Birgitta spoke the words fluently, natural to her, but Adam heard them as a foreign language.

'Schles... what?' he almost shrieked, before arresting himself. 'That is quite a mouthful. My name is Warkin!'

'Yes, you don't have to tell me that, I know it.' she replied. 'Well, two years after the wedding, in 1865, Queen Victoria visited a place called Kingston Lacey. There she was to present a Victoria Cross to the parents of a deceased, but very brave, young soldier by the name of William Bankes. He had died in India, but the Queen was determined that he should have a V.C.'

'Still not sure of how that connects you to Mr Granger at The Manor House.' said Adam.

'Well, listen!' said Birgitta, 'Your Dr Russell, Major James' grandfather, had been in India and tried to save the life of young William Bankes. He had reported on his bravery in his despatch to the London newspapers, acting as a doctor and a correspondent. That is how the Queen got to hear of Bankes and why Dr Russell was invited to Kingston Lacey, for the presentation of the medal to his parents.'

'Getting closer,' said Adam,

'Jonathan Redman was a loyal valet to Dr Russell. He had been with him since 1856, when he was thirteen, beginning in the kitchens and working his way steadily to become a valet. He was proud of his position and always kept himself, and the doctor immaculately attired, presentable and a credit to the household at East Hambley.

'Like me and young James,' said Adam, 'though I began in the gardens.'

'Adam, you have no idea how the similarity between you and my darling Jonathan has been treasured by me all these years,' said Birgitta.

'Well, Jonathan, aged twenty-two, was just under six feet tall, nearly always smiling, but courteous, with wavy brown hair brushed carefully, with a centre parting and delicate hands, which he washed regularly after every separate task performed. He was so very good-looking.'

'I think I can guess the next bit,' said Daisy, hoping their baby Jonathan would not wake up before the end of this story.

'The first evening we were at Kingston Lacey, we were in the servants hall and Jonathan was cleaning a pair of brown leather brogues belonging to the doctor. As he buffed away, with each shoe resting on his green apron, I went and sat by him.'

'I bet you did!' said Adam.

'You are making a very good job of the shoes,' I stupidly muttered in my broken English, trying to engage him I conversation. 'Your doctor is good man?'

'He is a good man indeed', replied Jonathan, 'and I am pleased to serve him.'

'Just then a bell rang in the servants' hall, and I jumped up to see which room it indicated. It appeared to be one of the bedrooms and I made my way out, saying I had to go, as my mistress wanted to dress for the evening.'

'And the rest is history, as they say,' said Adam.

'Indeed,' said Birgitta. 'I left the service of Her Royal Highness and Jonathan left The Manor House. We were married with a beautiful wedding at The Manor House, not unlike yours, and moved to Melton Ford in 1867. Jonathan, as I have told you before, then tragically died four years later.'

'In the year that I was born,' said Adam, '1871.'

'And that, of course, is how I knew Mr Granger from The Manor House.'

'And all this time, you let me believe that you had simply seen the Queen once in Weymouth?' said Adam.

'You were an excitable little boy,' she said, smiling. 'If I had told you every detail when you were eleven, I think your head would have exploded!'

'Yes, it probably would have.'

'Actually, of course,' said Birgitta, 'I was on the Royal Yacht, with The Princess of Wales, coming into to Weymouth, and then I was in one of the carriages, following the queen returning to Windsor.'

'All these years and you never told me that little detail!' said Adam. 'But look at us now. I thought my head was going to explode this morning. The Queen of England was here in my home!'

'You handled Her Majesty like a professional courtier!' said Birgitta. 'Oh! And by the way, I'd like baby Jonathan to have these as a christening present.' With that, she handed over two small, identical silver boxes to Adam. 'One was given by the Princess Alexandra to me when I resigned as her lady's maid, and the other to Dr. Russell, by the princess, when she visited Kingston Lacey. It seems that you have brought them together.'

'And now,' added in Daisy, 'there will be no stopping the stories Adam will tell!'

'I think we should, for the most part, keep our counsel,' said Adam, 'although I will probably write to Freddie and the others tomorrow!'

46

Where have we been?

Adam went to the crib, where the baby Jonathan was just waking up. He didn't cry, but looked up, even at just a day or two old, and seemed to look at his doting dad.

'You,' said Adam, as he carried crib and baby together up the stairs to the little second bedroom, 'are a very special and lucky little man. This morning the Queen of England came to our house, to see you. I mean it's not the kind of thing we should boast about, but let's be honest, that doesn't happen to every one, any day of the year, does it?

'So we are allowed to tell people. But we'll do it politely and quietly. And the queen asked if she could be your godmother! Well, of course, I had to think about it, but I told her, 'You'll do. If we can't find anybody better!'

'Well, I didn't really say that. It is a great honour for anybody to ask to be your baptismal godmother, so of course we said Yes.

'I never had much money when I was growing up. Well, actually, none. But you and your mummy are my treasures, and the events of this morning will be written down for you to read one day, when I have taught you how to read. And you had better pay attention, because you never know when it might come in handy.'

He placed the crib carefully in its place and sat down beside it.

'A long time ago, there was a little boy, quite poor, but rich in love and the joy of living, who ran along a country lane and made friends with one of the most wonderful ladies in the world. She taught him to be kind and honest, how to read and be inquisitive about the world. And that lady is sitting downstairs now in our house, as good as any Queen on earth!'

The baby's eyes were closing again, perhaps out of boredom, but probably because he was still tired at having been stared at all morning. Adam sang softly.

> 'Pussy Cat, Pussy Cat,
> Where have you been?
> I've been to London
> to see the Queen.
> Pussy cat, Pussy cat,
> What'd you do there?
> I frightened a mouse
> from under her chair.'

Adam looked up. Daisy was standing at the door, smiling for them both.

THE END